# Rough

## Geoff Crackett

**Rough**

Published by Geoff Crackett
Copyright © 2016 Geoff Crackett

ISBN-13 978-1535088121

Cover design: copyright © 2016 enigma graphics

All the characters and events in this work are fictitious and any resemblance to actual events or persons, living or dead, is coincidental and unintentional.

# PROLOGUE

## 1975

She was completely unaware of the activity taking place around her. She shook her head as though to clear it, but it moved in slow motion.

Her face was a promise of what might have been. Greasy hair glued to the forehead by sweat, tiredness shadowing the piercing eyes, a cut at the edge of her lip and a chipped tooth could not completely disguise a certain amount of natural beauty.

He watched, transfixed, from his seat outside the café. He had not ordered anything and had no intention of doing so. He was drinking the last of a can of beer that he had managed to talk some bloke into getting him from the off-licence. If he and his illicit can were challenged by a café employee he would simply move on. He had been nursing the drink for some time and had to force down the tepid, flat remains.

He could not take his eyes from her, but he was not interested in the potential of that dark auburn hair or the startling green eyes. As ever, he was weighing up how this situation might present itself as an opportunity for him. He looked at the large handbag that swung precariously from her wrist, seeming to cling to her rather than the other way round.

She bumped into a middle-aged man who showed his disapproval. It didn't register. She almost tripped over her own feet before slumping onto the concrete steps around the war memorial. She swivelled so that she was sitting on a step facing the street of shoppers. Facing, but not seeing. She leaned backwards and slid her elbows out behind her to rest on. The bag finally disentangled itself from her arm and bunched up next to her.

A flash of interest and mild excitement stirred in him as he stared at the bag and looked around. There were two men on the opposite side of the square, eating sandwiches and drinking tea from a shared flask, yet not speaking. A scruffy looking teenager was sat closer to his target. He wondered if the youth was a potential rival for the bag, but realised not when he stood and wandered away.

His attention shifted from the bag back to her. She had leaned further back and looked as though she might fall asleep. He didn't want that as she would attract too much attention and possibly be moved on, taking her bag with her. People walked past, absorbed by their Saturday afternoon activities. Some noticed her but most didn't. Of those that did, many pretended they hadn't, but some nudged each other and nodded in her direction, amused or appalled.

He saw her head sag forwards towards her chest and then jerk back upwards as her mind shocked her into staying awake. This happened twice more before she struggled to her feet and decided to move on. He wondered whether to follow her. Judging by the state of her the bag probably would not contain anything of any worth. Certainly not enough to risk him getting lifted.

She swayed slightly and took a moment to get her uncooperative legs under control. She leaned down to pick up her bag before being distracted by something on the ground. With great difficulty she leaned over and picked up a shiny coin, a fifty pence piece. She lifted it to her eye to take a look, as though she was a jeweller examining the authenticity of a gemstone. Pleased with her find, she stumbled down the steps and into the crowd.

He stared at the bag that was still resting on the concrete steps. A furtive glance around him. The café chair scraped on the concrete as he slipped it backwards from under him.

# PART ONE
## 1999

# CHAPTER 1

The telephone emitted its seventh ring. Leon glanced around at his two office colleagues. He was attempting to look preoccupied, as though answering the call would break his train of thought and ruin half an hour's concentrated work. The truth was he just didn't want to speak to anyone, and his co-workers were more than wise to the trick. In fact they had noticed during the preceding half hour that Leon was not hard at work but was struggling to keep his eyes open in between continuously straightening out his desktop stationery. They simply found this repeated trick of his annoying and were under no pressure to pick up the call as the ringing phone was, after all, the one on Leon's desk.

He reached across, having now missed the department's service level agreement target for answering calls by four rings. The double ring signified that it was an external call, which meant it was probably not someone he could fob off.

"Um, hello."

Both of Leon's colleagues looked at him. He had not only failed to identify himself but not even mentioned the university's name; another blatant breach of the service level agreement. Maggie decided then and there that she would raise these issues at the next senior support managers' team meeting. She wrote the date and time in the small notebook on her desk.

"Oh, er Leon Glover"

Maggie inwardly smiled. Leon was unaware of her, largely because he was wondering why a member of the local constabulary was on the telephone to him.

"I'm sorry, could you repeat that? I'm just a bit…"

"Alex Treadwell. Do you know him?" repeated the sergeant whose name Leon had already forgotten.

"Yes, he is one of the academic members of staff in our faculty."

"Is he currently at work?"

"I wouldn't know to be honest."

There was a pause before the sergeant continued. Leon tried to remember his name; Sergeant Hollins? Maybe not.

"I would appreciate a bit more cooperation here," said Hollins.

"I'm not trying to…I know he's not on the sick because I have a list here. Not that he would have told anyone anyway if I'm being honest with you. So, yeah, he might be."

"Can you find out for me if he has been at work?"

"I can look in his office, but if he's not there…"

"Can you do that please?"

"Can you hang on for two minutes while I have a look."

Leon opened the office door and stepped out into the corridor. He spoke into the cordless phone as he walked.

"His office is just upstairs, I'm on my way there now."

"Thank you," the sergeant's voice was a mixture of exasperation and relief that they might be getting somewhere.

The light was off and the door locked when Leon got there. He checked the nameplate on the door to ensure he had the right office. He decided it would not make much difference anyway as all the lights in the neighbouring offices seemed to be off too. He peered through the strip of glass, which all the office doors had for health and safety reasons. Even through the poor light it was a complete mess. Clothes seemed to have been piled up on a chair once they had been worn. A filthy coffee mug and cafetière sat on the desk next to an opened pint of milk in a plastic bottle. Leon was fairly sure he could see a pair of soiled underpants but decided not to investigate any further.

"He's not in but it looks like he must have been here quite…"

Leon noticed that the milk in the bottle was no longer milk. Even from this distance he could see that the contents of the bottle were a solid mass with mould growing on the top.

"No, forget that, he's not been here."

"OK," said the sergeant, "Can you let me know if he has been at work at all since last Thursday?"

"I know you think I am being awkward here, but there's no way of me knowing that. He doesn't really teach. Not if he can help it anyway."

"Is he on leave?"

"He'll not have filled his leave card in. He's *supposed* to but…"

"There must be *someone* there who can tell me that. What about a line manager? A Dean, if that's what they're still called."

"They'll not know," Leon was starting to sympathise with the officer's frustration, "I'll ask around. I think I know another one of the lecturers is quite friendly with him. But I don't know if he's here either."

Sergeant Hollins tone was becoming ever more sharp. "I refuse to believe that a full time member of staff can work there and nobody can tell me if he has attended work for the last seven days. How can nobody *know*?"

"Well, he's on an academic contract so…"

"Who's paying the bloke's wages?" snapped Hollins.

"I suppose you are," Leon responded, trying to be humorous. Even without visual clues he could tell that the sergeant was less than amused. "Just inasmuch as he pays yours I suppose," still Leon was met with silence and he wondered if he should just stop talking, "although I'm sure you turn up for work."

## CHAPTER 2

Leon clocked out. At least he thought he had clocked out. The university had recently rushed in a new electronic system of time recording at enormous expense without first checking that it worked properly. The system, and others like it, had been used as the excuse for getting rid of a number of support staff due to the projected reduction of administrative burden. The problem with this plan was that the university had performed the process backwards and let the staff go before implementing the technology. The clocking in system had actually served to increase the burden on staff due to the need to resolve hundreds of problems on a daily basis.

Because Leon was not convinced that the machine had just emitted the correct beep he would need to log into the system in the morning and, if necessary, manually amend the entry. This would then need to be authorised by an administrator before going to the Witch to sign off. He contemplated swiping his card again to make sure but then weighed up the risk of accidentally clocking himself back in again and decided not to. He found a pen and wrote the time on the back of his hand just in case.

Upon leaving the building Leon was now faced with a familiar problem. Having somehow made it through a day at work during which he had spent almost every moment fighting a fatigue that seemed intolerable, he would now start worrying about lying awake for the whole of the coming night.

A few pints were the usual answer. If he drank he could at least fall asleep at the start of the night. Even though he knew this was a poor plan he still went ahead with it repeatedly. He knew that the alcohol would possibly buy him a couple of hours of slumber, which would be of a low quality, but it was preferable to the alternative of getting no sleep at all.

He began to trudge his frequent path to the Oak. On the corner he noticed a young woman selling the Big Issue. He saw that this was a new edition as the face of a young man stared out from the cover. The man was clearly well known enough to be plastered on the front of a magazine but Leon did not recognise him. This was no surprise to him at a time when anyone was considered to be a celebrity and he was well out of touch with popular culture. The famous man was possibly an extremely untalented soap actor or once got to the last thirty contestants on the X-Factor. Or perhaps he was this year's Strictly Come Dancing contestant that no one had heard of.

What did surprise him was the fact that there was a new edition out today when he had thought it was due the following day. He almost paid the young woman for a copy but consumer loyalty won out over impatience and he decided to visit his usual vendor, Billy, near the Oak. He knew he would not open it until he got to the pub anyway so it made little difference.

On approaching Billy's patch he noticed a different man in his place. This man was much taller and younger, perhaps not even thirty although he already had some white hair speckling his biker moustache. For a moment Leon thought that the man showed a sign of recognition as he approached, but he dismissed it. Leon frequently thought that he recognised people in the street himself, a phenomenon he put down to his sleep-deprived mind playing tricks on him. The man with the moustache who was not Billy shuffled his pile of magazines around nervously. Possibly something he had learned to do in order to prevent the top copy from getting dog-eared and unsellable, and which had now turned into a subconscious movement.

"Where's Billy?" Leon asked as he handed over his pound.

The man simply shrugged his shoulders.

"Not a conversationalist then?" Leon smiled.

The man stared back at him, emotionless.

Leon felt like asking for a refund and going back to the woman near work but decided it wasn't worth it.

Leon took a gulp of ale and stared at the page in front of him. The pub was just starting to fill with people finishing work, most of whom would be gone within an hour, followed by a lull before the evening drinkers arrived. Leon had bought himself a pint of Black Sheep and found a corner table where he was not in any kind of thoroughfare that would result in him being disturbed. He still wished he had given his money to a more deserving vendor as he laid the Big Issue out on the table and flicked through it.

The Missing Persons page contained three faces that were looking at him. Each was haunting, if only in the context of the page itself. But Leon was only looking at one of them. According to the text, her name was Marie Holt and she had last been seen in 1975. Dark auburn, shoulder-length hair framed her attractive face and her green eyes bored into Leon as always. As striking as they were, he always imagined that he could see a world of trouble within them.

He placed his hand on her face and gently pressed the paper flat in order not to distort her features. His fingertips brushed along a faint edge beneath the surface. He picked up the magazine and turned the page. A scrap of paper fell out and slid onto the table. It was a badly printed flier of some sort which simply gave the details of a local soup run for the needy.

Leon turned it over and caught his breath. It had two words written on it, but that was enough to overload his senses and make his heart jump.

The message was "I'M OK."

Leon jumped to his feet and stuffed the magazine into his pocket and in doing so knocked his drink to the floor. Normally a spilt Black Sheep would have been bordering on tragedy but he barely seemed to notice. He was gripping the note so tightly in his fist that his knuckles were shining white beneath the lights of the pub. He bolted for the door.

The man was nowhere to be seen as he rounded the corner. He looked around in both directions, with little hope of spotting a retreating figure. Perhaps he was still around. The man still had at least fifteen Big Issues to dispose of when Leon had seen him. There was no way he could have got rid of them all in such a short space of time and he was unlikely to have packed up for the day without selling them. Leon called through the open door of the adjacent bakery to enquire if anyone had noticed the vendor move anywhere in the last ten minutes. The baker shook his head slightly, his two customers simply pretended he was not there.

Leon stared down at the note. His conviction that it was meant for him was waning. Why would it be? This wasn't a bloody spy thriller. There must be a hundred other explanations for a probably meaningless note to have ended up in a magazine.

But in *his* magazine, next to a picture of *her*?

He needed to go home.

## CHAPTER 3

Leon's head was thick with confusion and fatigue by the time he entered the terraced house that he could no longer afford to rent. He walked straight to the kitchen and looked in the fridge. The only beer left was a four pack of McEwan's Export that he had recently bought by mistake. Leon's lack of sleep frequently caused him to make such minor errors. He could picture the scene now in the corner shop. He would have reached for a brand he wanted, his eyelids drooping and his coordination all over the place. He remembered spotting the wrong beer in his basket while waiting at the till. The thought of going back to swap it was too much. Besides, someone else was standing behind him in the queue so there would inevitably be an awkward situation when he returned. Neither of them would know whether the etiquette was for him to be satisfied with his new position or be allowed to resume his old one. He didn't really give a shit about offending anyone; he just did not want to have the necessary conversation.

In the intervening time Leon had drunk everything else in the house rather than touch the beer, but now satisfied himself with the thought that this was the drink he used to choose around twenty years ago. It would be interesting to see how it tasted to his more mature taste buds. He had not even seen Export on sale for about ten years although, knowing his corner shop, it had probably been there since then. And if he was honest, it could taste like cat vomit and it would still be going down the hatch.

He reached for a can of the beer from the fridge, popping it open with one hand as he was still clutching the note in the other. He looked at the meagre contents of his fridge and wondered if there was enough there to form a sandwich. Then he realised it could wait; he had things to think about and at any rate, he had no appetite. Or bread.

He trudged upstairs to what he referred to as his study but was, in effect, the spare bedroom with a small desk in it. He slumped into the chair, finally releasing the note onto the desktop. He stared at it, motionless for some time, before pulling the Big Issue from his back pocket and folding it open at Marie's page.

He carefully cut out the whole page, making sure to have a nice, straight edge. He used four pins to attach it to an otherwise empty noticeboard.

Leon opened a small cupboard in the desk and retrieved a box file, opening it on the desktop. Inside was a collection of papers, at the top of which was a page from a different Big Issue; again the missing persons page. The same photograph of Marie looked out from it, the intensity of her eyes stealing any attention away from the men flanking her. They were two different men and this was a much older magazine page. There were two more similar ones beneath it.

Leon sat for a while longer. Everything looked too bright and slightly unreal, although he knew his body and mind were just reacting to tiredness. He looked longingly at the spare bed but knew deep down that it would bring him no respite.

He picked up the Export and took his first swig. It tasted like liquid fag-ash.

\*\*\*

1980

The day he had been waiting for had finally come. His mum seemed a little teary, as he would have expected. He knew that he was not a good son. He was too much trouble for his folks to bear. Too much alcohol, a certain amount of drug use, being brought home by the police, cautioned on two occasions. He had certainly calmed down in the last couple of years and work had given him some focus, at least until his enforced break. His parents' friends had no such issues with their own offspring and he had seen them looking at his folks with a mixture of suspicion and sympathy. But he was an adult and would make his own decisions. Even more so from this day forwards.

His dad was in the house but conspicuously taking a background role. It was as though he was going out of his way to demonstrate that this was just another day that deserved no acclaim or ceremony.

"Are you sure you've got everything, love?" his mum asked.

"Well, I can always come back if not can't I? It's not like I'm moving country is it?"

He wondered if that had sounded sarcastic and made a mental note not to snap at her any more. They would soon be out of one another's hair and, who knows; maybe he would develop a better relationship with both of them as a result.

Leon hoped that he could be nicer to his mum, in particular. She must have had a terrible time being caught in the middle of him and his father. The two of them shared the worst of their traits, she had always said. Both were stubborn and both got unreasonably irritated if they did not get entirely their own way. Worse was that following each argument the smouldering resentment seemed to burn for days.

His poor mother would have the almost impossible job of smoothing things over and, although she never would have admitted it, she would often edge towards his side. But that was before his hospitalisation. Some time afterwards, in a moment of unbearable frustration, she screamed at him that the accident had made him worse. Leon supposed that his face must have betrayed his emotions in that moment, as she never, ever mentioned it again.

The flashbacks haunted him every night as it was. The sight of the steel pole arrowing towards him as he looked up. The utter silence. The futile slow-motion of his attempted escape. The sickening crunch of his hardhat, a noise that had barely reached his eardrums before the blackness.

Leon's nightmares got even worse after he perceived that his mum had used it as a weapon against him. *Had* it changed him? He could not deny that the fights with his dad got more unpleasant as he recovered. The lingering anger would claw at his mind for weeks rather than days, leaving him completely incapable of forgiving or forgetting the most minor perceived transgression. But he put that down to the long days spent recovering under their stifling supervision.

He looked at the two bags on the landing. Not much for over twenty years on this earth, he thought. Two bags. He had seen homeless people with that much.

"So are you done then?"

"Think so."

"What about your box of stuff in the attic?"

"I'll just leave that I think."

He was about to say that he would not have room for it but then remembered that he would have quite a large room in the flat he was about to share with his mate Craig, and so far he had only a tiny amount of belongings. He was amazed at how much stuff he had simply thrown out as he sorted through the contents of his room. So much crap he had accumulated and hardly any of it worth keeping.

"If you're moving out you should do it properly," his dad grunted.

Leon had not even realised his father was upstairs. But the voice was definitely coming from the bathroom. How long had he been in there?

"Can't I just have a look through it next time?"

"He doesn't need to do it now," agreed his mother.

"If it doesn't get done now it will be up there forever," grumbled his dad, flushing the toilet.

Leon wondered if he had been talking to them through the door while taking a shit, and then decided not to think about it any more.

He considered whether his father was being belligerent in order to deliberately cause an argument. Maybe it would be somehow better for the old man if they left on bad terms. It might convince him once and for all that this was the best thing that could happen. If so then Leon was not going to give him the satisfaction. He shook his head at his mum, who shrugged her shoulders, and then grabbed the hook to pull down the attic hatch.

He knelt down next to the box, taking care to skirt the unboarded section in the corner through which he had once accidentally put his foot. That had been a bloody massive row, that one. He pulled back the four overlapping flaps from the large cardboard box, sending dust flying everywhere, including into his face and hair. He spluttered and silently cursed his dad for making him come up here.

This could all go out, he thought.

He dug through a collection of old magazines, an autograph book, a couple of childhood toys. There were also some school books at the bottom. Why had he kept those? He noticed that they would not lie flat; there was something beneath them. He lifted them out and saw an item that he had completely wiped from his mind. Something that would from this day forwards permanently be in it.

He lifted the purse out of the box. It was well worn and was partially covered in turquoise sequins that glinted under the dim light bulb of the attic. The rest had presumably rubbed off due to age and use. As a result, the purse had the look of a mange-ridden animal.

His mind travelled back to a time when he had been happy to live in the moment, care-free. But so much of it was at the expense of others. Acts for which, at the time, he had not spent a moment's remorse.

His twenty-year-old self, despite now despising his previous behaviour, suddenly envied his younger version's ability to simply not care about anything.

Twenty-year-old Leon, while looking at fifteen-year-old Leon as an entirely different person, was now landed with more than enough guilt for the both of them. All those people he had harmed – physically and verbally – and stolen from. How could he have done it so shamelessly?

Stolen from. He looked down at the purse. What would have happened to her? What part might he have played in her fate? How could he have given it so little thought? Was it ever too late to make amends?

\*\*\*

### 1975

As Leon's chair scraped back it tilted over and clattered off the floor. One of the staff inside the café had noticed him and was heading in his direction. He didn't care. He was leaving now anyway. He put his empty can of beer on the table, sneered at the man coming towards him and set off into the square.

He pushed past a couple of women who grumbled something about 'rude kids' and bobbed his head around, trying to keep the bag in his sights.

The handbag was large and burgundy in colour and, most importantly, was still sat on the step and attracting no attention from passers-by.

As Leon approached it he checked around to make sure that the woman had not realised her mistake and decided to come back. He knew it was unlikely but he was being cautious. He could not afford another run-in with the police. Turning back to the bag he was horrified to see that a middle-aged man was stooping over it, trying to look inside without actually touching it. The man looked around, confused, seemingly looking for anyone who might have left it. He was just about to pick it up when Leon grabbed it from beneath his fingers.

"Thank Christ it's still here," he panted, "Me mam's worried sick. I told it'd be here but she thought it would have been nicked by now. Thanks"

With that he sprinted off into the crowd as fast as he could, just in case the man decided to follow him. The man stared at where the bag had been, stared after the disappearing youngster, wondered if he should do anything and then decided not to. He didn't know what it was that he should do anyway.

## CHAPTER 4

Leon found a safe place to sit near the riverbank and poured the handbag out onto the grass. He immediately got up and threw the empty bag into a nearby bin. He did not want to attract any sort of attention and a fifteen-year-old boy with a large handbag might just be enough to do that.

Returning to the bag's contents, he poked through them. A large, turquoise sequined purse that had definitely seen better days, some tissues (some in a packet, some clearly used), a lipstick, an empty cigarette packet and a small, white prescription bottle.

Looking through the purse first he found several coins but, to his disappointment, no notes. The only other contents were some receipts, a bank card and a passport photograph of the woman. He lingered on the photograph due to her green eyes. Little did he know that in two decades' time he would still be using that photograph in the missing persons pages.

He rattled the white bottle and felt that it was full. The label informed him that it belonged to Marie Holt and was something called Diazepam. He noticed that the plastic seal had still not been broken on the top and he looked at the date; 25/05/75. Today's date.

Leon looked at it again. Today. What did that mean? It meant that the woman was ill to some degree and he had the medication that could help her. As he thought it over he stuffed the lipstick, tissues and cigarette packet in the bin. He zipped the tablets inside the purse and tried to shove it in his pocket. It was too big and he did not want to be seen with it. He decided that there was nothing of value to him, only to the woman. He wondered if he could just return everything to the steps at the war memorial. Too risky and probably pointless.

It was too late to do anything now, he decided. He threw the purse into the bin and, looking around, walked off.

***

1999

Leon gently pushed the contents around his desktop with his forefinger. He often wondered what had made him go back to that bin twenty-four years ago. The Leon from that time was not someone who would have dwelt on the situation for more than five minutes, quickly moving on to another self-serving endeavour. But go back he had. In the dark he had rooted around to find the shabby, half-bald purse, and take it home to his bedroom.

What Leon had learned in the years since he rediscovered his stash in his parents' attic was that Diazepam was more commonly known as Valium, used for anxiety and alcohol withdrawal among other things. Without it, sudden withdrawal could cause side effects as severe as psychosis.

Leon lay in bed, staring at the ceiling. He knew that shutting his eyelids would make things worse. Besides, his eyes felt so big that he was not sure that he could force their lids closed any more. His theory was that if he kept them open then tiredness, along with the four cans he had eventually drunk, would close them without him noticing. He'd had sporadic success with this tactic in the past.

His galloping mind gave him adequate notice that he was unlikely to sleep tonight anyway. He had lost track of time but knew that he had been lying there for a while now. His mind had got itself stuck in a groove and he didn't see how he could possibly free it. He had spent many nights thinking of Marie and building possible scenarios of what might have happened to her, imagining her now and back in 1975. In some they would meet up and he would have a chance to pour out his angst and apologies, in others she had come back to the square and broken down on discovering the missing bag. She had died from exposure. She had committed suicide. She had gone back to her loving family, pulled her life together. She was healthy, successful, happy. She was dead. She was dead.

He spun over on to his side as though trying to move out of the way of his thoughts. It did not work.

If she was alive then why had no one ever responded to her picture? Why did she not exist on the internet? He had wasted days of his life looking at people on the web who shared her name, but he was relatively sure she wasn't there. Was there any significance to the flier on which the note was written or was it simply the first piece of paper available to the author? Was the soup run connected to Marie?

For the millionth time he searched his soul to establish why it mattered to him. He could not have given a logical explanation had his life depended on it. Atonement, perhaps. All he knew was that it was an obsession. A compulsion he could not shake off any more easily than he could stop drinking. A compulsion even stronger than the one that meant he could no longer trust himself to go near a betting shop, taking longer routes while walking in order that he need not pass one.

He wanted to roll back over and look at the radio alarm clock, which had mocked him so often in the past. He hated it and the bad news that it inevitably gave him. But he found something strangely soothing about staring vacantly into the LED display. He felt that if he stared straight through it he could transport himself to another place. The insane product of a sleep-deprived mind that wanted to be taken anywhere that it might rest. On this occasion he resisted the urge to look.

Perhaps a drink of milk might help. But maybe he was about to fall asleep and the journey to the fridge would set him back. But milk was a well-known aid to sleep. Around ten minutes later he was stood with cold feet on the kitchen lino while swigging milk from the bottle. Not too much as he was worried about falling asleep and then being awoken by his bladder. His body told him that if he returned to bed now it would be impossible to stay awake.

Ninety minutes later he entered a phase that generally occurred at some stage during most nights; anger. He became annoyed with not being able to sleep, annoyed with himself, annoyed by people at work. Annoyed with her.

He needed to stop thinking. He moved his body by fractions until the angle made the pattern on the lightshade perfectly symmetrical. But now he was not perfectly in the centre of the bed. He would have to rotate the shade the next day or it would bother him the following night.

He listened to the quiet. He imagined that he could hear a clock ticking even though he knew that was impossible. He had ensured that there was not a ticking clock within earshot by throwing most of them out and placing the ones he could not bring himself to discard at the other end of the house.

The pipes might have been humming slightly, he wasn't sure. He had some sleep CDs that he could listen to on his Discman. He weighed it up. The 'nature' ones featuring rainfall, thunderstorms, waterfalls, oceans, and rivers rarely did the job. He had some spoken tracks by a thick-accented, quiet Scotsman. The man had been known to occasionally coax Leon to sleep, but the whispering Glaswegian did not have a wonderful track record, and it was equally likely that Leon would be frustrated by the fact that the recording was probably made by a chap who was at this moment fast asleep. At that stage, rather than providing soothing empathy the faceless voice would become the enemy.

He wanted to look at the note but would not allow himself. It would make him fully awake once more, he knew exactly what it said and, what's more, it was sat right next to the face of the alarm clock.

Rather than empty his mind, which was clearly now an impossibility, Leon knew he must think of something else which was less likely to cause an emotional response. As he let his mind decide what that would be, he felt an imaginary blanket descend upon him. His thoughts settled and quietened, his closed eyes relaxed and their eyelids thickened, cutting out all unwanted light. He knew he was very close but was trying not to think about it. If he could just stay exactly in this state then he would…

Cundy. The bastard. Cundy was smiling at him with his patronising fucking face. Leon had to open his eyes to chase away the image. He beat his forehead with his palms. He could not dwell on it; he must get back to where he was. Eyes closed, comfortable position.

He would get Professor Cundy one day. He would be standing there when Cundy got his comeuppance and he would relish every moment. Not for the first time he wondered about being a whistle-blower. The worst-case scenario was that he would be ostracised by colleagues and have his position at work made untenable. That would probably be no better or worse than his current working life. Perhaps he could do it anonymously. Either way, there were a lot of people he would like to bring down but he would start with Cundy and treat anything else as a bonus.

He wondered if he had enough information. There were numerous instances of abusing public money. Suspect expenses claims, ordering of unauthorised goods to his home address, taking university property home without returning any of it, unnecessary booking of hotels and travel, throwing out perfectly good furniture when he became bored of it. And that was all before looking into what he was actually doing to deserve his exorbitant salary.

Leon pictured his nemesis being shamed in the local press or, even better, escorted from the building without even having the chance to clear his desk. His colleagues were looking on, many of them spitefully pleased that a man who had made professor before them was being disgraced, while of course feigning sympathy. Some of them suddenly sweating over every publicly owned penny they had pinched and every taxpayer's pound they had frittered.

He rolled over to look at the clock. He was in his window of uncertainty. If he fell asleep now he would have so little sleep that he would feel dreadful when he woke up. He thought back over the last seven hours or so. He must have had *some* sleep. It seemed like he had been lying there for days but at the same time, he knew it could not have been seven hours of full consciousness. So perhaps it was better to get up at twenty past five as both the other options were so poor; he would stare at the ceiling for another hour or he might finally fall asleep and awake an hour later with his brain craving more of what it had finally achieved.

His mind was made up; he would get up, have some breakfast and coffee and watch some television. It would be light soon anyway at which point he would have no chance. It seemed a simple enough plan, except that his body wasn't in any hurry to move. He decided to give himself a count of three at which point he would roll his heavy head from the pillow and swing his feet onto the floor.

Three… Like the flick of a switch, Leon fell asleep.

## CHAPTER 5

He had not even reached his desk before he heard Kay shout down the corridor from inside her office.

"Leon, sorry, have you got a minute?"

He had not noticed her as he passed. She appeared at the doorway.

"Apologies for shouting," she smiled, "and look, you've not even arrived yet." She nodded at his bag and coat.

"That's fine, Kay, what is it?"

As always, Kay's office looked like it had contained a small explosion and she looked slightly flustered. Leon thought she always looked as though she had lost something important and if her desk was anything to go by perhaps she had. She ran a hand through her dark brown tousled hair.

"I need to get the workloads submitted today. They're nearly done but you know what my Excel skills are like. I'm sorry, I know how busy you'll be but would there be any chance…"

Leon held up his palms towards her to indicate that it wasn't a problem.

"Let me get a coffee and I'll be straight back."

He walked towards his office with Kay thanking him as though he were about to save her life. If only they were all like her, he thought. She had momentarily made him forget how fatigued he was and, although it now washed over him with a faint nausea, working with her for a couple of hours would be a welcome distraction. A new senior lecturer was approaching him. Leon could not remember his name but had seen him around a few times. He raised his face to greet the man, who noticeably turned his own face towards the wall.

"Knob," Leon muttered.

Leon sat with his third coffee of the day and a time check told him that it was still only ten thirty. Kay had briefly cheered up his day but now he was back to dealing with tedious crap. He kept catching Maggie and Frank looking at him, and then immediately looking away each time he raised his head. That meant that he probably looked as awful as he felt.

"Oh, Janet was looking for you when you were out earlier," said Maggie.

That potentially meant that he'd done something wrong. It probably meant that Maggie had told Janet that he'd done something wrong. He'd had suspicions of that for some time now. Either way, it would be bad news if she was on the look out for him. He looked at his phone and the display danced in front of his eyes. He looked up and tried to focus on Frank. It took his eyes several seconds to obey, as they seemed to have forgotten how to adjust focal length. He was so tired. Everything seemed like it was at maximum volume and he flinched every time someone closed a drawer too fast or coughed. He had jumped at one point when the printer had suddenly clunked into life on the table next to his desk. This wasn't sustainable. He must get some sleep. How would he manage to do it tonight? Put simply, he knew he wouldn't.

Leon admonished himself for thinking about tonight. It was something he tried to ban himself from doing. His longing for sleep was often so acute that it became an obsession that ramped up the pressure for the coming night. He knew that this just made the act of getting to sleep even harder.

He needed to occupy his mind with something else. The tedium of the tasks he had to get through at work that day were unlikely to do the trick. Besides, he knew what he would be thinking of for the remainder of the day. His note.

At lunchtime Leon wondered about going out to see if he could find the new Big Issue man. But walking to the café for a sandwich had used what little energy he had and it was more likely that he would find him after work. So Leon ate at his desk and worked through his lunch so that he could justifiably knock off a little early. No beer tonight. Just see if the bloke was there and then off home. He would need to buy some more cans for the house, though.

It was Billy. Stood there, grinning his daft grin with that missing front tooth, his demeanour totally unaffected by the dozens of people blanking him. He saw Leon and waved a copy of the magazine in his direction.

"Too late Billy. If you will have a day off then that's what happens."

Billy's smiled widened.

"Where were you anyway?" Leon tried to sound casual.

"Laid up with a stomach bug. You know it must have been a bad one to stop me, eh?"

Leon nodded in agreement. It was indeed most unlike Billy to miss a day, whatever the weather.

"There was a different fella here. He was on your corner."

"Well, there's nothing wrong with that if I didn't turn up myself."

"No, but, well... do you know who he was?"

"No idea, why?"

"Oh, er, I just thought afterwards that he'd given me too much change and I wanted to square it up with him, you know?"

Billy grinned, "If he's daft enough to give you too much change then he doesn't need it as much as the rest of us do."

"I suppose so. Still, if you do hear from anyone who it was, would you let me know?"

Billy looked inquisitively at Leon and then just shrugged his shoulders. Leon noticed the large stack of magazines that Billy had still to get rid of and thought about giving him a couple of quid, but he knew from experience that he would not take it. Often Leon stayed to talk to Billy for a few minutes and had seen him take an extra fifty pence or so from people who offered it. But he had always refused to do so from Leon. Perhaps it was because he considered them to be friends on some level and it did not seem right. It was a long time since Leon had offered in case it caused offence. He fished out the right change for a copy and passed it to Billy. Billy shook his head.

"You already got one."

"Lost it. And I need something to read in the pub in case someone tries to talk to me."

Leon and Billy talked for a few moments before Leon made to leave.

"I'm cramping your style, and I have a pint to drink."

He was about to leave when he had a thought.

"Have you heard of a soup run on Percy Road?"

"Yeah I know it," replied Billy, "I've been before. It's OK. Why?"

Leon did not respond to his question but opened his newly acquired magazine at the correct page in order to show him Marie's face.

"You ever see this woman?"

Billy looked confused but studied the picture as though anxious to help his friend, but eventually looked back to Leon and shrugged his shoulders. "I think maybe she looks familiar. If it's who I'm thinking of she doesn't look like that any more, though. Could be."

"Sleep rough?" Leon asked.

Billy nodded, "But I'm really not sure. The more I think about it…"

"Where."

"I don't know."

Leon was convinced he was a step nearer to finding her.

# CHAPTER 6

Leon looked at himself in the mirror. His gaunt face looked appropriate, as did the dark rings that framed his lower eyes like shadows. He was unshaven in such a way that could never be seen as an attempt at fashion. The clothes had been slightly more difficult. He had no problem at all picking out some things that were badly creased and had barely recognised some of them, so long had they resided in an unseen corner of his chaotic wardrobe.

The question was; were they *dirty* enough? He had thought not, so had earlier spent ten minutes treading his coat and jeans into the hardened soil that he laughingly referred to as a garden. He was fairly certain that Mrs Andersen had seen him from her upstairs window. God knows what that nosey cow had thought he was up to, but he didn't much care.

He decided eventually that he looked like the sort of person that people would try to avoid, and smiled grimly at his reflection.

The soup run looked confusing and slightly daunting. Everywhere he looked people were serving, collecting and eating food. Even though everyone seemed to know what was happening and how to navigate the process, after some time of watching from a distance he could not fathom out any sort of logical system.

What he did notice more than anything was that people seemed in relatively good spirits for folks who would have presumably spent the evening hungry if not for this piece of generosity. Perhaps their humour was simply lifted by this interlude and they would go back to being miserable once their bellies did not feel so full. Some wolfed down the contents of their Styrofoam containers without pause as though worried that it would disappear if they dawdled. Others savoured every bite, wanting it to last forever as they chatted to friends or acquaintances.

Some of the people taking advantage of the free food stopped to talk to those serving it, sometimes to the annoyance of others waiting for theirs. Others seemed almost aggressive to the helpers.

Leon inched closer to the action. The darkness and density of movement confused his eyes and made him blink long and hard. He decided just to go for it but then half way there he pulled up short. Someone walked past him, catching his shoulder as he did so. Leon looked up to see a thick-set man, well over six feet tall and in his late forties. He was accompanied by a younger woman.

"Watch out," the big man said.

Leon apologised and with that they were on their way, making a beeline for the food.

Leon found a section of kerb free and sat on it for a moment. After a while the big man returned with his partner and with little other space available, perched themselves close to Leon. The man nodded at him.

"Sorry," the man grunted. "Get grumpy when I'm hungry."

"No. My fault. Don't know why I stopped like that."

The man went back to his food.

"You not getting anything then?" the woman leaned forwards, peering past the bulk of her partner.

"Yeah, I'm just about to..."

"You're not hungry enough then."

Leon realised that she was right. There was free food a matter of yards away and he was sat without any. He must look suspicious.

"No. Yeah. Just had a dizzy spell there. Probably just hungry. I needed to sit down. Here I go."

With that, he heaved himself up and purposefully strode towards the temporary canopy. He stood there, unsure of how to proceed. The server, a young bloke in trendy clothing, looked at him.

"Not seen you before I don't think."

"Oh. Just erm... Lost my job that's all. And then it all went tits up and, well, the house."

"Woah, it's not an interrogation mate, I was just making conversation."

"Yeah, I know," Leon attempted a smile.

He felt the edge of the picture in his pocket. Patience. He wasn't about to cast suspicion on himself by dragging out photographs at the first opportunity. He thanked the man for the unidentifiable food he had served him and returned to his piece of kerb. As he sat, he waived his carton in the direction of the woman. She nodded back. A feeling of guilt sneaked up on him out of nowhere. If he ate this food would it deprive someone who might actually need it to survive? It was too late now; he just had to eat it or give up and go home.

Leon stared at his trousers, his fingernails, his shoes. He was comparing them to everyone else here to make sure that he fit in, although he had already realised that there was a wide range of appearances.

After a few plastic forkfuls he looked across at the pair.

"Not bad."

"S'fuckin' awful, mate, but it fills a hole," said the large man, shovelling a spoonful into his mouth hungrily. "Don't think I've seen you around."

Leon could not tell whether or not it was a question.

"I'm looking for someone." Should he have said that? Either way, the couple did not pick up on it.

"Anyhow, I'm Steve and this is Karen."

"Hi. I'm Leon."

"You know what you're doing round here then, Leon?"

"I'll soon work it out. I can look after myself."

They sat in silence for a while. Leon felt like he was being watched. He wondered if he had got all this the wrong way round. He had come in some sort of ludicrous undercover persona to try and hunt down Marie, but he had really been led here. What if Marie was watching him? But that was ridiculous; she could not even know who he was. If the note had been left for him by someone other than Marie then perhaps they could be watching him. Even more ridiculous and unlikely. Not for the first time since receiving the note, Leon started to feel ashamed of himself. The notion that anyone would give a shit about him was laughable, never mind that they should trick him into attending a soup run and spy on him while he did it.

Leon leaned forwards and put his head in his hands. He pressed the heels of his palms hard into his eye sockets until stars exploded in the blackness. He had to get some sleep soon. This could not continue for much longer without him simply shutting down all together and ceasing to function as a human being. He could feel his mind slowing down, before being interrupted by a few seconds of euphoria. Mood swings. That was it; he was going home. What the fuck was he doing out here anyway? He dropped his arms and was about to get up when a scuffle broke out in the serving area. Leon turned to look, just in time to see a middle-aged homeless man being led away by two men. One of them thrust a carton into his hand and said loudly, "Don't come back."

Leon looked at Steve and Karen and raised his eyebrows.

"Kelvin," answered Karen. Leon wondered if that was all he was going to get.

"Pisshead. He'll be back next time, same as every time. Bit of a running duel between him and Charlie over there. Leon looked at one of the young men on serving duty – the same one he had dealt with – who was being asked by several people at once if he was OK. He assured them all that he was.

"What's the problem?" Leon asked his new acquaintances.

"Kelvin just can't stand him."

"Why not?"

"Because he's a twat."

"Kelvin?"

"No, Charlie."

"Still, he's obviously giving up his time to do this so..." Leon tailed off.

"Thinks he's better than everyone else," offered Steve. "You've met them. Young dick-head likes to tell his friends how street wise he is, to tell birds how he is so kind-hearted, likes to tell himself he's better than us. Probably looks good on his CV too. Still, at least he's not a bible basher I suppose. Got more of those than we can shake a stick at."

"I still think anyone who gives up their time deserves *some* respect."

Steve had until this point been looking straight ahead into the distance. He turned to face Leon.

"You're new to this aren't you, mate? I don't just mean in the area, I mean you're new to all of this?" He swept his arm out to the side and behind, taking in the people around them.

"That obvious?" Leon's throat was dry and he felt in desperate need of a drink.

"Don't worry about it," said Karen. "Where you sleeping?"

Leon was ready for this one.

"Oh, just over on the Embankment. You know where the bridge meets the..."

Steve was looking at him with a look of surprise. Karen butted in.

"For Christ's sake don't tell us where. I just meant are you rough, B and B, hostel? You really are new aren't you?" she smiled. "Listen, it's really not a great idea to stay there, even if you have a good spot. It's full of psychos. Schitzos who are too far gone to live in the same buildings as other people. Thieves and violent nutters who are not welcome anywhere. All in all, not the safest area, especially..." she looked down, not wishing to offend him.

"I'm OK. I kipped in the multi-storey car park the other night. The security guards turned a blind eye. But there's others in there. It wasn't good." Leon had done his research.

"It's a well known smack-head hangout, Leon," Karen said. "I know a B and B not far away."

Leon though he saw Steve shake his head to himself in resignation. He guessed that Karen had a good heart and tried to help those in need. He suspected that Steve had not and did not.

"And I could just get in tonight? At this time?" Leon was genuinely surprised, even though he would be tucked up in his own bed, wide awake, within the hour.

"It's supposed to be referral only but I can get you in."

Steve shook his head again, making sure this time that Karen could see him.

"What?" she asked indignantly. "He's a straight-head. Clarence would kill to have another room taken up by a straight."

Leon had no idea what she was talking about but nodded along.

"Failing that," she continued, "I can recommend a hostel which is not rat infested and where you're fairly unlikely to get knifed."

She smiled which was a relief to Leon, but he was unsure as to quite how much she had been joking.

"It's really kind of you, Karen. Look, if you could give me the name of the hostel I'd appreciate it. Then I can see how the night pans out and have the option."

"Get there sharpish if you're going," grunted Steve. "You'll want to be hidden in your room by eleven."

Leon did not want to ask what would be happening after eleven. A woman appeared with a wedge of leaflets grasped in her hand, wearing clothes far too well presented to be a street dweller. She approached Karen and Steve and was about to offer them one when an entirely silent chain of events took place. Steve looked up from his food, the woman clearly recognised him and looked ready to give him a piece of her mind, Steve glared as if to dare her, she thought better of it, Karen smiled dryly at the woman and shrugged apologetically, the woman moved on.

Leon was so enraptured by this piece of theatre that he completely missed what the woman had said to him. He only realised she was talking to him at all because of the crucifix-emblazoned printout being wafted under her face.

"Hmm?"

"The Lord can help you. No matter how lost you are, He will show you the light."

"I don't suppose he could sort me out with a good night's kip could he?" Leon asked.

"Sorry?"

"Nah, nothing." He held up the leaflet in acknowledgement of its receipt and the woman moved on to find someone else. He wondered how many of these would soon be joining his own in the bin. Leon noticed that Steve was grinning. Perhaps the big lump was warming to him.

# CHAPTER 7

Leon stumbled towards work. As he entered the campus he looked in anger at a huge skip parked between two buildings. The rusty yellow vessel was overflowing with perfectly good office furniture. He thought about the people he had observed during the previous evening. The two that he had spent time speaking to. They were out on the street, relying on charity to be able to eat. Here was probably a couple of thousand pounds' worth of useable equipment being tossed away for no good reason.

He knew what the reason was, just that it was not a good one. Folks with any sort of clout in the university were constantly buying new gear. They would come back from meetings and be full of hell that someone at the same level as them had brought along the new model iPad. Why didn't they have the new model iPad? They must have one now. Leon knew that someone would have ordered a new piece of furniture for an executive office. It would not be exactly the same shade of veneered, overpriced wood as all the other desks, pedestals, and tables in that office. Rather than move things around the simple solution was to replace everything in a five metre radius until it was more aesthetically pleasing, even though no one would actually notice.

Leon decided that in the grand scheme of the day he was about to have to struggle through, this was not a particularly big deal. He would not "sweat the small stuff" which was a phrase he seemed to remember seeing on one of those hideous motivational posters somewhere, sometime. That was about as precise as his brain could be at the moment.

He had returned home from his 'night out' knowing he had wasted his time and feeling more than a little ashamed of himself. But for all that he had been somehow uplifted by what he had seen, which were human beings essentially being kind to one another. On the whole, anyway. There had been a general air of camaraderie among those benefitting from the generosity of others, aside from the commonly held opinion that Charlie was a twat. Leon was sure that this brief sense of warmth and contentment would help him to sleep. And it did. For three hours.

Entering the office Leon made a noise which could have not possibly passed as "good morning" but would have to do for now. He noticed that Maggie was not at her desk and then somehow remembered (surprisingly, as he tried not to listen to her) that she was away for three weeks on some sort of holiday with her smug husband. He made himself an incredibly strong coffee and had a flick through the purchase orders that had piled up on his desk. When did they even arrive there? He spent pretty much his whole working life at his desk so how did so many arrive when he was out of the office? Had he cultivated such a reputation of grumpiness that people waited until he was not there to throw them in through the door? He suspected that part of it was his propensity to question everything. As opposed to some colleagues in other faculties he was a stickler for financial regulations and believed that he had a responsibility to make sure that taxpayers' money was being spent in the right way. Many of the staff had such little respect for the source of the money they were trying to use that he took great delight in stopping them. It was sadly his favourite part of the job.

He looked at the first form on the pile; a research grant being used to finance a reflection pond for someone's home. He had never heard of a reflection pond and was not surprised in the least when he read further to discover that it was simply a pond to be installed at an Art Reader's house so that she could look at it and reflect upon her research. Normally there would have been a certain satisfaction to pissing on that particular bonfire. Now everything was too hazy. Leon's primary focus now was on just putting one foot in front of another until the day ended. Of course, he would still try to get it stopped but he didn't have the energy to stand up to any senior management once they waded in to support it. There were several of the usual nonsense; people who were completely I.T. illiterate wanting tablets to take to meetings, others wanting expensive notebooks so that they could no doubt take them home for their own use.

Then came the ones for which he had built up a useful knowledge over the years; someone trying to pay over a thousand pounds of university money for transcriptions to someone that Leon knew was his wife. Another trying to bring in her husband as an associate lecturer. Probably to cover hours that she was already being paid to teach.

Then came a beauty; a new member of staff claiming relocation expenses for moving to a new property that was actually further away from the university. What's more he was claiming not only for a delivery company but also for a specialist cat transportation company to move his kitten. Even in Leon's current state of mind he decided there was no fucking way this bloke was getting the cat money.

Leon begrudgingly picked up the phone and punched in the extension number of Andrea Reynolds about her desire for a reflection pond. He definitely needed more information on that one. He was dreading speaking to her as she had a reputation for treating the support staff like shit and he would have to bite his tongue. No answer. Not unusual as, if she didn't have lectures to do that morning she was unlikely to have come to work. He started to draft an email to her just to see if her out of office was on; it wasn't. He grabbed the purchase order and walked up the stairs to see her Head of Department.

Surprisingly he was in. Jeff Turner looked as though he had studied pictures of academic offices and tried to set his out in the same way. Leon had to wind his way through haphazard piles of books, while trying not to knock over things that may or may not have been pieces of art done by one of the staff, one of the students, or perhaps a school child. Maybe by Jeff himself.

"I was wondering if you'd seen this purchase order for Andrea?"

"Have I signed it?"

"Well, yes..."

"Then I've seen it."

"OK, yeah. What I meant was..."

"What you meant was; have I been signing off things without reading them?" Jeff smiled at Leon. Leon attempted to smile back but it came out as a grimace. They both knew that Jeff signed off everything without reading it and it had been a massive pain in Leon's arse for years.

"Well, anyway, I was going to ask her about it but I can't get hold of her."

"She's on sabbatical."

"No that was last semester. She'll be back now." Leon thought that it was typical of Jeff to not know what his own staff were doing.

"She's got another one."

Leon was surprised to see Jeff look rather sheepish; a look that he did not think the man was capable of. Something was definitely awry.

"But how does that work? She's work loaded to…"

"She didn't quite get as far as she was hoping so I've… look, Leon, don't make a big thing of this OK. It is in the interests of the department."

Leon could feel his frustration building again. It annoyed him that his academic colleagues got six months away from work every three years at the best of times, particularly as they rarely seemed to be held accountable for what they may or may not have done. But clearly some deal had been manufactured so that Andrea could have a further six months sat on her arse watching daytime television.

"So is she on another sabbatical?"

"Well, it's not officially part of the 'one-in-six' scheme."

Leon knew that if he pushed the issue that Jeff's sheepishness would soon be gone and replaced with defensive aggression. He left quickly.

Leon seethed over Andrea Reynolds. So she wanted them to pay for a pond for her garden while she skived off work. In what other career, he wondered, could you get full pay to not come to work for six months, admit that you had done nothing and be given a further six months as a bonus? Perhaps a reflection pond might inspire her to do some fucking work. He slapped the purchase order in his 'deal with when I'm less angry' pile.

There were times when he wondered whether he hated his job per se, or whether he would find it tolerable if everyone was treated equally. He thought about the senior manager who used the excuse of working on two sites to spend hours sitting in his parked car reading his Kindle; the countless people going on needless overseas trips because it sounded nice; the lecturer who was getting paid full time but was picking up a second salary for working two days a week at a private company; the staff who were essentially rewarded just for doing their job.

And then he thought of Alex Treadwell. The police had ended up breaking his front door down when the university could not vouch for his whereabouts. His neighbour had called the police as Treadwell had a history of 'eccentric' behaviour to the extent that several of those living around him wondered if he were fit to live alone. Despite this, the university clearly considered him fit to be in front of students. The next day he had returned home from an impromptu seven-day trip to Scotland. Other than the elderly aunt that he was visiting, not another soul knew where he had gone, including his employer.

Leon wondered how long it would take for someone to realise if he went missing. It would potentially take a couple of weeks from a social perspective; he quite often went off the radar for a while. As for work, who knew? Maggie was off for a while and, as of tomorrow morning, Clive was off for a few days. They might not even realise for a while when they came back. His line manager would notice at some point. Once he got caught, perhaps he could just feign sickness and claim that he had emailed or left a message and it had not made its way through.

As Leon thought about it, the notion became more and more attractive and possible. It even had a certain romantic quality to it. He knew that it was a ridiculous idea and that if his mind was not so rattled by lack of sleep it would be no more than a passing thought. He tried to get on with some work but it whirled round and round in his mind, fragmented, nonsensical. But appealing. So appealing.

Leon looked at the time, which was almost half past two. He stood up, grabbed his mobile phone and coat and walked out. He did not turn off his computer, he did not lock the door, he did not change his mind.

## CHAPTER 8

Leon walked briskly towards the park, as though he actually had a purpose. Perhaps he was moving quickly to get away from things rather than to move towards them. On arriving home he had picked up his mail and added it, unopened, to a pile of other unopened mail that was largely brown and unfriendly-looking. For weeks he had been too tired to even consider looking through them but he knew he would soon be in trouble if he didn't. Not today, though. Today was for riding the exhilarating wave he had created all by himself. He wondered quite how pathetic his actions would be judged by an external party; behaving like a school truant whose main justification seemed to be a petulant 'well everyone else does it'. He would undoubtedly go back to work tomorrow, even more tired after spending half the night wondering if he would be into a disciplinary procedure.

Closing in on the main park gates he stopped dead in his tracks. There was someone sat on the pavement on a dirty blanket. She looked up as a woman jogged past. Leon stopped breathing. It was Karen. His suit trousers and smart-ish jacket felt like they were glowing with cleanliness. He could not tell if she had seen him when she looked up at the jogger but he thought probably not as she had not reacted. He was only several feet away and was now stood motionless in the middle of the path. He spun around instinctively and crashed into a man who had been walking behind him. The man swore as he passed but Leon resisted the instinct to turn around and apologise to him. He walked off briskly, feeling Karen's eyes on his back but knowing that if she had not seen him so far then at least she had no way of identifying him from behind.

Once Leon calmed down he realised that he had been less worried about his 'cover' being blown than by Karen feeling let down. He barely knew the woman but for some reason he did not want to disappoint her. Perhaps it was that she had tried to help him and shown some sympathy for his imaginary plight, in stark contrast to her partner. He realised with some sadness that he had enjoyed the brief time he had spent with Karen and, even to an extent Steve, more than most social interactions of late.

He still had not moved the lightshade. Luckily it was still dark enough not to bother him, but he could still tell. He could have sworn that he could hear the clock ticking from the other end of the house. Not possible.

It was already turning out to be a long night as he had only fallen asleep for an hour and a half. He had woken at two thirty and was ignoring the guessing game of 'what time is it.'

What could he possibly gain from spending more time in the homeless community? He no longer believed that the note was any more than cruel coincidence. But Marie, if she was still alive and in the region, was clearly not a part of conventional society. If she were then someone would have spotted her in the missing person ads, or her name would at least produce something credible in Google.

If anyone was likely to have seen her or know of her it was someone within that dismal bunch of people he had seen the other night. And he simply had to know. It was occupying his every moment and he had gone too far with it to have any chance of retreating. He knew that it was one of the reasons for the break-down of his relationship with Sandra. 'That fucking woman', Marie had become known.

Leon had tried his best to keep the extent of his obsession hidden from Sandra but it was no good. She would catch him with his file; she knew of the missing persons pages; she seemed to be able to tell when he was thinking about her. It had driven her crazy and Leon did not blame her for that in the slightest. It had been quite some time before he had told the whole story to Sandra. One evening while quite drunk and wholly maudlin he had described his fleeting encounter. Sandra accepted that there was no issue of attraction for the woman, simply that Leon had to know what had happened to her. The issue was that she could not understand why he had to find out. And the truth was, neither did Leon.

Leon knew he had not been a good kid. He had done lots of things to be ashamed of, and some that he had never discussed with anyone. The only other people who knew about the burglary at the school, the property damage, nasty tricks and, worst of all, the accidental loss of James Blackwood's little finger, were his co-perpetrators. As they had grown older it seemed that they had all developed the same sense of shame and there was an unspoken rule that the events of decades before should be consigned to history, never to be mentioned. In that way, perhaps they would cease to exist. That certainly seemed to be the case as more years passed, the only evidence to the contrary being Blackwood's left hand.

But they had still festered away in the mind of Leon Glover. His guilt was never assuaged in the way that it was for his friends. Unless they were just as good at covering up as he was. During these long, lonely nights those events and those feelings would haunt him.

The episode with Marie seemed to him to thread its way through everything. He wondered to himself; if he could know for sure that Marie was dead and that her death had nothing to do with that day, would that be better than her being alive but him never finding out? The dark, desperate, selfish truth, one that he could never tell anyone and could not even admit to himself, was that he would prefer to know she was dead. Perhaps then he would move on. Perhaps then he would sleep.

But the real worry was that he knew his obsession was slowly growing.

Leon sat up in bed and switched on his lamp. He had taken enough of this shit. He decided there and then to take back control of his life. His contentment would not be dictated by some event which may or may not have happened and which he had no control over. If he did not stop this right now he was going to throw everything away including his job, his home and any chance of happiness. He should pull himself together and go back to work. That's what he should do.

Leon could hardly lift his head from the pillow, such was his tiredness. It felt like a bowling ball except that it was full of cotton wool. Eventually, he rolled his body off the side of the bed so that his head simply had to follow him.

He looked at the wardrobe and then to his unclean jeans and t-shirt that were crumpled in the corner. He walked over to them and dragged them on without any enthusiasm. He could not face the thought of wrestling with socks so padded downstairs to the kitchen barefoot. The cold tiles underfoot felt lovely to his feet; a relief that his body could feel any sort of sensation in its current numb state. He pulled open the fridge door and without hesitation grabbed the first can of beer he got his hand to, opened it with the other hand and put it to his mouth. Again, the touch of the cold metal woke up some more of his senses and he took a long series of gulps where he stood, emptying most of the can. He drank so greedily that some of the beer dripped down his chin and soaked into his top. He did not for a moment think about whether this was a good thing to be doing at seven o'clock in the morning and his foggy mind would not have been able to advise him even if he wanted it to.

Leon forced on a pair of trainers, deciding against the socks completely, and put on his coat. With that he walked out of the house, stepping over a folded piece of A4 paper which had the faint writing from a felt tip seeping through it in reverse. He didn't remember it being there before but he was too tired to be bothered about it. He shut the door behind him.

He did not know where he was headed as he walked along his street. He tried to make a decision but it was tough coming up with options, never mind selecting from them. That piece of paper definitely had not been there the previous evening and the post would not arrive for hours, which meant that someone had pushed it through the letterbox. It wasn't a takeaway menu or a charity collection bag; it was hand written. Leon realised that he had come to a complete stop in the path. After several moments and in lieu of having any other plan, he returned to the house.

Opening the door he stooped to pick up the paper and sat down on his front step. He decided he couldn't read while walking and did not want to go back into the comfort of his home from which he may never have the energy to escape again. He leaned sideways against the doorjamb and unfolded the piece of A4. It simply had three words printed in precise block capitals; YOU'RE GETTING CLOSE.

He needed to get out. Go anywhere. He shakily but precisely folded up the sheet into quarters and slipped it into his back pocket. He knew without checking that it was the same writing as the note in his Big Issue. He received a shot of paranoia that rushed through his veins and made the hairs on his forearms bristle. He looked around; across the street, up at windows, for passing cars, cyclists, the pub car park. Not a soul to be seen.

He checked that the note was still in his pocket, even though it was little over twenty seconds since he had put it there, and hurriedly rushed off in no particular direction. Although he did not know where he was going he needed to get there quickly.

## CHAPTER 9

"'Course it wasn't like that in the forces. Not a bit of it."

As far as Leon could tell, this was a complete non-sequitur, but he would be the first to admit that he had not been paying complete attention.

"You could trust each other for a start. No, trust doesn't cover it. Loyalty…and trust."

Even though Leon's last drink had been his can at seven that morning, he felt as though he had blanked out large parts of the day. Here he was, sat in a room that stank of animals, sweat and something that could well be piss. The chair he was sat in was not fit for a dog but it was still a damn site more hygienic than the sofa that his new acquaintance was slumped on.

"Got to watch your back now, young man. 'Course you got me to watch it as well now haven't you? Wouldn't normally say that but I can see I can trust you, see?"

Leon took a gamble that this was a rhetorical question and did not bother to answer. Upon noticing the man (Graeme? He might have said his name was Graeme) was looking at him he smiled weakly to acknowledge what was presumably a compliment.

Graeme (if it was Graeme) was overweight and sweaty with a drinker's pock-marked nose and a wheeze in his breath. Everything about him looked, if not downright dirty, then at least slightly grubby. His teeth were stained and it looked to be a little while since he had washed his clothes or himself. His hair was clearly thinning but was so overgrown and dishevelled that the baldness was the last thing you noticed. Leon wondered if some of the follicly-challenged blokes at work who clearly spent hours dragging their remaining hairs forward in a manner that fooled no one should take a leaf out of the book of the bizarre man sat opposite him.

"Aye, you'll be right. Look like you know what you'll do."

Leon tried to remember whether he had actually spoken since introducing himself half an hour beforehand. Since then his new pal had rambled in semi-coherent style in a voice that held a hint of Yorkshire accent but was mostly clipped. Leon suspected that he was drunk but he wasn't showing any signs of slurring or clumsiness.

It had been a long day. Head still reeling from his latest message and the guilt he felt from bunking off work, he had bumped into Karen and Steve. At least he told himself that he had bumped into them. In actual fact he had sought out the spot where he had last seen Karen and found them not too far away.

Having spent several hours with them, he had learned more about them. For starters, they were not a couple, as he had imagined. Reading between the lines it appeared that they simply needed each other. Karen needed Steve for protection and he needed her for company. Karen had been the victim of domestic violence over a great number of years before ending up on the streets. Steve had talked much less freely but Leon had garnered enough information to realise that he had suffered a relationship breakdown that had set off a chain of events, leading him from a well-paid job to his current situation.

Leon offered very little in terms of his own back-story but, caught on the hop, had claimed to still be sleeping on the Embankment and Karen had insisted on getting him indoors for the night.

"You need to get in a hostel. I can sort you a B and B for tonight if you can get the request in tomorrow so Clarence gets paid."

"*You* don't stay in a hostel. Or a B and B," Leon stated.

"Yes but we know what we're doing," she smiled.

"And before you get any mad ideas," Steve chipped in, "we have out hands full looking after two of us. We can't afford to be a threesome."

Leon had, by this stage, got used to Steve's brusque manner and had started to, very slightly, warm to him.

The end result was that Leon found himself in a bed and breakfast that seemed like it had last been renovated at some time around the war. He was not sure how he had allowed himself to be here. He had walked through the area many times in the past but never even noticed the building. If Graeme was to be believed then it was one of several similar places in the locale, although he claimed that this was one of the nicer ones. It was for this reason alone that Leon had decided to place the rest of his testimony under suspicion.

"So then Graeme," Leon took a punt and the man did not correct him, "any idea when you might have seen her?"

Graeme looked at him blankly through watery eyes. Leon nodded at the broken crate masquerading as a coffee table. Upon it was a well worn computer printout with a picture of Marie on it.

"Oh her, yeah. Well, I'm pretty sure I've seen her. You never lose your instincts you know, when you've had to be so sharp for so long," Graeme tapped the side of his sweaty head with two chubby digits. "Look ... I'm sorry I've forgotten your name already."

"Leon."

Leon had briefly considered inventing a new identity for himself but then decided that his adventure was already causing him enough problems without adding further complications.

"It's been a long time. Years. And that photo's much older than that. But yes, I'm pretty sure I've seen her."

"So is there anything you can tell me?"

"Why do you want to know? No offence... pal," Graeme (who had clearly forgotten Leon's name again) said, "but how do I know I'm not going to get this lass into trouble here."

"She's an old family friend. I just thought I would try to get in touch."

"Never tried to get in touch before you were on the streets I bet."

Leon looked at his feet and attempted to look contrite. It was not difficult to pull off as he just drew on the reserves of guilt he carried around with him. Graeme looked slightly fidgety.

"You got any drink?" Graeme asked.

Leon shook his head.

"Could you see your way to getting some?"

"I thought you couldn't drink in here."

"Clarence doesn't mind me. As long as I don't do it in front of the other guests, he knows I don't misbehave."

Leon sighed and stood up to go to the off-license.

"If it's who I think it is, she used to hang around with Vee. Even if she didn't then Vee will remember her. She's good like that."

Leon wasn't sure that this information was worth the can of beer that was currently nestled inside Graeme's jacket pocket. Unsure how to proceed once he got to the shop Leon had decided to only get one can of beer for Graeme for fear of looking like a spendthrift. Then came the brand; he had eventually plumped for Kestrel Super Strength, purely because he knew people referred to it as tramp juice. It had raised no reaction from its recipient so Leon was unable to ascertain whether it was his drink of choice. Leon patted the bottle In his own inside pocket.

"I don't suppose Vee lives here?"

"Clarence has his standards you know? Won't let smack-heads near the place."

Leon's heart sank a little. "Actually, I just meant in the area."

"Oh yeah. Not far at all. Last time I saw her anyway. She was in a hostel down near the front. I can show you where it is in the morning if you want. Show you where to get a decent lunch too."

Leon decided that Graeme must be quite pleased with his can after all.

## CHAPTER 10

At least it was a different ceiling to stare at. And this one had plenty of character. Mould spores decorated one corner while a wide crack provided an interesting division of a wide expanse of yellowing, peeling paintwork. There was the muffled noise of two men having a heated argument in front of the building while there was constant door opening, shuffling, coughing and swearing from the corridor outside his room. He dearly wished that he had returned home to at least collect his sleeping bag, but then its cleanliness may have raised eyebrows. Apart from his shoes and coat, he was still wearing all of his clothes. And it was certainly not for warmth; if anything the air was slightly muggy which helped stale odours drift upwards from the sticky carpet. The only window had been painted shut. The clothes protected him from the stained and frayed pieces of material that seemingly passed for bed sheets in this place.

Once Graeme had served his purpose Leon had been desperate to get away from him but through a sense of politeness, added to the fact that his help would be required in the morning, he had stayed a while listening to the hard-luck story. Apparently the drunken fellow had not adapted to civilian life upon leaving the army. He had seen too much for his mind to cope with. This had led to a turn of events which, despite Graeme not describing it as such, sounded to Leon like a nervous breakdown. Or at the very least, some form of post-traumatic stress disorder. Graeme had tried but failed to disguise his bitterness over the lack of support he had received from the institution he loved. He went on to describe in detail the similar fate of many of his former colleagues. Despite not being sure quite how much to believe, Leon felt real sympathy for this man who had clearly at one point been an infinitely more impressive human being than he was now. He wondered what made these people so susceptible to slipping into this sort of life. The same personality type that led them to the military in the first place? Difficulty living with the things they had seen and done? The fact that real life back home was so comparatively pedestrian? Leon had ultimately decided that he was happy to give some time to the former soldier who had fought for his country only to be disowned by it. In fact, it had eventually been Graeme himself who had called a halt to the evening's proceedings, presumably desperate to go and drink his reward out of sight of the other residents.

He fantasised about what the mysterious Vee might come up with. Perhaps she would lead him straight to Marie. Would she have an opinion on whether the notes were from her? Probably not. If she had a drug habit so hard that it prevented her getting into the Calcutta Bed and Breakfast then she was likely to be completely off her tits. He would see what the morning brought but decided he was likely to spend most of the night worrying about it.

He crashed into a wall of self-reproach. His home sat unoccupied while he lay in a wretched bed in an even more wretched building. And all so that he could chase after a ghost. What a fucking idiot. Maybe he had lost his mind and would soon be genuinely living on the street, shouting at passing cars and collecting up rubbish. He wondered how people could tell if they are in the process of such mental disintegration, or if they never know at all.

He looked at his watch whose hands glowed at him in the dark. Quarter past one. He decided that if he wasn't asleep by two he would simply leave and go home. At least there he could spend his wakeful, dismal, lonely night in the company of his television set and fridge. Surely that would be better than being confined to this small prison. He reached to the side of the bed for his bottle.

Leon was asleep before twenty past one and slept for six hours straight. He only woke then because the sun was shining onto his face through the paper-thin curtains that did not even reach the foot of the windowpane.

He felt excessively groggy and for a while could not even focus his eyes properly. He realised that perhaps this unexpected sleep had simply awakened his senses to the level of sleep deficit he was carrying around with him. He had made a token effort to repaying the debt but suddenly the rest of it seemed intimidating in scale. Nevertheless, he was grateful beyond words that he had had a night's sleep which many would find inadequate. He imagined that he could feel his mind relaxing slightly that it would not have to carry quite so much strain on his shoulders today.

He needed to find Graeme. What time would a person like that awake? He probably did not have anything in particular to get up for so maybe not until late. Leon wondered if it would be out of order to knock on his door. Not that he knew which door was his but he could possibly find out. He decided that if he just went down and sat in the lounge long enough then his pudgy friend would surface. Leon looked around for his belongings and then remembered that he was not checking out of a hotel; he was leaving a hovel disguised as a B and B and, upon putting on his shoes and coat, was wearing his belongings.

Leaving the room Leon felt his shoe bump into something and looked down to see a chipped and stained bowl at his toe, containing a sparse offering of cornflakes, and milk which had now largely slopped onto the floor. 'That must be breakfast,' he thought, and wandered off.

"You're up early."

"Not by my standards, believe me."

"Did you get your breakfast?"

"Er…yeah."

"Not the Ritz here you know?" Clarence seemed cheerful enough. Leon suspected that this demeanour was saved for his few paying customers. Leon had been far from welcomed the previous evening before paying for his night's accommodation in cash. He had explained that he was grateful for Karen's reference but that he had sufficient money to pay for one night. They made a pact that Clarence would say nothing to Karen.

"Will you be staying tonight?" Clarence asked, hopefully.

"No, I'll be going home."

"Eh?"

"Well, I say home. Obviously it doesn't have a roof, but it's all I've got at the moment."

"Look, if you've got no more money we can get you sorted for tonight. You can use my phone. It's just a local call. You don't seem any bother, compared to some of this lot."

Leon declined the offer, realising how difficult many of Clarence's guests must be if he was so desperate for Leon to stay and occupy one of the beds. There was no way he was staying another night in that room. His house suddenly seemed like a palace that he could not wait to get back to, once he had undertaken his mission for the day.

## CHAPTER 11

It was evening when he finally made it home. He swung his front door shut behind him and was about to collapse onto the sofa when he thought about how grubby he was and forced himself to strip on the way to the shower.

It was amazing how good the soap felt against his skin, the sweet smell of it permeating the air and making him feel instantly better. He wrapped a towel round himself and padded through to the living room. A look at the telephone answer machine. A solid red light refusing to blink. No messages then. Coupled with the lack of post it gave him a slight sense of isolation. No one knew where he had been for two days, which, if he was honest, both excited and scared him a little. Nobody from work had even bothered to check where he was or if he was all right. He was, for the time being at least, completely off the radar.

He had not been caught out so that meant he could still just waltz back in to work tomorrow claiming anything he wanted as an excuse. That was definitely what he should do but, with the new note and Vee, was he getting close? He needed another day or two if he could just drag this out a bit longer.

Vee had been a no-show earlier that day. Graeme held up his end of the bargain, although Leon was not even sure that the ex-solider had recognised him at first. It had taken a fair bit of prompting from Leon for him to remember their conversation about Vee; the woman who hopefully had a good memory and a sane mind. But Graeme had been happy to help, even though Leon claimed that he had no further money for drink. Graeme had stoically got over the disappointment and taken Leon down to the hostel in question. He spent the journey filling in Leon on some details about Vee in a manner that made Leon feel like it was a warning rather than just small talk. He painted a picture of an addict who was rather unpredictable. A 'repeater' who had ended up in endless programmes before messing things up and finding herself homeless again. A resourceful woman who was street wise and knew how to survive, even pretending to be a devout Christian in order to curry favour with certain charity groups.

Leon felt anxious about meeting her and when Graeme emerged from Albert House to inform him that no one had seen her for three or four days his disappointment had an edge of relief to it. But Leon now knew where she could sometimes be found and would no longer need Graeme's assistance.

Leon had spent another hour with Graeme before accompanying him to a day centre where a paltry lunch was available. Not for the first time, Leon was impressed that people were so willing to help the homeless but realised that it was not sufficient to survive on. They had parted company after lunch and Leon made his way home after assurances that he and Graeme would see each other "around." What surprised Leon about this was that Graeme seemed quite content that this constituted a firm plan and would definitely happen.

Leon went through to the kitchen and before he even went to re-examine his note, he moved to raid whatever there was in the fridge that might still be in date. It wasn't much. He was ravenous.

He could see Marie from behind, bobbing among the dense crowd ahead of him. He pushed into people but instead of his momentum moving him forwards, they all stood immovable and he bounced back from them. It was impossible. He had to instead run into gaps as they briefly appeared. This way and that he dodged, all the time looking up to make sure that he had not lost the back of her head. His heart would jump as he thought of her disappearing, before he saw her again through the smallest of spaces.

Slowly, agonisingly, he made up ground. At once he was upon her and reached out to grab hold. Her short coat, inadequate in the cold day, slipped through his grasp as she continued unaware of him, and he slipped back. Catching her again on legs which were losing their strength he reached out once more only to see his fingers fail to close properly around her shoulder, his hand a grotesque claw, too puny to grab up its promised bounty. He dropped back into the crowd, knowing that his legs had given up. He fell to his haunches and used his hands to drag himself forwards. Avoiding dangerous footsteps from all directions he gained momentum until he was running on all fours like a dog, and able to finally pick up some speed. Now he was making up the ground on Marie and leaped forwards, finally grabbing the hem of her jeans and forcing her to stop. As her head slowly turned round he held his breath. The sight that greeted him was initially too complicated to comprehend, until he realised that he was staring into the dark brown eyes of Sandra. His ex partner's face was full of anger until she looked upwards, her mouth falling open as she spotted something up above. Leon found it difficult to look up from his hunched position. Eventually he managed and saw a circular metal pole firing through the air directly over him. He only had time to squeeze his eyes shut and wait for the…

He jolted awake, unsure as to whether he had actually woken himself by crying out. He decided that was, perhaps the case. He was sweating and slightly breathless. He sat up and swung his legs over the side of the bed. He needed to get up and clear his head after what had just happened. Any attempt to go straight back to sleep would result in more madness of the type he had just experienced. He glanced at the clock. Forty minutes at most, based on the last time he had looked. Forty fucking minutes. He couldn't take much more of this. But he had to stay calm. Losing his temper at the situation would only guarantee no more sleep. A quick walk around the house, a glass of milk and then bed. Then he remembered he had no milk. Just a walk then. Maybe there was beer.

Back in bed, he tried not to look at the lightshade. What if Sandra had been the one? It was true that they had not been madly in love in a head over heels, running through a meadow in slow motion Hollywood sense, but then who was? Reality is stronger than fantasy. Even if it had not been perfect, perhaps it was the best they would be presented with in this life? That was probably more likely to be true in his case; he had to admit that much to himself. What would life have looked like in the long term? Children? Unlikely; both of them had described a lack of ambition on that front, but time can change things. Marriage? Even more unlikely.

Could they have been happy? What did it really mean to be happy anyway? Why did people equate contentment with certain factors such as a long marriage, high-powered job, successful procreation? He knew plenty of people with those things who were miserable as sin. So why this relentless, all-encompassing pursuit of "happiness"; a state which was by necessity transient? As a permanent state it was not a possibility. So why not aspire to something more attainable. Satisfaction perhaps. Could Leon attain satisfaction? Mick Jagger was more likely than him and even Mick had claimed to be struggling, so he didn't fancy his chances.

But it was surely possible to achieve some state of contentment where you didn't dwell too much on failures or sadness and didn't waste time chasing unlikely dreams. It sounded better to him than chasing ecstasy; running faster and faster on the treadmill of life until exhausted and disconsolate you dropped dead of a heart attack.

Leon often surprised himself by quite what a miserable bastard he could be in the middle of the night.

He wondered if he was capable of finding someone else. It was unlikely as long as the Marie issue was on the agenda.

There was also the practical side of things to worry over, of course. Sandra was the higher wage earner and had left him in a property with a rent that was far too much for him. He had heard that she had climbed the career ladder even further shortly after their break-up. Some sort of management position at a consultancy firm that he would never have truly understood anyway.

He knew he needed to move and find a flat but he could not bear the thought of the effort involved. As a result, he simply spent the same amount of time worrying about the situation while slipping further into the red due to lethargy. It wasn't even as if the house was worth holding onto. All the nice things had belonged to, and been taken by, Sandra.

The few belongings he had left, added to the lack of care he was treating the place with, meant that it was slowly taking on the appearance of a crack den. The only items he would miss were the fridge and the television.

# CHAPTER 12

Leon had decided to not procrastinate over his options. He eventually rose and pulled on his dirty clothes from the previous day. He pulled his sleeping bag from the cupboard in his bedroom and went on a treasure hunt around the house, pulling together any money he could find. Leon had a habit of coming home and emptying out the contents of his pockets onto any flat surface that might be within arm's reach. This habit had driven Sandra crazy and he even annoyed himself whenever he could not find his keys, but it was now literally paying off. Added to what he had in his wallet, he ended up with something over sixty pounds. Carefully secreting it around his clothing, including shoes and any inside pockets, he then set to work on ensuring that he did not give any of his coins the bulk or space to jangle. Satisfied, he left the house without any further hesitation. He crossed the street and walked down to the park, separating the battery from the rest of his mobile phone. He looked around to check that the coast was clear before crouching in the bushes near the tennis court. It was far too early for there to be any children around which saved him the peril of looking like a kiddy-fiddler. In the hard soil, well under the cover of the bush was a hollow that was completely covered by prickly leaves and further protected by a guarding patch of nettles.

Leon had once had to retrieve an errant tennis ball from this very spot and he had found it so inhospitable that he almost sacrificed the yellow Slazenger. A hideous slice had ricocheted off the net post and the ball had trundled into the spot where he was now depositing his house keys and mobile phone. Those were the days when he had played sport. And had friends to play against. And had not yet lost his marbles.

"It's supposed to prepare them for life on their own feet, in their own accommodation." Leon could tell by the tone of Karen's voice that she did not believe that any more than he did.

"That place couldn't prepare anyone for anything other than squalor and depression," he responded.

Leon was suddenly conscious that he was actually talking to a homeless person who had probably known both of those states more than he could ever imagine, and he had no desire to offend her.

The weather was what his mother would have described as muggy. The air had that dense and stifling feel that instinctively made people tell everyone in earshot that a storm was coming. This would be quickly followed by everyone in earshot nodding and muttering in agreement. 'Should clear the air at least'. 'We need it, to be honest.' 'It's been coming.' 'Shit I've left the washing out.'

Black clouds on the horizon intensified the sense of doom. Leon had several times thought that he felt raindrops but had been wrong. His brain appeared to have subconsciously told his skin that the sensation was on its way but his various components had got their wires crossed.

"The Albert's not much more than a night shelter really," Karen continued, "it's at the crap end – very basic but it is still supposed to have regular visits. I don't think many in there would engage with the programmes, though. Definitely not the regulars. There are, comparatively, good places for the homeless. It's not one of them."

"Don't ever end up there, or if you do make sure you get single occupancy with a good lock. If they only have a dorm you're better off sleeping in a toilet."

Leon had seen the regulars that very afternoon. An experience he thought was probably similar to entering the set of the Walking Dead. He had summoned up the courage to wander inside and have a look for himself in the hope of finding the elusive Vee.

Even the entrance had been horrendous. The smell was the first thing that had hit him; no building that held human beings should smell like that. It reminded him of animal cages at the zoo. The carpet did not just have holes in it, but entire patches that had been completely worn through, including what was supposed to be underlay. The walls were covered in stains, scuffs, and dents and the lights all hung shade-less and glaring brightly, as though proud of the disgusting state of the place.

In the absence of any people to question he had walked into a room that looked like it was supposed to be a communal area even though it had no chairs. It was currently home to half a dozen guests, who were lying against walls, on a beanbag, a backpack and a wooden box. None of them looked up as he entered. Most of them looked like they would not have been capable of looking up if their lives depended on it.

A shirtless man was tearing a strip off an A5 piece of card while muttering to himself. Leon noticed a small pile of crucifix-adorned cards in the middle of the room. Clearly someone had recently been in to sell the benefits of letting the big fella into their lives. The man curled up the strip and inserted it into the end of a roll-up that he had manufactured from the contents of a Drum tobacco pouch that looked older than the man himself. Leon wondered what exactly was in the roll-up and then decided that it was small fry compared to some of the activity the others had been indulging in. He was not even sure that a slight, blonde woman, lying on the floor with her head up against the skirting board, was breathing. She jerked with a cough that sounded more like a dog's bark and resumed her position. Leon assured himself that if she hadn't coughed he would have checked on her. Another, more realistic part of him said that he would have let her expire rather than go any further into that room.

Back out in the corridor he found a young man who looked terribly unhealthy, but not quite on the verge of death, so had asked him about Vee.

"Room twelve usually," was the extent of his response.

Completely in line with Leon's expectations, the woman was not in room twelve. Or at least he got no response. He noticed what looked like a syringe further down the corridor but decided that he had no wish to find out and headed back towards the entrance. As he got there the young man from earlier was still stood in the entrance. He was looking towards the stairs and nodded at Leon as he descended them, maintaining eye contact as though waiting for him. Leon's heart sank. What did he want? Had he decided that he now felt aggressive about being asked a question or had he realised that Leon could be a potential source of money? Either way, it was not a good development.

Leon tried to walk straight past him to the front door but the man stepped in front of him. In his peripheral vision he saw the man's hand move towards him and Leon instinctively grabbed him by the wrist.

"What the fuck do you want?"

Leon looked down. The man's hand did not contain the knife that he had somehow expected it to, but a harmless envelope.

"Sorry, I thought you... What's this?"

"Got to give you it."

Leon took the envelope. It was sealed so he ripped one end off to fish out the contents. Biro on lined paper but a glance was enough to tell him that it was the same author as the last two.

"Who gave you this?"

The man shrugged and Leon saw his own hands grabbing the man's filthy t-shirt. The man tried to push him off but Leon's grip was strong.

"Just some fella."

"Did he have a woman with him?"

The man shrugged once more and without realising it, Leon gripped him tighter. He shrugged again, to prove his point.

"What did he look like? And if you shrug I'm going to hit you. Hard."

Finally the man looked a little less casual and looked at Leon, weighing up whether or not it was an idle threat.

"Tall. Skinny. Big 'tache."

"Big how?"

"Like, not small," the man's mouth twitched at the corners. Leon tensed his arm as though about to bring it back and the man continued. "Horseshoe thing. Stupid."

"Lots of white bits in it?"

The young man looked as though he was about to shrug and then thought better of it.

"Maybe, yeah."

Satisfied that the bloke did not know anything further, Leon pushed him away, muttering a half-hearted apology. The man laughably smoothed out his disgusting rag of a T-shirt,

## CHAPTER 13

YOU HAVE MAYBE GUESSED BY NOW THAT I AM NOT MARIE. BUT I CAN TAKE YOU TO HER. I DON'T KNOW WHY, BUT I KNOW YOU NEED TO FIND HER.

THIS WILL HAPPEN IF YOU FOLLOW MY INSTRUCTIONS. IF YOU DON'T YOU WILL NEVER FIND HER. IF YOU TELL ANYONE OF THIS ARRANGEMENT THEN YOU WILL NEVER FIND HER.

STAY HERE TONIGHT. GET A BED. IT DOESN'T MATTER HOW OR WHICH ROOM. IF YOU STAY THEN I KNOW WE HAVE A DEAL AND WILL GET WORD TO YOU.

Leon just wanted to scream. He didn't know at whom or what but he could feel a build-up inside him that needed a release. Perhaps he should go and punch that bloke after all. He stood up from leaning on the wall and paced. He thought and paced some more until he could feel a pain behind his eyes. He knew he was going to follow the instructions so could not understand why he was thinking so hard about his options.

But the questions were unanswerable, infuriating and scary. Who was writing the letters? At least he had established that it was not Marie. How did this person know about him? Did the note mean that she was definitely alive? And, most bewildering and fundamental of all, *why* was this happening?

***

But this had all happened to him before. It had ended in death. But surely that made no sense. He had read every word of that note before and that realisation made him nauseous. A ball burned in his pelvis and rose up through his abdomen, spiralling and spinning everywhere. His chest, arms, throat, all were infected by the rising pocket of unwanted and uncontrollable energy coming up through him. He could hardly breathe in and his stomach felt as though he was falling through space. A demonic face swooped in from his peripheral vision until its semi-transparent features were right in front of his face. It passed on its way before being replaced from another swooping in from the opposite direction. It was wordless but its presence told him that he had been stood in this exact spot before and it was the end of him. Leon grabbed his hair and squeezed his eyes shut but it made no difference – he could still see.

Somehow, among the reserves of sanity he had left, he knew what was happening. He was having an epileptic seizure. He had not been looking after himself at all recently, which included taking his AEDs.

He opened his eyes and looked around for somewhere safe. The dizziness made this already difficult task impossible. He needed to keep the note – he stuffed it in his pocket. Confusion accompanied his dimming vision. Was he actually going to die? He didn't think so but it was becoming increasingly difficult to tell what was real. He had seconds to get himself somewhere. Using his last shred of coherent thought, he launched himself into the one place that strange behaviour would be unnoticed; the living room of the undead.

***

He remembered nothing beyond that but as he awoke he noted that he must have made it. He was sat up against the wall and feeling like he'd been gored by a bull. He slid down onto his side and his face nestled into the disgusting carpet. He had woken from a deep level of unconsciousness and was utterly exhausted. Another ball began to flutter up through his chest and he flinched. It dissipated, hopefully just an aftershock of the main event. He did his best to slide himself back upright.

Everyone in the room was lying in the same spot as on his previous visit. No one seemed to notice he was even there other than the shirtless man with the religious cigarette roach who looked up at him.

"OK?" he asked quietly.

"Fine," lied Leon who felt like he might spew.

"You were fucked."

"OK." Leon did not want to offend the man but certainly did not want a conversation.

"You went, like, AWOL or something. Tried speakin' to you but you weren't there. You kept pickin' at your jeans like there was something there but there wasn't. You were freakin' me out."

"Yeah, I'll do that," Leon wanted to get out of there but felt the need to lie down more than anything else. He fought the temptation and wobbled to his feet. "Listen," he said, "how long was I away?"

"Not long. Ten minutes. Maybe. Not sure."

Leon looked at this man who would presumably spend the rest of the day making rollies in among sprawled bodies, and doubted he had a great grasp of the passing of time.

The note seemed like it had been part of a dream. He checked it and it was pretty much as he'd remembered. One line jumped out - I DON'T KNOW WHY, BUT I KNOW YOU NEED TO FIND HER. Leon didn't know why either, he really didn't. He had sometimes wondered if it was an attempt to be a hero. He disliked being the centre of attention but often caught himself romanticising about his heroic (sometimes anonymous) behaviour saving people in distress. Is that what motivated his mind? Was it simply to create a sense of purpose in a life that somehow seemed to be slipping from his grip? Why this incident? He had done lots of other bad stuff too. It must have been finding the purse. Did some part of him think it would make up for everything? Or did he have some sort of abnormality in his brain that meant it operated in ways that were unfathomable to him? He guessed he would never know the answers to any of these questions.

The dorm was beyond his worst fears. He had to settle for a three-berth but it was so small that three occupants would be right on top of one another. Someone was sprawled out on top of one of the beds. The man had red hair and gaunt features that reminded Leon of Damian Lewis' character in Homeland while he was undergoing an extended period of torture. The filthy, thin mattress showed its stains through the equally dirty and thin sheet wrapped around it. Other than this, the man had no bedding at all. In fact, he did not appear to have any belongings. Leon supposed that even if someone did have belongings in a place like this then they would make damn sure that they were hidden away.

The Damian Lewis look-alike was completely out. Leon had made a significant amount of noise entering the room as he had not anticipated the tiny gap from door to bed and had kicked the metal frame quite hard. The clanking metal had been accompanied by a loud 'fuck', but not a stir. So Mr Lewis looked harmless enough. But then that proved nothing; he could be an absolute maniac once he awoke and the effects of his poison of choice wore off. Also, there was the unknown entity of dorm occupant number three, assuming there was one.

There was no point in trying to stay awake to size him up, as he might not even arrive. Leon wondered who he was trying to kid, as he was unlikely to sleep anyway.

He removed his shoes and rolled out his sleeping bag. He was still completely shattered from his earlier episode. The good news was that there had not been another. Sometimes in the past, before he got his medication sorted, a larger absence could be followed by several smaller seizures. Thankfully not this time. He had gone several years without any problems and was angry with himself for neglecting his tablet routine. He climbed in before starting to worry about his shoes, so he grabbed them and stashed them in the bottom of the bag. He could not hear a sound from his roommate so stayed as still as possible and held his breath. There was an extremely faint but definite sound of shallow breath. So he was alive then. Leon told himself to stop thinking that people in this place had died.

He woke in a whirlwind of panic, confusion and pain. The pain was due to a large hand which was crushing his throat.

"Where's your money?"

"W..." Leon realised he was incapable of speaking due to the pressure on his windpipe. It was dark but he could make out the shape of a large man. Broad across the shoulders but also carrying a large belly. His vest showed hairy arms, one of which was attached to Leon, the other ending in a ball of knuckles, ready to strike. Leon processed all this in a matter of seconds, along with a neck tattoo (never a good sign) that looked like it just might be an SS insignia (a very, very bad sign). At least the ogre had the sense to let go of Leon in order for him to respond.

"What money?" he gasped.

"You *paid* for your bed."

"So"

"So you got money."

"Which I spent on my bed, genius." Leon's anger at the situation had momentarily got the better of him and he immediately regretted it. Leon did not shy away from confrontation but he was clever enough to know when to keep quiet. Fortunately, the man did not even seem to register it.

"Give me your fucking money!"

Leon's hand slid into his left trouser pocket where he had some loose change. He knew it wasn't much but he was going to have to play the situation as well as he could. He pulled it out and pushed it into the ogre's hand. There was less than two pounds.

"There. Have it. Now fuck off."

This was a calculated risk. Leon reckoned that he had to act pissed off at losing all his money or the man would know that he had more. The ogre seemed surprisingly satisfied with his haul and popped it in his own pocket.

Leon was astounded to see the man then crawl into the still unoccupied third bed. He had just been robbed by one of his roommates who now seemed content to sleep only several feet away from his victim.

For once, Leon decided that laying awake all night would actually be the preferred option and he lay on his side, heart pounding, staring over at the ogre. He'd already had a couple of hours before being strangled awake so that was just about manageable. The beat of his heart bounced into the flattened mattress but he did not dare roll over for fear of taking his eyes off his assailant. Confusion reigned; should he safeguard himself and get out of this shit hole, or would that prevent his secretive pen-pal from providing further communication? The ogre appeared to be snoring already. Almost four o'clock. Leon decided to give it an hour and then go downstairs to sit in the communal area. God knows what went on down there in the early hours, though.

Twenty to eight. That couldn't possibly be right. He was so confused that he had to talk himself through the positioning of both hands on his watch before he would believe that he had slept for a bonus three hours and forty minutes. He remembered the ogre and flicked his head in the man's direction. The ogre was sat on the edge of his bed noisily blowing his nose into a large handkerchief. Perhaps that was what had woken Leon. The man was preoccupied with his nasal housekeeping and had not noticed Leon's movement. Leon decided to play dead and closed his eyes, hoping that the man would soon be gone. He very slowly slid his hand, palm flat against the mattress, under the hood of his sleeping bag to get slightly more comfortable. The fingertip of his forefinger was pricked by something and the image of a dirty needle was the first thing that sprang to the forefront of his mind.

He jumped up to look under his sleeping bag. He didn't care about the ogre at this point. He thankfully found a small, plain brown envelope without any markings or writing on it. He must have prodded the corner of it.

Leon sat upright on the bed and held the envelope with both hands. Something small but heavy slid inside the envelope and settled at the bottom. He glanced across at the ogre, who was now watching him. The man's eyes were almost lost in the shadow of the long, thick, single eyebrow that crossed the whole of his forehead.

"Did you put this here?"

"Hmm?"

"Is this anything to do with you?"

Leon was too annoyed to be worried. Someone had obviously got way too close to him as he slept and the thought of it was freaking him out.

"What are you talking about?"

"This," he waved the letter, "wasn't here when I went to sleep. Did you put it there?"

"Why would I?"

Despite his Neanderthal appearance, the ogre spoke surprisingly clearly.

"Who's been in then?"

"I didn't see anyone. I came in, went to sleep. I've not seen anyone else apart from him." The ogre nodded at the inanimate body on the other bed. "I suppose someone could have been in."

Leon stared at him. He now seemed to be conversing quite normally with Leon, almost trying to be helpful. Surely it could not be that he had no memory of violently robbing him only several hours ago. Could it? He looked into the ogre's face as though looking for confirmation either way.

"In this place, *anyone* could come in. It's whether you wake up or not. Not much chance with that one, I'd had a few drinks, not sure about you…"

So that was it; the ogre had been blind drunk last night and didn't remember anything. Leon wondered if he should say something and then realised he was worried about upsetting the bloke, which was clearly ridiculous.

"Yeah, about last night. No, I didn't wake up when someone brought this in. I only woke once when you. Look, you probably don't remember this but…"

The ogre was staring at Leon with a confused look on his face. Leon though he detected one end of the brow rise a little.

"You woke me up."

"Right."

The man must think that he meant *accidentally* woke him. Must happen in these co-inhabited environments all the time.

"You woke me up on purpose. Took my money."

"Yeah," the ogre looked at Leon as though he was crazy for bringing this up. "Let's have a look at him."

With that, the ogre moved across to Damian Lewis and rolled him onto his side, which took some effort as he was as lifeless as a corpse. Perhaps by this stage he *was* a corpse, Leon thought, and wondered if he should have done something about it.

"Well he's certainly not your man and it definitely wasn't me so… What is it anyway?" he asked, nodding at the envelope in Leon's hand.

"Private," muttered Leon.

"Suit yourself. Just trying to be helpful."

Leon looked at him, getting more confused by a social situation the likes of which he had never experienced before. He hoped that he would not spend days mulling over ways to take revenge on the ogre. He did not have the time to spare on such a pointless exercise. But he knew that he would. He gathered up his sleeping bag and left.

# CHAPTER 14

THE ENCLOSED MAP SHOWS THE POSITION OF A WAREHOUSE.

ON FRIDAY AFTER 10PM YOU WILL BURN IT DOWN. NEARBY WILL BE AN OLD GREEN FORD CORTINA. IT WILL CONTAIN SEVERAL CANS OF PETROL. THE CAR NEEDS TO BURN TOO. THE ENCLOSED KEY WILL GET YOU THROUGH THE GATE. IF THE BUILDING IS STILL STANDING ON SATURDAY MORNING THE DEAL IS OFF AND YOU WILL NEVER KNOW.

IF ALL GOES TO PLAN I WILL FIND YOU. DON'T FORGET YOUR LIGHTER.

Leon looked at the map. He knew the run-down area of the quayside that was depicted although he had never been to the specific location of the warehouse in question. What the hell was happening here? This had escalated all of a sudden. He thought that he really needed to take this to the police. But then what? He would have to own up to his frankly insane behaviour. The police would do nothing on his word and, if he was honest, he couldn't blame them. And then what? He would break his contact with the mystery writer and that would be the end of it. Was he actually considering it? He didn't think so. Leon's mind was crashing; there were too many factors clashing with one another and he could not stop them gaining momentum.

He weighed up his options. It was Thursday morning, which meant that he had almost two days to come up with something before ten the following night. He decided to walk and try to think. The problem, as usual, was that he could not afford to go anywhere that he might be recognised so he shuffled off, sleeping bag over his shoulder, along the river. He was vaguely aware that he was heading in the direction of the warehouse but decided that was just coincidence rather than a subconscious need to see it. The fresh air did little to clear his foggy thought process, which seemed to have benefitted little from the previous night's unexpected sleep. He didn't feel like he was capable of making the most inconsequential decision, never mind one that he knew, if he got caught, would be a life-altering one.

After an hour of trekking and contemplation, he knew that he only had one lead; he had to find the Big Issue seller with the biker moustache. One problem was that Leon did not even know if the man was legitimate. He tried desperately to remember if he had been displaying an official vendor badge. He couldn't recall and admonished himself before deciding that no one ever really noticed that sort of thing.

It wasn't much of a plan. He was going to have to spend two days randomly wandering through the city, asking homeless people if they knew a man with a large moustache. A man who may not even be homeless himself. The words 'needle' and 'haystack' did not even seem sufficient. But it was that or commit arson so he was probably going to do it. He noticed that the option of giving up and going home had not entered his head.

He was tired, emotionally drained and completely demoralised. He couldn't even go for a pint. He had walked into a bar without a moment's thought and been taken aback when the barman simply shook his head at him. Leon wondered if the man's attention was on someone else, and then he caught sight of himself in the bar-length mirror on the back wall. The man looking back at him was hardly recognisable. Dirty hair, sallow cheeks, darkened eyes. His clothes were unpleasant and he had a sleeping bag hung over his shoulder by its cord. He had not been much to look at for several years anyway due to his lifestyle and sleep patterns. He now looked like death.

He was surprised at how quickly his metamorphosis had occurred. It was not even that long ago that he had been considered reasonably good looking. At the time he started seeing Sandra he knew that there were a few of the girls at work casting glances in his direction. If any of them glanced at him now they would undoubtedly not see beyond the tramp that he had become. A tramp who had no individual features that anyone would notice; those were not necessary as he could now be quickly and conveniently pigeon-holed as belonging to a certain section of society. This was what the barman had seen and that was why he had been forced to leave, ashamed.

He was safely inside the Five Cups, which was a far less discerning boozer, with a pint of bitter and a window seat. His paranoia told him that the barmaid was still looking across.

Leon had stashed his bag behind a wall near the train station and visited the toilets on the platform there. As public toilets went they were pretty good and he had felt like he was in the lap of luxury in comparison to the facilities he had recently been forced to use. He had stripped to the waist and used the soap dispenser and scalding hot water to clean himself. Through embarrassment he had hidden his face each time a passenger had entered.

He knew that going home for some clothes made far more sense – after all, he was trying to smarten up an outfit that he had chosen to make scruffy – but he could not bring himself to go there. He had earlier started to worry that work may report him missing. As he was actually accountable for his whereabouts at work, unlike that wanker Alex Treadwell, it must be raising alarm bells by now. The last thing he wanted to do was create a situation where the police were looking for him. So he had gone back to excavate his mobile phone and, perhaps rashly, rung Jonathan, a bloke he sometimes went for a drink with, from the Finance department. He had informed a slightly stunned Jonathan that he was not coming back, and please could he let everyone know. Leon had hung up before the conversation had recovered, removed the battery and re-buried the phone.

The barmaid had taken a long look at Leon when he had entered. So long that Leon was about to turn around and wordlessly leave before she had eventually said: "'Can I get you?"

But she glanced at him too many times while pulling his pint for him to feel comfortable. He surveyed the clientele of the bar which was mostly single alcoholic gamblers; typical afternoon fare. He had certainly fallen if they were more acceptable as customers than he was. He did not blame the barmaid in the slightest; he wouldn't have served himself.

He had got nowhere with his pursuit of moustache man and was having to ask himself some soul searching questions around the issue of whether or not he could burn down a building. How much would it trouble his jumpy conscience and, more importantly, could he live with the repercussions if he was caught at the scene or arrested afterwards? He could imagine himself as the subject of an amusing mini article in a tabloid newspaper. Having left a ridiculous clue at the scene of the crime he would be labelled the 'world's stupidest arsonist' and there would be a photograph of him arriving at court for everyone to laugh at.

His recent irresponsible behaviour was one thing, but it was a hell of a leap into crime. He was onto his second pint of Tyneside Blonde which he knew was silly but he didn't care. He now had a severely limited amount of money and he would need to find much cheaper ways of getting drunk if he were to get by. The Five Cups was a cheap bar but two pints was just reckless. There was also the danger of being seen by one of his new friends and 'outing' himself as a fraud. There was no chance of them coming in and getting served, even if they could afford it, but he would need to be careful as he left. In the meantime, he should stop worrying and enjoy the remaining two-thirds of a pint.

Leon loved pubs. He always had. There was something he found very comforting in them, and it wasn't just the alcohol. These days he usually drank through what he considered to be necessity rather than pleasure, and he had been aware for some time that he now had a fully blown alcohol problem. He believed himself to be a functioning alcoholic although he had never actually looked up the definition for fear of scaring the shit out of himself. The fact that he could go for several hours during the day without a drink was all he had to cling to in his attempts at denial. So his drinking habits had changed from enjoying company in the pub over a few drinks, with the occasional shared bottle of wine midweek with Sandra. Before he knew where he was he was using alcohol to induce sleep and drinking with anyone he could persuade to come to the pub, or on his own with cheap booze in the house. Often the cheap booze also made an appearance *after* the pub, and the distinction between weekday nights and weekends had blurred.

But in addition to his dependence on alcohol was the draw of the pub as an environment in which he felt more at home than in his own house. Even if he did not speak to any other patrons, they shared a bond in that they had all chosen to get away from the stresses and difficulties of their life for a short period. It was a haven where no one could damage them – unless you bumped into a psycho and got glassed of course. But Leon's fondness for public houses was not completely blind; he only frequented ones with the right sort of atmosphere and a minimal psycho count.

He tried to ignore his current predicament and sank back in the leather wingback chair. He forced his shoulders downwards in an attempt to make himself relax. He faced out of the large window that almost covered one end of the building and placed his drink on the small coffee table next to him. He was going to savour his drink and take his time, even though there was a deep-seated craving within him to swig and gulp until it was gone. He wished that he had brought something to read.

Leon stared aimlessly through the window, the outline of his own reflection mingling with real objects in the outside world. He scanned the front wall of the building across the road, watching the people walking back and forth, going about a multitude of tasks. One person stood stock-still in the middle of it all, staring straight across towards the Five Cups. Leon sat bolt upright as, through his reflection, he picked out a brown and white moustache. Dirty clothes, damaged shoes. For a moment Leon danced with his mirrored self, trying to get a proper look, before leaning forwards and pushing his forehead against the cool glass.

A car horn blared as Leon dashed across its path. He was barely aware of what was going on around him, so terrified was he of losing sight of the moustachioed man. As he approached him it was clear that the man had seen him coming. Only at the last minute when he saw the anger in Leon's face did he move away. Leon stopped right in front of him and at once realised that he did not even know what to say. For a moment they stared at each other.

"So who are you?" Leon started.

"I'm no-one. Just a bloke." The man tried to appear calm but was clearly rattled by Leon, despite being the taller man.

"Who gave you the note to give me? The notes?"

"A bloke. I don't know him."

Leon had to consciously stop himself from hitting the man. He tried to get a grip of himself and calm down; if he didn't then he was going to get nowhere.

"So you gave me notes? Two?"

"Yeah, I dunno what they were, though."

"From *who*?"

A few passers-by had obviously noticed the aggressive body language and tone of one of the two scruffy guys in the path. Some slowed as they passed, hoping to hear something interesting or funny that they could take back to the office and share with colleagues. Most assumed the two men would be drunk which increased the likelihood of comedy value. The common perception would definitely be that Leon was the perpetrator.

"One from a woman, one from a bloke. I didn't ask. Why would I? Someone offers you some easy cash in this life and you don't make a fuss."

"Tell me what they looked like. Both of them," Leon's aggression was getting the better of him once more and he was raising his voice.

"Why should I?"

"Because it's important."

"Not to me."

Leon's fist was approximately half way towards its target when his brain took over and tried to pull the punch. The result was a not very hard contact that was just about strong enough to cut the man's bottom lip against his teeth but not enough to really hurt him. The man dabbed his finger against the tiny cut, unperturbed. A few people on the path had actually stopped to watch at a safe enough distance that they would not actually get caught up in the action. Leon's vision was beginning to spin and he felt light headed. The lack of sleep and food, a bit of beer, a shot of embarrassed shame and a dash of adrenalin had combined to produce a cocktail of confusion.

A voice called out to them to stop, and another threatened to call the police. The rest of the gathering crowd silently wished that the two voices would shut up so that they could watch a good scrap.

"I'm... sorry. I don't know where that came from. Look... I need to know," Leon sounded almost pathetic.

"Fuck you. I didn't agree to *this*."

The man shoved Leon in the chest and barged through a small group of on-lookers. Leon stayed where he was for a moment until most of the rubber-neckers had dispersed. He glared at the few remaining with a challenging look so that they soon left too. His legs felt weak and, looking down, he could see his heart beating against the fabric of his t-shirt. Once he had collected himself he glanced around to see that everyone had gone back to what they were doing. They would soon find something more interesting to look at. Leon crossed the road back to the pub and looked up at the window seat he had occupied only a matter of minutes ago. To his dismay, his pint had been removed from its ledge. He kicked at the wall in frustration and set on his way. A thought struck him; what had the man meant? 'I didn't agree to this.' Agree to what?

## CHAPTER 15

He had no chance to escape as he and Steve noticed each other at the same time, making eye contact in the process. This was difficult; both men would probably choose to have a quick nod, no conversation and move on. Relief all round. Besides, if they spoke he might have to admit he was looking for Karen.

In deciding whether that would be acceptable Leon had noticeably slowed to a snail's pace. So that was it then. He could not simply walk on now or it would look like too much of a conscious decision. He stopped. Steve was sat leaning back against the fence with a small bowl in front of him containing a paltry collection of small change.

"All right?" said Leon, in that half asking, half greeting sort of way.

"Aye."

So far just an ordinary bloke-chat, then.

"Much happening?" Leon ventured.

"Nope."

"Well I'll not cramp your style; you'll not get much if I'm stood here."

"There's nowt happening anyway," Steve nodded to the spot on the floor next to him without actually offering up any of the blanket he was sat on.

Leon's heart sank. He contemplated saying that he was busy but then realised that would just raise more questions than it answered. He sat. He looked about and saw a set of coloured but very faded juggling balls. Next to that was a large red yo-yo.

"What's going on there," Leon asked, nodding at the equipment, "Get a bit bored, do you?"

"I like to try and earn my money where I can," said Steve.

"What, you perform?!"

"Yeah, what's so surprising about that? The kids love it. You know, seeing the big scruffy man juggle."

"Why are you not doing it now?"

"Who for?" Steve glanced up and down the road.

"You just don't strike me as the type to entertain kids."

"Got a daughter of my own…" Steve trailed off.

"Yeah, no, I'm sure…"

There was a long pause, eventually broken by Leon.

"So how old is your daughter?"

"She'll be eight now."

The phrasing left Leon in no doubt that Steve no longer saw his child.

"Been three years," continued Steve, responding to Leon's thoughts.

"So what happened? Sorry, I'm probably not supposed to ask that. I'm still learning the ropes of this homeless chat thing."

Steve smiled.

"Nah, it's fine. Her mum kicked me out. I don't blame her; I must have been a complete twat to live with. I didn't always behave well and she just had enough. From that point on I just turned into one of your classic street stories. Couldn't function, started drinking, lost my job, got in debt, etcetera, etcetera. Whenever I start to feel sorry for myself, which is quite a lot, I just remind myself that I deserve it."

Leon decided not to interrogate him on the 'bad behaviour'.

"So are you not allowed to see her? Your daughter, I mean."

"I probably could if I went about it the right way, but I'm not letting her see me like this. It kills me not to see her but it would definitely finish me if she saw what I'd turned into. Once I get myself sorted out I'll get back in touch with her."

"Must be hard."

"Yep…" Steve drifted off, "…but I am sticking to my guns. Get sorted, and then see her," he paused, unsure whether to go on. "I went to watch her once. Through the school gates. I just watched her playing. She looked happy. Anyhow, I got chased off by one fella who had come to pick his kid up. Thought I was spying on the kids I suppose."

Leon took a sideways glance at Steve. It was difficult to imagine anyone chasing him anywhere. He was shocked that the big man had opened up so much in a very short space of time. Perhaps he was even grateful to talk about it. Steve had possibly forgotten to be grumpy and accidentally revealed a side of himself that was normally concealed.

"I know what you're thinking; you've never heard me talk this much."

Shit, maybe this bloke could mind-read.

"I normally let Karen do all the talking. She's better at it."

"Where is she? Do you share this pitch or take turns?" he realised that in the excitement of getting Steve to talk he was now asking multiple questions.

"We don't always see each other during the day. Apart from anything else, it's hard to earn money when there's two of you. Always meet up at night, though. The streets are lonely *and* dangerous on your own at night. Anyhow, give us a look at the picture of that lass again."

Steve seemed to be hurriedly shutting the door that he had let swing right open. Leon pulled out the picture and passed it to him. Steve studied it and shook his head slowly.

"You having any luck so far?"

Leon shook his head in return.

"Just be careful if anyone reckons they know anything OK? They probably just see you as a chance to get some smack, booze, or whatever else they are into."

Leon felt an overwhelming urge to tell Steve about the notes, and about everything. Maybe leave out the part about having a house and lying to Steve and Karen about being on the street; that bit might not be well received. He wanted to pour it all out and share his burden. For some reason he stopped himself as it was about to come tumbling out of his mouth.

Steve was in the middle of warning him about trust and here he was almost telling everything to someone that he hadn't even liked very much up until half an hour ago. But then Steve had shared his own weakness with Leon, and surely that was a sign of trust. Maybe that's why he had done it. Perhaps he was just trying to lure Leon in. Perhaps he was lying. Even by Leon's standards he realised that he was being very cynical and decided to take Steve at face value.

Steve passed him back the picture, "So why you looking?"

"Hmm?"

Steve nodded at the crumpled paper in Leon's hand. Leon realised that, because his latest friend had gone soft and confided in him, he was going to be expected to return the favour. Of course, he had foreseen such a circumstance and practised scenarios. In his mind, however, he had always been in control of the situation and he had given details on his own terms in order to progress his search. Now he was on the back foot.

"She's too young to be your mother, and maybe a little on the old side to be your partner, although I'm not ruling that out. Sister *possibly*, although there's no resemblance," Steve began.

"You seem very interested."

"Just keeping the brain ticking over. Have you not found that yet? Doing nothing all day rots your brain. You only think about where money and food is coming from. That's stressful but it doesn't work the brain, you know? It does you fuck all use to think about what's in front of you so you find other things."

Leon was just pleased that there had been an abrupt change to the conversation.

"So I'm going to go for sister."

Bugger.

"Or cousin. No, sister."

Leon made a noise which was supposed to mimic the incorrect buzzer from Family Fortunes but actually sounded like he was in pain. Steve looked at him and he decided not to explain the groan he had just produced.

"I don't actually know her," admitted Leon.

"Okay, you're clearly just a weirdo then. I don't want to know."

Leon was surprised but noticed Steve was grinning. How the hell had there been such a transformation in this bloke's personality? He was aware that some people warmed up once they 'got to know you' but this was extreme.

"No, I just want to get in touch with her. Yeah, I've never met her but I know she's important to me to find out things. She can explain some things about my past that I can't make any sense of."

"Could you be a bit more vague please?" Steve responded sarcastically, "You sound like one of those bellends that wants to go travelling to find himself."

"Fair enough."

"We all need something to keep us going, though. So fair enough if that's yours."

"What's yours then?" Leon realised he was pushing his luck, delving deep into Steve and trading so little in exchange. He made a mental note to back off.

"I got two. I need to see my little girl and in the meantime I need to keep Karen safe. That's it. The reasons that I am still alive in one sentence."

"Are you really not a couple?" Shit - he'd gone even further across the line this time. He should leave after this one.

Steve nodded slowly and silently. Leon was unsure if he detected regret, sadness or just certainty. Leon did not want to ask anything further and Steve seemed to be thinking.

"I've noticed," Steve eventually offered, "folks in this way of life often fit into one of two categories in terms of the other sex. I reckon it's a bit like prison. Some completely lose any libido they might have had. I mean, who would want to get intimate with someone when you both look like you need a fucking good bath? Some others are at the opposite end. They just try to fuck anything that moves and do it by force if necessary. And don't ever think you're not at risk from them by the way, just 'cause you're a fella. Anyhow, I'm in the first lot. Karen seems to be as well. It's never been part it."

"Oh. It's just that you're so, you know, close," Leon was so intrigued that he kept forgetting to not ask any more questions.

"She stopped me killing myself," he said bluntly and abruptly.

Leon looked at Steve's bulk and pictured the petite Karen. 'How the hell did she manage that?' he thought. Luckily Steve's mind-reading abilities were still intact.

"She talked me round. Made me look at my picture of Agatha."

Leon momentarily wondered who Agatha was and then realised it must be the little girl they had been speaking about. He just pictured Agatha as an old lady's name, that was all. He was about to ask if Steve and his missus had been big fans of Ms Christie's whodunits but realised it was not the time.

"So if anyone hurts her, I'll kill them. It's a simple rule."

Steve smiled but Leon believed him without hesitation.

## CHAPTER 16

It was reasonably dark although the lengthy walk there had allowed his eyes to accustom themselves to the gloom. He felt light-headed and at one point sat down for a moment and practised deep breathing. The only light was from the moon as it peered through wispy clouds, and a dirty yellow streetlight which was really too far away to be of any use.

He looked at the battered old Ford Cortina at the roadside. He looked at the poorly maintained fence next to it. He looked at the large building inside the fence, which seemed like it was doing well to remain standing. He wondered what could be inside that was so important. Or maybe it was empty and the building itself was the important thing. Whatever the reason, the place was in a terrible state and certainly did not look as though it could be useful in any way.

He felt like he was dreaming. He was watching himself walk around; he could see what he was doing but was not sufficiently sentient to process information or make his own decisions. He knew that this was just his nerves getting the better of him. This was a very extreme situation and his mind was attempting to shut it all out to deny responsibility. He shook his head and nipped himself hard under the arm. He was back. He was now simply light-headed and nauseous which, although unpleasant, was better than having some sort of out of body experience.

How had events brought him to this point? He could barely piece everything together in his mind. The details no longer mattered. He had a purpose and he had travelled too far in its direction to simply stop. But there was no way he could go through with this insane errand. He pushed the button on the boot of the Cortina and had to pull it upwards, hinges squealing in protest. Part of him expected the boot to be completely empty, perhaps save for a towrope or a tattered atlas. That would be a normal thing to see. But no, it did actually did contain a number of ten-litre petrol cans, tightly packed against each other. His heart sank at the reality of them. He ran his hand over the smooth black, plastic exterior of one and his reluctant mind had to concede that it was definitely there. But that still did not mean he was going to use it.

His hands were slightly shaky as he pulled out the key and tried it in the lock on the fence's gate. It opened far more easily than the car boot. So far nothing was going to enable him to say he could not do it. It was going to come down to a straight battle between his obsession and his conscience. And he knew his conscience would win. Perhaps he could manage to switch off his conscience. Leon had often thought about how to do that very thing many times in the past.

He'd had bad thoughts before and occasionally got worried by them. What if he drove across the carriageway and mowed down that bloke at sixty miles per hour? What if he grabbed that child and threw him over the side of the bridge? What if he ran at that old lady and punched her as hard as he possibly could, square in the face? Horrible deeds, horrible thoughts. But it was perhaps the obscenity of them that made them so intriguing. And it was on these occasions that Leon, like the vast majority of people, could rely on his conscience coming into play. But sometimes he felt convinced that he could do it. Just for a short time switch out all other influences and just carry out the task, completely ignoring any soul-crushing remorse and life destroying implications that would follow. Just do it to see what the aftermath may look like. He had almost convinced himself that he could do these things; often scaring himself into grasping for his conscience to rescue him.

He dragged the gate open.

Leon stood looking at six large petrol cans on the floor in front of him. For some reason, he had pulled the gate shut behind him. He guessed that if someone did inexplicably happen to be passing this way they were likely to spot the bloke with sixty litres of petrol stood in front of the building whether the gate was open or not. The thought made him pull up the hood on his sweatshirt. He had returned home in order to pick up some clothing that was dark and might conceal him. In addition to this, he was worried that he may end up stinking of petrol or smoke. If he actually set fire to it of course; that was still unlikely but he wanted to cover every eventuality.

He kicked the can nearest to him gently and it made a pleasant sloshing noise. He walked towards the warehouse, back to the containers, over to the fence, in a large circle and then returned to the petrol, kicking the nearest container hard in frustration. He swore as his toes met the heavy object and his ankle jarred painfully. More circling was required to walk it off.

Leon walked across to the front of the building and tried the door, which was not even fully shut. He had to lean into it with his shoulder as it pushed against corrosion and rust. As he entered he realised two things; one was that by not dragging in a petrol can with him he was simply procrastinating, the other was that he was a fucking idiot for not bringing a torch. He pulled a cigarette lighter from his pocket. He had noticed that the car boot contained two large boxes of cook's matches but he had not brought those either. The lighter would not catch. Typical; he had remembered to bring a lighter but not checked to see if it worked. After repeated attempts the lighter's flame flickered to life and the light played gently up the interior walls. There was very little to see. The interior simply confirmed what the exterior had suggested; that the building had not been used in any meaningful way for years. The smell was quite unpleasant too. Stale, damp, rotten.

A shelf had a crumpled newspaper lying on it. Leon unfurled it and was surprised to see that it was only two months old. He screwed it tightly up and lit one end. The eeriness of the building simply intensified. Leon could not tell whether his fear came from his spooky environment or his task. He tripped and as his hands shot out in front of him the flaming paper came to rest close to a pile of cardboard boxes. He ran across to stamp out the flame in case it took hold of the boxes, before realising the irony of his actions.

Leon lay down on the patchy grass. The sweat poured from his brow, stinging his eyes. He could feel his hair was plastered to his skull and his sweatshirt had long been discarded. He did not even know where it was, so frantic had the last hour been. He must remember to find it.

The first two containers had been by far the worst. He had dragged those as deep into the building as he could manage. Over the unseen and hazardous floor it had been tough, but pouring them out had been harder. He had felt incredibly vulnerable in there too. He'd had no idea what was happening out on the road and upon exiting had breathed a sigh of relief that he did not have an audience. The distribution of petrol had become easier after that as he did not have so far to drag it; the last one he had simply tipped over a few yards inside the entrance and listened as its contents fought to escape from the small hole, glugging frantically.

He looked up into the sky. The night had got darker. The moon was obscured and the streetlight did not seem to have much impact on its own. He thought about what he had done. From a moral perspective he argued that he had, as yet, done nothing wrong. From a practical point of view, he thought everything should be fine. He had not risked the staircase to the first floor, partly because it looked shot and partly because he could not bear the thought of carrying the petrol up there. And he had not quite made it all the way through to the back of the ground floor, but there was a hell of a lot of wood in there. It would burn, he was sure.

Leon could not help feeling that he was completely wasting his time out there. He had carried out this ridiculous errand but there was no way he would be able to go through with the key stage. His head spun and he was pleased to be lying down. He could see stars and was not sure they were real. Confusion in his brain. He spotted his hoodie top on the ground and sat up to tie it round his waist.

He struck one of the large matches and watched it burn. He held it between himself and the warehouse, as though watching it alight. No one would miss this building. But he did not know what was in it other than a worthless ground floor. He could easily get away. But he would go to jail if he didn't. He pulled his picture of Marie out of his pocket and stared into her eyes. She was going to switch off his conscience for him. Just her. She was all that existed.

"Shit," Leon jumped at his own voice. He had not noticed the flame creeping down to the base of the oversized match and burning the tips of his forefinger and thumb.

He lit another and stared at her as he walked to the entrance. He kicked the door open. He put her back into his pocket although her image was still just as vivid in his mind. He opened the box of matches and carefully slid in the lit one, ensuring that it ignited the other tips, all lying neatly next to one another. He had a memory. They used to do this at school. They even had a name for it. Genie? Whatever it was they would shout it and lob the box into a group of people. Normally girls. Genie?

He tossed the box forwards and it landed on a piece of filthy carpet, soggy with petroleum. He had left the matchbox slightly open and smoke curled up through the gap. He thought it had possibly gone out but then saw a glow and a dry hiss as a couple of previously unlit matches joined in the party. The lid of the box started to char, and then lit.

Leon stood in a sort of trance. Although he knew what he had done it again seemed as though he was watching someone else carry out his own tasks. He felt an urge to go and retrieve the matches. His legs tensed as he inched back and forth, about to pounce one second and then retreating the next. What had just happened? What was he *doing*?

He started walking forward to get the matches, shaking his head at himself and wondering what he had been thinking about. As he approached he noticed that a single, small flame was beginning to dance next to the box. It gyrated, trying to build up energy. It was certainly *next* to the box rather than connected to the box. Leon held his breath. He possibly had enough time to stamp it down and kick the matchbox out of the door before it expanded. But then how much petrol did he have on himself? Common sense disappeared and he rushed towards the fire. At that moment, he heard a loud crackle and the flame shot upwards and sideways. He stopped in his tracks, inches from the fire and ran back outside. The left boot and hem of that trouser leg were on fire. He threw himself to the floor, wrestling with his clothing. He untied his sweaty t-shirt and attacked his ankle with it. Content that he was no longer on fire he sat and watched the building.

A distant siren pierced the quiet. Leon had no idea how long he had been watching the warehouse get ravaged by the fire that he had started. Judging by the fact that much of it was now either burned or collapsed and flames were tearing through the first floor, it had obviously been quite a while. He must have been hypnotised by it. Why the hell was he still here? He located his sweatshirt again and checked that he had not left any other belongings. The road was now too risky as an escape route. He had waited too long and put himself at risk from the approaching emergency services. He ran towards the opposite fence, which was in an even worse state of disrepair than the front one. He found a gap and yanked hard at it in an attempt to create a big enough hole for him to squeeze through. The hole got bigger. He had time. The siren was getting closer but was still obviously some distance away.

That was when he remembered the car. Shit, the car. The car had to go too. That was part of the deal. It would have his fingerprints all over it too. Running in the direction of the siren seemed crazy but he had to do exactly that. As he sprinted all sorts of things flashed through his mind; he should have done this as soon as the building was on fire, maybe even before; he had used up all the petrol; how do you set a car on fire?

He remembered seeing a programme on television where someone had lit a roll of newspaper and put it in the petrol tank of a car they were trying to destroy. Or was it a rag? He didn't have the paper any more anyway. And there was a high probability that the Escort didn't have a drop of petrol in it.

He picked up the sound of a second siren, different to the first and much more distant. He arrived at the open car boot, still with no semblance of a plan. There was nothing of any use left in there. Frustrated, he slammed the boot shut and grabbed his hair with his hands, his eyes wide with fright. He could see something through the dirty back window. Running round to the side of the car he saw that there was a seventh petrol canister sitting on the back seat. The siren was getting louder. From his position on the roadside, he expected to see headlights appearing over the brow of the hill at any moment. He tipped the can onto its side, removing the cap so that its contents spilled out into the foot well. Once it was a bit lighter he dragged it out and did the same in the front seat. He could now definitely see headlights coming towards him, the initial siren becoming frighteningly close.

He used all his remaining strength to take the petrol can on one last journey, this time to the boot where he threw it in on his side. He was soaked in petrol by this stage. The smell of it burned the lining of his nose and his eyes stung. He wiped his sweating face, which only served to transfer large amounts of petrol from his hands directly into his eyes. He was full of panic, his breath coming in ragged sobs. Through the tears he realised that he was illuminated. A police car had emerged from a vale and was headed his way with its red and blue lights cheerfully dancing in the darkness.

Matches. He needed matches. He had burned one box. Where was the other? In the boot. Probably soaked through. He grabbed his lighter from his pocket. He flicked it. A brief spark and then nothing. Again and again, the lighter refused to work. This couldn't be happening. He was going to have to run and leave the car. But what would be the repercussions of that?

The police car was almost there as the lighter produced a flicker, then a flame. He held it down in the Escort boot until it lit. His hand burned as he fought through the pain barrier in order to ensure the job got done. The police car was screeching to a halt but as the driver saw the fire start in the Escort he moved a few yards out of the danger zone.

Leon was running. He was running as fast as he could but it did not seem fast enough. He heard two car doors slam shut and at least one set of feet chasing after him. As the police car engine shut down and the siren turned off Leon could hear the second vehicle on its way. He was amazed that he could even take in this information but he felt like he suddenly had more awareness than ever before. His senses were finely tuned. The sound of the policeman running, the distant fire engine, the smell and taste of petrol, the cold air against his now damp skin, the gap in the fence.

Leon knew that he did not have time to stop and try to further expand the space in the fence. He was only going to get one chance and he had to trust that he had done a good enough job earlier. He hurtled towards the weak spot that did not look big enough now. He charged into it headlong and felt wire scrape his cheeks, stick in his arms and snag his clothes. The fence's sharp claws tried to close in on him and trap him but his momentum carried him until he ended up in a heap on the overgrown grass on the other side. He risked his first glance back and saw a silhouette against the fire. The man was trying to get through the same hole in the fence but had not approached it with the same level of commitment and had got himself tangled.

Leon knew, however, that it would not take the policeman long to escape. He pointed himself downhill and ran fearlessly down the treacherous and dark slope, his sights set on the distant lights illuminating the river.

He tripped. He fell. He rolled. He was OK.

## CHAPTER 17

He awoke within an hour having nodded off shortly before dawn, but it did not seem worth lying on the sofa any longer. The night had been a mixture of adrenalin, guilt, fear and anxiety. He had managed to dispose of his clothes in a black bag, which he had dumped in a neighbour's bin. A long shower, which included washing his hair three times, had taken care of the smell. He wondered how long it would be before the gas stopped warming the water and the electricity stopped powering the shower. Presumably once the standing orders could no longer draw any money from his account and the companies received no response to their threats, printed in red capital letters.

He wasn't exactly sure why he had come back to the house, other than a desperation to wash. The need to hide had made him feel especially vulnerable on the street but then this was perhaps an even worse option. The house made him nervous. People might discover him here and the whole place reminded him of responsibilities of his old life that he had decided to leave behind.

On autopilot, he picked up the TV remote and put on the news. There were new messages on the answer machine. He unplugged it and went to the toilet. He could not bear the thought of anyone having contact with him. Upon retrieving his house keys last night he had not even touched his mobile phone, leaving it in the dirt.

Re-entering the living room, flicking on the kettle en route, he stopped in his tracks. There, staring at him from the television set was the moustachioed Big Issue man. Leon's mind did a somersault. Through the confusion, he caught words from the field reporter; 'homeless', 'known locally as James Potter', 'suspicious'. The camera cut from the still of the man to the shell of the burned out building that Leon had not long ago lit up.

Leon struggled to make connections. He saw his fingers crawling across the computer keyboard and noted without feeling that his broadband had also not been cut off. After some frantic searching, Leon established several things even though there were very few details. His fire had made the news, police were searching for him and the fire brigade had been too late to extinguish the blaze. They had, however, pulled the dead body of James Potter from the wreckage who had, it was presumed, died from smoke inhalation. Again, a photograph showed Potter with his greying moustache. Leon threw up on the floor between his feet. He had to sit down on the floor where he ended up lying for a while.

He thought back to the rather public fight that he had with the dead man. Who had seen them? Who would remember? Who could identify him?

The photo-fit of the arsonist he had found on-line was so generic that it could have been anyone. But he supposed there was always a slim possibility that someone might identify him from it. And as for an alibi, he was screwed. People could testify that he had been missing for some time and no one had seen him at any point last night. Where had a photo-fit come from anyway? Surely not the copper that was chasing him.

And what did all this mean? Could it be a coincidence that it was this man? Surely it could not.

He thought about the phrase, 'If you can't do the time, then don't do the crime'. He needed to man-up and accept responsibility for his actions. He had done it and, even if he had been pushed, he had no one to blame but himself. He had no idea that the man had been inside, but then he had not checked either. He wondered if he should go and hand himself in. He tried to think what the 'old' Leon would do, the Leon that wasn't fucking crazy.

He knew that he was going to have to do something to stop his mind going round in circles. His brain had formed a track on the inside of his head and his thoughts would be trapped in an endless cycle around that track unless he did something drastic.

He decided to go to work.

Frank almost dropped his cup of tea as Leon walked through the door.

"Leon. Jesus. Where have you... I mean what... What the fuck has been happening?"

The fact that it was the first time Leon had ever heard Frank swear barely registered. He was in such a daze that Frank could have been sat there naked and he would not have noticed. He *was* aware of what he looked like. He had stopped off in the gents to check and it was perhaps the familiar environment of work that made him realise how much he had changed since he used to work here. That was how he thought of it now; 'used to work here'.

The man in the mirror was at least a stone lighter than the Leon his colleagues were used to seeing. His face had a haunted look, the eyes dull. The attempt at a shave had left unsightly patches and the scratches across the face from the fence could not have been passed off as shaving scars. Unless he had been shaving his nose and eyelids too. The drooping eyelids betrayed an exhaustion beyond comparison. Dirty fingernails just completed the picture. He should have done something about those.

"Leon, say something. You look..."

Leon realised that he had still not answered Frank but he didn't have the energy to do so. He suddenly could not fathom why he had come here and wondered if it was a sign of oncoming madness or a complete emotional breakdown. No sleep and exceptionally high stress levels seemed like an ideal combination to bring either of those on.

Frank picked up the telephone and, barely taking his eyes off Leon, punched in a four-digit extension number.

"You should have lost your job. You would have if I hadn't intervened," Janet snapped.

Leon knew there was no way that the second bit was true. Janet had never liked him much.

"A lot of people here have been very worried about you as well. No one knew where you were. People have been ringing and texting. Two of the girls from exec support called round at your house. Couldn't believe the mess they saw through the letterbox, mind. So what's up? Jesus, Leon," Janet continued, without even waiting for an answer that would probably not have come anyway, "You look like shit."

Leon stared emotionlessly at the paperweight on Janet's desk. He wondered how paperweights had ever taken off as a desk accessory. They didn't seem awfully necessary in an indoor environment, where desks were generally found. He wondered how easy it would be to kill someone with it. He was aware that Janet was still talking and decided to listen for a while.

"You need to see a doctor. Go home. You shouldn't be here. That's no shape for somebody to be at work. I am going to ring Occupational Health. Have you seen a doctor yet? Go and see one. Will you? Go on then. Jesus, Leon, you look like a tramp. You need to get sorted out."

The only thing Leon took from the conversation (if it could be classed as a conversation when he'd not actually spoken) was that he was not welcome at work and needed to go. Before he knew it he was crossing the threshold of his own house once more and crawling to bed, James Potter clawing at the inside of his head.

Had he dozed off? It appeared that he had, and in the middle of the day. Not for long though, he thought. It seemed as though he had heard a noise but he did not remember what or where from. He rolled onto his back and exhaled long and hard. He jumped as the doorbell chimed. That's what the noise had been. As he clattered clumsily towards the front door he heard a pat as something was dropped outside and then the unmistakeable sound of running feet.

He opened the door and scanned the street. A young kid ran towards the street corner and disappeared. There was no way of telling if that had been his caller but it seemed likely. Looking at his feet, Leon saw a medium sized jiffy bag. He picked it up and retreated inside.

Sitting at the table, he tore open one end of the padded envelope and tipped it out onto the beech table top. A small tablet container rattled as it fell. He felt inside the bag and was unsurprised to feel a sheet of paper. He unfolded it and laid it out flat.

SOMETHING TO HELP YOU SLEEP. DO NOT TAKE MORE THAN TWO AT ONCE. WILL BE IN TOUCH SOON AND WE CAN COMPLETE OUR DEAL.

Anger brewed in Leon's gut. He had done what he was asked. He had dropped himself in shit infinitely deeper than he had expected, leaving mental wounds that would last a lifetime. And still no straight answer. At that moment, he hated the author of the notes more than he had ever hated anything or anyone. The frustrating thing was that he or she had no physical shape, no face.

Leon had no doubt as to the illicit nature of the tablets that he popped into his hand. An unmarked receptacle with a broken seal containing six pills. It reminded him of Marie's pill canister all those years ago. Did tablets even come in pots like this any more? He was pretty sure you could only get things in blister packs now. A friend had once told him that suicide rates from sleeping tablet overdose had plummeted since blister packs were introduced. It seemed that people couldn't be arsed with the faff on in order to kill themselves. Survival by lethargy.

He put three tablets back and popped three in his mouth. He poured some water and downed them before crawling back into bed and closing his eyes.

Although he felt confused by the darkness, and hung-over, he felt much better when he got up at half-past four the next morning. He had slept for hours and hours and felt better. He did not know how much of that was a placebo effect of the pills but neither did he care.

He rose and made himself a cup of tea, drinking it in his leather chair and staring out into the still darkness.

## CHAPTER 18

As he reached the front door, something in his bones told him that this really was the last time he would ever leave this house. The pile of ominous-looking, unopened letters in the hall was growing ever larger. He kicked them away. It was over. There was no way he'd be able to stay now even if he wanted to. Those letters no doubt informed him that he was evicted, that his utilities were being cut off, that he was due in court. Or perhaps they were all harmless, even good news. He was never going to open them. It was like a really shit version of Schrödinger's cat. He locked the door behind him and stared down at his keys. If he ever tried to return here, the locks would probably have been changed for new tenants anyway. He considered throwing them in the first bin he came to but then stuffed them in his pocket.

He needed human contact and he didn't care whether it was Steve, Karen or both of them. He wanted to find them and never let them go. He was floating aimlessly and needed to tether himself to something, anything. Just to provide some respite.

The sleep had given him a little more energy than usual and he was very glad to not feel like he was running on empty, even if it was just temporary. The more he thought about it, he actually felt quite good. It was so easy to get into a mind-set of feeling rubbish that it was difficult to notice when he wasn't. He wondered what the hell those tablets had been. The only thing he did know about them was that they definitely were not a placebo. He pressed a couple of fingers against the bottom of his back jeans pocket and felt the reassuring bumps which let him know that the remaining three pills were safe. He would need to use them wisely.

His sleeping bag felt heavy over his shoulder, which was unsurprising considering its contents. He had wrapped the bottles in a minimal selection of spare clothes in order to stop them clinking against one another. He had not been sure about the bulk of the bottles but then had decided to bring every drop of booze that was in the house, including some he had purchased that morning. His haul comprised several cans of beer, two bottles of red wine (one opened) half a bottle of brandy, and some unidentifiable shite he had been brought back as a present from a mate's holiday about seven years ago.

He decided to go and sit by the running track and have a couple of beers. He removed his watch and stuffed it in his pocket in case it talked him out of his plan. It didn't matter now. And besides, it would make the sleeping bag lighter.

He blinked once and then the confusion set in. Closing his eyes he could still see bright red as the bright sunlight warmed his face. As he built up to forcing open his eyelids he soon became aware of other things too. A ball of pain sat pulsating within the right hand side of his head, its nauseating epicentre directly behind his eyeball. He seemed to be lying across his sleeping bag rather than in it. God knows what he was lying on beneath that but it had contorted his lower back into such a shape that he was going to have to slowly and painfully roll over in order to try and address it. And then there was his mouth, which felt like it had received a coating of glue to its interior and then blasted with dust. His tongue peeled free of his palate and begged for moisture.

He finally opened his eyes to see a motorway flyover stretching out above his head. He was on the Embankment. At least he could genuinely say that he slept there now, he supposed.

Something that felt like a thunderbolt hit him square in the chest. It was the now regular recall that he had killed someone in the fire. He took a moment in order to force himself to function.

There was no one around and the place looked like a dumping ground. Which it was. He realised that it was probably late enough in the day that most of his new cohabitants had moved on to get on with their day. How long *had* he been asleep? He felt in his pocket for his watch but it was gone. He instinctively grabbed for his back pocket and discovered that his pills had gone too. Then he had a very hazy memory of taking those even though he knew he shouldn't. Luckily he had fallen unconscious in such a way that his sleeping bag and its contents would have been difficult for someone to steal from under him. His mouth was actually becoming painful. He could not swallow or produce moisture of any sort. His throat constricted and he retched painfully.

Looking around it was clear that there would be nowhere to find any water. He moved his back, which was so painful that it made him call out in pain. He fished out a warm can of lager from the foot of his sleeping bag, opened and drank from it greedily. The first sip of the fizzing liquid caused considerable discomfort but after that it was heavenly. He finished almost the whole can in one go and then lay back down as his throbbing head began to spin.

Images were coming to him. They had no chronological order or sense of significance. He had a reasonably clear memory of sitting with Steve and Karen; they had both been there. He was pissed by the time he'd arrived and they had mentioned it, but in an amused way more than anything else, he thought. He hoped he had not annoyed them too much. It certainly would have hampered their chances of any money.

On second thoughts, they probably didn't make any money at all. Leon remembered childishly pinching Steve's things again and again. Trying to juggle. Losing one of the balls. Karen finding it. Steve being pissed off. Not good.

He had got into an argument with a bloke. He had no idea what that could have been about or how serious it had got. He thought he was still with Karen and Steve at that point but, even with a stretch into his memory bank, he was not at all sure. Part of him didn't really want to remember.

He definitely could not recall leaving them so it was impossible to tell whether he had upset them or even sufficiently annoyed them that they would not want to see him again. Perhaps he had told them he wasn't homeless. What if he told them about the fire?

Leon knew from experience that alcohol induced memory loss always brought out the demons. The worst-case scenario was always willing to step forward and present itself to him as the most likely, if not the only possibility.

But this was more serious than previous situations where he had imagined the blanks being filled in by making a clumsy pass at a colleague or calling someone a twat. This was actually dangerous. Why the hell had he got so drunk? Perhaps that would raise suspicions on its own. Getting that drunk cost money. Had he taken his pills in front of them? He was sure he had taken them late on but then as he couldn't remember coming to the Embankment then how could he trust that fragment of memory?

Leon shakily got to his feet. He looked around for somewhere to stash his meagre belongings for the day. The place really was horrible. The floor, or at least what could be seen of it, was more dried mud than grass and much of it was in the intimidating shadow of the fly-over. The amount of broken glass was staggering; it looked difficult to find a human-sized piece of earth without glass on it for someone to lie down. Perhaps they didn't bother. Looking back down at his site for the previous night he noticed that he certainly hadn't bothered. Collecting up his sleeping bag he saw that as well as a decent sprinkling of glass he had also been fast asleep on two crumpled beer cans, a teaspoon and something that looked like it might be dried shit. Either this level of waste built up in a very quick window of time or the council had just given up all attempts at dealing with it. The weight of his bag told him that he still had a reasonable amount of booze in the bottom. He could not see anywhere reasonable to hide his things so decided to look in town.

His head felt the size and weight of a medicine ball and he had to be careful how he stepped through the mess for fear of losing balance. A wave of nausea was followed by a soul-crushing melancholy that stopped him in his tracks. His first thought was that he needed a drink to pull himself through it. His body hurt, his stomach cramped and his nerves jangled. His hands were shaking and he felt a cold sweat chilling his brow. He ached for a drink and the more he thought about it the worse it became. All he could picture in his mind was alcohol. Its form changed and it did not matter to him if it was beer, spirits, wine. He just craved it with an intensity bordering on desperation. He could not cope with the situation he was in and his throat constricted in warning of the tears that may soon follow. If he just had one drink – a strong one – it would surely sooth his nerves sufficiently to get him through to the afternoon, maybe even the evening. It would stop the hurt and let him progress with things. On balance, it seemed as though he would actually be helping himself by having a large brandy.

His second thought was that he was on the edge of some pretty dangerous behaviour and needed to hold off the alcohol for as long as possible. He decided that he would not have a drink until lunchtime if possible. Not that he knew when lunchtime was of course. The sun looked high in the sky so perhaps it was soon. Which was good because then he could have a drink.

## CHAPTER 19

Leon had not seen Steve and Karen for two days, since the barely remembered afternoon together when god-knows-what had happened. In fact he had, not spoken to anyone in that time. He had sat on street corners and slept in shop doorways. He had been given spare change, moved on by the police, verbally abused by charvers and approached by evangelists with the promise of redemption. In short, he was properly homeless.

To say that he slept in shop doorways was not entirely true. Sleep had been harder to come by since the night of the fire. It was elusive and when it did arrive he would soon be awake due to the myriad of noises of the street at night; disturbances in the street, alarms going off, the aforementioned roaming constabulary. He thought that the physical exercise might have exhausted him as he had spent many an hour wandering the streets, aimlessly trying to find some clue to Marie without having any structure at all to this 'plan' of his. He needed to get back on track if he was ever to find anything. The rest of the time he had sat on benches and corners mulling over his problems.

His experience with the police had left him badly shaken. His paranoia about the warehouse was gnawing away at him from the inside. His body was now home to two dark rats that were restless, twitchy and causing him physical pain. One rat lived in his stomach where it scuttled back and forth, trying to find its way out of the darkness. It fed on doubt and guilt and shrieked out to be placated. Its sister lived in his head and scrambled his thoughts and senses. This one feasted on fear and refused to be ignored. They both could only be calmed by alcohol.

His initial reaction upon having the torch shone in his face was to lash out. A visitor to his shop doorway in the middle of the night was unlikely to be a welcome one and he did not want to give anyone a chance to better him. But no sooner had this thought registered than he heard the voice of the young copper informing him whom he was dealing with. And in an instant he was transported into a terrifying scenario; he had been recognised somehow, he was to be arrested, charged, convicted in court, imprisoned for murder. Life over. He would sooner be dead. These thoughts flashed through him, fully formed but fleeting, before he realised that he was simply being told to move on, which he had; all of twenty yards down the street to another doorway once the copper and his colleague had rounded a corner.

Leon had heard no more from his mysterious correspondent who he had come to think of as the 'Mystery Man'. Even if he ever discussed his situation with another person he would never admit to his little nickname out of embarrassment over its dramatic nature. He did not know why he assumed that it was a man but that was how he had pictured his pen pal from the start. A weak but power-hungry, sorry excuse for a human being who was loving his little project of operating Leon like a puppet. A spiteful man who had probably been mercilessly bullied and was now taking his revenge on anyone he could.

Mystery Man's silence left him with some serious decisions to be made depending on how things panned out, but he would definitely have to develop a contingency plan in case he never heard from him again.

Leon had no idea of the time but one of the shop shutters across the road was being opened by a teenage girl who could not have looked any less pleased to be arriving at work if she had tried. He grabbed his sleeping bag, which was now almost empty, and shuffled away from the front of 'his' shop. There was a small fountain at the end of this particular street with its hexagonal base shaped by concrete steps. It was as good a place as any to sit and try to pull himself together. As he sat there a pair of police officers strolled across the street. He watched them while pretending not to watch them, and noticed one of them speaking to her colleague and looking in his direction. Again, his instinct was to run but he knew that would be disastrous. But he had no way of telling whether they were casually thinking of moving him on or whether there was an arrest warrant out for him. He mulled over the fact that you could never normally find the buggers but now that he wanted to keep out of their way there seemed to be hundreds of them. After what seemed like an age, they wandered off.

Activity built up around him as the shops opened, staff arrived, shoppers started to wander in. He had a feeling it was a Saturday which was a theory backed up by the lack of people running around in suits grasping massive containers of over-priced coffee and shouting into mobile phones to colleagues that they would be seeing in the office in three minutes' time.

Leon became aware that someone was looking at him from a distance. The woman seemed unsure of whether to approach him and as he stared back at her he realised with dread that it was Claire from work. Claire was a frumpy old do-gooder that he had never liked even though she had no harm about her. She was definitely coming towards him, her husband hanging about in the background. What the hell was he going to say to her? He lowered his head in the hope that she might take this as a message to leave him alone. As her feet entered his field of vision he realised that had not worked. She shuffled cautiously up to him and he decided to bite the bullet, looking up and discovering that she seemed to be avoiding his eyes too. From a safe distance she leaned slightly forward and gently lobbed something in his direction. He looked down to see a shiny one pound coin spinning between his filthy boots. He looked back up at Claire's retreating back.

What had just happened? Presumably, Claire had seen the state of him, realised his predicament and decided to give him a pound. It was a new low. She would barely be able to contain her excitement about getting back to work on Monday. By half past nine the entire building would know about it, he was sure. He wondered why that thought bothered him, and then realised that it didn't particularly. What lingered with him more was that sense of detachment with which she had approached him. It was as though he was a different person to the one that she knew to talk to. This different person had crossed a line and was now a figure of either contempt or pity. Claire, having the nature she did, was of course in the sympathetic corner, but had treated him like a lame dog rather than a work colleague. He would still rather that than have to talk to the boring bugger, though.

He watched her walk away along the street, talking to what he imagined to be a very long-suffering husband. The amount of banal shite he would have had to listen to over the years would be nobody's business. Leon imagined he had adopted the technique of many men who had found themselves stuck with the Claires of this world; an ability to appear attentive while thinking about anything else, dreaming of a world away from this source of pointless chatter. She would be wittering on now, explaining that the tramp on the steps worked at her place just a couple of weeks ago. He looked at himself through

Claire's eyes and realised just how different he was. He started to wonder if she had even recognised him. Perhaps she just was in the habit of giving money to the homeless; it was certainly something he could imagine. It was too much of a coincidence to choose him, though, surely.

Claire slowed in the street, pulling her husband to a standstill by his coat cuff. As she looked in her wallet he looked exasperated and seemed to try and move her on. She leaned towards the window of Costa but Leon could not see why. He stood up on the step above him and saw a homeless woman and a dog. The woman was smiling at Claire and holding up a pound coin she had just been given.

Blocking out the craving, Leon wanted to not drink today, he really did. He checked his supplies secretively. He had got used to doing everything furtively by this stage as anyone could be watching, waiting, ready to take what little he had. There were only two bottles in the base of the bag now. One was vodka and he could not quite see the other one clearly. His mind hurt. He did not know how that was possible but it was definitely his mind that was occupied with a dull ache rather than his head. It told him that he could not cope with another day on his own. He needed help and that help was lying inside his sleeping bag just waiting to be a friend to him. It would take him to its bosom, caress him and see that everything was manageable. It was difficult to be sure whether he would rather be dead than get through the whole day dry. The notion of sobriety seemed so unbearable that he felt his chest tighten in worry about it. This was not the first time of late that he had felt his only chance of peace was to get drunk.

What he really needed was to get hold of some more of those pills but that was as impractical as it was inadvisable. He wouldn't know where to start looking for drugs, although he knew a few people in his previous life that certainly would. As appealing as that was he knew that there was no going back now, at least not in the short term. He could hardly just rock up on one of their doorsteps, 'Hi Craig, not seen you for months but I just thought I'd give you a knock. Hope you're well... Anyway, as you can probably see I'm a tramp now so I wondered if you could get me any drugs to help me sleep in shop doorways.'

The other problem was money. Although he had eventually squirrelled away a few quid it was becoming increasingly apparent that it would not last forever and he needed to be careful. He had decided that he would need to spend a few more nights indoors, especially as the nights got colder, and that would need cash. He could not see how he would get away with claiming benefits without revealing himself so it would have to be quiet words in landlords' ears and piss-stained mattresses for now. He had some belongings in the house and he had considered selling them but it seemed that going back and doing anything at the house would quickly spiral into having to deal with other elements of his old life. That was just exhausting to even think about. It was gone. He was gone. He was one of the disappeared.

The pain from his mind intensified and he could feel it scratching and crackling, hugely uncomfortable. His hand snaked into his sleeping bag and grasped the neck of the vodka bottle. It reassured him and made him think of a shopkeeper's hand surreptitiously closing around the handle of a baseball bat beneath the counter, out of sight of the scrotes who had just come in to take his money.

In general, he needed to get away from the crowds as the swarm of activity was beginning to confuse him and make him feel ill. He needed some company to soothe his nerves and get him thinking about something else. That meant either talking to a stranger, which was a no-go in his current state, or finding Karen or Steve. *If* they were still speaking to him. He knew that if they weren't, and if he had lost the only companionship available to him, then he would be struggling. Either of those plans would require a drink to brace himself. At the thought of the vodka sliding down his gullet, his stomach reached up a grasping hand to welcome in the tepid alcohol. The rats were definitely awake.

One step at a time; get away from the shoppers.

## CHAPTER 20

The vodka buzz was now wearing off and he stared longingly at the bulge in the bag's dirty nylon that he knew contained more. Sure enough, he had taken a drop of Dutch courage before searching out his friends. The welcome he had received was vague enough that he had no idea if they were offended, disappointed or indifferent. He had half hoped that he would only find one of them – perhaps they would be more likely to open up on their own, having a quiet word in his ear about his behaviour.

Or perhaps he was, as normal, being utterly melodramatic, all was fine and if he broached the subject they'd wonder what the hell he was talking about. This lifestyle must have put them in direct contact with some pretty unpleasant characters that drank and used substances to extremes and had behavioural patterns to match. But then they had set themselves up an arrangement that avoided that.

Leon decided that, unless he was told otherwise, he'd not done anything bad and all was fine. He did not sufficiently understand the street code yet but he suspected that passing judgement was frowned upon. They had not asked where he had been the last few days either. Ah, fuck it, it was all fine and that was the end of it. This casual attitude was all the easier for the booze which had nestled warmly into his gut, quietening the rats.

Leon normally didn't give a monkey's what anyone thought of him. He knew lots of people who said that and didn't really mean it, but Leon did. Admittedly there were a small number of people who he valued too much to be overly casual about, but it normally did not phase him at all to be disliked. He was a social animal by nature but if someone decided they didn't enjoy his company he would simply move on. Nor was he one of those "I say what I think and if you don't like it that's tough" types who seemed to use their mantra as an excuse for acting like a dick-head. Strangely, his laid back attitude had often led to people being socially attracted to him.

Here on the street was a different matter, though, and at the moment he needed Steve and Karen.

Karen leaned forward, "So how are you doing then?"

Leon could tell from the seriousness of her tone that this contained subtext but his brain had taken some hammering over recent days and he wasn't feeling too sharp.

"With everything... the life..." she spelled it out for him having seen the vacant look on his face, "finding a kip, you know, that sort of thing."

"Oh I'm not bad," he could not help notice Karen's raised eyebrow at this point.

"Because you know you don't seem to be doing that great to the casual observer."

Steve gave her a look.

"I'm still finding it OK up on the Embankment. I can handle myself and it's not too bad if you can drink enough to stop worrying about getting stabbed," he smiled. Karen only half returned it. Perhaps he shouldn't have mentioned drinking. Still, in for a penny, in for a pound. "Speaking of which, does anyone fancy a drop?"

He pulled out the Smirnoff and waggled it in her direction. Steve held out his hand.

"I'm afraid it's not at optimal temperature and it seems to have a couple of floaters in it." Steve did smile at this point and took a decent glug before handing it to Karen. When it arrived back with Leon he took a couple of gulps and stashed it away again. The alcohol felt so glorious as its warmth spread that he felt like hugging himself around the middle as if to show his gratitude. He felt the warm sun on his face and leaned back against the railings to lap it up. With a start, he jumped up and decided to leave them to it.

"Y'off?" asked Steve.

"Yeah, think I'll make a move. I'm in the way and I seem to have got my own pitch at the minute. I want to get there before someone thinks it's a green light to nick it."

Steve nodded sagely.

"See you at the soup run tonight?" Leon asked them both.

They nodded back.

"See you there," replied Karen.

The Christmas illuminations strung up from the street lights were the same ones that the council had been using for years. As a result, their shoddy appearance struggled to convey a sense of celebration or festivity, particularly while dangling above a crowd of people that would probably spend Christmas Day rifling through bins for unwanted mince pies. The best lights were understandably saved for the city centre and this year were augmented with large hanging signs implying that the forthcoming millennium celebrations would be the party to end all parties.

For the first time in a while, Leon actually felt like he had eaten enough food. He didn't think he had eaten any more than previous evenings and wondered if it was that his stomach was simply getting used to receiving less, shrivelling up like a prune. He had spent a couple of pleasant hours chatting with Karen and Steve over polystyrene bowls of something or other. The conversation had started on the usual topic of what kind of meat could be in it but they had soon given up guessing and moved on to more notable topics. Leon was surprised at Steve's grasp of current affairs. Leon felt like this new life had sealed him in a bubble where nothing in the wider world was brought to his attention, and he did not seek it out. Steve, on the other hand, talked passionately about the Russian invasion of Chechnya, the European Court of Human Rights recent decisions, and the potential impact of the millennium computer bug. Leon wondered how he did it as he had never seen him with a newspaper or a radio. Leon supposed that he had no idea of Steve's situation off the streets; he may be living in a bedsit with a new-fangled flat-screen TV for all Leon knew.

The conversation had somehow moved once more onto Leon's sleeping arrangements at which point Karen had adopted her serious and motherly persona. She was definitely worried about him. She did not say it specifically but Leon got the distinct impression that she was concerned about his rapid decline in health. She had surprised him greatly when she said that he could come and "live with" them for a little while. Strictly just to get him off the Embankment and see him through until he found something he was happier and safer with. The most amazing part was that Steve did not seem put out in the slightest which made Leon sure that they had talked it through beforehand.

Leon agreed to think about it and now, surveying the area he now considered home and which probably had as relaxed an atmosphere as the aforementioned Chechnya, he wished he had accepted the offer immediately.

It was a struggle to sleep that night, largely because he was not particularly drunk. Across the road he witnessed his first robbery. An intoxicated man was held up at knife-point and had his money taken from him. The man was in his late thirties and was wearing an overpriced but tacky t-shirt of the kind that passed as trendy, but was more suited to a man ten years younger than him. He stood out like a sore thumb in an area such as this and had presumably got lost trying to take a short cut home. He was now skint and, if nothing else, would have a story to tell his mates in the pub. No doubt in the retelling he would be considerably braver than the snivelling wretch who had begged for his life this evening. Leon had felt no sympathy for him; it was his own fault.

The two men that had robbed him had done so in a very unsubtle and clumsy way. Leon could not hear the conversation other than the whining of the late night reveller but he knew that if the man had his wits about him he could have easily seen this unfold and avoided it. The robbers had approached him from two sides at once. He had to give them the fact that they had attempted some form of tactics. By the time the man noticed them it was too late to avoid them. The transaction took place in less than a minute. Leon was interested by the fact that the two shuffling figures only took cash. They rifled through a wallet, removing the money before throwing it at the man's feet. He shakily retrieved it. The man would certainly have had a decent watch, possibly even a mobile phone. Even at the distance Leon was he could see the man's chunky necklace glinting but the robbers ignored it. Cash in hand, they left.

Surely having committed the crime they should have taken everything they could and made cash in multiples of what they had. But it had all been about desperate immediacy. Leon could imagine the desperados just being relieved that they had sufficient to pay for tonight's hit. Tomorrow would have to be a repeat performance at which point they would again fail to take full advantage. Was it a lack of intelligence or an obsession with calming the twitchy storm inside them as quickly as possible that clouded the thought process? Leon plumped for the latter.

Speaking of which, he needed a drop. He now only had a small amount of vodka. If he rummaged his feet around he could feel both of his boots and the bottle. It was as though his toes could extract the calming relief by osmosis through the thick glass. He could sense it slosh rhythmically. He told himself that he might need it the following day but he knew that he was going to drink it at some point tonight.

Leon adjusted his position so that he could force his index finger into the small, tight watch pocket of his jeans. He could feel the notes stuffed in there. There were still a few in addition to several more that he had in other locations. He did not know exactly what time it was and could not see his watch in the dark, but he knew it was late enough that no off-licences would be open. There was a 24-hour supermarket about half an hour's walk away but he had been refused entry the last time he tried there.

He looked around to make sure he was not being watched and then shuffled awkwardly down to grope for the elegant neck of the bottle. He could not get his fingers past the two boots that floated around in there. Finally, he got hold of the bottle. Such was his position that his shoulder muscles began to cramp. He grimaced from the pain but refused to let go of his prize. He forced himself out, teeth clenched and a guttural groan emerging from him. He sat up and spun the thin metal bottle top before massaging his screaming muscles.

He was floating; he knew that much. He didn't know what he was lying on or where he was. It was clearly small due to the extreme rising and falling. Spreading out his hands and feet did not meet any resistance so he assumed that it was some form of raft. He listened out for clues but could not hear a thing. *Literally* not a thing. He banged his heels down on what he was now sure was a wooden base. He heard nothing as a judder moved up his calves. He was obviously profoundly deaf. The darkness made him wonder if he was also blind. Perhaps the sense of movement was the only thing left available to him. Up, down, sideways, up. Was that all he had left?

Eventually, he managed to lift his upper body, pushing his elbows beneath him to rest awkwardly on. He strained his eyes and noticed that there was a difference in colour. The inky blackness in the lower half of his vision must be the sea while the more bluish darkness above must be the sky. No stars. Blinking a few times his vision improved remarkably quickly and he saw the raft beneath him. Lying across it, just below his feet was a long oar. What use could that be? He had no idea where he was or which way he would go.

The raft's movement seemed to be intensifying and yet he managed to kneel up. Now that his eyesight had improved, his surroundings were clearer, but nearby was a blackness so dark it was noticeable even in its surroundings. And he was slowly and inexorably moving towards it. As he gazed more widely he saw the sea swirling towards this vacuous epicentre. He was in its grasp and was being clawed in. But he was still on the periphery; perhaps he could save himself. He rose to the crest of a wave and saw the nothingness. It had no bottom. It was deeper than any seabed could possibly be and it greedily sucked in water.

He had to act quickly. He stood and leaned down to pick up the oar. He stood upright again and upon trying to row realised that the oar was not in his hands. He tried again and found that he could not pick it up.

He stared down at his hands, or at least the space where his hands should have been. The moon broke through a cloud and illuminated the two stomach-churning stumps held out in front of him. They tapered towards rough looking stitching which made the ends of his arms look angry and infected.

He screamed. At least he thought he did. The deathly silence continued. Stood on the raft, despite the oscillation of the ocean, he held up his forearms to the moon. Their silhouette emphasised their uselessness. He wanted to scream louder but did not try. He had insufficient breath for that anyway as he gasped for air. The sea sprayed against the hot skin of his face as the sea's movement knocked him to his back and the raft dipped violently. He was in the grip of the black hole now. He began to descend into the oblivion, staring upwards at the swirling water above him.

Somehow, a face appeared over the edge of the void and looked down at him. The eyes glowed and the teeth shone. The skin was burned and the hair still smouldered, but it was the moustache that told him for sure that he was looking into the face of James Potter. Potter's grin widened as he reached out and dropped something into the abyss that was stretching out further above him. Leon strained to see what it was, but by the time he realised, the metal scaffolding bar was rocketing towards him. He tried to grab the side of the raft to haul himself out of the way, but of course he had nothing to grab with. He closed his eyes and waited for the...

He gasped and his eyes shot open in panic.

Leon groggily took in his surroundings and did not recognise them. So violently had he been wrenched from one world into another that, for a split second, he could not even recall who he was; what he looked like, how he sounded, why he was here. Then it rushed back. He was on the Embankment and he was a fucking loser who had thrown away his life in order to sleep in a shit-tip and scrounge food.

"You awake, pal?"

Following the 'p' of 'pal', Leon felt a fine spray of spittle land daintily around his nose and mouth.

An old man was leaning over him. Leon blinked, suddenly feeling very vulnerable, cocooned in his sleeping bag.

"The fuck you want?"

"Just trying to help you," the man sounded annoyed with Leon's less than friendly welcome.

"Yeah?"

Leon noted that the man was not as old as he had first supposed. It was a phenomenon that he had gotten used to now; the street made everyone look a decade older than they actually were. With this bloke it was the beard that did the trick. Leon looked and saw how disgusting it really was. Even in the moonlight he could see that it was mostly white and grey with streaks of nicotine-yellow in it. But it was not the colour that struck him. The beard was thick and matted. It almost looked like dreadlocks except that at least deadlocks were divided into separate entities. This just looked like an entangled mass of filth. Leon wondered how the man could bear to swallow any food that had brushed through it on its way to his cracked lips.

He sat up, not taking his eyes off the man for a moment.

"I asked what you wanted."

"Just trying to help you is all."

Leon looked at him doubtfully.

"Scared off two fellas who were coming over here to sort you out. I heard them talking 'bout you and head over."

"Why would they do that? I've nothing to steal."

Leon pulled his arms out from his bag and looked at his hands. Moved them, just to make sure.

"Who knows what they were looking to take from you or do to you. You know what it's like here, son."

"So what happened?" Leon was highly sceptical about this Good Samaritan's story.

"Scared them off didn't I?"

Leon looked at the man's slight frame and his scepticism moved back to distrust.

"I'll ask you again then, what do you want?"

"Why do you think I want something?"

"Everyone out here wants something."

The man attempted to look hurt but Leon was having none of it.

"So you just woke me up to tell me about your good deed did you? Well, thanks. I'm going back to sleep."

"Suit yourself."

The man stood and began to shuffle off. Leon laid his head down, sure that he was done with sleep for the night now.

"'cept you *don't* sleep do you?"

The voice was so quiet it was almost a whisper. But it was enough to make Leon sit up. He was not even sure if he had heard it, but he must have done.

"The fuck d'you say?"

"No need for that, lad," the man muttered without turning round as he shuffled off down the bank.

"Come here!"

At this, the man slowly turned and Leon wondered if he was imagining the slight look of satisfaction on the face behind the monstrous beard. The man walked all the way back to Leon's feet and looked down on him. Leon sat like a coiled spring, ready to leap up if he needed to?

"Am I right?" the man asked, measured and soft.

"Why do you ask?"

"I have lived on this streets all my life. It teaches you to read people."

"Save the sixth sense bullshit."

"Fair enough. You look like you've never slept in a year, son. I know what insomniacs look like and you, my friend, are undoubtedly an insomniac. Take a look in a mirror; you couldn't look that buggered if you tried."

Leon thought about this and guessed it made sense. He started to think about exactly how buggered he really was. He had given up his life to find a woman he had never met, he barely slept and could only do so at all by using alcohol or drugs which left him getting only the shallowest, phoniest of sleeps. He was effectively now a barely-functioning alcoholic. He was being tormented by someone he did not know and as a result was distrustful of everything and everyone around him. And the real crowning glory was that he had killed a man. All things considered, he was unlikely to be looking his best.

Without being invited, the man sat next to Leon and he just decided to let him. After some time, Leon realised that they were not actually sitting in silence but that the man was talking. He decided that this background droning had been there for some time so it was clearly some sort of monologue that did not need his contribution. Leon tuned in to hear selected snippets about the dangers of living rough and how those that looked after each other survived.

Leon started to wonder if this episode was going to conclude with the man making a sexual advance on him. Hopefully not; that was a confrontation he could do without.

The man looked round at Leon.

"So do you want some pills? Help you sleep?"

Leon was now convinced that the man's motives were sexual. Who knew what would happen once he was out for the count. On the other hand, the offer seemed tempting.

"I don't have any money."

"That doesn't matter."

"Why would you give me them?"

"You not been listening, lad?"

Leon decided not to admit that he had not.

"We need to look out for each other if we are to get through this life. It's a favour; I happen to have lots of them. Another time when you have something that would help me out you can return the favour."

Leon looked into the man's eyes.

"Don't worry, I'm not going to touch you up once you're out," he grinned but Leon was far from assured. "I don't have much on me but I can give you a couple."

Leon thought about it. This was a potentially dangerous situation and he did not trust the man any more than he trusted anyone else out there. What would happen once he was in his debt? He had no way of knowing whether the pills were the real deal or rat poison. On the other hand, he remembered the blessed relief that the tablets from the Mystery Man had provided. His reserves were on empty and perhaps just one night of deep, dreamless sleep would give him that impetus, as it had last time. Leon stared into the man's face, weighing up his options and oblivious to any social discomfort which might have been caused by close-range staring.

"Not sure," was all that he finally mustered.

Leon thought that the man was getting a little agitated; he was fidgeting. A bad sign. But he was, again, probably imagining it.

"Suit yourself," the man replied nonchalantly.

He wondered if the man was *too* nonchalant. Perhaps he was trying hard to act that way. Leon felt the effect of his paranoia but, even though he knew it was there, he was not prepared to fully disagree with it. The man made to get up which triggered a craving in Leon's gut for the tablets.

"OK, wait. Supposing I do get some off you, what then?"

"Don't worry about that. It's free. That's it. A gesture."

The man felt in his pocket.

"A couple more of these fellas and you'll be right as rain."

The man's voice trailed off towards the end of the sentence and he made a big show of trying to get his hand inside the pocket.

"What do you mean, 'more'?"

"Hmm? Let's have a look; they're in here somewhere. Ah, here we are," the man carried on.

"What do you mean '*more*'?" Leon was losing it. His mind seemed to lose a grip on reality and he was floating.

The man looked to stand up by which stage Leon was fully out of his sleeping bag. He grabbed the man's coat and prevented him from standing. The man tried to swing out of his grasp but Leon held on tight and the two of them rolled to one side with Leon ending up on top.

"Let me see," Leon growled.

"I was just trying to get them if you'd let me…"

Leon jammed his hand in the man's pocket and drew out an unmarked medicine container. His cold fingers fumbled with the child lock until it popped off onto the floor. Leon emptied the contents into his palm and saw eight small, round, white pills. He held one up to the light. It seemed identical to those he had received from the Mystery Man. The man tried to retrieve them from Leon.

"I didn't say you could have all of them. You can have two. You can't have mine."

Leon clenched his right fist around the one tablet, letting the rest fall to the ground as he wrapped his left hand around the man's throat, using his legs to pin him. He felt the man's body bucking against him but, even in Leon's current depleted state, he was still the stronger man by far. He was about to hit him without any further ado when he had an urge to check the area for witnesses. He could not put himself in such a precarious position again. What if this man ended up dead by daybreak? By the time he had checked in all directions his blood had cooled and he rolled off the man and onto his knees.

## CHAPTER 21

Leon had established that the man with the giant facial dreadlock knew nothing and, against his better judgement, had acquired four pills and swallowed two of them after finding a new place to bed down. He didn't want the bloke to find him again. Sleep had quickly followed.

That sleep, however, was violently interrupted as a booted foot slammed into his ribs. Leon awoke instantly and his brain engaged with what was happening. Perhaps this was partly because he had expected it to happen eventually. Before he had taken a defensive stance the boot crashed into him again. Leon's initial thought was of relief that his assailant had connected using his instep; a good toe-ender would have at least cracked a rib or two. As he rolled away in desperation a second foot connected with his face from the opposite side. The shock outweighed the pain but he knew that would come soon. The kicks rained in for what seemed like an eternity. Leon could not help but think that he should be feeling more pain than he was, and put it down to the drugs. He surprised himself when annoyance became his overriding feeling rather than fear or pain.

"Will you just fucking *stop!*"

Amazingly they did. Then the bloke in front of him gave him a final half-hearted kick in the chest for good measure. He rolled onto his back and panted heavily, looking up at the two men. Individually they were nothing to be impressed by. Leon was pretty certain that he could take either of them on their own. But he knew better than to tackle two people at once. They looked down at him. The man who had got in the final kick bobbed twitchily on the balls of his feet. He seemed unsure as to whether stopping at Leon's behest showed weakness and that maybe he should have another pop. He was the smaller of the two, wiry, crazy hair, buck-toothed with a feral look about him. The man who had started the onslaught had covered the lower half of his face with a dirty scarf of some description.

"What do you want?"

"What you got?"

"Fuck all," Leon responded, gambling on aggression as his best form of self-defence, "haven't even got any booze left."

Leon thought about his cash. He wriggled, trying to look as though he was struggling to get out of the sleeping bag while actually attempting to remove the bit of money that was in his coat. He got some of it and shoved it down the front of his pants, tucking it at the base of his balls. That was all he had time to do for the time being but he knew there was a ten-pound note in his inner coat pocket.

"Empty your pockets," the feral one instructed.

Leon did as he was told. Thankfully his caution was paying off as he now had nothing in his main pockets.

"Shit," Feral continued. The two men looked at each other.

"Shit," Scarf echoed. "We'll have this then."

He tugged at Leon's sleeping bag until it was off his legs, swinging it over his shoulder. Both men looked at him again, exasperated with their paltry haul. They turned and walked off.

"My boots are in there," Leon pleaded.

"Great. What size are they?" Scarf muttered - through his scarf - causing Feral to emit a wheeze that could well have been a laugh.

At that, Feral returned to Leon. "We'll have your coat as well."

"Oh, *come* on," Leon protested.

There was no response. The two men stood where they were until Leon had removed it and handed it over. He watched for a few moments as the men casually sauntered out of view. He looked at his now cold feet. He looked at his now chilly torso where a coat containing ten pounds had recently been. He looked at his legs, which had been covered with the sleeping bag; a sleeping bag that had come to seem like a part of him. He looked at the desolate waste land he was on and thought that he could not have felt more vulnerable at that moment had he been naked. Exhaustion took over as the adrenalin wore off. He collapsed backwards and, defeated, went back to sleep.

Maybe the eyes. A little. No... he was looking for it. His face was inches away from the newsagent window as he peered intently at the photo-fit picture displayed from the inside. Also included on the poster was a picture of moustachioed James Potter who was equally unrecognisable. The picture had clearly been taken in the man's previous life when he looked comparatively vibrant and healthy. Passers-by were highly unlikely to recognise him, never mind the generic, pixelated attempt to capture Leon's features. Leon wondered about the source of the picture. Had someone seen him that night that he was unaware of? Presumably. Unless, of course, this was a picture of someone entirely unrelated to the incident. Perhaps some curtain-twitching resident had decided they wanted to be involved in the hottest case in town and had reported some unfortunate innocent that they considered to be a bit of a wrong-un. The accompanying text was vague enough that it could easily have been someone else; dark clothing, medium height, 25 – 40. Could be anybody. Leon tried to convince himself that the picture actually had been based on someone else's features. And despite his paranoia he had to admit to himself that he could not be identified by the picture even if it was based on him. It did, however, leave the possibility that someone *had* seen him and, despite their apparent ineptitude for description, would recognise him if the opportunity presented itself.

"Getting a good enough look at him there?" A cheerful voice boomed from the side of him. Leon looked up to see an elderly man with a rosy face and bright white hair looking at him with a friendly smile.

"Oh, just wondering if I knew him, that's all. But I don't," Leon added with what was perhaps too much certainty.

"I don't know what we're coming to, I really don't," offered the man, tucking his recently bought newspaper under his arm.

Leon nodded sagely. The man nodded back, maintaining eye contact. As Leon watched, the man's eyes flicked to the poster, then returned to Leon. Leon spun round and walked away, feeling the panic rise up in his chest like icy bile. After a short while, he sneaked a glance back to see the old man studying the poster.

It was just a small report on page four. The 'story' was that the police were following up some promising leads, but surely that was just an empty statement to let the public know that they were still interested in finding the killer. He tried to think as an impartial reader and decided that was the case; they had nothing, would not be too bothered about the death of a tramp and the story would soon go away. Of course, the less logical, more emotional part of his brain was screaming to be heard. And even the logical side had to concede that the story was interesting enough to hang around for a while until something more exciting happened.

So, a small, picture-less article in the local rag and no mention at all in the free national paper of which copies could be found strewn around every public transport stop in the area. The local paper he had picked up from a bench outside the off-licence. So then he had found himself a pleasant spot in a quiet area of the park near his house from which to enjoy his two newspapers and two cans of Kestrel Super Strength.

The thick tasting lager only partially satisfied him. What he could really do with, he decided, was a few more of those pills. He had taken the second two the previous night and was feeling anxious that he would be a nervous wreck that evening without a couple more to settle him. He was self-aware enough to know that this was a disturbing development but it was just to get him through a sticky patch until things, his nerves particularly, settled down.

He knew that he could not wait until the disgusting beardy might seek him out again with the offer of further addiction or ambiguous nonsense.

Half way through Leon's second can he realised that he must find something to do for the rest of the day. He had seen a spot several times in recent days that he had started to think about using. It was off the main shopping centre in one of the side street called St George's Road. Part way along that was a cut between two shops where one could sit out of harm's way but still in sight of the passers-by. The other advantage was that there were no other patches in the whole street meaning that he would have it to himself. He did wonder if there was a reason for that but then decided that there was no point worrying over something that might not be an issue.

It would give him a focus for the day. He needed to think about something other than spending the rest of his life in prison. He needed to stop drinking for the rest of the day and, most importantly of all, he now needed to start getting some money.

## CHAPTER 22

After experimenting with several approaches Leon settled on what he described as 'vocally unobtrusive but physically obvious'. He thought that giving people too much notice that he was after their change might make them more likely to busy themselves with something to look at across the road or have a sudden urge to check their phones. He found that he had more luck when people noticed him once they were close by and had to make a snap decision. This particular city central location had the added benefit of being in an alcohol-free zone.

After several hours, Leon had slightly more faith in humanity than he did at the outset. He started out with nothing for people to drop coins into which made things a bit awkward. Fortunately, a nice old lady had bought him a coffee, which he had only to pay for with five minutes of conversation. The poor old dear had not seen her son for over twenty years since he left home after a family row. He had been about Leon's age at that point and so she thought she should help him. Leon thought it was something along those lines anyway as she had been rambling fairly incoherently at various points. But as well as a hot drink he had gained a paper cup with which to entice the public to part with their change.

From that point on he never looked back. Around a dozen people had dropped in coins ranging from coppers to pound coins. Two more free coffees, a pasty, and a ham sandwich were also donated. Another bonus of his current spot was that it was within spitting distance of a small bakery. It was also close to a coffee shop but that could now be said about anywhere in the civilised world. The ham sandwich man had been slightly weird and had hung around wanting to talk about model tanks. Leon had also been interrupted by two Mormons, harangued for scrounging from the state, asked if he wanted to be a in band and given a hug, all by mid-afternoon. All in all, it was more eventful than he imagined it would be. He was a few hours in before he wondered if he should feel in some way ashamed by what he was doing. Ashamed of begging, of his appearance maybe. Or ashamed that he had a choice in all this.

Leon knew enough about street life by this stage to know that if he came back to the same spot each day for a while it would unofficially become his pitch. And that seemed good.

He got to the soup run too early. He did not know how he had got it so wrong as he had got used to maintaining an idea of the time from passing the clocks on display in the town, but the young woman struggling with the wallpaper table informed him that he was almost an hour early.

"So how come *you're* here then?" he asked her by way of conversation.

"My time keeping is obviously as bad as yours isn't it?" she smiled.

It was a stunning smile, her mouth seeming to have more than the normal amount of teeth in it, shining from a pretty face. Leon's dormant libido stirred somewhat. Perhaps it was not quite yet extinct. The more he looked at her the more he suspected there was still some life in the old dog yet.

Leon grabbed one end of the wallpaper table and flicked out the legs.

"Thanks. I'm Ysanne."

"Leon. I've not seen you here before."

"No, I usually work on a run over on the North side. I've not worked this one for ages."

Leon looked around and saw that there was not a single other person around. It was too soon for even the early-bird diners and Ysanne had only brought the table with her so would have to wait for her colleagues.

"Can I ask you something, Ysanne?"

She nodded.

"Why do you do this? It's not a trick question or anything. I'm genuinely interested."

"Can I be corny and just say I want to pay something back?"

"But who would want to pay something back? Especially if you've received less than your share to start with."

"Ah, you're one of those deep types." No teeth but a definite smile.

"Not really, just get a lot of time to think about things these days."

"Well, seeing as you ask, I should probably be dead by now. And I'm not. I've got another chance. Don't look panic-stricken; I'm not born again. I was never born in the first place as far as all that's concerned."

"Go on."

"Well, I don't normally talk about this stuff, and I don't even know you..."

"I told you – I'm Leon. Go on."

Ysanne smiled. Teeth.

"I hit bottom, had issues. Anyway, turned out I had a guardian angel who talked me round."

She seemed to look towards the bridge in the distance, at this time of night little more than a hazy silhouette, although Leon could have simply imagined it.

"I still don't know who she was," she continued, "but she cared enough to do something. She didn't stand by like most people would."

Ysanne was back in the present and looking more than a little embarrassed by her admission.

Leon's heart was beating fast. The guardian angel had been Marie. He was convinced of it. He realised that, such was his current plight, he had not even thought about Marie for a couple of days. He did not have time now to look into how he felt about that.

"What did she look like?"

"Why?"

"Oh, er... I just knew someone once and I wondered if it might be the same... Here, I've got a picture."

Leon started looking through his pockets at which point Ysanne seemed to be wondering if she was talking to a nutter. She looked around and was grateful to notice a pair of colleagues arriving together.

"OK, so I have to get some more stuff ready now. It was nice to, you know..."

"Here, look. Please just take a look," Leon pleaded, passing his picture to Ysanne.

Ysanne looked at it for a moment. Leon stopped breathing.

"Nope," Ysanne hurriedly handed it back and moved away from him.

He was obviously losing the plot.

\*\*\*

Leon sat, lost in thought, hunched over a bowl of meat stew. He felt clean for the first time in ages. Looking down at his trousers he realised how much his standards had changed in this regard. That afternoon he had been to the day centre that Graeme had once introduced him to. In addition to getting a feed, he used the facilities to wash himself and his grimy clothes. Using a toilet with running water, toilet paper and a light had been an added bonus.

Karen and Steve soon arrived, holding their own supper.

"So you're in the paper then," grunted Steve as he sat down. Karen followed suit.

It took a couple of seconds for Leon's preoccupied mind to order those few words so that he could understand them. Once the final piece slotted into place he felt himself go numb. "What? What are you talking about?"

"Newspaper. People read them, get informed of the news."

"Steve, what are you *talking* about?" Leon could feel the symptoms of panic coursing through him.

"Local paper. Front page, no less. Wasn't he Karen?" Steve was actually enjoying this.

Karen, not expecting to be asked to contribute so soon, had been trying to separate a mass of greasy meat that seemed to be linked together by a web of gristle. Unable to do it easily, she had just popped the whole lot in her mouth. Considering her mouth was now over-full and it was far hotter than she had realised, this was not an ideal time to be asked to contribute. She simply nodded.

Leon put his stew down next to him, his appetite completely gone despite the fact he had not eaten much earlier. He forced himself to take deep breaths. The warehouse, the fire, the moustache, the charred body being wheeled out, the car, the petrol canisters, the police, the chase. He had been identified after all. The photo-fit had worked. He had been too cocky and dismissive of that picture from the start. He would be the last person able to tell if people would think it was him. Prison, inmates, mental deterioration.

He wanted to run. Just stand up there and then and sprint away from Steve, the others, and the temporary food supply. Why were Steve and Karen so calm about it, he wondered. Had they already informed the police who were now watching the three of them? Perhaps Steve was wearing a recording device and there were a crew of them sitting in the back of a van, waiting for him to convict himself of murder. Surely he was just being a fucking lunatic who had watched too much television.

"Why am I in the newspaper, Steve?" Leon asked in no more than a croaky whisper.

"People are looking for you," Karen almost sounded concerned. Perhaps she was. Perhaps she and Steve were going to help him escape. Leon looked around and thought that most of these people now knew he had killed one of their own. If the police didn't get him then one of them would. Perhaps prison would be better than a filthy broken bottle sawing slowly into his jugular vein, the lifeblood pooling in front of his eyes as he realised that his final resting place would be among dog shit and hypodermic needles. Why had he not been confronted or attacked already, he wondered. Presumably, the thing that was saving him was that most of the people there had not read a newspaper in years. Why would they? He already knew for himself that any knowledge of what was happening in the 'normal' world was a complete waste of brain space. You may as well tell someone the football results from the Danish second division for all the impact it would have or use it would be. If anything Leon found that it just increased the feeling of alienation by creating memories of a life left well behind. The only use for newspapers that his current peers had, other than the ever-inquisitive Steve, was insulation to keep themselves a fraction warmer at night and help them to stay on the right side of that precarious line between life and death.

Leon stared pleadingly at his friends, willing them even to give him the worst news possible rather than stay in this agonising state of dread.

"Obviously someone has reported you missing," said Steve.

Leon's mind, up to this point being tightened in a vice, escaped its constraints and billowed outwards. The relief was intense. That was it! He was in the local news because of the fact that he had gone missing. That in itself would have ordinarily been bad news but by comparison it was like being told he had won the lottery. His secret was still safe and for that he could not have been more grateful. He wondered who had reported it. It had to be someone at work as no one else would panic at not getting hold of him after only a few weeks. He was notoriously bad at answering telephone calls or emails and if anyone actually called at the house, a rare event, he was usually in the pub. Karen was talking but he didn't give a shit what she was saying; he could have jumped for joy.

But this was still serious. At least Karen and Steve, if not more people, knew that he had a home, a job that he had simply walked away from. How would that go down?

"My debts..." he began before realising he had nothing to offer.

"Stop," snapped Karen, "no one needs an explanation."

"But you must be wondering. You must think..."

"No one cares, you're not that interesting, you know. You can't be if no one's noticed you gone until now." It was sometimes difficult to know whether Steve was kidding or not.

"I know, but I couldn't afford..."

"Be quiet Leon," Karen interrupted him again. She pointed to the crowds of people around them, "I probably know most of this lot. Enough to talk to anyway. They all lived in a house at some point and a lot of them had jobs. Most of them had wives or husbands, children, cars, dogs, whatever. Something happened to every one of them; bankruptcy, divorce, getting arrested, getting caught cheating, mental breakdown. We all have something that made us arrive at this point, some more willingly than others. But none of these people care why you're here. You just *are,* so get over it. If you want to tell us about your life at any time I'll be glad to listen. But I don't want to know just because you want to explain why you're in the paper."

"I just told you 'cause I thought you'd want to know folk were looking for you," Steve sounded as though he had taken Karen's monologue as a personal scolding.

"Anyway, I'm off to see if they've got any of this crap left," she waved her polystyrene tray, "who wants some?"

## CHAPTER 23

"You want something that'll just chill you out or something that'll properly knock you out? Because believe me, some of this will put you out of commission 'til Wednesday"

Leon did not know how long it was until Wednesday but that did not sound ideal.

"Just to sleep. Just want sleep," Leon could sense that his voice was slurred but did not care.

The dealer coughed and it sounded like a marble rattling around in a tin can. He reached into the inside pocket of his coat and Leon could not help but stare at the stick-thin, sinewy forearm which was left uncovered by the vest and leather waistcoat he wore. It looked as though it might snap if he snagged it on a pocket. This urban apothecary's wares were out on display; a wide and varied choice. Leon had no idea why the man had even bothered to do this as Leon was clearly going to buy whatever the dealer told him to, regardless of how recklessly stupid that was.

"This is exactly what you're after," he held up a small sandwich bag with a couple of dozen pills in it.

Leon reached out to take it and the dealer whipped it back, his tightly covered skull split horizontally by what Leon guessed was a smile. The sight was hideous and Leon half expected the top half of his head to simply fall off backwards, tearing the paper-thin skin. Leon dropped his bottle of lager, which he could not remember acquiring. Luckily it was virtually empty.

"Steady on, man, steady on," the dealer held his hand out, "Ten."

"No way. For how many?"

"One."

"Stick it."

"You need to be careful what you're saying, man."

The dealer's eyes bored into Leon, who did not doubt his menace for a second. He had not even ruled out the possibility that they were being watched from the shadows by some equally grotesque partners in crime.

"Thanks anyway," Leon began to walk away, swaying slightly. He desperately wanted something. Although he was pissed he knew that the rats would not allow him to sleep after an initial bout of unconsciousness had worn off. He was still sleeping better on the whole since he left home, but these things were relative.

"Come 'ere," the man grunted.

Leon walked back to him.

"New customer discount. Give us a tenner an' you can 'ave two."

Leon still looked doubtful.

"I look after me customers."

The dealer shook two pills onto his dirty palm, his long talons closing round them. Leon momentarily considered lamping the man and taking what he wanted. There were several things that put him off, including the possible accomplices. His drunken reactions and the knife he had noticed in the man's waistcoat were paramount, but there was also the fact that this bloke looked like one of those slight, skinny men who moved like a cat and turned out to be a frenzied, freak-of-nature, lunatic fighting machine.

Leon could not find the street. He knew he was close and was starting to get frustrated with himself. The pills felt so conspicuous in his pocket that he imagined them the size of golf balls. He was drunk. Perhaps he should just go back to the Embankment, take the tablets and get his head down. But he realised that he had finished with the Embankment for good now. He did not know what he had been thinking about to begin with by going there. If it had been to see if Marie was there then he had established very early on that she wasn't. If he had been subconsciously trying to prove something to himself then he had surely managed that too, and he had to admit a slight satisfaction that he had survived the most notorious spot in town. He knew though that there was just as much danger, possibly more, in those dark corners of the city where no one could see you take a beating. He had generally been impressed by the level of camaraderie among the homeless population but it was no secret that each of them had one main priority; to look after themselves. And there was a minority who adopted this philosophy wholly and ruthlessly. Besides this, the Embankment had become intolerable now that he had lost his sleeping bag and coat. The weather was starting to get noticeably colder of late. Although his will was being eroded day by day Leon knew that on the sliding scale from self-preservation to self-destruction, he was still clinging on at the end of the former.

Elmsfield Road had to be around here somewhere. When Karen had given him the address he had barely listened to her directions as he was certain of its location. Now he was starting to wonder if he had confused it with another street or if that was even what Karen had said in the first place. He had turned so many corners that he did not even know what direction he was facing. He turned the corner at the end of a street, certain that he had already done so about ten minutes previously. And there it was.

If the neighbouring houses seemed in a state of disrepair to Leon as he passed them, then number 43 looked fit to collapse. Paint and plaster had fallen from the sills and door so that their original state was unidentifiable. Leon noted that he could have pushed half a finger into the gaps between some of the bricks and there were several pieces of fallen roof slate in what had once been a front yard and was now an overgrown mess complete with beer cans, crisp packets and a fragment of a TO LET sign. The building looked drunk, as though its two neighbours were holding it up. This sight was made more concerning by the fact that the neighbours themselves appeared to be only slightly more sober.

No one answered Leon's knock at the door. He stood back to look at the house once more. He had already established that there was no sign of life but he concentrated on each window before returning to knock louder. He opened the letterbox to peer inside and was met by a thick musty odour. It was difficult to make anything out but there was definitely a distant source of light that he could see showing through a quarter inch gap at the bottom of a door at the far end of the corridor. He banged louder with the heel of his fist and moved backwards, frustrated.

Eventually, a young man answered the door with none of the caution he had been expecting from an illegal occupant of a property.

"Yeah?"

"I'm Leon."

"Yeah?"

The lad did not look more than twenty-five. He wore heavy, oversized boots that looked large at the end of his spindly legs, which were clad in holey jeans. He had dirty blonde, spiky hair and looked fresh faced. Leon wondered if this kid was new to the life. It had not yet left its mark on his features, scarred his face and twisted his posture. Leon was suddenly aware once more of how the street had remoulded him both physically and mentally. He was convinced that even if he were plucked from his position now and dropped back into his old life he would never look or feel the same as he had. Instinctively his hand rose to rub the lengthening bristles on his chin. He knew that it looked pretty bad. He had always been a very poor beard-grower which was why he had rarely before let it get beyond a shortish stubble, even during spells of fairly heavy drinking when his appearance had not exactly been at the forefront of his thoughts. After experimentation, he had noticed that he had asymmetrical bald spots that made him look ridiculous. He would have quite liked a shave now but it seemed like an unnecessary extravagance and besides, the itchiness had stopped and he had developed an automatic technique of flattening out his moustache with forefinger and thumb before eating.

"Is Karen in?"

"Nope."

"I'm not in the mood for this. I'm Leon. I don't know if she mentioned I was coming."

The kid looked Leon up and down.

"Nah."

Leon could feel his finger nails digging into his palms. He took a step towards the door and was pleased to see a moment of worry flash across the kid's face. The lad went to close the door and Leon knew he would be able to shut it before he got there. He was aware enough to realise that, although he could have quite happily throttled this little prick, he did not want to upset a possible friend of Karen and Steve before he had even crossed the threshold.

"Let's start again. Is Karen in?" Leon asked patiently, even managing a slight smile.

"I already said she wasn't."

"Steve?"

This time just a shake of the head. Leon could feel himself boiling over and wondered if this was worth it.

"You can wait out there for them if you want," and with that, the kid had shut the door. Leon found a spot in the yard where he could sit back against the wall and popped both pills in his mouth.

Just over an hour later Karen and Steve arrived to find Leon sat on the front wall, having searched to find a section that he felt might take his weight. There was no apology for their tardiness and he did not expect one. They were, after all, doing him an enormous favour at their own inconvenience. They let him in.

They moved through the corridor and Steve opened the kitchen door to reveal numerous candle flames flickering violently in the sudden draught, creating a disorientating effect on Leon's initial sight of the room and its occupants. The door shut and things settled down. Although the night outside was now dark and the kitchen was a big place, the candles gave off a reasonable light; certainly good enough to read by if he was lucky enough to get his hands on a book at any point. Leon had once been a voracious reader but his disengagement with his hobby correlated directly with his increased appetite for alcohol. He had tried to force himself to read once the drinking started in earnest but he had found it pointless as each time he picked up a book he had no memory of the narrative that had brought him to that point.

Five pairs of eyes turned to face them. Karen did the introductions.

"This is Leon that I told you all about."

Leon glared at the young kid who gave him a look of feigned innocence. Leon again contemplated decking him and going back on the street.

"This is Sue." A woman with greying hair who could have been sixty. She had a copy of the local free newspaper on her lap.

"Alice P." The stick thin, mousy haired girl was child-like except for her eyes, which locked on Leon's. He could tell instinctively that she had already seen more than one lifetime's worth of badness. She was whittling a piece of wood into a sharp point with a penknife.

"Jane." Dark hair, possibly forties, she had a walking stick next to her. She and Alice P looked like they had been chatting as the three of them had entered.

"Alice M." Her hair could have been auburn or dark and her age was too difficult to guess as she was sat towards the rear of the kitchen area. She was trying to fix a frayed dog lead. Leon looked around for a dog but did not see one.

Each of the women in turn muttered or nodded a greeting.

"And this is Guy. He's not long joined us himself," Karen finished by introducing Leon's new nemesis. Guy looked slightly miffed that Karen had 'outed' him as a newcomer to the group. Leon wondered if she had done it on purpose and was glad that she had. Guy raised an index finger. It appeared to be in greeting but Leon had no idea what he was doing so simply ignored him.

It was clear that the room had originally been a kitchen and dining room, knocked through into one larger room. The door from which they had entered brought them straight into the dining area and the kitchen was at the back where Alice M sat motionless. The room was now, however, just a general communal room where this bunch of people sat doing whatever it was they did.

"Florence is probably upstairs asleep and we also have Jim and Felix when they come home."

Leon knew that this was a three-bedroom house and wondered what the sleeping arrangements were. He did not ask as it was really nothing to do with him and he would find out soon enough. All he knew was that Karen and Steve had offered him some floor space in their own room, which was how they had convinced their housemates to take in another guest. Perhaps they felt guilty at having the least populated room in the house and it was preferable to let Leon in than share with one of the others.

"We'll show you where you'll be," Karen said to Leon and they left the room.

Rather than going upstairs as he expected, they went straight past the foot of the stairs and entered the only room at the front of the house on the ground floor. Leon guessed that this had originally been the living room.

"We're just in here."

Leon had a bizarre feeling like he was in his previous life being shown to a room in a nice countryside bed and breakfast. When the door opened he would see a deliciously comfortable double bed with crisp white sheets and pillows so thick you had to flatten them down to get your head on top.

Steve expertly fumbled in the corner of the room and quickly lit a candle that was in a brass holder. He placed a glass cover on it that caused the flame to recoil, recover and jump back to life, invigorated. The room was larger than Leon had imagined but not particularly welcoming. Steve seemed to see his expression.

"Not much is it?" he smiled. "Just somewhere to lay your head, so it doesn't need to be five star."

"No, it's fine. That is, it's great. I really appreciate it. I couldn't face the thought of another night outside and I can't bear those other places."

Leon continued to stand and there was a moment of silence.

"Oh yeah," Karen said, "that's you down here."

Near the bay window were two old mattresses, one at either side of the room, which clearly belonged to his two friends. A few paltry belongings were pushed against the wall. Karen was pointing to what was essentially an empty corner of the room. But it had a carpet and two walls. The room had a door and the place had a roof. To Leon, it felt like he had hit the jackpot.

"Brilliant. Thanks."

"There are a couple of blankets we're not really using so we left them next to the fireplace. Help yourself," offered Steve. "I think Alice M's dog might have slept in one of them so you might want to check 'cause it's a smelly little shithouse that one."

"*He*'s called Clyde, and he's a nice dog," said Karen in a way that told Leon this was not the first time this conversation had happened between them. Leon was fairly sure the blankets were not 'spare' at all but were a charitable donation, but he was not going to argue.

"So do you normally hang out through there?" asked Leon, nodding back towards the kitchen.

"Just do what you want," answered Karen, "we normally just get back late, come in here, play cards, read, whatever."

Leon noticed three paperbacks next to the mattress she had just sat down on. Steve sat on his own bed and Leon simply stared at them. How had these two found each other? Leon had never believed in all that soul-mate nonsense but these two had found something amazing in each other. It was made all the more intriguing as they were not even in a relationship, at least not according to any standard notion of one. He suddenly felt like a gooseberry between two platonic friends. He wondered if he should go through to the kitchen to get to know his new pals. He knew though that he was really going to speak to them in the hope that one of them had drink. The last few hours had kept his mind preoccupied in order that any cravings were pushed out of the light. But that was then.

He hoped that sleeping indoors would reduce his need for booze. Perhaps subconsciously he had simply needed the buffer against the reality of sleeping in the open air surrounded by predators. But he knew deep down, in a place that he did not care to explore or question, that his realistic aim was simply to maintain his status as a functioning alcoholic, rather than delude himself with higher aspirations. If he could avoid degenerating into a pissing-yourself in-the-street type of drunk that would be good. He would try to get some sleep.

After only half an hour of lying on the floor in his new corner, hoping to catch up on some sleep, Leon realised already that the ache was coming back. The drugs still had not had the slightest effect and he was annoyed with himself for buying them. The nerves networking through his body were breaking through their protective casings and crackling through him. Anything that he could not find in the kitchen would have to be sought elsewhere. It had been naïve of him to turn up without his medicine.

Having borrowed a book from Karen that he had no intention of reading, he grunted some greetings and plopped himself down on a vacant piece of floor with his back up against the wall. Looking around it was difficult to see where to start. He decided that Guy might be the best bet but there was no way he was going to cosy up to him unless things got really bad. Alice P. Definitely. The skinny young kid with the world-weary eyes. He shuffled slightly in her direction. The silence in the room was eerie and yet everyone looked fairly comfortable in their own skin. All except Alice P who looked like a deer; twitchy and coiled to make a run at the slightest sign of danger. The advantage of the candlelight was that he could watch her with less chance of being noticed. Her head snapped upwards.

Shit.

"What? What is it?" she asked quietly, speaking quickly.

"Sorry, no, I was just wondering what you were making," Leon responded. He nodded at the pocket knife and small pile of wood shavings. The piece of wood was about two inches in diameter and five or six inches long. The end that Alice was carving was now flattened like a blade and had a fearsome point. The knife she was using had seen better days but was still functional.

Alice looked as though she did not want to talk. She glanced around at the others and Leon noticed that none of the women had altered what they were doing. Guy was making no attempt to hide the fact that he was listening to them and this seemed to bother Alice.

"Just for self-defence," she lifted the wood and blew what was presumably a wood shaving away.

"Oh, OK. Why wouldn't you just use the knife?" Leon immediately wished he had not asked. He had heard his own voice and thought it sounded like he was taking the piss out of her. Alice's eyes flicked once more around the room.

"You never know what's going to happen," she said in a voice so low that Leon had to lean in to hear her.

Leon assumed that was the end of the conversation and decided he should probably see what the book was in his hands.

"You men think you've got it hard. You should try being a woman out there."

"I can't imagine."

"No."

Leon realised that they were virtually whispering.

"Sorry to just come out and ask, but you don't have any drink on you, do you?" Leon decided to make his intentions clear, lest she should mistake his attentions as something else and stab him between the ribs with a sharpened stick.

She shook her head without lifting her gaze up from the wooden blade.

"Okay, no problem. Listen, I've got a couple of quid left from today. I'm going down to the off-licence. Do you want a drink?" Leon chuckled to himself, "look at me - asking a girl out for a drink."

Oh God, it could be shiv time after all.

Alice P did not show any indication that the notion was amusing. Leon thought she looked like she had seen no reason to find anything funny for a long, long time. He wondered what had happened to her and decided he was better off not knowing. He stood up.

"All right. Well, I'll see you about Alice."

"I'll come."

As they left, Guy glared at them. Leon wondered if he was annoyed that Leon had made a friend so quickly or jealous because it was this one. This made Leon wonder if any of the gang thought he had designs on young Alice. What if she wanted him to? He looked at her. She was so skinny that her body could have belonged to a boy, giving her an air of asexuality. He was just thankful for a chance of a companion for a while and had no other hopes. He felt in his pocket for money and wondered if she would be happy to swig from a shared bottle because that was probably what she had just signed up to.

## CHAPTER 24

He awoke feeling like a car had hit him. In the dark, it took him many seconds to realise where he was and he was relieved to find that it was Steve and Karen's room. He had no recollection of returning. Any move he made was painful in the extreme. His right hand throbbed with an intense heat that made him wince.

He could remember sharing a drink with Alice. Too much drink. He had glugged it greedily, Alice barely getting a look in to her apparent indifference. Leon had assumed she had come for the same reason he had asked her - pure and simple companionship. It was an attempt to have some sort of social interaction in a world controlled by self-preservation and paranoia. While the conversation had never reached free-flowing levels he had enjoyed being with her enough. Attempts to recall events from later in the evening were met with a familiar and total blackout, as though the plug had been suddenly pulled on his brain and it had just now been plugged back in. The reboot was certainly shaky.

He started to picture the worst-case scenarios. He had probably made a clumsy pass at the twitchy young girl who had decided against her better judgement to trust him. She would have run home and explained her anger to their housemates that Karen and Steve's lecherous twat of a mate had made a move on her. In that case, he would have to leave after only a single night with a roof over his head. Balls. He soon stopped creating depressing scenarios because his hand forced him to. As he gradually came round it became more scorching. He tried to form a fist and an agonising spear of pain shot through the fleshy part of his palm. He was slightly alarmed and desperately wanted to light Steve's candle to investigate. There was no way he was going to risk waking his roommates on his first night there, although he was sure he probably already had the previous evening or early morning, or whenever the hell he had actually got home.

The pain was unbearable. He curled his fingers again and a rush of nausea came from the pit of his stomach with a ferocity that made him clap his left hand over his mouth. He felt some sort of bandage wrapped around his hand. He had to see what was wrong. He extricated himself from his sweaty nest of sheets and padded in his boxer shorts through to the kitchen, closing the door to his room as quietly as possible.

Wandering slowly through the inky darkness of the kitchen, Leon headed for the rear of the room where he had spotted a box of matches and a couple of candles the previous evening. He walked slowly, exaggerating each step and waiting for a crunch of shin on wood or a shock of sole on upturned plug. He pictured his ridiculous walking style from the point of view of someone looking at him through night goggles. The thought of what a ridiculous sight he would make made him smile despite everything.

He gingerly peeled off the filthy, unidentifiable rag that had formed his makeshift bandage. The flickering light of the candle did not help an awful lot except to confirm that he was quite badly injured. The gash was deep and wide and as he gingerly moved his thumb it seemed to yawn like a muppet's mouth. In the limited light, the blood was black. On the plus side it did not appear to be bleeding freely any more but the dried blood on his hand, forearm and clothing told him it had done. He sucked in air through his teeth. Now that he had seen how awful the wound was the pain seemed somehow more intolerable and the throbbing seemed to beat up into his forearm. He stared into the darkness in front of him.

"Jesus Christ," he muttered, "Such a prick."

A pair of eyes materialised in front of him. The irises appeared black in the gaunt face. "Bad then, is it?"

Leon's heart almost jumped through the top of his head. He was aware that he had shouted out some sort of yelp.

"Alice. What the fucking hell? You nearly gave me a fucking... What you doing in here anyway?"

"Couldn't sleep," she answered, as though that were somehow a logical excuse for being sat in the pitch dark of the kitchen. "I sometimes come in here."

"You been here the whole time?"

"If you mean the whole time you've been staring at your hand then yeah."

Alice swept up another couple of candles from somewhere, lit them from Leon's and popped them in a pair of pots. They both leaned into the centre of the table to examine his injury.

"What happened? Last night," he asked.

Alice was not listening to him. She was peering intently at what used to be the palm of his hand.

"This is bad. We're going to need to get this seen to."

"How? I don't have anything. Any papers, anything."

Leon tried to quickly weigh up his situation. He wondered how likely it was that he could give bogus details at the hospital and successfully avoid recognition as 'Missing Leon Glover'. In addition to that, although his nerves had calmed significantly on this matter, the more people in the real world that he met increased the small chance of him being recognised as a killer. It was fine on the streets as no one really paid too much attention to anyone's past or future, only to their present, and even then details such as identity were of secondary importance.

Alice stared at him and in the candle light Leon could feel her deep, troubled eyes once more boring through his own retinas and into the recesses of his skull. "You're not in America. You turn up at A&E bleeding to death and you're going to get treated even if you *are* a street bum."

"It's really painful."

Alice gave him a shrug that told him that she did not give a toss how much pain he was in.

"What happened last night then?" he asked. He decided he might as well get all the pain dealt with at the same time.

"If you mean this," she nodded to his hand which he was still resting, palm up on the table, "then I've no idea. This was after I came home."

"Hmm, so what else happened?"

"We had a drink. You started being weird. Kind of morose I suppose you'd call it."

"Oh. Sorry."

He sneaked a look at her and she simply looked straight back. He wondered if she was bothered by anything.

"I just remember sitting by the corner having a drink," he said.

"Yeah, and it was fine. I knew you were getting really pissed but that didn't bother me. Then you started banging on about some woman."

"Marie," Leon almost whispered.

"Dunno, I wasn't really interested to be honest so I stopped listening."

"Oh..."

"Anyhow, then you disappeared. I thought you'd gone for a piss and then you came back with another half bottle. You were all over the shop. Started going on about having something to help you sleep. As if drinking your own body weight in cheap whisky wouldn't have done that. You wouldn't go home when I told you to and I could only see the rest of the night going one way so I left. Looks like I was right to."

"Sorry. Not much fun. Anyhow, I think I'll head down to A&E then."

Alice looked as though she was trying to work out something in her head. She looked down at the table and sighed.

"Come on then?"

"You don't have to come," he said, surprised.

"No, but even in this light you look like shit. You're white and shaking like a shitting dog. I don't think you'll make it. Anyway, I can't sleep and I've got nothing better to do."

"Well, er thanks."

"Shut up and put your trousers on."


Stitched and bandaged, Leon sat in his wheelchair and stared at his gauze mitten. He worried that the local anaesthetic would soon wear off and was anticipating the pain. He felt light-headed and slightly sick. He wondered what and how much they might give him in the way of prescription drugs.

"Come on then, Colin," Alice smiled.

It was the first time he had seen her smile. Properly, at any rate – there had been a few forced smiles that could have meant anything from sarcasm to pain – but this was a real one. It changed her face and made her whole appearance somewhat softer. He wondered what she was talking about until realising that she was calling him by his hospital name.

"Don't I need to…"

"We're going. Unless you want to hang around and fill in more paperwork of course. Once you've got your medication you can head off. It's sort of a rule."

He could feel Alice looking at him even though she was pretending not to. He supposed she was wondering where the money came from for his never-ending supply of booze. Most of his float was now gone and so it was largely bona fide begging cash. He screwed the top back on the bottle and placed it, rustling in its bag, below his dangling feet. They were sat on the wall just along from the off-licence, not far from where they had spent the previous evening.

"Don't worry, I'll give you plenty of notice before I lose my mind this time," he grinned.

"Don't *you* worry, I'll be long gone before that."

"It's just medicinal. My hand hurts."

She looked at her watch in an attempt to make it look like she needed to be somewhere. Leon noticed that she was not even wearing a watch, just a couple of frayed wristbands.

The whisky spread and calmed the rats inside him. His muscles relaxed and any feeling of embarrassment about his previous behaviour was subdued. Didn't take much, he thought.

"Wonder what I got up to then. Must have been good."

"If you want my bet you found a pusher, couldn't pay and managed to get your hand in the way of getting stabbed to death. You wouldn't have had a cut that clean and deep from anything other than a decent knife,"

Leon simply noted this as an interesting hypothesis, rather than it scaring him, which he knew it should.

"Have to remember to defend myself with my other hand tonight."

She didn't seem to find it funny. He leaned forwards and swiped up the bottle, unscrewing the cap. Alice looked and wondered why he had even bothered putting it down in the first place.

"You need to take it easy with that."

Leon took a long swig.

"You've got enough tablets in that bag to subdue a horse. You don't need to be necking booze on top."

"I'll be right."

"I can see you've got some sort of romanticised self destruction thing going on, but you need to calm down. I'm assuming it's a recent development otherwise you'd be dead already."

This was the return of the world-weary, cynical Alice P that he had mentally summed up at their first meeting. He wondered how much was a defensive front and how much was her genuine character, refined by the street.

"It's nice that you care," he grinned, swigging again.

"I just don't want the cops turning up when Karen and Steve find a dead body in their room."

"Nice."

He had a vague recollection of curling up to sleep in his blankets, which meant that he had not got completely out of control. He could remember Alice leaving and him lingering on his own. He could also remember bumping into that twat Guy back at the house. It was fairly safe to assume that hadn't gone awfully well. Leon struggled to be civil to him without three-quarters of a pint of scotch and a bucket of prescription pills inside him. Best not to worry about that.

He blinked several times and decided that he had once more awoken in the middle of the night. Too late to have a nightcap and way too early to think about getting up. He needed to piss and had a mouth like sandpaper. He struggled out of the room in silence and went to take care of the former. Luckily there was a tiny toilet located under the stairs between his room and the kitchen. He imagined someone, a family, at one time loving this house. The family had made it their home and were happy. Happy in their home, with each other. 'A spare toilet under the stairs?' 'Why, that would be wonderful dear.' These people had put time and effort into this simple but costly attempt to improve their living conditions. They had been tragically proud of it, looking forward to friends coming round for dinner. 'No need to go upstairs, we have one under the stairs now… I know it's great, isn't it?'

Leon could picture them vividly in his mind. The house had probably had dozens of inhabitants over the hundred or so years it had been standing, but these were the ones he was now emotionally connected to. The ones who had put in the spare toilet.

He fumbled around in the dark, suddenly sad about the state of disrepair the house was now in. He was thankful that the lack of light prevented him from seeing the awful mess of this, the smallest room in the house. He knew it was now mouldy, the toilet seat hung on to its porcelain base by one wobbly plastic screw. The carpet had long been pulled up and the smell was getting towards unbearable. He flushed as he fumbled his way out and cringed as the plumbing gurgled and spluttered in its attempt to refill the cistern. He was sure that given the choice all his cohabitants would rather have had stale urine in the filthy toilet than be awoken at this hour.

Leon felt his way to the kitchen table, lit a few candles and filled a cracked mug with some water. He sat down to drink it and stared into blackness. He thought briefly about going to get one of Karen's books to bring back through but then decided it was not worth straining his eyes. He thought he heard a noise and held his breath, listening. Probably his imagination but he leaned forwards as though it would improve his hearing. He was sure he heard someone move.

"Alice. That you?" His voice was only marginally louder than a whisper.

No answer. He pushed the mug to one side and clenched his fists.

"Alice, stop pissing about. Are you there?"

He had probably just heard the house moving. The plumbing was far from the only thing that made its presence known. The building creaked and groaned constantly, grumbling about its years of mistreatment. Leon picked up his mug once more and took a swig.

The flat of a hand slapped against the mug, bouncing it across the table and was followed immediately by a sickening crunch as a fist connected with Leon's eye socket, knocking him backwards off his chair.

What was happening was as quick and disorienting as it was violent. Leon scrabbled to his feet and saw a hand dip into the orb of light around the kitchen table, thumping down a half litre plastic bottle. A head bobbed into sight and in the time it took for the candles to be blown out Leon saw that it was balding with grey stubble for hair. In the half-light a pair of dark lips pursed just before the flame went out. Leon's fists were up in front of his face and he was up on the balls of his feet. Instinctively he shifted to his left so that he was not in the same spot as he had been. It only made him feel slightly less vulnerable. He tried to calm his breathing so that he could hear as well as hide. He was surprised to hear footsteps moving away from him, across the room towards the door.

"Come here," Leon growled, his anger overpowering his common sense.

"Sit down. Move back to the table and just sit down." The voice was male, younger and better spoken than he had been expecting, but with a rasp to it, like someone trying to shake a chest infection.

Leon felt that he was starting to panic. He felt so vulnerable stood there in the complete darkness, at the mercy of someone that was a complete mystery to him. Still, he felt his way back to the table. He scraped back the chair loudly and clattered it into place. He thought he heard a noise from upstairs and was unsure of whether an interruption from one of his housemates would be a good or bad thing at this juncture.

"What do you want?" he asked in a loud, clear voice.

The man in the dark saw through his intentions immediately.

"Keep it down. The last thing you want is one of your mates coming in to see what the noise is, believe me."

"Okay then," said Leon in a much quieter voice, trying to sound calm, "what is it you want?"

"You need to hear what I've got to say so I'll just tell you now, if I hear that chair move an inch, if you try to light a candle, I'm gone."

"Understood." Leon had no intention of testing him.

"On the table in front of you is a bottle full of liquid. It looks like water and it's fairly tasteless but *do not* drink it. Do not let anyone else drink it. The only person who can drink it is the man you are going to give it to."

"Fuck you."

The man continued, completely ignoring Leon.

"There is a small plastic pouch there as well."

Leon had not seen a pouch. He silently slid his fingertips across the surface of the table. They snagged a couple of times on the crevices in the mistreated wood before touching the folder.

"There are a couple of things in there but the most important is the picture of the man you need to see. He goes to the soup kitchen at Berkeley Square, you might even recognise him."

"Hang on…"

"Just be quiet. This is easier if you just let me speak. In answer to your first question, there are a few reasons why you'll do it. Firstly, we'll hook you up once it's done. You'll have as many drugs as you want. Probably a lifetime's supply the way you're carrying on. You can spend months on end not knowing what day it is. You'll have enough to top yourself with if that's what you want to do; I don't care."

"Talk to me somewhere I can see you, you coward."

"Secondly, you'll finally see your woman."

"You don't know where she is, you've never known. I think I always knew that really. I've come to terms with it,"

"I know exactly where Marie Holt is. This is it. One job. It's the end of the road, Leon."

Leon flinched at the mention of his name, and hers. Hearing it somehow made the situation more real and made him realise how much responsibility was being put upon him personally.

"Thirdly, and this one might seal the deal, if you don't do this one last thing that will see you walk free of everything, you will be going to jail. A witness has just decided to come forward. She saw you set fire to a warehouse, Leon. And we both know that means she saw you kill someone."

"Except your stooge saw nothing," spat Leon, "so if she was ever to get on the stand the worst defence lawyer in the world could pull her apart."

"But not before she'd pointed the finger in the right direction for the police to find out that you actually did it."

Leon knew he was right.

"I've still got the note. The note telling me to do it."

"That's bullshit. Even if you did have it, it could have been written by anyone, including you. But I know you haven't got it. I'm going now. You've got four days. I'll find you to complete our business. And just in case you were wondering, the folder and its contents have nothing incriminating about them, including finger prints."

"Hang on. Even if I did decide to do it, how the hell am I supposed to persuade a complete stranger to drink a bottle full of unidentified liquid?"

"Use your imagination. I would have poured it into a vodka bottle myself if I didn't think you'd get confused and drink it yourself, you pathetic fucking drunk."

"Okay. Just thought I'd ask."

Leon heard the man retreating further and stood up, making his way in that direction. Still unaccustomed as he was to the layout of the room, he stubbed his unprotected toe on the corner of a chair and silently grimaced.

"Sit yourself down. You don't want to see what I'm carrying here just in case I need it. We've already had one run in and I don't want to have to put you down."

Leon's hand twitched involuntarily and the hot pain of his palm sent out a dull ache. This must be the his assailant and, therefore, he must have a knife. Perhaps this was not his first attempt to talk to Leon. He did as he was told and sat back at the table.

"I'm not going to do it, you know? I just don't care any more."

"It's all in there. The backup. Insurance, if you like. How *are* Chris and Sophie doing? Because they are reason number four."

The names took a couple of seconds to sink in. Chris and Sophie. Lynn. He and his sister hadn't spoken in over a year. They had not fallen out as such; it was just that they had drifted apart. He knew they would pick it all up again one day but that day had not yet arrived. A few years ago, when Kevin had walked out, Leon had been a regular feature at their home, but even then he was painfully aware that the support his sister needed was of an emotional rather than a practical nature. For most problems that she cried over, Leon would be able to come up with an idea that, to his mind, was helpful. He could fix the shower that had just broken or take an afternoon off to collect Sophie if Lynn could not get off work. He could remove the last of Kevin's belongings and (even though he could not trust himself to call at the flat of his brother-in-law and his ridiculously young new girlfriend, for fear of harming Kevin) drop them somewhere for collection. But he knew that is not what she really needed. She wanted someone to hold her, to say 'I know' and truly empathise with her. This was not in Leon's skill set and, as a result, he felt more of a helpful handy-man than a shoulder to cry on. He had told himself that was fine. After all, she had her friends for that.

He pictured Chris and Sophie and realised that he could only bring up vague images. It had only been a year or so and he could not recall their faces with any real clarity. Under normal circumstances that might have saddened him, but now it just added to the swirl of anger that he could feel rising up from the pit of his stomach. Thick, lava-like fury splashed upwards and was in danger of completely consuming all his other senses. He had hold of the edge of the table and his nails dug into the top so hard that, short as they were, they felt in danger of snapping.

The dark air was overwhelming and thick. He struggled to inhale it and his mouth opened wide. He needed to breathe. He needed to get oxygen in and rid himself of the carbon dioxide that was sending his anxiety level into the stratosphere. As he stared into the blackness he could see shapes and colours dancing in front of him. There were patches as though he had been partially blinded by a camera flash. He knew he was in danger of losing it and felt that he was going to pass out. In. Hold. Out. Keep breathing out. More. Until it hurts. Wait. Now in again.

He did not want to give the man the satisfaction of an angry response but the lid might come off if he did nothing to relieve the pressure. He heard his own voice and was surprised by the hoarse, quiet, measured tone of it.

"If I so much as find out that anyone has been looking at those two kids I will find you. *You*. I don't care about anyone else. I won't have a thing to lose. I will kill you."

The man chuckled. "That's the spirit."

And with that he was gone.

## CHAPTER 25

Leon staggered through the Embankment, his flaming torch flickering and crackling in front of him. Purely based on the lack of life, his experience told him that it must be around four or five a.m. Pitches were either empty or housed unconscious bodies. Any earlier and there would still have been people up to a variety of activities, none of which would have been particularly wholesome.

Even prowlers were absent. There was only one person scavenging on that desolate ground and that was Leon. He realised that even in this corner of the world that had no rules he must be a worrying sight, stumbling around with a flame streaking the darkness above his head.

The moment that Leon's guest had vacated the house there was only one thing on his mind, and it was not his niece and nephew; it was something to sedate his mind. He relit a candle and searched the kitchen for booze even though he was pretty sure there wasn't any there. After going through every option he could think of he had gone for the one place he knew there would be alcohol at this time of night, even though obtaining it would be dangerous at best. Taking a single match from the squat, some rags from a bin, a stick from the front yard, and finding a car petrol cap with no lock, he had fashioned his 'lynch-mob' torch.

An unconscious body; a possibility. But there was no sense in moving it and potentially waking it up to find no alcohol and an ensuing fight. Eventually he saw it; a skinny young kid, half in a sleeping bag. On a night this cold he must have been hammered to pass out without snuggling completely inside the bag. Barely visible was the neck of a glass bottle. The reflection of Leon's flame danced playfully on it and as he approached he saw amber liquid gently lapping in time with the man's snoring. He reached down and slid it ever so carefully from the man's grasp. As the base slipped out of the crook of his arm the arm bumped down and the man sat upright. Leon placed the flat of his hand against the man's head and pushed him back down, ready for the fight. The drunk simply passed out once more and Leon moved on.

Upon finding a bench well away from the Embankment Leon took a deep swig and felt the liquid begin its job. Only once the elation had dwindled did he reflect on the despicable act he had just carried out. The kid had potentially begged for days to afford the bottle and he may have needed it every bit as badly as Leon. And he had just stolen it from him. After a few moments of contemplation the overriding message from Leon's rats was, "Fuck him. We only care about you. It's survival of the fittest." Leon decided to go with this; it seemed the only way to cope with his actions.

The concealed plastic bottle pushed into his ribs, which had become much less protected of late and were very visible on the rare occasion he saw himself shirtless. He put his hand into his pocket and felt it. It felt heavier than he knew it really was. He slid it out and placed it on the bench next to him as he took another generous swig of bourbon. The alcohol was reanimating his mind. Not so much the amount he had this far imbibed, but the promise that it brought with it. The message received by his brain was that he could relax. There was plenty. He stared at his stolen booze and realised that he should not get too complacent. There was not a huge amount in there and he would at some point have to get more. He screwed the top back on, the hollow scraping sound of aluminium tightening against glass pleasing him as it always did. He slowly placed it on the bench and examined the plastic bottle with its seemingly innocuous and transparent contents. He lifted it and, holding it close to his face, stared through it. Such was the contoured shape of the bottle that he could not see anything, but he could certainly ascertain that the liquid was colourless. There was no sediment and it would easily pass for water or vodka just from its appearance. It had a safety cap on it and he wondered what the bottle had once contained. Presumably something fairly toxic. Turps or white spirit? Presumably (and hopefully) it had been well cleaned out to get rid of the scent.

He got the top off and sniffed the contents. There was a smell that could be described as musty, and he also detected, bizarrely, a slight fruity smell, but nothing overpowering. Certainly mixed into something stronger it would leave no trace. He considered that the bourbon he had just been drinking could have affected his sense of smell, but there was definitely something there. He sat back, open plastic bottle grasped in one hand, glass bottle of booze in the other, staring straight ahead into the night.

He wondered if it would hurt to drink from the wrong bottle. The end result did not scare him. Quite the opposite; it carried some appeal. But he was not ready to spend an indeterminate amount of time in agony. He imagined a white heat eating him from the inside, stripping him bare, choking and suffocating in increments of agony, alone in this shit-hole. But the rats wanted it, he was sure of that. It would satisfy their desires once and for all. They would be quiet. Blissfully quiet. Forever.

He was scared to realise that the more pertinent question was what exactly was stopping him from doing it. It would remove any threat to his niece and nephew. If he were gone then no one would have any reason to touch them. It would simply end what had become the most pointless of existences.

He lifted the bottle up once more and took in its aromas.

He would not have to search out more booze tonight or any other night. The tiredness and the cold would be banished. He would never again have to beg strangers for money and be treated like a dog for doing so. There seemed something victorious in leaving all that behind on his own terms. And of course there were the rats. How he would love to kill them, even if it meant harming himself in the process.

He lifted the bottle to his mouth. He tilted it a little and felt the liquid settle against his upper lip, which was pushed tight against the opening.

To never have to worry again, about anything. He knew he was 'one of those people'. People stayed a while in life. Some of them made a difference, often a big difference. Doctors saved lives, teachers educated another generation, scientists made unprecedented discoveries. And then there were those who were truly exceptional; folks who composed songs to span the centuries, discovered cures for deadly illnesses, could play sport better than anyone else on the planet, could win wars, inspire the masses, sometimes sacrifice their own lives to make the world a better place. The world kept turning in order to accommodate these people. But at the other end was the human debris. It was needed to even everything out. Without the masses the aforementioned achievers would not be special. And to balance out the geniuses there needed to be the people that should never have been here. The ones simply taking up whatever valuable resources we have in this world. The leeches. Him. Him and others like him. They shouldn't be here. He shouldn't be here. It was just the order of things and he was unlucky to have been born who he was, but there was no sense crying about it. He accepted it there and then. Accepted what he was.

Leon's upper lip slid up and over the bottle opening and the liquid rushed into his mouth. It definitely had a taste of some sort but his numbed taste buds barely recognised it. Leon felt like he was not in control of his movements and had handed over to someone else. He swallowed.

## CHAPTER 26

She woke with a start, at a sound like a gunshot. Is that what it had been? She sat in silence, waiting for a repeat and trying to work out whether or not she had just heard it in a dream. It seemed so real but the memory was becoming rapidly less clear. There was a rustling noise above her and she leaned out of her room to get a look. It was too dark. Probably pigeons nesting on the beams beneath the bridge. She withdrew her head and continued to listen, but there was nothing happening.

She had been like this ever since the incident with the young men. Boys really, she had to admit, but 'young men' made her feel slightly less foolish for some reason.

She lay down and pulled her blankets tight up under her chin. It was a bitterly cold night; one of those evenings when even the insulation of her room did not put up enough of a barrier to protect her. Her room was actually a cavity hidden under the base of a bridge. She laughingly referred to it as her room and she knew how lucky she was to have found it – most in the city did not have anything near as luxurious. Amazingly, considering it was actually quite near the riverside footpath, no one had ever discovered it. At least, that is, to the best of her knowledge. Certainly no one that would be a threat to her or her belongings. For three years she had spent most of her nights there, each morning carefully covering any sign of the opening with branches and anything else she could find. A few times some council workers had cut the grass along the river bank but, whether through laziness or lack of necessity, had never bothered with any of the sparse foliage beneath the bridge.

She felt relatively happy there. After many years living rough in the centre of the city she had tired of sleeping with one eye open and had moved out to the suburbs. This seemed a much safer place; a place she could stay for a long time. But that had been before the *Boys*. At least they hadn't discovered her room. Sure, they had spotted her under the bridge, but just on the bank, and they were probably unlikely to come back if she was honest. That did not stop her worrying about it when the dark descended and she would lie staring at the decayed concrete above her head.

She had been sat on the bank eating a sandwich that someone had bought for her from the bakery. She generally did all right for herself in terms of food. There was no local homeless population to speak of in the area and as a result she was well known, almost popular with some. Some local residents were donators to her cause and, although there were no day centres or soup runs the local village hall was sympathetic to her and she rarely went dangerously hungry. Any time she approached that level she simply went back to the city for a day.

Unfortunately, along with this level of familiarity came a risk to her home being discovered. She was always cautious entering or leaving her room but was often seen in the vicinity of the bridge and the river in general, so people knew she was sleeping around there somewhere.

The sun was lowering in the sky as she picked out the crumbs from the sandwich packet by pressing down on them with her forefinger. As always she looked around casually before heading to bed.

Just as she was about to make her move, in the distance she spotted a group of five males heading in her direction. They were sufficiently far away that she could have probably made it to her room without them even noticing her, but she had self-imposed rules and caution was the basis of many of them. So she waited. As they neared she could see that they were perhaps sixteen or seventeen years old, definitely from some of the more affluent families in the neighbourhood, of which there were many. They had fleece tops over rugby shirts with the collars turned up. Two of them even had red trousers on which was often a sign of a spectacular level of poshness, and almost always a sign of a dickhead. As she watched they slowed and seemed to be having some sort of discussion, glancing in her direction. She could not explain why but she got a cold, nagging feeling in her gut. As they got closer they dallied, as though they didn't actually want to reach her, and she now knew that something was awry. She did not scare at all easily and life had hardened her to the point where she was almost incapable of being intimidated. Nevertheless, she felt that some sort of confrontation was coming and tensed. She would fight her corner if need be, scare the shit out of these posh kids and they would be on their way. She had a hard exterior but it was not entirely authentic and she noted her heart begin to pump harder.

She crumpled the sandwich box in her hand and looked at the floor, hoping they would simply pass by. After a short time she realised they had stopped only a yard from her. Keeping them in her peripheral vision she did not look at them but continued to look at the wrapper in her fist.

"Hope you're not going to drop that."

The voice was every bit as middle class as she expected it to be. She looked up to see one of the group stood in front of the others. Her green eyes scanned theirs. None of them looked quite as sure of themselves as the one that had spoken. She did not answer.

"Isn't there anywhere else you could go and be a scrounger?" the same youth asked viciously.

She continued to ignore him. He took a step forwards and kicked her, reasonably hard in the thigh. She showed no pain and decided that this was a key moment. He had scored a minor victory in front of his pals, she had not given him any cause to get angry, and they might just move on to laugh later about their run in with the village tramp. That was how it *could have* worked out. But it didn't.

The fact that she had not cried out in pain seemed to infuriate the young man. A couple of his friends chuckled and the other two looked surprised by what had just happened.

"You kick like a girl, Jamie," one taunted. She saw something change in Jamie's eyes. She decided that if he took another kick she would feign injury in an attempt to appease him. It was against her nature but she knew she had to ignore her fighting impulses and play it clever. She would take the kick and hope it would be the end of it. As it turned out, acting hurt was not necessary. He took a two-stepped run up and swung his leg as hard as he could, every sinew aimed down into the one extremity. The toe of his shoe caught her just above the pelvis and up into her rib cage. There was a crack as the pain jolted up through her body. As she keeled over onto her other side she cried out in genuine pain and the side of her face landed in a patch of grass. She felt dizzy and sure that she had broken a rib at the very least.

"Jesus Christ, Jay."

Her vision blurred and then focussed on the sandwich box which now lay a couple of feet down the bank.

She was rolled roughly onto her back and her assailant straddled her chest, pinning her arms down with his knees. The time for acting the victim was clearly over and her street-wise self needed to emerge. Jamie was so far up her torso that she was able to arch back her neck and thrust her own knees into his back. This took him by surprise and she took her opportunity to push her shoulders up. Jamie bucked up into the air and she groped for freedom. But Jamie was a large kid; a rugby player she would have bet. He grappled with her to regain the upper hand but he was struggling. Before she knew it her ear was ringing loudly from a flat-palmed strike to the side of her head. She was vaguely aware of a commotion going on among the group.

"I'm going."

"What's wrong with you?"

"He's gone fucking mad."

"She's just a tramp."

This was all background noise. Her good ear picked up a much nearer voice. "Give me a hand for Christ's sake." It was Jamie, panting and struggling.

The next few minutes seemed to last an eternity and were as confusing as they were painful. She could barely see the group behind Jamie's bulk but two of them helped to pin down her arms. Her legs kept flailing. She knew she was stuck and overpowered but her defiance and stubbornness would never allow her to submit.

There was shouting towards the other two boys who clearly were reluctant to help.

"I'm not getting involved," called a more high-pitched voice from out of sight. Jamie, turned his head back over his shoulder and growled, "You already are involved. Now get that leg."

Jamie looked up and down the bank, making sure they were not being watched. She knew the area enough to know that they were unlikely to be.

She thought she got a few decent kicks in which may have even caused some pain if not damage. But eventually she was under control. Jamie looked down at her with contempt.

The youth holding down her right arm looked terrified. He kept glancing at the other two boys she could see and was doing his best to avoid her eyes. She remained silent.

"You're disgusting, you know that?" Jamie sneered. "Have you got no self-respect?"

She would not satisfy him with an answer. There was a pause. Her right arm holder still looked worried. The kid on the left arm, however, was warming to the task.

"My friend Clive back here," Jamie nodded his head backwards, "has never been with a woman."

Her stomach lurched.

"Don't tell her my name," the high-pitched voice was back.

"Why, what do you think she will do about it?" asked left arm.

"Get yourself up here and have a look at her Clive" said Jamie.

" I... I don't want to. This is..."

"She's not as bad as you'd think once you get a look at her. You know, once you look past the filth."

Left arm leaned behind Jamie and dragged Clive into sight. He looked mortified as he was forced to look at her. She stared into his face, knowing that he was her best chance of getting out of this. Left arm seemed to take on the job of look-out, scanning the horizon for walkers.

"This is not right," said Clive, sheepishly.

"*Right*? Look, my brother told me she gives blow jobs for crack at the bottom of the village," offered Jamie in a manner that seemed to suggest that this made their actions more palatable.

"Who the fuck has got crack in this village?" Clive shouted, his anger giving him confidence. "Old Langley? The vicar, maybe?"

What followed was fifteen minutes of hell as she helplessly listened to the boys discuss what to do with her. She was certain that if the others abandoned their leader she was tough enough to keep him at bay, but they did not go. Clearly Jamie had a certain amount of hold over all four of them.

Jamie clearly knew he was at a point where he had to do something or walk away. His frustration gave way as he grabbed hold of her long sleeved T-shirt and ripped it open from the neck to the navel. The effort made him breathless. But she felt that this was a power play as much as it was anything sexual. His troops had dissented and he was losing his power over her, which had largely been built of fear. Her silence was now perceived as mocking him and he needed to re-assert himself.

As sure as she was of this, the sight of ten pubescent eyes hungrily taking in the sight of her bare chest weakened her resolve.

Eventually she had been relieved to take another blow to the side of the head before being thrown into the river. As she bobbed back up in the water and headed to the bank she saw only the backs of the boys, their body language reading anywhere between fury and relief.

Ever since, and for the first time since her early days of homelessness, she felt vulnerable in her room. Waking with a start in the night had become normal. In the safety of daylight she was fairly sure that they would be unable to find her cubbyhole and she thought it was unlikely that they would return anyway. Jamie would be the only one who might want to get some sort of closure but she had seen his type many times before; he needed to be surrounded by numbers. But during the dead of night she was not so sure. She scrunched up the yellow cagoule that doubled as her pillow. She closed her eyes and listened to the ebb and flow of the river, trying to remind herself of a time when she had found it so relaxing.

## CHAPTER 27

Leon's eyes bulged and his stomach and raw throat felt like they were being turned inside out. Down on all fours he could barely make out through stinging watery eyes the puddle of bile in front of him.

He had choked off the first gulp halfway through. He spluttered, inhaling some of the drink, which seemed to make things so much worse. Amazingly he had the presence of mind to stand the bottle upright – his mind was at least telling him that he might still need it.

His reaction had been instantaneous – clearly he had no idea how much his subconscious wanted to stay alive. He had heard of theories that all suicides, successful or otherwise, provoked a last minute reversal of the desire to leave this world. Of course this theory was difficult to prove, as the study group would only include those who had been unsuccessful, but he suddenly had his own primary research to draw on.

His fingers were jabbing their way down to his oesophagus before he knew it. He wondered how much damage might already have been done. Perhaps he would be maimed, brain-damaged, or simply die more slowly and in more agony than if he had downed the lot. All he knew for now was that he needed to get it out of him. With little food to propel it out he retched and retched until he was in considerable pain.

Eventually he sat up. His throat and mouth tasted of poison. He knew that was not possible but that is how it felt. He retrieved the bottle top from the floor, tightly screwed it back onto the bottle and lay on his back, panting from the exertion.

He was still shaking uncontrollably with his body tensing so much that it ached. He was so light headed that he felt that he might pass out. He imagined all of this as being symptoms of his impending death, but at the same time he was fairly sure it was just his body and mind's way of 'coming down' after the events of the last ten minutes.

The moment seemed important; almost like a rebirth. Everything that was now happening to him would not have been, had he killed himself. He felt like a ghost, left there to replace the body he had just disposed of. Stuck in some sort of purgatory on earth. Perhaps this was the moment that some spoke of; an epiphany from which his life would begin anew.

Such grand designs were rapidly dismissed by the rats who were building themselves up into a frenzy. They had built up a ravenous hunger and were baying to be heard. Physically and mentally exhausted though he was, they needed to find some poison of their own to feast on.

Perhaps killing himself really was the only way of ever stopping them; the ultimate Pyrrhic victory.

If Leon had died then it would not have saved the man whose picture rested in his pocket, he knew that much. 'They', or 'He' would have got someone else to do it. It may not have even saved his nephew and niece now that he saw things a little more clearly. They would just assume the job had not been done and act accordingly.

The angry frustration started to build and he could not stop it. It had a force of its own which pumped the blood faster through his veins until he felt like they were standing out. His teeth were clamped so tightly that he had a dull ache across the top of his head and his fingernails dug into the palms of his fists. The rats retreated into their holes, satisfied with this as an alternative, and he could not feel them move as his heartbeat thudded in his ears. He pushed the back of his skull into the ground with enough force to lift his shoulders from the floor. And he screamed. An anguished cry like an animal echoed through the nearby bridge.

He knew what he wanted. He wanted to find the man responsible for all this and kill him. He could do that. If he could find him he would find the courage to kill him.

Leon slumped again, too tired to sustain the anger. He suddenly felt so exhausted that he could have fallen asleep there and then except that the rats were once more stirring. They gnawed to get out and he curled up on his side. He closed his eyes tightly in a vain attempt to stop the tears from squeezing out.

The streets seemed quiet and he wondered what sort of time it was. He could not decide whether or not to go back to the squat. He really could not cope with having to speak to anyone, even Steve or Karen. And he needed to find some booze. He considered looking for a dealer and robbing him. He did not have his own weapon and realised that there was a good chance of being stabbed but at the moment it was on his shortlist of options for the night.

Eventually a man emerged from the 24-hour supermarket with a case of beer under his arm. He looked so hammered that he should probably not have been served the box. Leon had located himself outside the front doors, visible to exiting customers but not employees, for such an event. He barely needed to ask before the man opened the box and placed two cans of lager in front of Leon, almost losing his balance as he did so. Leon muttered a thanks and the man muttered something unintelligible before weaving his way towards home. Was he stuck living from drink to drink for the rest of his days? If so he should have just died.

The lager was just a stopgap until he came up with a better plan. He knew that at this time of night (whatever time it was) there would be security guards on the entrance to stop thieves getting out and people like him from getting in, so stealing a bottle of whisky was off the list. He wondered if he ran in to the drink aisle how much of a bottle of vodka he could neck before it was taken from him. Probably not much if he was honest. That plan was so bad it did not even make the shortlist.

The weather was decent so he found a shop doorway in which to drink his two cans, hiding them on the rare occasion that someone passed, just on the off chance of being given some money. He was given none.

For what now felt like the hundredth time he examined the photograph of the man he was to kill and the time and place he was expected to do it. Was he going to kill the man or was he going to create a situation where the man killed himself? Splitting hairs was not going to allow him to justify it.

The photograph betrayed nothing of the person. So what could it be that he had done to cause this… mess? He could be anyone. Just someone like Leon who had lost his way and ended up on the streets. Because that much was certain; the man he was looking at was a street dweller. Leon was by now convinced that the death he had caused in the fire was no accident. He was being used as an unwilling hit man. How the fuck had that happened?

Leon felt sure that he had seen this distinctively red haired man at the soup run a while back. If it was the chap he was thinking of he had pushed in and then acted in an extremely aggressive manner to the volunteer. Or was he simply projecting a desire for this man to be a 'bad guy' onto a vague memory? He might just as easily be a thoroughly decent human being who might one day achieve something with his life. Leon might like him. The more he thought about it he was less concerned with the man dying and more concerned with any potential suffering. If the poison simply lowered him into a sleepy death it would be much better than the visions he was suffering of a thrashing body, eyes bulging, finger nails clawing at the throat, choking on his own vomit, unable to breathe while his organs collapsed in on themselves. Overly dramatic as he supposed his picture to be, even the slightest suffering would be down to him, and that was nightmare-inducing stuff, even for a man who could barely sleep at the best of times without demonic visions of some sort.

There was also the fact that if this went wrong and Leon was to spend the rest of his life in prison, then he would be better to kill Mystery Man himself, rather than the ginger man. At least as he spent year upon year in a cell he would be able to look at his own reflection with something more than disgust. But this sort of thinking was wasting his time. He had no idea who the guy was and, even if he were to somehow work it out, he did not have time before his deadline. If he wanted to get to

Mystery Man then it would have to be after, and in addition to, the ginger man.

The picture was shoved back in the pocket. The beer was not working quickly enough. He looked at the instructions for his mission. Scotch Plaza, Eastern entrance, third bench along on the left. 6 a.m. on Thursday 24th. The specificity scared him. How did they know the man would be there or how would they get him to be there? Was Leon going to be watched? Set up? Killed?

Once again, anger built within him that he was dancing so obediently to their tune. He knew one thing for sure; if he had to do this, if he really, really must, then it would be on his own terms. He would take responsibility, find the guy and potentially commit an act from which he would never mentally recover. He accepted this fact and knew that even if he ever rebuilt his life, the shadow of this awful act would forever darken his life. A shudder ran through him as he realised that he was seriously thinking about doing it.

This realisation was fuel for the anger, the anxiety and the rats, who needed more than a couple of crappy beers to feed upon. His mind was floating out of control. He decided that he would walk in the general direction of the squat and attempt to find some hard booze on the way. At the very least that would give him the slightest sense of purpose to his wandering.

He was alerted by what sounded like a woman in distress. It was more out of interest than a desire to be of help that he rounded the corner to see what was the source of the noise. A man had his hand around the throat of a young woman. His hand was pushing up against the underside of her jaw, fingers and thumb forcing the flesh of her face to crumple upwards. Her retreat was impeded by the lamppost that she was stood against on her tiptoes. The man was growling something at her as she whimpered. He lowered his voice as Leon approached, as though trying to keep the conversation private. The man had presumably been drinking as his attempt to reduce the volume was fairly laughable. Leon tried not to listen but still gathered that the man was threatening to throw the woman out if she ever did 'that' again.

Leon wondered whether to get involved. Just as he decided not to he looked at the woman and her eyes flicked in his direction. They met his, just for a second, but he felt that he saw a glint of terror in them, and acceptance of her fate. She was powerless. She looked back to her assailant and tried to gurgle something to him.

Leon walked across to the front wall of a house that was in such a state of disrepair that the top two rows of bricks were laying loose on top of one another. He lifted one that he liked the look of, feeling the heft of it in his palm. The man was, as yet, oblivious to his continued presence even though he fancied that the woman was trying to tell him that someone was there. He walked towards the man, jogged the last two steps and swung the brick into the side of his head.

The sickening thud was quickly followed by another as the man's limp body collapsed against the path. Leon threw the brick away and straddled the man who was semi-conscious. He clenched his fist. That was when the woman started screaming.

The noise provoked a moment of clarity, which came just in time. He calmly stood and left, trying not to let the woman get a good look at his face. Despite this he could not help himself from a sideways glance in her direction. It would not have mattered had he told her his name as she could not tear her gaze from the barely conscious man on the floor. Probably her partner, thought Leon. She'd go back to him and probably get throttled again the following evening.

## CHAPTER 28

He kept his distance and watched from behind a couple of trees. Two early birds were hovering as the serving tables were being set up. It had started to rain and the young woman was trying to erect some sort of canopy. She skilfully pushed together all the requisite pieces of plastic piping as a man worked at setting up a huge metal vat, which was in the back of the van they had arrived in.

Leon got a good look at the two keen customers. They did not look out of the ordinary. One was probably in his late fifties, allowing for Leon's margin for error at gauging age, but his case was not helped by the leathery skin that seemed to have been stretched out and then snapped back into place, never to fit properly again. Definitely a heavy smoker. The other man was much younger and looked sufficiently fresh faced to indicate that he was new to life on the streets. Leon wondered if he had looked that green at first. The two did not appear to know one another.

Leon recognised the woman. Ysanne, he thought her name was. She really was beautiful, now that he had time to stand and observe her. She looked tired and what he remembered to be her best feature – her wide smile – was yet to appear, but Leon still could not take his eyes off her.

Ysanne was struggling to stretch the waterproof covering over the plastic shell that she had assembled. She simply wasn't tall enough. She glanced back towards the van and saw that her colleague was busy. She swiped some now wet hair from her eyes and battled on. Leon's natural impulse was to go and help her. This would have been his reaction regardless of who it was; he had always been ready to help out wherever he could. But on this occasion he could not afford to draw any attention to himself whatsoever. He looked across at the two men, expecting one of them to come to Ysanne's rescue. The younger one shoved his hands deep in his pockets and the leathery one proved Leon's theory by producing a cigarette that he eventually managed to light.

Once it became obvious that neither had the faintest intention of helping, Leon found that he had to turn away from the scene or his frustration would get the better of him. He wondered how people could do that. Was it laziness or were they just completely oblivious? He decided that awareness was probably not high on the list of attributes for a man who was stood waiting for free food while smoking cigarettes that he could not afford.

He walked a circle and by the time he returned Ysanne's colleague was helping her with the finishing touches of their shelter. Both were quite wet by this stage and still being observed by their two spectators, plus a couple more, equally unhelpful, newcomers.

And then suddenly there he was. The ginger man. Thomas McCann, Leon now knew him to be. Here. Now. Panic filled Leon's chest. This was what he had been waiting for but the gravity of the situation had not fully hit home until this moment. Thomas stood behind the other four in what was becoming a fairly ramshackle queue. Leon leaned back against a tree, trying to get his breathing under control. He realised how tightly he was gripping his bottle when he could feel his fingertips throbbing to the beat of his heart.

He looked down at it. A slightly grubby vodka bottle around half full. He had stolen the bottle from a drunk near the Embankment when it was three-quarters full. Leon had decided that his liquid would need to be camouflaged. He had wanted whisky or something with a stronger taste, but vodka was what he had to work with so it would have to do.

He had planned long and hard over the amount to leave in the bottle. Too much and Thomas may decide to share it. Or he may drink it over too long a time period, perhaps even a couple of days, leaving him ill rather than dead. Too little and it would taste wrong, or the aroma of the poison may filter through. He was pretty sure that the taste buds of most street people were shot to bits and no one would tell the difference. Still, if he was going to do this he had to do it right. He had decided on leaving a quarter of a litre, to which he had added the 250 millilitres or so of his own brew. Of course this had the added bonus of giving him another half litre of vodka with which to calm himself.

He spun the top off and breathed it in. He had done this dozens of times, convinced that the next time it would stink of deception. Again, he imagined he could smell something amiss and took another deep sniff. He told himself that there was nothing suspicious.

Leon was slowly winning the battle with his panicked breathing. One more deep breath, an extra turn to really tighten the bottle cap, and he strode from behind the tree before anything could change his mind.

As he slipped behind McCann no one even looked in his direction.

"Hello."

This did not even register with Leon, such was the speed with which jumbled thoughts were running through his head.

"Hello, are you with us?"

He looked up and was horrified to realise that Ysanne was talking to him. It had not occurred to him that she would remember him. She smiled. There it was; that smile. Despite the situation his spirits jumped at the sight of it. The smoker remained intent on sucking the life out of his cigarette but the other three turned their heads to see the object of Ysanne's attention. Leon pulled up what was left of his collar and looked at his feet until he was sure they had turned back away from him.

"Haven't seen you for a while," she spoke cheerily while putting out plastic food cartons.

"No, not been about much."

Why did she remember him? Did he stand out? Was it just the fact that he was sociable towards her?

Leon was desperate to talk to her, mainly because there were so few pleasant people in his life that the thought of chatting with Ysanne seemed like it would satisfy a burning desire in him. But he could not afford to draw any attention to himself at all. His intentions of being invisible were already in tatters. The fact that she had recognised him meant that one too many people already would be able to identify him. The vodka bottle felt like a giant beacon in his hand, drawing attention from miles around. He was going to bail out. The thought of that was so welcome that he could have cried out in relief. But if not now, then when? Was Ysanne a sign that he shouldn't do it? He could not start believing in 'signs' now that it suited him; he normally would have put that sort of thought down as 'superstitious bollocks'.

Things weren't totally fucked, he decided. He could still follow through with the plan. No one was going to die right here at the soup kitchen. He would be fine.

Ysanne looked unperturbed that he did not seem pleased to see her, but busied herself with some plastic spoons rather than spend any more time on him. Leon was desperate to say something, for some reason deeply caring what she thought of him. It didn't matter what she thought of him. His life was screwed anyway so any thoughts of being friends with someone like her was just fantasy.

He used one sleeve to surreptitiously wipe down the body of the vodka bottle, stuck it under his arm and wiped the neck and top. Now holding the neck from inside his sleeve he tried to bide his time and appear nonchalant. They were still way too early for the food to be served but the five men in front of him were unconsciously edging further forward as though it might speed things up. He knew that he had to act quickly before anyone else turned up. He slid the bottle onto the edge of the table and nudged it towards McCann. Now he was caught in no man's land. He needed to disappear but also had to ensure that the bait was taken. Then came a godsend, which of course he didn't believe in either.

A police siren blasted into action with a suddenness that made everyone start. Within a split second the light from the accompanying blue lights danced across the buildings around them. The car was over beyond the other side of the square but seemed to head in their direction.

"Shit," Leon blurted, loud enough for the other men to hear him.

He turned on his heels and ran off in the other direction. As McCann turned to watch him depart the vodka bottle was directly in front of him. He seemed unsure, as though the rapidly escaping Leon might return. Eventually he picked it up and looked at it as though he had never seen one.

Leon peeked back at the square from behind a corner he had just rounded. The police car had veered away and its lights and volume were already diminishing. The ginger man was still studying the bottle. Leon sprinted back towards him. He did not know what had caused him to do so, except that he couldn't do this. He was not about to kill someone. He thought he could do it but he couldn't.

The young man in front of McCann had spotted his prize and looked agitated about it. He glanced across to the metal vat and then back to the bottle. Something told Leon that trouble was afoot and not a second later the bottle had been snatched and was speeding away in the young man's hand.

"Oy," McCann called half-heartedly. He looked about to run after the other man but then seemingly could not be bothered.

Without thinking, Leon tore back across the square and down a street where the man had disappeared. As he passed them, the smoker and McCann caught each other's eye. The smoker shrugged before lighting another cigarette from the dying embers of his last one.

It was a dark alley with tall buildings on either side and Leon could hear, rather than see, the man running. He was quite far ahead; of that, Leon was absolutely sure. Not only had he a good ten seconds head start on Leon, but also he had perhaps ten years on him. Leon's eyes acclimatised slightly and he could see the distant shape of his prey. Perhaps, if he was not actually gaining, then at least he was surely keeping pace. For now, until the lack of fitness began to tell.

Up ahead he heard a hollow thump and detected a plastic bin bounce sideways. A second later was the sound of the glass bottle bouncing on the tarmac. Leon held his breath, waiting for the tell-tale sound of glass breaking which could have quite incredible repercussions. Whatever happened he needed the bottle. He needed the option. The bottle bounced again and Leon felt a surge of relief and hope. But then came the noise that confirmed his fate. The crunch of shearing glass followed by its dull tinkle as it scattered across the tarmac with its liquid contents.

Leon stopped at the broken bottle, looking forlornly at the floor. The neck of the bottle was still spinning and out of the corner of his eye the man was pulling himself to his feet. Leon reached down and stopped the rotating section of bottle. He could make out a single word on the tattered label: Hardys. It was a bloody wine bottle. He looked up. The man was running again, the shadow of a bottle still visible in one of his pumping fists. The man seemed to move more slowly, which was evidenced by a pronounced limp. This enabled Leon, who was back in pursuit in a flash, to make ground and a swell of hope spurred him on. He needed it to overcome the dual aching of his lungs and thighs. His shortness of breath was now causing pain right across the front of his torso and it felt like fingers were digging into his collarbone.

The man was within his sights just as Leon tripped and skidded forwards onto the ground. He knew that what had impeded him was irrelevant yet he still glared back to see a black bin bag that he had split. Cursing, he leapt to his feet and took off again. He knew that he had skinned his good hand fairly badly but there was no time to think about that. With the loss of momentum came a loss of belief. How the hell was he going to catch him now?

The alley was about to open up onto a street that ran across the end of it. Leon could see the orange glow of streetlights. He somehow found an extra burst of energy, realising that his chances would reduce significantly once they entered somewhere more populated. He put his head down and pushed as hard as he could. Looking up again it seemed as though he had actually gained, but the guy was nearly there. Leon watched the man, now silhouetted against the dirty, luminous orange light as he lunged for the street as though he were a sprinter striving to cross the finish line. Leon knew he was a beaten man and his engine began to splutter.

But just as the young man reached the end of the alley, a black shape sped into view. Leon just had sufficient time to realise that it was a bicycle before it clattered into the running man with a sickening thud.

The bike's front wheel buckled and sent its rider skidding across the path. The cyclist's head clattered against a waste bin, which sent him windmilling into the path of an oncoming car that did well to swerve around him. Leon watched the scene in slow motion, noting that the rider's helmet had just saved him from serious injury, perhaps death, at the hands of the bin, which was cemented into the pavement.

The walls of the alley were alight with flashing red. Confused for a moment, Leon wondered if the police could possibly have arrived so quickly but then he noticed that the bike had come to a stop with its rear light pointing towards him.

The young man had bounced sideways and backwards into the alley at the impact and was groaning and grabbing various parts of his anatomy as if he were trying to establish which hurt the most. Leon ran towards him, briefly wondering why the bicycle had been on the path rather than the road and then deciding not to worry about it. As the young man struggled to his feet, Leon grabbed him by the collar and dragged him backwards into the light with sufficient force to put him on his back. He took a step back and kicked the man hard in the ribs, figuring that would buy him enough time to find the now missing bottle in the darkened mouth of the alley. He got on his knees in the general vicinity of where the man had ended up. He had not heard a breakage but then there had been a bending bike, a head clattering a bin and a swerving car to compete with the noise. And he was fairly sure that it had not been dropped en route. He looked back at the man who was struggling for breath and so far completely incapable of retaliation.

Leon could not see a thing along the edge of the wall, despite the flashing light teasing him by almost lighting things up. He ran his hand along the join of wall and ground. His fingers swept through all manner of filth of varying textures. For all he knew he was probably currently groping in dog shit. He got it. The bottle.

The young man was trying to get to his feet as Leon went back to him, carefully resting the bottle on the floor. He knew that he could just leave him be. He could walk away, formulate another plan and never need to cross paths again with the man in front of him that had caused him such anguish. Instead he felt that something took control of his decision-making. Leon knew that he could rebel against it if he wanted, but this mysterious force seemed to know what it was doing so who was he to argue? He picked up a piece of timber from a small pile of wood that had once been a pallet. The man just had time to raise his arm and prevented the plank from doing some serious damage to his skull. He howled in pain as it cracked into his forearm and he slumped backwards. Leon circled him, swung it into the back of his legs like an ice hockey slap shot. He lost track of everything around him. He could not hear the man's pleading above the thumping in his own head. He had no idea how many times he hit him, or how much damage he inflicted. He just knew that he felt compelled to do it. It was necessary for some reason that he could not quite reach but he knew was there. The unknown force was making him do what was needed and logic could be investigated later.

"Hey…..hey."

Leon had no idea the voice had been there calling in his direction. He swung round, his face a mask of madness and the wooden plank raised high above his head. The cyclist's jaw dropped.

"Listen, you need to just calm down."

Leon could barely believe the cyclist was talking to him. Why was he talking to him? He stepped towards the cyclist. Even though Leon could not see his features in the gloom, he could sense the fear coming off him.

"You're going to kill him," the voice quivered.

Leon stepped up to him and tightened his grip on his makeshift club. The cyclist turned and ran, tripping on the twisted carcass of his own bike as he sprinted across the road.

The break in proceedings had brought Leon out of his hypnotic state and he stumbled back into the dark alley. The awful flashing red light disoriented him and he squeezed his eyes shut. He could still see its ghost flashing inside his eyelids.

He looked across at the man he had just beaten to a pulp and heard him groan. Leon collected the bottle and wondered if the cyclist had called the police yet. He started walking. He walked and walked, gradually slipping back into reality. Eventually he was shaking so much that he was forced to sit in a shop doorway before his legs buckled underneath him and he threw up.

## CHAPTER 29

As he sat on a bench under a tree at the edge of the square Leon considered the possibility that he may be suffering from some form of psychosis. His life seemed to have shifted away from reality. How could he tell if he had lost the plot? He decided to work it out later – he had important things to do for now. He had chosen a place under a large overhanging tree as it provided further murkiness against the black clouds hanging overhead. The downside was that his seat was thick with bird shit but that hardly mattered. In front of him was a square that was slightly below the level of the surrounding roads and paths. What had been designed and originated as a recess of relaxation and relief from the surrounding rat race had now become a complete tip. The small patches of plant life had long dried up and shrivelled. Takeaway cartons and cigarette packets swirled around with the wind, unable to escape from their crucible of dirt.

There would nevertheless be numerous visitors throughout the day. At this time of the morning the place was empty. Lunchtime would see depressed white collar workers sit with their limp sandwiches, bitching about their colleagues. Late afternoon would be the time for the disaffected youth to spend a few hours repetitively attempting skateboard tricks that they would never master. After a few more hours had passed the kids arriving would be slightly older and large bottles of cider would replace the boards. As for the night creatures, well they were a law unto themselves.

But the visitor Leon was waiting for had, he was assured, a very reliable schedule. He should arrive some time shortly after six a.m. and he would sit on the bench directly across from him for an hour or two. Leon could not work out what this place offered that would tempt someone to incorporate it into a regular schedule but each to their own.

There was still at least five or ten minutes to go and Leon knew he was fidgeting. He needed to look more natural. Risking an even more thorough coating of bird droppings, he lay back lengthways on his bench, adopting an impression of relaxation. But within seconds he was back upright, leaning forwards, elbows on knees.

What would happen?

The bottle rested in the corner of the opposite bench, cupped in the recess between backrest, seat and arm rest. Not obviously apparent to a passer-by. Of course, there were barely any passers-by at this time of morning but Leon had learned his lesson from the soup run. He could not afford to risk any more cock-ups. They were very much at the business end of things now.

With his hands cupping his chin he looked around. He was fairly certain that, somewhere, someone would be watching him. Someone would be waiting for a report that all this had 'gone down' and a first-hand account would be required. But he couldn't see a soul. Was he being paranoid? On this occasion probably not. It seemed only logically that someone was keeping an eye on things.

He spotted the hair first. The copper-coloured mop bobbed into view and Leon realised he had been miles away in thought. He jerked up and felt utterly unprepared. Why had he not planned things better? He was leaving everything to chance and was about to blow it. He looked at his feet and hoped that the shadow from the tree would do its job. Glancing up periodically he saw McCann go straight for the bench. For the hundredth time Leon wondered if all this was one big set up. The man immediately noticed and picked up the vodka bottle. He held it by the neck and swilled its contents around.

This was a key moment. Would the man's train of thought lead him straight back to the soup kitchen? Spirit bottles don't just get left all over town. Once is chance, twice in the space of two days is a bit much. McCann looked left and right. Nothing. Leon was straining every sinew to stay still although he did not know whether he wanted to stay and watch or run away. Inevitably McCann's gaze lifted in his direction and latched onto the shady figure under the tree. His body language seemed unsure. Leon was rigid. The man's gaze was unbroken. He had blown it.

All this effort and he had made a complete mess of what should have been a very simple task. Why had he sat there like that, in view? Fucking idiot.

A big, fat raindrop landed on the concrete outside of the canopy of his tree. This was quickly followed by another. Having tested out the location, the clouds seemed to decide that this was an acceptable place to dump their load and the heavens opened. Leon looked up as the tree above his head rattled with quick-fire rainfall. Although he was covered, McCann was not. He looked to the skies, pulled up his collar and stuffed the bottle in his pocket. He stood up and Leon was horrified to realise that the only possible place to take shelter was next to him, on the bird shit bench. He would possibly recognise him. The face from the soup run queue. The bottle. The game was up.

McCann walked across towards him and Leon looked at the floor, his chin digging into his breastbone in an attempt to hide his features. He was going to have to wait until McCann sat down and then simply stand and walk away into the rain. Suspicious but perhaps his only hope of remaining anonymous.

McCann was only feet away and Leon was getting ready to leave. Trying not to move his neck, Leon saw him walk right by, past the bench and off into the rapidly soaking streets. Leon could not help but turn to look at the man as he trotted off into the distance. In between furtive glances all around, he glugged greedily from his bottle.

So much for spotting the coincidence and getting suspicious, thought Leon. No one rough could afford to turn down free booze. The need for it would override any other urge. And it should be drunk as quickly as possible to negate the risk of losing it.

He looked around again to locate a pair of eyes that would confirm he was being watched. A pair of eyes that, now that McCann had taken the bait, he hoped was there. He wondered to what extent they would check up to ensure the man's death. Would the fact they had seen him drinking suffice? He also wondered if he would ever hear back from the men who had tormented him. Would they fulfil their obligations, or would they simply try to get him to do more of their dirty work? Either way, he was finished with them now. Leon lay back on the bench and closed his eyes.

He spluttered into life and jolted upright, immediately checking the surrounding area and wondering how long he had dropped off for. What a bloody time to sleep. The nervous energy had presumably left his body as McCann left the square. He had a terrible thought that someone may have robbed him in his sleep and thrust his hand into his pocket, relieved at the discovery that they had not.

## CHAPTER 30

Leon sat with his back to the war memorial. He wasn't sure what had made him come here today but maybe in some way he felt that the end of his journey should be signified by returning to where it all began. He wished he had never been here as a fifteen year old boy. He regretted many things in his life but among them was how he had been as a teenager. A good-for-nothing antisocial nuisance would be a very kind description. A horrible little shit would be nearer the mark.

He looked across at the café where he had sat all those years ago. The place had become even more run down and now seemed to specialise in some awful form of pizza, hugely unappetising pictures of which were plastered over one exterior wall. The tables and chairs outside looked so old and rusty that any one of them could well have been that upon which young Leon had sat, sipping his can. A slight movement made him realise that there was a person sat on one of the chairs that he had not initially spotted. It was a kid in his early teens. He was sat, almost motionless, staring out across the square. He was scruffy looking in his baggy tracksuit and huge white trainers. Leon shuddered. If this was some sort of sign then he did not understand it.

He did not know what to do. And it was not on a 'what shall I do this afternoon' level; this was on a gigantic, existential level. He was every bit as inclined to kill himself as he was to attempt rehabilitation. If he could suddenly appear as a clean, healthy version of himself, living in his own house with some sort of simple job, then he would accept that willingly. But there was no magic portal and the thought of alcohol withdrawal and continued abstinence, joining a housing project, engaging in voluntary work just seemed to be a journey too exhausting to be worth it. He couldn't do it. If he stayed on the streets he would die soon enough. If he stayed drunk the winter would pick him off with ease.

But this seemed the most cowardly of all his options. He was effectively taking any decision-making out of his own hands and assuming all would be sorted out for him by fate. That he would rather die than act. Pathetic.

Leon brought the vodka bottle out of his pocket and unscrewed the lid. Leaning forwards, he poured a tiny amount onto the stone step between his feet. The concrete was warm from the early autumn sunshine and he wondered how long it would take to evaporate. He poured a little more. He wondered if he should really be doing that. What if a pigeon pecked something up from on top of it, or a dog curiously licked it? He decided that he didn't care enough about that to stop and he poured a larger measure.

He thought of McCann. He had probably by now finished his vodka and would be oblivious to how close he had come to death. The poisonous vodka, which he had been due to imbibe, was currently dribbling onto the steps in front of Leon. He had kept hold of it in case his plan did not work out but there seemed little sense in keeping it now. There was just one more piece to fit into place. He would be back at the square at 5 am the next day to leave a note in the same place on the bench as he had left the vodka. This would inform McCann that he had 24 hours to get out of town before the men who killed James Potter in the fire came after him. The deadline was arbitrary but he had decided it might focus McCann's mind. So long as no one saw the man between now and him leaving then Leon was in the clear.

He was feeling a little self conscious about the growing puddle at his feet and looked around to see where he could pour the rest of the liquid. After days of carrying it around he was suddenly anxious to get rid of it. He was amazed to find that the rats were stirring even at the thought of a drink that would kill him. One way or another they would be the death of him. He didn't dare leave the drink in a bin in case someone took it. He knew from personal experience that people are so desperate for drink that they will think nothing of taking unknown, unlabelled liquid from a public bin. He screwed the lid back on just in time before it clattered on the hard floor. Leon was not even aware that he had dropped it.

His eyes were fixed on a yellow cagoule or, more specifically, its wearer. She had walked to the opposite corner of the steps and taken a seat on the lowest step. A shopper waved hello to her. He had only caught the slightest glimpse of her profile, protruding from her hood. But it was enough to convince him. Within seconds, a detailed argument had taken place inside his head. It couldn't be her and yet he *knew* it was. He tried to stand but realised that he would have to give it a moment before he was capable. He tried to remind himself of how many times he had been wrong before.

An elderly lady walked across to the woman, put some money in her palm, squeezed her hand shut and chatted for a moment. The cagoule wearer, whom Leon could see only from the back now, waved the old lady off.

He realised that he had absolutely no idea how to proceed from this point onwards. She was sat only twenty metres away and he could not decide whether to approach her or not. Surely it was enough that he had seen her. She seemed OK. At least he had not sentenced her to death by throwing away her anti-depressants. All those years of dark thoughts on that score could be wiped away. If he spoke to her he would have to confront what he had done and she would think him insane. The best thing would be to go. But then that would be the end of the road. A journey that had cost him so much couldn't end just like that, could it?

Thinking of it in those terms presented a moment of clarity. His relationship, his job, his home, his *life*; all gone. And then there he was looking at the back of someone's head from the other side of a monument. Looking at the back of someone's hood to be more precise. This could not be that. Would he need to speak to her to her give him the peace he so desperately sought? Or was this pilgrimage about more than that? Could he rest now or did he need to more to atone for a perceived crime that she would probably have no memory of?

The deciding factor was that he needed proof. He had completely convinced himself that he was looking at Marie. But then he wondered if he would be so sure when he played this moment back in his mind later, which he probably would do a million times. So purely in an attempt to convince his future self that this was Marie, he shakily stood up.

He shuffled forward one shoe and then the other. He felt like he was pushing against an invisible opponent. He blocked out his own thought process and took another step.

At that moment a police car rounded the corner on the other side of the woman who must be Marie, its lights flashing. Leon felt like he was in a bubble. He could not hear anything around him and wondered if there was a siren he was oblivious to. Two male police officers jumped out. They moved towards her. From behind there were no tell tale signs of tension or worry as she remained sitting. Leon inhaled deeply. What if they took her away before he could check? The brisk manner of their approach, coupled with the lights, signified that they meant business. Could he take the risk that they might whisk her away? He was certain of one thing, which was that he was not going to involve himself in the scene. He could not afford to get embroiled in an arrest. But then, what if this was his one and only chance? He stood motionless as the officers walked up to her. She still did not seem to have even acknowledged them. They walked straight past her. What the hell?

One of the officers looked up and locked eyes with Leon. And with that the horror of realisation hit him. They had not come for her. The two men were only a few metres from him. He looked around. The streets were reasonably busy. He could make a run for it, weaving among shoppers. It was, in all honesty, the only play he had.

The second copper met his stare and they began to speed up. Leon stepped back onto the step beneath him and spun on his heel.

He was picking himself up off his backside. He wasn't entirely sure what had just happened but he was fairly sure he had just bounced backwards after running into a man behind him. He must get up quickly. He did not have time to look but the police officers could only be a matter of seconds away. He looked up to see the shadow of a large man in front of him. Presumably the brick shit-house that he had just run into. As he stood, Leon shielded the low sun from his eyes and realised that he was looking at a third police officer, with a fourth stood behind him. As he stood, the large policeman put a hand on his shoulder and began to speak. Leon only heard snippets from inside his bubble as he was also seized from behind and hands were rummaging through his pockets. Arrest. The bottle was retrieved from the floor. Manslaughter. Out came the picture of McCann. Arson. Where was Marie?

Leon was cuffed and led to the car that he had seen arrive. As they passed, Marie lowered her head from the police. A street dweller's instinct.

"Marie," Leon croaked in a hoarse whisper.

She probably had not even heard. The police moved him more quickly.

"Marie."

She looked up and he craned his neck backwards to see her. She may have just been looking at someone talking in her direction rather than responding to her own name. He still did not have proof. He wriggled to get free of the police's grasp and spun round. Two of them wrestled him to the floor and dragged him roughly back up. The cuffs dug into bone and flesh.

Her furrowed brow reflected the one he had looked at for so many hours. For so many years. The hair was shorter, the skin a little more creased. Her eyes looked up at him from the floor. The bright green eyes with no bottom.

# PART TWO
## 2016

## CHAPTER 31

It was a small dog. He didn't know breeds of dogs but he was pretty sure that it was a Yorkshire terrier. A wiry little bugger. For some reason, he instinctively ran out into the path of an oncoming BMW, one palm outstretched in the direction of the car, using the other to scoop up the wayward dog.

His attention had initially been attracted to the fact that only the dog's head was protruding from the old lady's wheeled shopping bag that she was trundling along behind her. The bag looked particularly full and he wondered if it might not have been better to let the poor little sod out. Or perhaps it had become so accustomed to travelling in such comfort that it now refused to walk anywhere.

As the lady approached the zebra crossing, the bulging contents of the bag took its toll on the cheap zip that was keeping it all contained. As the dog wriggled, the zip slowly yawned open and an orange plastic Sainsbury's bag had leaned forwards and begun to tip its tinned contents onto the pavement. At this, the terrier had half fallen, half jumped out and trotted down the path, its owner oblivious to everything that was happening two feet behind her.

Leon started to walk in her direction in order to let her know about the escapee and offer to pick up the spilled shopping. As he was half way there the dog, by now several yards up the path, glanced across to the other side of the road and started to follow its nose. Leon saw what was about to happen next and wondered if years of being tugged along in a shopping bag had removed any streetwise senses it may once have had. And sure enough, with a little skip, the dog ended up walking into the road without a care in the world.

Leon made a snap decision. Fortunately the BMW started to slow for the upcoming pedestrian crossing where the old lady was now waiting to cross. The driver, however, had clearly not seen the dog and would have squashed it flat if not for Leon's intervention. The car's brakes screeched a little as the driver stamped on the pedal, and a couple of horn blasts soon followed. Leon stepped back onto the pavement and watched as the driver - a middle aged, overweight man – screamed abuse at him. The loud music and closed window made the words hard to understand but Leon's very basic grasp of lip-reading helped him identify a few snippets. It looked for a moment like the man was going to get out of the car. Leon took a step in that direction and stood up tall, although his attempt to look intimidating was slightly hampered by the quivering terrier tucked under his right arm. Nevertheless, the man moved his car up to the crossing. Leon looked down at the dog and it stared back up. Maybe it wasn't such a bad dog. At least that was what he thought until it started to wriggle and bit him hard on the hand.

"You're an angel. An angel."

"Really, it wasn't a problem."

By the time he had caught up with the old lady she had crossed the road and was still walking. The confusion of being handed her own dog and shopping had taken some time to subside. Now she was sitting on a low wall, carefully restocking her bag as Leon handed her the items. He handed her the last tin. Peaches. So old people still loved tinned peaches then.

"Thank you. Now would you mind just getting hold of Muffin for a minute while I get this sorted?"

"Hmmm. He *has* bitten me once," Leon showed her the mark on the webbing between his thumb and forefinger. A couple of drops of blood had squeezed through the tiny punctures in his skin.

The lady seemed to neither see, nor hear his protestations. He picked the dog up.

"Did you not even hear the car braking?" he asked, still puzzled.

The fact that she did not even hear his question was answer enough.

Eventually, he handed back Muffin who was returned to his rightful place on top of the woman's food.

"You can always trust dog lovers," she offered.

"Actually, I'm not that much of an animal person. I'm just glad you've not lost your pet. I wasn't really that bothered about the dog itself." He immediately wondered why this had come out of his mouth, but this time her lack of hearing came to his rescue.

"And now you've got to know little Muffin here I bet you're already in love with him. Everyone that meets him is."

"Well, it did bite me so…"

Again no response.

"OK, well you seem all set, so I think I'll be off."

"Just a moment," she pulled out her purse and started looking through the coins contained within. Leon realised with horror that she was trying to give him a pound for rescuing the bloody dog. He sloped off as she was still routing through and pretended not to hear when she called him back.

The day was crisp and bright; a picture book spring morning. It was definitely cold enough to justify a coat but Leon was in short sleeves. He normally was these days. He loved the feel of the elements on his skin. He breathed in and hoped that the rest of his short journey would be uneventful.

The bell made its welcoming tinkle above his head as he entered the café. It was an American style diner that he had liked on his first visit and had become a regular. This was partly because of the pleasant atmosphere, even more partly because of the lovely Grace who worked behind the counter, but also because the food was reasonably good while being extremely cheap. The coffee was particularly good and now that he had become accustomed to the staggering prices people paid for a cup these days he realised this place was not too bad by comparison.

It was fairly busy today. Another attraction was the eclectic mix of regulars that frequented the place. There were office workers who sipped coffee while pretending to conduct business on their iPads and laptops, pensioners in to take advantage of the numerous OAP discounts, mothers on maternity leave talking to each other about baby shit (literally), and a variety of others. While most of them chose to use the numerous circular wooden tables, Leon liked to sit on a high stool at the counter. He even had a favourite one, and was disappointed on the occasions it was already occupied.

Levering himself up on the counter with his forearms, his legs scraped the tall chair in behind him until he was comfortably positioned. As he waited for Grace he stared at the mirrored wall behind the counter. He had looked at himself so seldom over many years that his appearance always seemed a slight surprise to him. He had never been the slightest bit vain, even in the old days, but he had to admit that he had developed a propensity for studying himself when opportunity presented itself.

He stared at the reverse image of the man that he believed to be him. His hair was short and his face clean-shaven; something that he was very particular about. His checked shirt was freshly ironed and smelled faintly of washing detergent. He was heavier than he had once been. This was partly because he had bulked up somewhat due to many sessions with the weights. But he knew it was also partly due to middle-aged spread. His belly, while not large, was definitely bigger than he would have liked and as well as the extra creases around his eyes, he could not deny that his face was carrying a little weight too. But on the whole he thought he was in pretty good nick for someone almost half way through his sixth decade.

Leon's gaze shifted from his own image to the contents of the fridge below, in particular the various bottles of beer standing in rows and proudly advertising their contents. There was a minor stirring from the rats. It was not too bad these days and generally manageable, but it always amazed him that they were still alive. He suspected that as they had not yet gone then he was stuck with them for life, but they were much weakened. Tamed? Perhaps. He had starved them and took satisfaction from having done so. There were rare occasions when they twitched into life but he generally had the mental strength to quieten them.

"Leon."

He realised that Grace was talking to him. He looked at her.

"Wandered off a bit there didn't you?" she smiled. Leon nodded. "Coffee and…?" she asked, beginning to pour a coffee from the percolator.

He looked at her and, as always, looked a little too much. She must have been in her mid-to-late forties, he supposed. Long dark hair tied back under a work cap, beautiful pale blue eyes and a round, welcoming face with a ready smile. He knew she was single and they often engaged in fairly flirtatious conversation. At least he thought that was what they were doing. He would not have been altogether surprised to learn that she thought him backward, slimy or sinister, so loose was his remaining grasp on social niceties and interpersonal skills. No, he was pretty sure she liked him, although on what level he did not know. He had even thought about asking her out before realising that his baggage was too heavy to inflict on anyone decent.

Leon quickly thought about what day it was. The cooked breakfast was excellent but in order to prevent himself sliding into clinical obesity he had restricted himself to one a week on a Friday. Today was only Thursday. Bugger.

As Grace walked to the hatch to request Leon's porridge he watched her bottom wiggle in her snug jeans. He had previously been caught doing this by two other customers and by Grace herself when she saw him in the mirror once. At that point he realised that he needed to either stop doing it or stop caring about being caught. As Grace had not told him off he went for the latter. It was sometimes the highlight of his day.

As he scraped the bottom of his bowl and picked up his second large mug of coffee he glanced up at the oversized wall clock. Quarter to nine. That meant two hours until he had to check in with Jenny, and eight hours until he had to be at home. In between he would undoubtedly check the situations vacant at the job centre, pop back to the flat for lunch – he could not afford the extravagance of two meals out in a day – and call in to see Gary. Gary owned a bed making business down behind the train station. He had been giving Leon a few hours here and there, cash in hand, depending on how business was going. Trouble was, Leon rarely knew from day to day whether his services were required. Gary was a decent enough bloke but unreliable and as Leon still did not have a mobile phone, he needed to go in person to find out.

He also needed to go and buy a tube of zinc white and one of ultramarine. He could only really afford two this week so that would have to do for now. And using them would account for his time once he had to return home. That was the only way he got through the evenings, otherwise he thought he would have lost his mind by now. Television had become some sort of wild beast that he did not particularly want to understand. It had become far less simple and much more shit, and he could not understand why most of the programmes, made from paper thin premises and starring talentless morons, were even being broadcast.

He would have never imagined that oil paints would be his thing but he had started some time before, scraping by on whatever scant offerings were available for him, in terms of both paint and canvas. Now that he could buy his own it was his one extravagance. Not that he could have met the cost of another once his coffees had been taken into account. Thinking about his paints made him instinctively look at his fingernails where he saw signs of the previous night's forest canopy; cobalt green and terre verte. He had been working on this one for weeks. It was amazing how much care and attention one could apply to a task once time became something to fill rather than ration. It was the one time when Leon's mind was truly quiet. Every bit of his attention was on the scene in front of him, usually open landscapes which made him feel so free that he almost sensed a dizziness.

Now he just had to decide how to spend the time in between. That was how he felt about his current life. Filling in blocks of time. He looked along the counter; one customer he recognised and one he didn't. Tomorrow morning he would arrive at the same time, Grace would pour him a coffee and his day would pan out exactly the same as today, minus the appointment with Jenny - thankfully they were becoming less regular.

Marking the passing of time. This was not what he had planned. Not what he had spent all that time thinking of. He looked at the bite mark on his hand. It looked redder and angrier than it had half an hour previously.

It was time.

## CHAPTER 32

His painting had not gone well. Immediately after getting home he decided that he should have got a different colour from the ultramarine. It was not right. Not for the next part anyway. It would no doubt come in useful later but he should have got something darker. He knew that his irritation was disproportionate to the event, but he was still cross and it affected his concentration. He gave up after twenty minutes and decided to wait and start in a better mind-set the following evening. He at least amused himself by wondering if his was an artistic strop.

Things had got progressively worse from then on. He had noticed over recent weeks that his sleep patterns were getting less reliable again but he had continually put it out of his mind. Thinking about it could only make things worse after all. But he had known.

The bed was fairly comfortable, particularly considering some of the places he had previously slept. The darkness and comparative lack of noise were difficult to get used to. Admittedly there were occasional disturbances to contend with but nothing major. All in all, very decent sleeping conditions. But he knew the insomnia was whispering to him. It had decided to return and haunt him. So the night had been spent going through his myriad of coping mechanisms. Getting out of bed to walk around before returning. Going to fetch a drink of milk, gulping it down and then hopping back into bed. Distraction practices were not working at all – each time he forced images into his mind, insomnia's whispers eventually drowned them out.

As so many times in the past, it was the demon's victory. Each time he returned to bed he could sense its presence lurking below the sheets, in the air. For the first time in a while he really wished he had some drink handy. The rats had been aroused by the whispers of the night. They were not desperate to feed, but just emerged to remind him there was an easy solution. He listened to the dull sounds from neighbouring rooms. Faint conversation, the muted thud of music. Any of the people responsible for those noises were likely to have something to drink. It wouldn't do any harm to just have a little in order to get him to sleep. He sat up in bed to think through his options. He was so tired that his bones ached and his head felt too heavy. It flopped back onto his pillow. Even if he had the desire to go scrounging from strangers in the middle of the night he had not the energy. And he knew he couldn't fall off the wagon after all he had been through.

And so he was trapped. A body that could not move due to fatigue and a mind that would not let him sleep. That was the irony of insomnia; you could not even use that extra time productively. Even if he had managed to drag himself out of bed to sit at the window with his laptop he could not have done anything remotely constructive. But more than anything, the thing that kept the reluctant night-owl pinned to his mattress was the delicious prospect of the sleep that would not come. Leon fooled himself yet again that if he blanked his mind and thought of a black void he would win. That was the thing that no one tells you about insomnia – it's so interminably fucking boring.

His mind emptied and felt at peace. Out of nowhere, James Potter's face appeared, his hair and moustache burning brightly, the anger in his eyes even brighter still. Potter visited Leon at night much less frequently than he once had, but his presence was still as startling as ever. When he came there was no escape – his spectre could climb under Leon's eyelids, making him impossible to escape from. Potter's mouth opened in a silent scream. Leon jumped up in bed and was unsure if he had actually shouted.

He stumbled and looked down to see if he had tripped over a body. His peripheral vision was not functioning properly so he could not tell what was beneath him. It was just a bin bag. He thought about the fact that at one point he would have torn the bag open to see if it contained anything worth having. Thank fuck he was past all that. At least he was for the time being. He should go home. He did not even really know what he was expecting to achieve out here on the Embankment. He was highly unlikely to find them. He had spoken to two or three people – he didn't know exactly which and trying to remember took his brain through a labyrinth that just made him even more tired. He could not even remember the conversations except that they had been of no use.

The sun was just beginning to poke out its face from beneath the horizon, entering the space it had already begun to illuminate. Its appearance gave a new dimension to his sense of surreal timelessness. He was so tired that he felt like he was tripping. He slumped to the floor and lay down to look at it.

He was walking along a pavement outside oppressive looking high-rise office blocks. He had no concept of where he was or what he was doing there. He felt himself listing to one side, moving inexplicably towards the road. His right foot planted too close to the edge of the path and he pushed off strongly to steer himself back across to the left. It did not have the desired effect and his left foot only served to push him out once more to the right. He tried to repeat his action and plant his right foot firmly enough to correct his gait. He knew to the accuracy of a fraction of a second that his foot had hit fresh air rather than concrete. His head whipped down and saw his right foot dropping off the side of the path towards the road. The kerb was enormous; at least twelve inches high. This was going to hurt.

His right foot flicked out with such ferocity that his whole body jerked. His eyes shot open and it took him a couple of seconds to realise that he was lying in the dirt on the Embankment before the sun had even risen fully. Idiot. He patted his right jeans pocket and felt the outline of his wallet. He opened his eyes and realised that he had almost fallen asleep again, hand still on wallet. He had to get away. With a huge amount of effort he rolled over onto all fours and got to his feet. Gingerly making his way down the slope to the road that was just starting to show signs of life, he saw movement to his left. He looked and saw a tramp twitching into life under a tent of cardboard. He sat himself down next to the man with a thump that startled him upright. Bright blue eyes peered out of a dark, grimy face. The man was utterly filthy. Had people really looked like that when he was on the streets? Had he simply got used to seeing poor wretches like this? Had he himself looked like this horror show? He found it hard to believe but would have to admit he did not know for sure.

"I'm Leon." He looked straight out ahead towards the town. He had seen the alarm in the tramp's eyes and did not wish to spook him any further.

"I'm David Beckham. The fuck do you want?"

Leon considered standing up and calling it a day but something – not just the tiredness – made him stay.

"I'm looking for some old friends. Just asking around in case anyone has seen them."

"What's in it for me?"

"Fiver."

The tramp paused.

"Who are they?"

And that was the transaction agreed. Simple as that. No consideration for the fact he might be getting fellow street-livers into trouble. Five pounds was enough to erase all concern.

"Steve's a big lad. Really big. Scottish. And the woman's name is Karen. If you know one of them you'll know both of them. They're joined at the hip. Or at least they were. It's been a long time," Leon's voice trailed off to follow his memories.

"Oh, aye, I think I remember him. In fact, I think I seen him. Recent, like."

"Oh right. Where?"

"Gets to the day centre fairly regular."

Leon looked the tramp in the eye.

"You have no idea who I'm talking about, do you?"

"Yes, I do. Don't come asking me questions and then calling me a liar," the tramp complained indignantly.

"What colour hair's he got?"

The man looked deep in thought. "Dark?" he asked, hopefully.

"Piss off," Leon rose to his feet.

"OK, so I don't know him. Hardly my fault. Can I have a quid?"

Leon started to walk away and then stopped.

"Do you know someone called Vee? Everyone knew her. An old dear, God knows what sort of age she would be now. I know she lived in a guest house down on Main a long time ago."

Leon figured that in the absence of any information about Steve or Karen, he might as well try to find the woman in the know. The matriarch of the homeless. If anyone knew then she would. That was in the highly unlikely event that she was still alive.

"Vee, yeah, everyone knows Vee," the man said, a little too enthusiastically.

"How do I know you're not lying again?"

"She lived on the first floor at that place you're talking about. Long grey hair, tied back."

The tramp was much more sure of himself and Leon decided that he was probably genuine. The tramp looked up at him.

"Fiver?"

"Three," said Leon. The tramp realised from the tone of his voice that there was no invitation to barter and nodded.

"And that's if you can tell me where to find her. Do you know?"

"I can tell you, but I want the money first."

"You definitely know where she is."

"Definitely."

Leon found three pound coins and placed then in the man's gnarly hand. The tramp shoved them deep in his pocket almost the second they hit his palm.

"Well? Where will she be?"

"In the cemetery."

## CHAPTER 33

It was two days later that Leon found Guy.

He had done a full day's work making a bunk bed for Gary the previous day and had a few extra quid in his pocket. He was having a mid afternoon coffee in a place called Beans. He unfurled a crumpled copy of the Big Issue onto the small circular table in front of him and placed his gigantic cup of white Americano on one corner to keep it flat. He felt like the magazine was a thread to the past that he could keep alive, although he was not entirely sure he wanted to. There did not seem an awful lot to be nostalgic about.

He had no intention of looking up old friends and was avoiding bars, which were realistically the only place he was likely to bump into anyone. It was best for all parties if he simply let them get on with their lives oblivious to what had happened to his. Only four of them had been to visit him and he had been surprised by their identities. He had found it strange that in a time of crisis those he thought he could count on most had been absent while those less close had lent their support.

As he turned the crumpled pages he wondered what had happened to Billy, his regular vendor from years gone by. In all probability he was dead too. He felt like he was chasing ghosts, trying to grab hold of fog. But he knew from experience there was no point trying to convince himself to abandon his fool's errand. He would go on with it no matter what. Addiction. Obsession.

Today was an empty day except that he had to check in with Jenny at three. She was a nice enough woman but it was a pain in the hole. Their meetings were not the constructive counselling affairs that Jenny seemed to believe them to be. But she was doing her best and, if her spiritual help was somewhat lacking then her practical assistance was appreciated. She was helping him structure plans in a way that he would not have managed his own. This was largely because she knew the system and he didn't, but it was also because she had good organisational skills and a desire to help.

With her guidance, it looked likely that he could get on a programme that might get him his own place. That was dependent upon getting a job but, again, Jenny was on the case. Ideally, any real employment would allow sufficient flexibility for him to supplement his income with some cash in hand work from Gary; he was loath to give that up as he was enjoying it.

He pictured his future flat. It was small, unfussy but comfortable and felt like home. The living room was laid out simply with a suite and TV and a few photographs in frames. His easel stood in one corner. It had a good enough stock of paint that he would not be forced into a strop if he accidentally bought the wrong shade. Leon was stretched out on the sofa watching a film. From the kitchen, Grace walked into his imaginary living room. This surprised him sufficiently that he bounced back into reality. What had all *that* been about? Here he was, trying to embark on the mission that had kept him going for years and yet he was fantasising about playing happy families with Grace. He had certainly fantasised about her before, but admittedly not in such a domestic scenario.

This was confusing in the extreme. He decided not to think about his daydream room again if he could help it. He would continue along the road with Jenny's help and see what happened. He needed to keep all his options open.

He found himself staring at the barista who was bouncing around behind the counter, deftly tamping down coffee into a filter handle with one hand and pouring copious amounts of milk into a takeaway cup with the other. He had on an apron in the shop's burnt orange signature colour. That was just another touch that added to the confused personality of the establishment. With its local notices and garish displays, it seemed unsure as to whether to pitch itself as a community-based local business or attempt to emulate the look of a multi-million-pound identikit corporate juggernaut.

Next to the bouncing barista was a similarly attired young woman, possibly late teens. She was taking the orders and repeating them to her colleague who was all of four feet away from the customers that had uttered them in the first place. She had a sullen, almost huffy face and was utterly unsuited to a job that involved interacting with people. Her demeanour said to the customers 'I hate my job and I hate all of you for making me serve you.' Leon decided she must be related to the owner in some way.

The man had one of those thin beards with a tuft on the chin and a separate moustache. It was the kind of facial sculpting that always made Leon wonder two things; how long must it take to look after, and how did the chin hair make acceptable a tache that on its own would have been the subject of ridicule? To complete the look the man had a scruffy but styled haircut and trendy wire-rimmed spectacles. He was in good shape and had rolled his short sleeves up so tightly that it looked uncomfortable, in order to show off the tattoos which adorned both arms. The man looked a little old to be in his line of work – possibly early forties – but Leon could imagine that the he was the recipient of attention from many of the female customers, perhaps even some of the male ones.

But the reason Leon was staring at the man was not admiration, but a sense of recognition. He could not place him but knew he had come across him before. The harder he strained to remember, the further the answer wriggled from his grasp, like a half-remembered dream one tried to retain upon waking up only for it to agonisingly float back into the ether.

He let it go. It could be anyone; a face from the past, which would probably mean it had changed considerably, someone from the inside, maybe even someone he had seen working in another shop. He had done that for as long as he could remember; spent ages trying to place a face in the street before realising it was a barman who had tolerated his presence in a pub at some point. He looked back to the Big Issue and turned the page. After reading the same paragraph twice he realised that he had still not taken in a word of its content. And then it hit him. He flashed his gaze back to the barista. It *could* be. Was it? No, probably not. Back to the magazine. Funnily enough, it was while looking down at the page that the certainty arrived. It was definitely Guy – the little shit from the squat.

Take away the beard, the glasses, lengthen the hair, remove some of the bulk; it was him. Leon's instinct was to look down to hide his face. He had no idea why. Guy had already served him his drink and clearly didn't recognise him, and even if he had it was immaterial because Leon was going to have to talk to him anyway.

After twenty minutes or so the queue shortened, another staff member that Leon had noticed arrive a little earlier popped behind the counter and Guy went out to collect a few cups and saucers. Leon looked at the opening times that were printed on the shop window. In reverse, he saw that the place opened at 7.30 and closed at 6.00. It was 2.25. If Guy had started at 7.30 that might well constitute a shift. Leon stood and left.

Guy threw his apron on a shelf and pulled on his coat. With a half-hearted 'cheers' to his two co-workers he left, stuffed his hands in his pockets and walked away down the street. After a few minutes, he became aware that someone was walking quite close behind him. He ignored it until the person pulled alongside him. Rather than overtake, this unwanted companion simply fell into step beside him. Eventually, Guy looked up at his face.

"Can I help you with something?" There was no answer. "Hey, what do you want?"

"I'm a bit upset you don't recognise me."

"I don't know you. Leave me alone please," a brief tremor in the last word betrayed the fact that Guy was beginning to feel more than a little unsure of the situation. "I know you've been sat in the coffee shop for a long time, that's all."

"Come on. Take a look. Have a good think."

Guy sped up and Leon had to trot to keep up.

"OK, slow down. I'll tell you."

Guy looked at him and nervously waited for an explanation.

"We were in that squat together," said Leon.

Guy swallowed and looked down.

"I think you've got the wrong bloke."

"Well, you're called Guy, for a start."

"You were just in Beans," realised Guy, "and you've read my name on my badge."

"You didn't have a badge on. I know because I looked for one."

Guy walked away and crossed the road, stepping in front of a car that honked and swerved. He got across and was visibly dismayed to find Leon still at his side.

"Fuck off or I'll call the police," Guy growled.

"No you won't. You don't want to open up all that. I'll leave you alone if you just talk to me for two minutes."

Guy thought hard about the offer and then nodded at an empty bus shelter. They entered and sat next to each other on the long, thin plank of a seat.

After ten minutes of evasive answers from Guy, Leon had managed to establish that he had seen Karen and Steve once or twice after the squat. The younger man had clearly decided that Leon was not going away until he had some information, and he seemed to open up a little.

"I haven't thought about any of that shit for years. It's a different life; hardly seems like it really happened. I look back on it now and realise that I was just playing with it. It must have been a bit of a rebellious streak of some sort. I was a complete prick when I think back."

"Yeah, you were," Leon smiled a little.

"I wasn't the only one as I recall."

"I'll take that," Leon's smile almost grew into a grin.

He was actually warming to Guy. Guy the elder seemed decent enough. He had pulled himself together somewhat and made a fist of things. Guy the younger had an attitude, sure, but Leon had probably been too judgemental and intolerant too.

"Can I buy you a drink while we talk?" Leon asked, nodding to the nearby Ship Inn.

Guy looked surprised at the offer. Clearly he had believed that the talking had now finished. He hesitated, and then shook his head. Leon had no real desire to go into a pub and have his customary soft drink, but he thought it may have relaxed Guy a little.

"So, Steve and Karen…?" continued Leon.

"I don't know much, honestly. They split up."

"I find that hard to believe."

"I say split up – I never knew what the deal was with them anyway. If they were a couple."

"Not in the conventional sense," offered Leon.

"Steve left the area. I'd lost touch with them years before but he got caught in this paedophile sting. It was difficult not to hear about that. He was all over the local news," Guy had lowered his voice as a couple passed behind them on the other side of the Perspex.

"No fucking way. I'm not having that."

"I didn't believe it either. Most right-minded people didn't. But that doesn't stop the dickheads raising a lynch mob. There was this little vigilante prick. He was posing as little girls on line and trying to trap paedos in the act. He was weird, seriously weird. Anyway, he had set up a trap in some disused house. He filmed Steve coming in for the meeting, passed it to the police and plastered it all over the internet."

"And how was Steve supposed to have accessed computers?"

"Well, that was just one of the reasons that the charges didn't stick," said Guy. "Steve argued that he had seen the house door open and, realising it was not being used, had snuck in for a look as a potential squat. Wrong place, wrong time type of thing. I even heard that the real fella that had been doing the grooming turned up later and missed all the action. But you hear all sorts when something like that happens don't you?"

Leon nodded, "So what happened?"

"Like I say, there was no real evidence at all. But I know he got the shit kicked out of him a few times and it would have taken a few to do that to him, wouldn't it?"

Leon thought about his image of Steve. A huge, strong man. He had always seemed to be a gentle giant but Leon had always assumed that the big fella could have caused havoc if he needed to.

"Again, I just know that 'cause it was in the papers."

"So he left?"

Guy nodded. "I've definitely never seen him again anyway."

"And what... Karen wouldn't go with him?"

"Nah, they'd stopped talking years before that. I was still at the squat. I don't know why. I don't know if I knew at the time but if I did I've forgotten it now. I left soon after"

"So when was the last time you saw Karen?"

Guy shrugged and stood up, flattening out his trousers where they had crumpled on the bench. Leon noticed a sudden change in the man's body language. The defensiveness had returned.

"Look, I've got to go. It's been lovely and all..." he said sarcastically but without malice.

"Where's Karen?"

"I dunno. Sorry, have to go," he started to leave.

"I'm going the same way as you, I'll walk with you," said Leon.

"You don't know where I'm going."

Leon gave a shrug of his own as he stood and followed Guy out of the bus stop.

The two men walked in silence for a couple of minutes. Leon sneaked a look at his watch and saw that he was now pushing it in terms of his meeting with Jenny. He had to act quickly as he knew this was a once only opportunity. He had to break Guy down within the next few minutes or that was it.

Guy walked with his fists jammed into his pockets, staring straight ahead and clearly wishing that his companion would leave him alone. Leon had decided that the best plan of attack was restraint, despite the pressing time that made him want to rush. He kept the silence going as long as possible until it became an entity that they could both sense in the air. Sure enough, Guy was the one to break it.

"She was around for years. Probably still is."

"So you saw her."

"Few times," Guy nodded.

Leon knew instinctively that there was more to this.

"What's the story?"

Guy paused, clearly weighing up his choices. It seemed that the desire to get rid of Leon as quickly as possible won out.

"Look, I'm not proud of it. Of what I did. I was on the street a while after you left. When I got sick of it I just asked my parents for money and got on my feet. I could have done that at any point but I was a twat, OK?" Guy was getting angry.

Whether that was with Leon or with his younger self, Leon could not tell.

"I would see her around after that. I would pretend I didn't even know her," Guy muttered, looking at his feet as he walked.

"She would ask me for help whenever I passed. Money, somewhere to stay. She looked a state. A real fucking mess. I didn't help her. I cut her off. She would try when I was on my own. When I was with other people she wouldn't even look at me. She was being decent. I wasn't," Guy almost seemed to be speaking to himself.

"I saw her around for years. She looked worse as time went by. Probably a few years now since I saw her but she was completely screwed. She looked ancient, no front teeth, skin and bone. I know I could have helped her but I didn't. Happy?"

Leon wondered if he was meant to offer some words of reassurance at this point. He did not.

"So there you go," offered Guy as a summary. He turned up the next street and it was obvious that the conversation was now well and truly closed.

"So where is she?"

"Dunno," Guy called back without turning.

"A guess?"

Guy was walking away quickly. Again he did not turn around but his low voice drifted back to Leon.

"If she's still alive there's only one place she could be."

## CHAPTER 34

The meeting with Jenny had been much more productive than usual. Sure, she had tried to slip into touchy-feely mode every now and then but he could live with that and, besides, he had to engage with this process so he may as well do it positively.

She had found a *possible* job opportunity. Hard work for shit pay but what could he expect considering the way his life had turned out? A labourer at a place building canal boats she had said. It actually sounded ok, certainly better than being cooped up doing some sort of meaningless office job. Finishing a day's manual work feeling exhausted but with something to show for it, some well-earned money in the bank, and the camaraderie of others. He had not had that kind of job satisfaction since well before the university. He couldn't even remember how long it was since he had worked on the site. Then the university job came up. It wasn't that he was excited at the prospect and it certainly wasn't that he was desperate to escape his job at the time. It has simply seemed like what he *should* do. A ridiculous rationale in hindsight. He had some A levels on his CV which made him a little more educated than some of the lads he was working with. He knew that didn't mean he was any brighter or gifted that them – it just meant he had been given more of an opportunity, but he felt that that he ought to go into something where he could get a career. Get on a ladder of progressively demanding and fulfilling jobs, make something of himself, never look back... fucking idiot.

So if he got this potential job, or indeed any job, he could then be lined up for a rental place. It would be next to nothing but when you are starting from actually nothing that would demonstrate progress. He pictured it. Coming home from building canal boats, kicking off his work boots and collapsing on the sofa, hearing a door open, turning to see... Grace. Jesus, he had to stop this.

It was freezing cold and he had to pull down the cuff of his jacket to cover his left hand. The hand was particularly chilly because its fingers were wrapped around the neck of a bottle of Smirnoff. A snowflake chose the bridge of his nose as its final resting place and gently brushed its freezing kiss on his skin. He looked up and saw more flakes, sparse but noticeable, drifting down to catch their forerunner.

While staring up into the dark, snow-speckled sky, he stumbled down the hill a little and cursed as he struggled to stop his descent. He managed to do so and peered around him. This was going to be much harder if the snow got heavier although, on the plus side, it would make him harder to notice.

His quest so far had taken in in two threats of physical violence, several unpleasant bouts of insults, the offer of a blowjob and countless requests for some of his vodka. A couple of brief conversations had actually cost him a measure of the drink.

Eventually, after a long time he found the spot. The snow had thickened and was beginning to lie on the sparsely grassed ground. All around him the Embankment dwellers were curling up tight in sleeping bags, competing for sheltered ground, pulling extra protection over themselves or simply leaving. As Leon knew, walking around to stay awake until better shelter could be found was far less dangerous than drunkenly sleeping out in the cold in this sort of temperature. It was turning into the sort of night where some of the exposed homeless simply wouldn't wake up.

He wiped away the snow and sat down on the hard ground. He shivered and looked at his bottle, which was now minus the series of payments that had led him here. He looked down at the sleeping bag next to him. It contained a body that was motionless, head on a carrier bag of unknown content. Leon looked at the woman who was either oblivious or indifferent to his arrival. She lifted a can of Tennent's to her lips without moving a single muscle outside of her drinking arm, her head still on its side. Quite a skill, he thought.

That arm and part of her face were all he could see, but the face was ravaged. The eyes were so opaque that he wondered if he was looking at a blind person, the flesh was sallow and slack and she had a bright scar running under the full width of one of her milky eyes.

"Hello," Leon tried to catch her attention, unsuccessfully.

He tried again and she simply turned away from him in such a manner that he still did not know if she was aware of him. He touched her on the shoulder and she twisted away.

"Look at me."

There was no response and the two stayed as they were for a while with Leon wondering what his next move would be. Eventually, the woman took another noisy slurp of lager and turned to face him. She looked not to have the energy to care why a strange man had sat next to her. She had clearly endured so much that anything that might be thrown at her would be met with indifference. The eyes focused a little as Leon stared intently into her face.

His spirits sank. He had always known that in all likelihood this would be a false lead but he had hoped nevertheless.

She wiped her eyes, then her mouth, with a disgusting sleeve and hoisted herself up a little. Another drink from her can, draining and then discarding it. She looked expectantly at his vodka and Leon thought he saw her finger poke in its general direction. He didn't offer it. He continued to stare at her face. Nothing. Nothing at all. He felt that he'd maybe had a fractional moment of recognition and he told himself that he was just hoping too hard. It didn't seem to be her; he would have to accept that.

"Do you recognise me?" he asked. Nothing. "Do you know who I am?"

He had wasted his time. He stood. Even if it had been her, the woman in front of him appeared almost catatonic. He started to pick his way downhill. He thought he heard a noise from the woman's direction and turned to look at her. She hadn't moved. He set off again.

"Leon," came the rasping whisper.

No mistaking it this time. She was pointing at his bottle.

Leon did not want to rush things unduly but she had been sipping his vodka for ten minutes and he still hadn't had a sound out of her. Maybe she had insufficient breath left in her to talk again. It was a possibility. Everything else about her seemed to have rotted away so there was no reason why the lungs or vocal cords would not have been affected. And if she did not have the capacity for speech beyond one word then this was a waste of time. He looked at the trembling claws that occupied the space where her hands should be. They were shaking, either because of the cold or something else.

Watching someone drink was hard for him, even though he should have been concentrating on the task at hand. As he heard the liquid being swallowed the rats twitched ever so slightly. He wouldn't have cared quite so much except that the noise of her swallowing was utterly disgusting, like spilling water onto loose gravel. She held out the bottle to Leon and her lips parted in what could have been a smile. Her four front teeth appeared at first to be completely missing but on closer inspection were revealed to have simply eroded to stumps. A wave of nausea lapped at the back of his throat.

He looked at her face and it seemed to rush towards his own. As the heat rose within him, a further face – much more transparent and indistinct – swooped in from the side, followed by another from the other side. He knew that they meant doom. He could not have explained how he knew that but something primal within him accepted that he had seen them before and they brought death.

In fact, he had been here before, not just in this physical spot but also in this actual situation. Sat with her. He looked at the extended bottle. She would withdraw it in a moment. She did. He *had* been here. He knew there was another demonic face to appear. He knew how it would look and how long it would appear for. He knew that it would swoop into her. It did just that and she did not even notice.

His head felt as though it had no mass whatsoever as it threatened to lift upwards and his mind began to rotate within it. It detached from his consciousness and left him completely out of control. Another demon joined the party. He could just about see her face which he knew was only three feet in front of him, but it was like trying to watch someone while on a merry-go-round.

The terror started to build at the realisation that he was slipping from reality. Could it be real? Had this been building up for all these years just waiting for this moment? Had Death erred in not taking him when he slept here and this was some sort of punishment; was his brain now about to split open as payback?

At the moment of near acceptance, something familiar kicked in and, in the context of what was happening it was almost a relief. A hot ball started spinning inside his lower midriff. Much like a star's transformation to a black hole, all the energy of his being had been compressed tighter and more densely until it had nowhere else to go. It rose gently through his stomach and up into his chest. Although the sensation was awful he now realised with a little relief what was happening to him.

It was amazing really; after all that time rough when he had no access to medication and only one episode he had now been back on the required dose for some time. But that was the secret that epilepsy held from him; while medicated he never knew whether it still lived within him, simply held at bay by the Lamotrigine, or if it had left for good.

Now this was happening he just had to see where it took him. Perhaps if he relaxed he would be ok in a few minutes. Or at least after the absence he was about to slip into.

He was stumbling along the Embankment with a torch but it had very little battery power and was barely any use at all. Driving rain stung his eyes. He tripped over someone and looking down saw that it was the Big Issue seller with the moustache. He got up and started to run, almost immediately tripping again over a ginger haired man who he had been meant to poison.

He screamed silently and found that he could not get up onto his feet. He rolled away down the bank. The moon appeared from behind the clouds and revealed at the top of the bank a woman sleeping on the bare ground. She was curled up and had her back to him but the yellow cagoule glowed with a fierce luminescence. He clawed frantically to propel himself in that direction, his legs providing only the weakest of assistance. Half way there. He could hear men behind him, closing in. Then they were right behind him. He would be at the yellow coat soon if he could keep going. A hand grasped at his ankle and he looked back to see the moustachioed man grinning with sharp teeth.

"Leon," his voice rasped like sandpaper, little more than a loud whisper.

Leon struggled forwards.

"Leon."

He blinked and looked down at his right hand, which was picking at something on the knee of his jeans. It was as though the hand belonged to someone else. He had no cognitive link to the actions it was making, nor could not see what purpose it was serving as there was nothing there to pick at.

"Leon," the voice was on the verge of exhaustion, so long was it since it had been used. He turned to look at the woman's face. She seemed more bemused than concerned.

"How long?" he asked.

"Mm?"

"How long was I, you know… not here… forget it."

Leon felt completely drained and more than a little confused. He looked around him and saw that everything looked exactly the same. Perhaps the snow was a fraction deeper, but probably not. She was in the same position sipping at his bottle. But time was liable to stand still here so it wasn't possible for him to give an accurate guess. All he knew was that he had definitely been away for a while. He felt dreadful and he recoiled in fright from the waves of déjà vu that still persisted.

There was no time to worry about himself, though. He needed to concentrate.

Her restraint with the drink was noticeable to him. She was not drinking as greedily as she should have been, but nor was she in her right mind. She was either already drunk, high or over the years had completely lost it.

She handed him the bottle as if they were two old friends sharing a drink. He supposed they were. He took it and sipped some down. Just to keep up appearances, he told himself. The liquid felt hot as it burned its way down his throat. Shit, he could have drunk the rest of it right there and then. He quickly handed it back and vowed that he would not take so much as another sip.

He still could not see any trace of the woman he had once known. She looked at him, leaned forwards and squinting to try and get a decent look at him through her uncooperative eyes. And suddenly there it was. Something about her crow's feet or her wrinkled up nose perhaps. He wasn't sure, but there, hidden in this seemingly other woman's face was Karen.

"S'wa happened t'you then?" she slurred and wheezed at the same time.

"I'm sure you know exactly what happened to me. What happened to you?"

"Ah, I been fine, good."

"I see that. A picture of health," Leon said. The sarcasm appeared to go straight over Karen's head. "Where's Steve?"

She went quiet and he thought she was not going to answer.

"No seen 'him f'years."

"Seems a shame."

"Nah, din't really like 'im," she took a long gulp from the bottle. That was more like it.

Karen lay back and stared straight up into the snow. Leon saw at least one flake land directly on her eyeball and she did not react in the slightest. He pulled his coat around him and hugged himself. Karen shut her eyes.

"Oy," he poked her hard on the arm, "stay awake."

Her eyes flicked open again and he took the vodka from her hand. She unzipped her sleeping bag so that she could sit upright, keeping herself closer to the bottle.

"So how did they find me?" he said.

She stared blankly at the bottle. He started to move it in her direction and then pulled back.

"I need you to concentrate Karen. How did they find me?"

She took her eyes away long enough to look at him and give a shrug which conveyed that she did not understand what he was talking about.

"The squat. How did they find me at the squat.?"

She looked at the bottle.

"Guy?" she asked unconvincingly.

"Wrong. I didn't know Guy until I was actually at the squat. He sends his regards by the way."

"Twat."

"Well, anyway... They'd lost me when I moved in. Someone told. Someone let them in the house. So they could only have approached someone they knew I'd had previous contact with. And only two of those knew where I was, didn't they, Karen?"

"OK. Was Steve. Din't wanna tell ya, but..."

Karen seemed to be drifting back towards unconsciousness. Leon leaned across and tempted her with the bottle, just to keep her sharp.

"Why did you and Steve split up?"

"He got accused o' kiddy-fiddlin'. 'E did one after that."

Karen leaned across to take the Smirnoff and Leon once again moved it just out of her reach.

"You'd already gone your separate ways before that."

Karen stared at him, her eyes suddenly sharper, whether by surprise or anger he could not tell.

"I know everything."

"So why ye botherin' me?"

"I just wanted to see if you'd have the balls to admit it."

"Fuck yesel'!"

"Fine," said Leon, standing up.

"No," she wailed, eyes fixated on the vodka. Leon waited a moment.

"Whad'ye want us to say? Sorry? Cos 'm not."

"How much did they give you?"

"Fifty. Like a say, m'not sorry."

"Fifty quid. You ruined my life for fifty fucking quid."

He sat back down hard and lay on his back, the snow melting into his coat. He breathed deeply and watched his exhalation leave his mouth, move upwards and mingle with the snow coming in the other direction. He felt his energy escape with his breath. He could have fallen asleep there and then in the snow, on the Embankment, next to Karen. He looked across at her. She was still only focused on one thing. Her sleeping bag remained open and was filling with snow. Her thin jumper was soaked through and her hair was decorated with hundreds of flakes. His teeth started to chatter and he realised that if he left her out here she would most likely die tonight. He pushed the bottle out to his side and she picked it up.

"Needed money," she stated, very matter-of-factly, "they'd a found ye anyways. Might aswell o' got mesel the money."

He sat up again.

"Knew wha' you were fr'm the start," she continued. " A big fraud." There was no slurring with the last statement. It was the sound of years of festering resentment being poured out. Leon looked at her, one eyebrow slightly raised. "Even afore ye was in the paper I knew ye wasn't really homeless."

"How?"

"Seen ye keys. Seen ye dressed smart. Aft' that a folle'd ye couple times. Y'ad a house."

Leon sat and thought. He could see why she would have been angry. Someone who lived on the bones of her arse, scrimping and begging every day just to stay alive for another 24 hours. Watching some prick waltz in and out of a house while pretending to be like her. The fact that he was well on his way to being evicted from that particular house would matter little.

"How'd ye know was me?" she asked.

"I only suspected but you've just told me for sure."

"Wanker," she said, as though feeling stupid for being tricked although, in Leon's opinion she looked incapable of such awareness.

"And presumably you told Steve what you'd done. That's why he left. Or he worked it out." This was more of a statement than a question.

"Told 'im. A while after. He knew summ'n was off. I could never keep anything from 'im. I's worried he'd kick off I never shared the cash wi'im?"

Leon looked down and shook his head.

"Fucking hell," he muttered quietly, "everything that lad did for you and you hid your money from him. He'd have given you the shirt off his back. He probably did for all I know."

This all hit him harder than he had expected; the fact that Karen had always know of his deception, the fact that she had sold him out, the fact that Steve had left her, the fact that here she was living back in hell on earth.

"He didn't leave because of the cash, though. You were a part of him Karen. I know he wouldn't have left you over money."

"'E n'ver e'en asked bou' the money," her speech was becoming increasingly slurred and unintelligible as she swigged on the vodka.

The drink was clearly just topping up a body that already had the needle hovering over the danger zone. She was starting to keel again.

"A jus' tol' 'im wha' I did to you n' he went. No arg'ment, nuthin. Just off. Broke me 'eart."

"Who did you tell about me, Karen? Who asked you?"

There was no answer. Karen looked in the middle of passing out. Staring at her, Leon assumed that it was the event that had led her to this current predicament. She would have lost everything when Steve left her side, including her protection. God knows what had happened to her without that. And even more importantly she had lost her constant companion. The life was hard, but it would have been ten times harder for her on her own. Some people could handle it. In fact, he had known lots who only managed because they were going solo. But not Karen. She had been alone once but having found Steve, Leon knew there was no way she could go back.

"Who did you tell?" he asked more aggressively, "I need to know who it was."

He shook her, took the bottle and moved to pour out the remains.

"No, no... giz it."

Karen squeezed her eyes shut.

"Colin or summat. Clive. Summin'. Clive?"

This was hopeless.

"What was he like?"

She looked at the still precarious bottle and seemed to have a small moment of clarity.

"Posh lad. Young. Goin' bald, Shaved."

Leon was panicking. She could actually remember. He had a very small window of opportunity here and the stakes had suddenly heightened. He managed to resist the urge to shake her.

"What did he sound like?"

"Posh. A said. Croaky, though."

Leon's memory flashed back to a dark place. A place so dark that he could not see anything. In his mind, his senses of hearing and touch seemed to be heightened to compensate for the dark. He was quickly into the scene, so often had his thoughts gone back there. Over the years, he had rebuilt every aspect. The flickering candlelight, the pain, the overwhelming confusion, anger, and helplessness. He had recreated it so many times that it had now become difficult to establish what was real and which elements had fraudulently stolen in with time and repetition. But the voice was there, as clear as the very first time. Young, well spoken and an underlying rasping, chesty quality.

It was him. He was agonisingly close now. But Karen was nearly spent. He pushed the bottle into her hand. Perhaps the action of drinking would prevent her from passing out.

"Who *was* he?"

"Follo'd him once. Worked at accsy firm on Al'zander."

"What? Say again," he asked frantically. He was shaking her now, "a what firm? Karen?"

"Accounts. Fuckin' ell. Gerroff us."

An accountancy firm on Alexander. It was something, but it wasn't nearly enough. A posh bloke in an accountancy firm, Christ, it was *nothing*. He shook once more in desperation. Her eyes were closed. That was it.

Leon sat back and looked at her. Her hair, now laid back on the ground, was white with snow, her eyebrows too. Her closed eyed were sunken and in the half light her lips looked dark blue. Her sleeping bag was also collecting snow. Her arm had relaxed with the rest of her and the vodka seeped out onto her chest. He looked up and almost immediately had to look down again, so heavy had the snow become. He saw a white blanket spread in all directions.

One thing he was sure of was that Karen would die out here tonight. But that wasn't his fault, was it? She had been very intoxicated when he arrived. Lying out in the snow. But she had opened her sleeping bag in order to accept his drink, got progressively drunker and now soaked her top in vodka.

He weighed things up and decided he had no problems if she died, after what she had done to him. Her days were numbered anyway if she was living like this. The thought of actually contributing to her demise was not as easy to deal with.

He noticed that there were no wisps of condensation escaping her lips and leaned across her. He couldn't hear anything. He leaned in closer and thought he could just detect shallow breathing. He lingered a little longer, just to make sure.

"Carl," she coughed. Leon jumped in shock.

Her eyes rolled back. Within seconds Leon was on top of her, knees either side of her frail body, trying not to put any pressure on her with his backside. He dragged her upwards by her collar and her head simply arced backwards as it would if she had a broken neck. There were only a couple of inches left in the bottle, which he threw onto her face. She spluttered and he shook her hard. He looked up and saw a pair of eyes peering at him through the snow from further up the bank. He couldn't make out the features of his spectator and so decided they could not see him either. He picked up snow and rubbed it into her face, already raw due to the weather. He shouted her name and, miraculously, she started to return to him. She mumbled something incoherent that may have just been an extended groan.

"Carl," he was bellowing now, "Carl who? What was his name?"

"Weather's…"

"Weathers? Carl Weathers? Are you taking the piss?"

"So cold… too cole. S'weath…" she was tailing off again.

"His *name*."

Leon was aware that he was attracting attention to them now but continued to gamble on the curtains of snow around them.

"Wallers."

"Wallace?"

"Wallers."

She was gone. He lowered her limp, unconscious body to the floor.

Leon stood up. He rubbed his face and realised how soaked he was. Freezing water dripped from his hair onto his face and ran in rivulets down the nape of his neck. He could barely feel his fingers and he was just starting to feel the chilly damp in the toes of his boots. It was funny how soft you got, he thought, once you weren't on the street. Slight discomfort seemed far worse when you weren't spending every night in abysmal conditions, fighting to stay alive and safe.

He looked down at Karen's body. The snow lay everywhere on her now. He thought about what she had been to him. He knew she had been genuine at the start and remembered how she had helped him enormously. She had shown him a kindness that no one else had. He knew that Steve would almost certainly have not taken him in if not for Karen. Sure, he and Steve had become friends but the big man had not provided the warmest of welcomes.

Then he considered what she had done to him. His life was heading for the knacker's yard anyway, but she had made sure it was ruined. She had led them to him. The kitchen, the poison, his niece and nephew. For fifty fucking quid. The amount shouldn't matter, but it did. His emotions were in turmoil as he looked down on her, and he could feel them competing against each other for his attention - hatred, sympathy, warmth. Mainly hatred if he was honest. But could he really leave her out in this? He looked at her face and, just as when he arrived, could see absolutely no trace of the old Karen, just this woman that had mercilessly betrayed him. He stood indecisively. He kicked hard against the sole of her foot; one of the few parts of her still covered by the sleeping bag. She jerked and her eyes flicked open before closing again. He started to walk away.

Despite the anger, he stopped and returned to her. He pulled the sleeping bag around her and stood up to look at his handiwork. Probably wouldn't make any difference. He reluctantly took off his coat and wrapped it round her too.

That was all she was getting from him. Part of him was still so resentful that he considered retrieving the coat. He hoofed the empty vodka bottle away in frustration, turned and walked down the Embankment before he could change his mind.

He had given her a chance, the rest was up to her.

## CHAPTER 35

Leon felt a strange sensation bubbling in his guts and realised it was nerves. He had just asked a woman to go out with him. On a date. Wow. He couldn't remember really doing that before, but he had just done it with absolutely no preparation. It had simply popped out of his mouth. One part of his brain had clearly seen an opportunity, thought it was a good idea and gone for it, all without checking with the rest of him. And now he had butterflies. Bloody ridiculous. His age, with his life. Butterflies for God's sake.

He was nursing a cup of coffee on his high stool. He and Grace kept catching each other's eye as she was serving customers and then looking away. He wondered if he had caught her on the hop and she had just said yes in a panic. No, it was fine. Anyway, he had said it was just to have a bit of a laugh, which gave the impression he didn't expect anything too serious. She probably felt the same. What was the problem? There was just something that told him he shouldn't have done it. Not just at the moment.

They had arranged to meet at the park on Thursday evening and then possibly go to the cinema or for food. It was all quite an informal arrangement except for the fact that they were to meet each other near the tennis courts at five.

Leon had become aware that the modern way was to not organise anything properly as everyone had mobile phones. This led to everyone making half-arsed plans and then ringing each other at the last minute to explain why they were not there. It seemed to him that, for all the advancement in technology, the old fashioned method of just turning up when and where you were supposed to seemed infinitely better. So they had arranged a time and place. Grace knew that he did not have a mobile, and she also knew that he didn't drink, which meant that there was no need to explain why he was not taking her to a pub, which seemed to be what every other man on earth would suggest when asking a woman out. So that was ok as she would not think he was weird. Or she *might* think he was weird, but it was ok because she had known beforehand.

Naturally, he had asked while there were no other customers, taking his customary seat just after opening time. Immediately after doing the deed he desperately wanted to leave but thought that would appear odd so he stayed for his coffee. Within a short while, there were four other people sat around sipping drinks and nibbling on muffins the size of their own heads. This made any exchanges between Grace and him even more awkward so he had decided to take his leave at that point.

He looked around the room he had been showed to and wondered how anything so run down could possibly class itself as a customer-focused business. The chairs at each of the semi-private cubicles were tiny, and the cubicles themselves packed in tightly, giving one an experience of what a battery hen has to go through on a daily basis. There was only one other occupant of the room, despite its ambitious capacity for fifteen. She looked surprisingly normal and he realised he was being judgmental. She was in her early twenties, in casual clothes but relatively well presented. He had imagined the place would be full of overweight, filthy young men with long greasy hair and an off-white complexion.

Internet cafés had begun to emerge before Leon went away but they had been shiny, futuristic affairs with the alluring promise of a revolutionary experience and a chance to be at the cutting edge of a technology-enhanced society. The peak had come quickly and then the inevitable decline as everyone and his dog could afford to have a service at home that was at the very least comparable to the cafés, often better. The advantages of surfing from your own home were numerous, including not having to spend a fortune on coffee, and being able to surf in freedom, safe in the knowledge that you could while away the hours looking at pornography without fear of someone noticing it over your shoulder. Undoubtedly this would explain the absence of the men he had half expected to see.

The establishment that Leon was currently visiting could not be classed as a café. It had no food or drink on offer for a start. It was simply a back room of a shop that sold computer equipment. He felt seedy just being there. The sort of place that anyone seeing you leave would think 'I wonder what he's up to?'

But needs must, and here he was. He really fancied a decent coffee. Fat chance.

Leon's lack of IT skills had led him to require help twice and the surly youth in the shop was clearly not happy at being dragged into the back to perform a job he seemed to think below him. He also clearly had no tolerance of people that were not as au fait with technology as he was. He explained in impatient, patronising fashion how multiple tabs worked in the browser, and how the printer worked, with an extra warning about the cost of using it. Leon wasn't especially worried about the printer – he was definitely old-school and had brought a pad of paper and a pen. The youth looked at that in a way that made Leon wonder if he'd ever seen one before.

The search was excruciating, and Leon had to keep reminding himself that he had all the time he needed, while trying to keep his mind away from Grace and on the task in hand.

Investigation into Carl Wallace was bringing up little more than a man, far too young, that had been in Australia for eight years.

He searched for accountancy firms on Alexander, of which there had been several over the years. A painstaking process of elimination found that there had been four in 1999, but finding a list of their staff would be impossible.

He started to doubt himself. He had tried variations; Karl, Walls, Wallis. What if he had completely misheard Karen? What if she had invented the name, either because she couldn't remember the real one or out of malice? What had she said first – Colin? He couldn't start again. She had been barely conscious when she gave him the name – perhaps she was already in a dream-like state and in an alternate world was calling out to an ex-boyfriend. He was searching for a needle in a haystack. In a field full of haystacks.

Several times Leon stood up to leave before wandering around the small room and sitting back down. He had been in there for the best part of three hours and for the last two and three quarter hours had been alone. There were no windows and he felt like he was losing touch with the outside world. In all his time previously stuck in a small enclosed space, he had always had a window to let him know that he was still part of a real world.

Leon's driving force though, was that this was his only chance. He started looking more closely at the four firms' names on his screen, unsure of what exactly he was looking for. He tried to be methodical and search for a Carl at each in turn. Billingham Walls Chartered Accountants brought up nothing. He had already established that the Walls in question was not Carl and had spent ages looking up any details of Walls' family with no success. The company had closed down in 2007. Miller and Lamb was next – a company still operating out of the same premises.

He typed into the search engine, eyes flicking back and forth to his notes, determined not to make a silly mistake. He typed in "Miller Lamb accountants" and a page full of links popped up. A glance told him that they were all high level, external-facing stuff – web pages intended for prospective clients, explaining that the company could change their lives in a way no one else in the world could, without actually detailing how – that type of thing.

Leon returned to the search bar and added a suffix to his previous search "Carl Wall..." And as he hit the second 'l' something amazing happened. Something that had happened billions of times the world over, before and since but which, to Leon, seemed at that moment magical. The search engine, like an impatient pensioner finishing a spouse's stuttering sentence, auto-filled the rest of the line; "Miller Lamb accountants Carl Wallers."

And there in front of him was very possibly the name of the man he wanted to find. He had to remind himself that this could still be a complete wild goose chase, but it didn't feel like it at that moment.

Then out of nowhere Leon was hit by a pessimism that had somehow stayed away so far. What was he doing? Even if he had found what he was looking for here, why could he not move on and have a life? He could go back to his seat in the diner, ask Grace if there was any chance she was free tonight rather than waiting, bollocks to whoever might be sat in there listening, take her out, see if anything happened, move on regardless. That's what a normal person would do, he was sure. Someone without a personality disorder.

But this was what had kept him going all these years. He had stared at those walls for so long. He had tried to look beyond them at the sky, the sun, the clouds. Sometimes he had managed but his focus always returned to the bars he was trying to stare past, bringing them into sharp focus, like tinkering with a camera's autofocus.

Nothing to do but think. Eventually painting had soothed the tempest in his head, but his access to that was limited and there was still too much time to let his mind click back into the channel it had forged so deeply. A channel that had become perfectly circular and led eternally back on itself. Spinning out of control, passing thought processes and ideas he had experienced thousands of times before. At times, he had been convinced that his mind would snap from the perpetual motion it had found itself in. How he tried to derail it, distract it. Just stop it. It had not worked.

In the end, he had simply accepted and tried to work with it. He addressed the things going on in his head that scared him so much. Once he did that it was much less scary. He felt that he had at least part ownership and control of them. He worked with them and formulated plans and strategies for when the opportunities presented themselves. Compulsion. Obsession. His old friends were back. And everyone would pay.

## CHAPTER 36

Leon sat watching from the McDonalds across the street. This was the third day running and he fucking hated McDonalds to begin with. Unfortunately, it was the only place with the view that he needed. A view of the front of an accountancy firm called Garrison Hall.

He had realised over the last few days what a vast and terrifying place the world wide web could be. No one was safe out there. As he worked on Carl Wallers a whole world had opened up; a world where even a comparatively private man like Wallers could be dissected, explored and potentially exploited. And Leon was just a novice – he couldn't imagine what the little shit at the internet café might be capable of finding.

Photographs emerged, some of them candid or at social occasions, and the man probably was oblivious to the fact they were out there in a public forum. So now Leon knew what he looked like. Carl was around fifty and had a shaven head that he suited even though it had clearly been a necessity rather than a style statement. He usually seemed smartly dressed and even the pictures of him in more casual attire showed a man who spent a lot of time and money on his appearance.

Leon knew from his profile page at his new firm and something called LinkedIn – the purpose of which escaped him

–that this was definitely the man who had once worked at Miller and Lamb.

The Garrison Hall site had of course allowed Leon to find out its address, which was now directly opposite him. The firm was based in Liverpool, which meant that Leon had needed to take a reasonably long bus journey for each of the last few days. An inconvenience but one that he told himself could have been far worse.

Wallers' reported appearance at various charity events had allowed Leon to establish that he had a wife named Claudia who was pretty and appeared much younger than him. They had a twelve-year-old daughter and an eight-year-old son. The daughter, Chelsea, had a Facebook account on which she had not activated any security settings. Leon, therefore, knew that the family had recently returned from a very nice holiday in Lanzarote. He knew the name of the hotel, saw pictures of what and where they had eaten, and knew that one of the prawn dishes had made Chelsea sufficiently ill that she had missed a trip in a glass-bottomed boat that she was a little upset about. Chelsea and her brother Carl (how imaginative – perhaps they couldn't think of another name beginning with 'C') were now back at school; a school for which Leon now had a name and address.

Staggering.

Leon looked at his watch. He looked down at his limp burger and cold chips and wondered how it could legally be sold to people as a meal. If someone had told him that they had never been near a cow or potato respectively he would have had absolutely no problem believing it. He couldn't take any more of this; he was going to have to act today.

On both previous days, Wallers had left the front of the building between one and one thirty. On both occasions he had emerged while talking into a hands-free headpiece presumably connected to his phone. On both occasions, he continued to talk until he had disappeared out of sight. Leon had been taken aback the first day. He knew who he was looking for but it had been a big moment to see him in the flesh. But Leon knew that this was still not definitely the right man. He was going on the word of Karen who'd hardly been a reliable witness. Not for the first time, he pushed her quickly from his mind.

On both occasions, Carl had taken over an hour to return. Leon supposed this was one of many perks afforded to people once they got into senior positions. On Tuesday, he had walked in a different direction to Monday.

And now there he was again, out on the pavement in front of his building, striding purposefully away. Leon did not rush to pursue him. That wasn't his plan. He wanted to have some control over the situation and that did not involve following Carl into a situation he could not predict.

The reception area was bright and plush. Colourful walls and modern soft furnishings made it obvious that this was a firm aiming to attract the young wealthy rather than the old wealthy. The receptionist was also young, busty and attractive in a way that made one want to submit a freedom of information request to see the selection process.

Having signed in at the ground floor under a false name, Leon had run up the three floors rather than take the lift. He trotted across to the desk and waited a moment for the receptionist to notice him. Leon was not badly dressed but the receptionist seemed to have an inbuilt radar that let her know this was not a person of significant interest to her or the company. As a result, she took her time with something on the computer before turning to smile at him.

"Can I help you, sir?"

"I'm after Carl. I've not missed him have I?" asked Leon, emphasising his breathlessness.

"Can I ask what it is about?"

"Is he in?"

"I'm afraid…"

"I got held up. Rushed here as fast as I could. I'm Jason. Did he mention I was coming? Was supposed to meet him here so we could go out."

"No, no he didn't. I can make you an appointment, or you're free to wait in reception until Mr Wallers is available. But I can't tell you when that will be as he has gone out."

"Can't you ring him?"

"I'm sorry, no. I don't disturb Mr Wallers while he is out of the office unless it is…"

Leon wasn't listening. He was inwardly sighing with relief that he had got the response he wanted.

"If you are a friend of Mr Wallers then I'm sure you will have his number. I'm sure that if you rang him from your own phone, Mr…"

"Cook. I can't. That's part of the reason I was late. I had to take my phone in to be repaired. Oh bollocks."

The receptionist looked at him sternly. Leon apologised and then looked around, wondering why it should matter if he swore in an empty room.

"Can you just look in his diary then? I don't know where we were going, he just said to meet here."

"I'm sorry but I'm sure you understand."

"Well just look and see if it mentions me then. At least then you'll know I'm legit," he tried to give a winning smile but he was feeling stressed by the whole situation and he was genuinely a little out of puff from climbing the stairs. He ended up looking like he was trying to keep a fart in.

"It's not that I don't think you're… look, hang on," she said, clearly now looking for the quickest route to getting Leon out of there.

The receptionist started tapping on the keyboard, her fingers moving across the keys and back and forth to the mouse with astonishing speed. She muttered something to herself, which sounded like she had found what she was looking for.

"So am I on? Jason Cook," Leon leaned over the counter as far as he could.

"Mr Cook," she snapped, "I'll have to ask you to move back." She tilted the screen away from him.

"Yeah, sure. Sorry. Just I'm a bit anxious to see him. Seemed important when he rang. Anything you could do to help would be great, honestly."

The receptionist was completely unaffected by his helpless act.

"So am I on there?"

"No."

"Bollocks. Sorry. Where is he then?"

She just raised an eyebrow. She didn't even need to answer that one. Leon held up a hand, thanked her and walked away. What a waste of time. He rounded a corner and headed in the direction of the lift. There was no way he was taking the stairs again. As he bounced silently across the grass-green thick carpet, he passed the gents toilets and a fire alarm on the wall next to it.

Leon checked the toilets were empty and came back out. Without thinking any further he jabbed his left elbow into the small red box, shattering the glass. He realised immediately that he had been a little over enthusiastic as a jolt of pain bounced through his arm. He was immediately distracted from that as the sirens wailed into action. He disappeared back into the toilets, jumped into one of the two cubicles and sat on the cistern, feet on the seat and door ajar.

He soon heard the commotion of a small crowd of people jostling towards the staircase, one voice was trying to sound authoritative and give helpful instructions while the others betrayed a mixture of annoyance, excitement, and slight concern. The main door to the gents crashed open.

"Anyone in here?" called a male voice.

Leon stayed silent as someone had a quick look, saw nothing and then left, the door closing behind him.

A few minutes later, Leon slipped out and headed to the receptionist's desk, praying that she would not have had the time or inclination to lock her PC. Fortunately, a wiggle of the mouse showed that she hadn't as the screen came back to life. A package called Outlook was on the screen and appeared to be showing someone's diary. Unfortunately, Leon could not ascertain whether or not it was Carl's. He scanned it for clues. It was full of hour or two hour blocks of activities and names that were presumably client names and meetings. He looked through the lunchtime activity. There were a couple of lunch appointments in previous days but this person was an early diner and the times did not correspond with what he knew of Carl's recent movements. He looked around to see how he could find the correct calendar. He didn't have a clue. The alarm stopped. Shit. That meant they would shortly be on their way back in. he didn't have long.

He tried to slow himself down and be more methodical. The answer had to be somewhere in front of him but time was slipping away. He was sure he heard movement out on the staircase. There it was. On the left hand side of the screen were a list of a dozen names. One of them was Carl Wallers. He clicked on it and another calendar appeared. Unfortunately, it appeared as well as the original and presented a compressed mess. He got rid of the other diary and looked to find out where Carl was. A small line showed the current spot in the week and corresponded to a slot named "Market". Bloody useless.

Leon had a look for the next two days and heard a rumbling from the direction of the lift. How come their fire procedures were so bloody slick? He had never known anything like it. He got rid of Carl's calendar and sprinted towards the lift that was now definitely on its way back up. He heard a ping and the lift doors began to open right in front of him. He just had time to dive to his left and back into the toilets.

He had what he wanted. It meant another trip to Liverpool the next day but at least he didn't have to go to McDonalds. It was perfect. A minimal amount of research would find out the exact establishment, and it would be ideal for a one-to-one chat. Carl wouldn't even have his mobile phone.

## CHAPTER 37

He had over four hours before he was due to meet Grace, which was plenty, even considering the unreliable nature of the bus route home. He looked down at his feet and a bead of sweat ran down the side of his chin and plopped onto the boards between his bare legs. His hair was hot against the skin of his forehead and ears and he felt more perspiration beginning to build. He wondered if he should get out of the steam room until he needed to be in there. He could be sat in there for an age waiting and at the rate he was going he would be fit to pass out and look like a prune by that point.

He made his way out and wandered over to the plunge pool. He took a scoop from the ice bucket next to it and dumped into the water. Looking at it, he wondered if people ever had heart attacks from moving between such extreme temperatures. He'd never heard of it happening and presumably the Scandinavians had been doing this for generations without worrying about such nonsense. They probably would not have even bothered with the shorts that were currently sticking to his legs.

He looked around and was pleased to see the place was almost empty. Several people were using the swimming pool but he had noticed that admission for that did not include access to the spa facilities. He had seen no one else in the steam room and only a pair of men in the ornate arches of the steamy baths that had soon left. He supposed that working people could generally not afford the time, and out of work people could not afford the money, to be in a place like this on a weekday lunchtime.

Without further ado, he jumped straight in. As his head emerged he eventually regained the ability to breathe and got out. What a strange exercise, he thought, and then headed back through the baths to the steam room to get another sweat on.

This time, he did not have to wait long. He climbed up to the top level of the slatted, tiered wooden benches. It was considerably hotter up there but the gathering steam made him difficult to see. He had started to worry about the prospect of Carl not being alone for this particular part of his extravagant weekly schedule.

He heard the glass door being opened and detected someone shuffling in. Leon could only see the top of the shiny head as the man sat down. The newcomer lifted his legs onto the bench, rotated sideways and lay down with a groan. Leon could see that he was definitely looking at Carl Wallers. A small crescent-shaped birthmark curved downwards from the outside corner of his right eye. Leon recognised it from the photographs he had seen. Carl eventually sat back up and leaned forward, head bowed.

Leon coughed deliberately and Carl jumped.

"Jesus Christ. Didn't see you up there. Nearly shat myself."

Leon froze. The voice. It was well spoken with a trace of an indistinguishable accent. Although it had deepened over the passing years it remained a touch higher in tone than one might expect from him, but its main characteristic was a rasping undertone, as though he would shortly clear his throat. It was him. Leon had conversed with that voice. He had argued with it, despaired of it and, yes, been afraid of it. It had contributed to his unravelling. It had always remained a bodiless voice in Leon's imagination. It had been attached to several imaginary people over time but had always ended up being a separate entity; simply a tantalising ghost. And now it had identified its owner as Carl Wallers of Garrison Hall Chartered Accountants.

Leon stayed where he was. Now that Carl knew he was there he would be able to see a lower torso and pair of legs but little else. Carl chuckled slightly, trying to emphasise that he was over his small fright and it had been insignificant.

"What are you hiding up there for anyway?"

"I like it up here."

Carl shrugged and lay back down on the bench.

"I know you," said Leon.

The bald man tried to ignore him.

"Yeah, I know you," Leon repeated.

Carl sighed and sat up again.

"I couldn't tell you because I can't see you, can I?" he said sharply. He clearly wanted to be left alone now.

"Miller and Lamb. You're an accountant."

Carl suddenly took notice.

"Bloody hell. You're going back a bit."

He looked up, waiting for Leon to move down out of the steam. He didn't.

"I hope you're not expecting me to recognise you by your feet."

Still no movement from Leon.

"You came to see me in 1999."

"I came to see you? That's not how it works. You must have come to the office. Anyway, no matter. Great to see you." Carl was bored now and trying to shut down the conversation. "Sorry that I don't remember you."

"No problem. It was very dark."

Carl had heard enough from the weirdo he was sharing the steam room with. He stood and headed for the glass door. Leon needed to catch his attention. He was also aware that he needed to start things moving a little quicker. The heat was becoming quite unbearable.

"Sit down Carl."

Carl stopped dead in his tracks. He moved as though to approach Leon but then stayed where he was.

"You've got a good memory for names."

"I never knew your name then."

"You're sounding like a fucking madman. Do you actually want anything?" he asked, anger changing his voice.

"You came to my house. My kitchen. It wasn't a very nice kitchen. We sat in the dark and we had a chat. You gave me some photographs and a bottle."

Carl had been staring up, trying in vain to see a face to go with the legs. He didn't move but his face changed enough to betray him. Leon felt unadulterated pleasure as he watched Carl's expression move from irritation to confusion, and then finally a flash of horror. He quickly recomposed himself.

"I don't know what's going on but you're babbling like an idiot. I'm going," he said as he got as far as putting his hand on the wooden handle."

"Sit down Carl," growled Leon, threateningly, "and listen to what I have to say. If you don't I promise you'll regret it."

Carl sat back down.

"You've made some sort of mistake. I don't know what you're talking about but I'm not whoever you think I am. I never met you in a *dark kitchen* and gave you a *photograph*," Carl emphasised the words to try and make it sound like an even more ridiculous accusation.

"Shut up. Listen. Listen but don't react. You don't want to see what I've got up here."

Carl looked as helpless as he did angry.

"Not nice is it? Firstly, don't tell anyone about us meeting. Not Claudia when she gets in from pilates. Not Chelsea and little Carl when they get home from St Cuthberts in Hallwell."

"At this, Carl moved up and down like a coiled spring. Even in the semi-dark Leon could see his knuckles whiten as he gripped the bench."

"I'll fucking kill you."

"It won't make any difference," said Leon calmly, "I'd be unlikely to expose myself like this if I was working on my own, wouldn't I?"

"What do you want?"

"I want you to tell me who sent you. I want you to tell me who ruined my life."

"You come in here, threaten my family and ask for help? Are you out of your fucking mind?" Carl was shouting now. "My *family?*"

"As I said, not nice, is it?" Leon maintained the calm approach.

There was a long pause while Carl gathered his thoughts. There was no way Leon was going to break the silence. He wanted Carl's thought process to reach a conclusion. Sweat was, however, now pouring down Leon's face, stinging his eyes. His bare flesh felt like the hot wood was slowly roasting it and his breath was becoming increasingly laboured.

When Carl finally spoke it was little more than a whisper, "Why would I tell you anything?"

"Because if you don't I'll unravel all of this. I'll name you. I'll name you as accessory to attempted murder. That sort of thing sticks even if it's not true. Imagine trying to disprove it if it *is*. Only you know what else will come out at that point. What else you did. If you were prepared to get involved in something like that I would bet there are a hundred other things you wish you'd never done. Maybe you're still doing them, how would I know? How is Carl junior going to feel when he finds out who his old man really is. Prison won't be easy for a man used to the finer things in life. And that's just while you're in there. How are you going to cope when you finally get out, divorced, limited access to your kids."

Leon had prepared this little speech in order to make it as impactful as he could, and it seemed to be working. Carl was crumbling.

"I'd bring you down with me. What about that?"

"You can't. I've served my time. I've got nothing to live for anyway, not like you." Leon thought about Grace and quickly dismissed her image.

"You don't have anyone else with you."

"Feel free to risk it, but I have warned you." He knew Carl was broken. "Give me his name."

"I don't know it."

"Give me his name."

"Why would he tell me? I used to get the money from someone else."

"You're not naïve Carl. You're a clever man. Not as clever as you think you are, but you're too clever to do anything that dangerous without the leverage of knowing who you're doing it for. Tell me his name... You know who he is, and I would bet he doesn't know that you know. Think about your kids."

Carl did think about them, for a long time.

Leon did not know how much longer he could stand this. He had promised himself that he would not show Carl his face but he felt light headed. Leon's other fear at this stage, due to the length of time that had passed, was that sooner or later someone else would join them in the steam room. Quiet as the spa was the room could not remain unused. Leon leaned forwards in an attempt to lower his head. He felt as though he were breathing through a hot, wet towel. He grabbed the edge of the bench to stop himself slipping forwards and then had to pull himself backwards to lean against the wall, which felt like an oven.

"Not here."

"Hmm?"

"I'm not talking here. I want some time to think about it."

"What's to think about? What about your kids' safety?"

"You'll get what you want. I'll see you at eleven p.m. in the car park behind the bowling alley. It's over at the Collins retail park."

"Oh, and try taking some responsibility. You were responsible for your own actions."

With that, he was gone.

Leon descended, almost tumbled, down the benches and managed to wait about another minute before swinging the door open, gasping at the air. He was gambling on the fact that Carl had immediately left the spa. As he approached the plunge pool he glanced around and saw no sign of a bald head, just a couple heading for the Jacuzzi.

Not even stopping to add ice, he jumped into the already freezing water and felt as though he was having the heart attack he had earlier wondered about.

## CHAPTER 38

So he had missed his date. *This* was why people had mobile phones. The thought of it made him feel quite sick. An image of the lovely Grace sitting at the edge of the tennis courts as arranged. What thoughts must have gone through her mind about him as she waited, doubt turning to realisation and then resentment? Would she hate him now? In his imagination she certainly did. She would build up ill feelings towards him that could never be fully undone. She would decide not to even speak to him again. Leon felt a desperation to return home and try to find her, although he knew that after the diner closed he had no way of contacting her.

He was aware that if he were to develop a relationship then there would come a tipping point where he would have to admit to his past. This put a lot of pressure on the early stages. He would have to make such an impression early on that it outweighed the bombshell he would eventually drop. Perhaps this was another reason he should not try to pursue it.

There was also the slight problem that the buses had now finished for the evening so he was stuck in Liverpool overnight now. He could not afford the luxury of a hotel room, which effectively left him without anywhere to sleep. It didn't worry him too much. It would be just like old times, he thought wryly.

He realised, however, that he needed to stop worrying about that as there was a far more immediate and threatening issue to address. He had bought a paperback and sat in the bar of the bowling alley for an hour until eight o'clock, sipping soft drinks with way too much cordial in them, on an uncomfortable chair with an incredibly sticky table. It wasn't so much the hideousness of the place that had led him to leave as the possibly paranoid thought that Carl might guess he was in there. He knew that he would have had to leave at some point anyway as he had discovered it shut at ten p.m. during the week,

So he had left the unread book and moved to the equally horrendous family themed pub across the other side of one of the roads that found its way into the heart of the retail park. The inside of the pub was a soulless vacuum. Colourful menus and artificially cheerful staff were an echo of the previous hours when the place had been full of families so devoid of imagination that they thought this place would be a good option. It was even worse than sitting in the bowling alley – the pub was virtually empty whilst the alley had at least had customers.

At quarter to eleven Leon had been glad to see the back of it, even if the nerves were cranking up to a worrying level.

He stood at the edge of the car park, which had been submerged in darkness since the bowling alley closed and its staff left. He pulled the hood tightly around his head. The retail park had at least come in handy for one thing when he had purchased the cheap coat. It was slightly too large for him which meant that it could easily slip over his existing jacket and provide cover for his face. He paced around with his hands in his pockets, trying to burn off nervous energy as well as keep warm. The quiet was broken by the sound of a car approaching. Leon saw a pair of lights approaching in the distance.

By the time the car swung into the car park and the engine was switched off, Leon had stepped back into a concealed doorway. He wanted to size up the situation properly before stepping into it. The black car reflected the streetlights from the nearby road, which partially lit up the gloom. The car looked sporty and expensive, but Leon did really not know cars and could not see the maker's badge.

Carl stepped out and closed the door carefully behind him, looking around. He wore a thick winter coat and Leon wondered if he might be concealing some sort of weapon. Leon scanned the surrounding area for more vehicles or people and saw no sign that Carl had brought an acquaintance or the police. Unless someone was lying down there was no one in the black car either. Leon walked forwards as quietly as possible. Carl saw him emerging from the shadow of the building and seemed to get a fright. He certainly seemed edgy which made Leon's confidence swell a touch.

"Take your hood down," Carl grunted. Leon took another step towards him. "Take it off or I leave. I want to see you."

"If you leave now then I'll go through with everything we talked about."

"I don't believe you. You won't gain anything by doing that."

Leon shrugged. "Believe me, at this stage just fucking you up is a good enough reason."

Carl mulled this over. "The hood. Now."

Leon paused before lowering his hood. He felt like he had somehow lost an advantage, but it was a small enough sacrifice to help him achieve what he needed. Carl looked him over without a hint of recognition.

"Would it jog the memory if I let you smack me about a bit by candle light?" Leon asked, his voice thick with resentment.

Carl's hands were shifting in the large pockets of his overcoat. Leon was convinced that he saw something. A knife, perhaps.

"Why me?" asked Leon.

"I don't know."

Leon shook his head to show his impatience. He dearly wished now that he had brought a weapon of his own. Why hadn't he thought to do that? Idiot.

"OK, how did you find me?"

"Some homeless skank you were shacked up with."

"So you didn't know anything about me before that?"

"No."

"Did your boss?"

"Of course," Carl shrugged.

"And who is *he*? Tell me his name."

"No."

"Carl, we both know why we're here. Don't start pissing about."

"I won't tell you his name."

It was dark in the car park, but Leon knew fear when he saw it. The man in front of him was suddenly scared of something or someone. Leon had to assume it was the man who had charged him with visiting Leon's kitchen seventeen years ago.

"Then we are wasting our time."

"I said I won't give you his *name*."

There was a pause while Leon weighed things up.

"I am assuming we still have a deal?" asked Carl.

"Depends how far we get. Obviously, I've got questions."

"Come and sit in the car."

Leon did not even respond. There was no way that was going to happen.

"How do you know him?" Leon thought this was as good a starting point as any.

"We were introduced. Twenty years ago I had a reputation. I was known as being very professional, and it wasn't just for my accountancy skills. You need to understand this was a long time ago. Before I met my wife. I'm different now. It was a lifetime ago."

"Carry on."

"He gave me a job to do. Nothing major, but he was pleased with my work, so he gave me more. It was never anything too bad. Or at least I told myself it wasn't."

"You gave me poison to kill a man."

"That was the point when I realised things had gone too far. Well, it was the fire to be honest, although I didn't have a lot to do with that, and I didn't know I was leaving that stuff for you. I tried to get out of it. I'm sure some of the things I'd done before had led to bad things happening, but I never really had them on my conscience. But he wasn't daft. He knew that job – you - would maybe be too much for me, but I was stupid. I let myself get into the position where he owed me money for previous jobs. Then yours came up. I really needed my money and I knew he would withhold it. It's not really the sort of deal where you can take your boss to court for not paying salaries. So I did it and promised myself that was me finished. Of course, the irony was that by doing that I had proved to him that I was capable of a lot more than I had been doing."

Carl seemed lost in painful memories. Leon made the effort not to let it affect him. He could not afford to have the smallest amount of sympathy. He had to forget that Carl was even a human being and view him as a thing. A thing that needed to be used and dealt with.

"So things escalated after that?"

Carl nodded. "Did some stuff I wish I could take back. I can't explain it. He gets this hold over you. You feel helpless and scared. I've not had a feeling like it since, until you threatened my kids," Carl looked up at Leon. Anger suddenly cast a shadow across his face as he remembered why he was having to help this ghost from his past.

"I'm sure you know this is just business. You must remember how it works," Leon wondered for a moment if he had overdone it. He needed to keep his own feelings in check. But Carl seemed to slump again.

"I made my escape not that long after we… met," he said. "He threatened me with a lot of stuff but we reached a compromise. I won't tell you anything about that because to be honest, it's got fuck all to do with you."

Leon was trying to read Carl's state of mind but it was almost impossible. He seemed to be fluidly moving from angry, tense, provocative, resentful, to submissive, resigned and sorrowful. Leon hoped that as they moved on Carl would start to feel a cathartic effect of unburdening himself. But he was clearly a hard man to get under the surface of. Or at least he had been once.

He was growing increasingly confident that this was not a trap. If Carl had a weapon or an accomplice he would have revealed it by now and overpowered Leon. There was no need for the conversation to have got this far if that was the plan. On the other hand, Leon did still have concerns that Carl was trying to get him off guard, perhaps convince him to sit in the car where someone was crouched down behind the passenger seat, waiting to help dump Leon's body in the car boot. That was what would have happened in the movies.

"So what do you know about him?"

"I have never met him and I swear that's the truth," began Carl.

Leon's heart sank. Was he really going to leave this situation empty handed? Why had Carl even brought him here? He could have delivered that news in the steam room. Perhaps he really was about to get ambushed. Leon started to hope they would kill him quickly before getting rid of that thought.

"He doesn't work like that. Why would he? You put layers in. It creates safety, makes you untouchable. And people are more scared of you if all they know is myth and rumour. It almost creates an air of legend."

"You know, though."

"Like you said today, I'm not stupid. I got in too deep in the end but I can look after myself enough to get my way out. The fact I'm still around means I know what I'm doing. I know about him."

Leon stood in the car park for the next twenty minutes just listening. He did not notice the cold for a moment. Occasionally he would stamp his feet or stretch a leg up behind him but he did not even realise he was doing it, so intently was he concentrating on Carl. If the bald man had, in fact, brought an accomplice he could have walked up behind Leon banging a drum without being noticed.

Carl provided an almost uninterrupted monologue, comprised of first-hand knowledge, his own research and a little folklore thrown in. Carl insisted on referring to his former taskmaster as Alan. He insisted that he would reveal neither 'Alan's' real name nor the name of his companies. Leon listened as the tale of the man behind his demise unfolded.

Alan's story was of a local lad turned good. Or evil, depending on one's personal experience. He had grown up with various foster families in the area, many giving up on him as they discovered his angelic exterior masked a difficult and manipulative child who bullied and made life miserable for his carers' other foster children and biological offspring.

Thrown out of Technical College within months, young Alan had soon made a name for himself wheeling and dealing in pub car parks and on the edge of markets, flogging unwanted and often stolen goods. He became a colourful part of the city's street life and got away with his cocky behaviour because the local villains enjoyed his cheeky but charming demeanour. But already stories started to emerge that the nineteen-year-old Alan had sinister methods of dealing with his competitors.

Alan's dealings became more profitable and legitimate, outwardly at least, over the years. He started by buying a small independent petrol station which was losing money and in a terrible state if disrepair. Within two years it was a thriving business, which he sold at a sizeable profit. This he used to set himself up again until, some time in the late 80s he had set up a business consultancy firm.

Many questioned the wisdom of this. Alan's experience, after all, was entirely with small independent business. The industry of business consultancy was not huge at that time, but the visionary Alan had no doubts and ploughed everything he had into his new venture.

The company flourished at the same rate as Alan's profile. There was indeed a market for his product. The only existing consultancy firm in the city saw its most successful staff leaving in their droves to join him. Rats deserting a perfectly sturdy ship in order to join one they had been convinced was shinier and more exciting, even though it was still being built by a captain who had not yet taken to the seas.

He became something of a local media darling, interviewed by local papers on a monthly, sometimes weekly basis as the firm shot into the stratosphere, local businesses paying for consultants they had previously no idea that they needed. But persuaded by Alan's convincing nature and profile, everyone wanted a piece of the action. Everyone in a profitable business decided that Alan's staff could come in and help them achieve even more. Everyone in an unprofitable business was told that they could be saved if they gave Alan the last of their dwindling profits to come and rescue them. Times were good.

But Alan had a secret, and this is where Carl had needed to tread carefully and work hard to uncover things. At first, Leon wondered why Carl would reveal these details; things which he could easily and reasonably have claimed not to know about. But at times, Carl's body language and tone of voice betrayed a burning hatred of Alan. He wanted him to pay, and it seemed worth making himself more vulnerable in order for that to be achieved.

Seventeen years ago he had got married to a local girl from a successful family that owned stables and riding outlets, most of which she stood to, or had already, inherited. It was seen as a perfect match – two attractive people at the height of their powers. The romance was enhanced by Alan's status as the orphan boy come better-than-good. His new wife soon got pregnant and, by the time Leon got arrested, she was close to giving birth.

Alan's secret was safe and, as long as he could control the urges within him, he could put them in the past. The ugly secret that must never reveal itself was that Alan had a liking for boys. Vulnerable young boys. During his early business success, it was thought that he had managed to get involved with a small and select circle of like-minded businessmen. Combining their resources and intellect they had devised safe and ingenious ways of satisfying their desires.

A rumour had started to circulate about one of the men in the group that owned a chain of sportswear stores. Alan had been at a party where he heard people talking about the man's sexual preferences and he panicked. He distanced himself from the group and never associated with them again.

But it left Alan with a problem. He still had a need that seethed inside him. He had enough money to buy anything he wanted in life and it seemed illogical that there was not enough money in the world for him to safely acquire his greatest passion. He knew that in the absence of his former acquaintances he would need to go it alone.

Alan bought a small flat near to his offices sometime in the mid-eighties. This, he reasoned, would cause no suspicion as his home was now out in the leafy suburbs and he often stayed late at his work. The flat was in a quiet area. It was a little run-down for a man of his wealth but he figured he could explain that by its convenience. Some people were a little surprised by the place but he never invited visitors and no one seemed to think any more about it. It was simply Alan's bed and wardrobe for the night when he worked too late.

The first boy to come back was fifteen years old. Alan had promised to look after him, give him money. The boy was blindfolded for the last part of the journey. Alan made him clean himself up before taking what he wanted. He did give the boy some money but he left, once more blindfolded, led by the elbow, in pain, dehumanised and defiled. Mental bruises that could never heal. The boy was called James Potter.

James Potter. It was a name that had stayed with Leon for a decade and a half, hardly a day going by when it was not at least a passing thought. James Potter. The man Leon had killed.

"I don't... don't understand," Leon stammered.

"Just listen," Carl snapped back.

"How do you know all this?"

"Because I'm good. Nothing's a secret if more than one person knows about it"

Alan had been excited by his success. The key now was to manage himself sufficiently that he did not lose control. He had discovered a perfect set up. He had a venue. And he had a supply of young boys who had found themselves on the street. Kids cast out by families, kids running from previous physical, mental and sexual abuse. Damaged kids with no one to turn to. It was better than perfect.

Alan paced himself, the anticipation being almost as good as the act. No one knew how many people had been lured back to that flat with the promise of money, some hot food, and warm water. The desperate hope that they had found someone that cared about them and wanted to protect them, was too alluring to resist.

All that Carl had gathered was that one night, around six weeks after James's visit, Alan was on the prowl again. He was walking around the seedier end of town where he tended to dress very much 'down' with a baseball cap pulled tightly down on his head when he found a sleeping bag from which was protruding nothing but a shock of thick, red, rumpled hair. Beneath the hair turned out to be a pale, scared face. A face that looked like it didn't belong on the street. A face with teeth that looked too clean to be on the street. The face of another fifteen-year-old kid by the name of Tommy McCann.

Leon felt nauseous. He was starting to understand where all this was heading. Many, if not all, of the pieces were being clumsily shuffled into place.

Carl was in full flow now. After his initial reluctance, he was talking as though he and Leon were old mates sat talking over a pint. Perhaps that catharsis Leon had been hoping for was emerging.

If Tommy was to be believed he had almost died that night at the hands of Alan. Lured to the flat by promises, he was savvy enough to know that it might be lies but he simply had to take the risk. He was terrified of being right. Right he was, but his terror had been based on imagined events far less traumatic than what unfolded. After cleaning himself up Tommy had been fed and seemed to be receiving the altruistic hospitality he had been promised. But within moments, everything had turned upside down. He found himself tied to a bed upon which he received terrible beatings in between even more terrible sexual violation of his frail young body. The last thing Tommy could remember before passing out in his own blood was wishing for death.

Tommy lay tied to the bed, face down and naked, for three days after that. Alan would return now and then to give him water and try to make him eat, which he refused to. As he left each time, Alan would turn on the television for him to watch.

Most of the time Tommy could not see it through his tears. At night, he would be violated. He was still on top of the same sheets, wet with blood and tears. He knew that under the bedclothes was plastic sheeting, which he somehow found even more dreadful. In his mind, it confirmed preparation and the ability to erase Tommy's existence.

During those three days Tommy's mind broke irreparably. Whose wouldn't? Seventy two hours that lasted an eternity with no end in sight. Nothing but pain, degradation, and starvation. Literally the only hope was that death would come.

Late on the third evening Alan had untied Tommy. The boy was rather puny to start with and the chance of him being able to cause Alan any sort of physical problem now was negligible. Alan helped him into his clothes, which had been laundered along with his sleeping bag. He took several notes from his own wallet and stuffed them into Tommy's pocket and snapped the blindfold around his face.

Tommy barely had the ability to place one foot in front of another as he was led away from what he considered to be Hades' deepest corner of torture and suffering. Upon being roughly dumped on a street corner he lay for a while without removing the mask as he heard Satan's steps retreating. Eventually, he removed it and looked into a dark sky. The stars were shining but they would never again look the same to him. Nothing would.

Many years had passed. For Alan, that meant continued business success, married life, and impending fatherhood. For James Potter, it meant withdrawal, solitude and a life of crime. For Tommy McCann, it meant a descent into mental illness which peaked and troughed indeterminately.

This horrendous equilibrium was broken by chance one day when Tommy shuffled past the window of an electrical retailer. There, on a wide screen TV was a local news broadcast. A man was being interviewed. He had a big grin on his face and a glint in his eye. Tommy looked for horns and saw none. But he knew it was Satan. He opened the shop door and wandered up to another television set, turning up the volume with a remote control that was securely attached to the display. Satan had seldom used his voice during his stay in hell, but the sound coming from the television chilled his bones. The shop assistant did not even have a chance to evict him before Tommy ran screaming into the street.

Tommy ranted about the man on the TV for days and days, but no one paid any attention. Until one night at a soup kitchen, he was talking to another man in the queue. Tommy was known in the homeless community for talking a lot. Some days it made sense, others it didn't. That particular evening he was quite intelligible. As Tommy talked about being taken to a flat by Satan, he described what had been promised him compared to what had happened to him. He now knew who the man was. He had been on TV.

The man next to him was not listening to this teller of tall tales. But someone was listening. James Potter was listening three places forward in the queue.

Despite Tommy's difficulty in articulating what he had found out, James was convinced by his story and made sure that the two stayed in contact for several days. During that time, he spent his time in front of shop windows with TVs. He removed newspapers from bins and sneaked into newsagents to thumb through local papers until he was thrown out. Having now spoken at great length with his new friend, James was convinced that they had both been led to the same place, by the same man. What he was far less convinced of was that Tommy had seen him being interviewed on television.

Nevertheless, he had bought into it – after all, what else did he have to fill his days? One day Tommy and James were sat opposite the electrical store. They were sharing a sandwich. As James picked at a crust, trying to savour his lunch, he felt Tommy jump backwards and begin jabbering about the devil. Looking up, James saw him. He raced across the street just in time to see a banner displaying the man's name.

Over the next few days, armed with their newly found information, James and Tommy found out more about Satan, although James had to do most of the work. Tommy had periods of clarity but on a bad day was incapable of helping. They found out the name of his company, where it was. Their plan was not to go to the press. Their plan was far more risky, but potentially far more lucrative. Their plan was to blackmail Satan. Not on an on-going basis; that would certainly be too dangerous. They would aim for a large one-off payment and would somehow have to convince him that they would not come back for more.

The obvious difficulty at that point was getting to Satan. Visits to the business premises were predictably unsuccessful. Eventually, they discovered where he lived and simply called at his house. After all their plotting it had been ridiculously easy. Satan's wife had answered the door and informed the pair of tramps that he was not at home. They had just waited there all day for him to arrive home, accosted him as he got out of his car and told him who they were. He had denied all knowledge and threatened them, angrily when he discovered they had spoken with his wife, albeit without disclosing the purpose of their visit. Before they left he agreed to meet them that night.

The men made their demands and got agreement, although they were deflated to hear that even a man of Satan's means could not procure that kind of cash easily. Alan employed all his powers of persuasion to explain to them that he could provide them with a longer-term income by giving them work to do. They agreed to meet again in a week once all parties had time to consider things. Although the two men agreed to this week-long break they felt that their advantage of surprise had slipped a little.

Alan was already looking to the streets for his answer – the place he felt he could find someone desperate enough – when he was presented with a possible answer. Alan was told about a man with what was described as a potential personality disorder and an all-consuming obsession with finding someone that was most likely either homeless or dead. He was perfect. The irony was that, although he had people out looking for his puppet, he was presented with this man's story at a work gathering.

"You know the stupidest thing?" Carl asked, rhetorically. "I know that he never thought it would really work. It was opportunistic at best. I think really, he just set it away while he made a better plan B. I never thought you'd be unhinged enough to do any of it either. When you look at it, why would you? Why *did* you?"

The last question was emphatically non-rhetorical Leon looked at the floor and squeezed his eyes shut. 'Normal' people wouldn't have done any of it.

"Of course, then you lit a match. Literally," continued Carl, "and you were his bitch from that moment on. So was I. I suppose both of us have had to live with how our lives turned out after that."

"Get on with the story," Leon growled. He did not want Carl eliciting any empathy from him.

So Carl continued.

Within a short space of time, James had started working for Alan and was dead, leaving the mentally inept Tommy in over his head. He scuttled into hiding, afraid that he would meet the same fate as James. He had nowhere to go. If he now went to the police he did not even have James to corroborate his story. It would be the solitary word of an unhinged, penniless tramp, with no proof, against that of a successful pillar of the community with access to any legal help he required. His only slight hope was that others may break their silence upon hearing his story. Tommy did not even know if there were any more victims and so went into hiding in order to save his own life. And even that would not have worked if Leon had not switched bottles.

Carl looked spent.

"Please just keep me out of this now. I have told you everything I know. I am a good man now. I'm not the same person."

"Did you put him onto me in the first place? When I still had a life? A home?" asked Leon.

Carl shook his head. Leon believed him completely after he had just poured out his story.

"Who did?"

"Don't know," Carl whispered. He was done.

He wandered round to the driver's door of the car and opened it.

"Wait. Does he know that you know any of this?"

Again, Carl shook his head and got in.

"I'm fucked here. I'm asking you. For my family."

With that, he shut the door, started the engine, and began to pull forwards. Leon rapped on the window. The car stopped. He saw Carl pause and then reluctantly open the window.

"One last thing," Leon said, "Where's Tommy?"

"I don't know."

"Carl. I've just been watching you talk for twenty minutes. I know when you're lying. Don't forget I'm still in charge."

"He's still there. I sometimes make business trips back there and I've seen him once or twice. He doesn't know me of course.

You'll never find him. Now leave me alone. I expect to never hear from you again.

## CHAPTER 39

He was outside the diner before it opened at 7.30. Matt, the cook, had opened up and let him in ten minutes early as long as he 'didn't expect anything to eat yet.'

Shortly after that Carly, the waitress had breezed in, seen Leon, and stomped past him to hang up her coat without a word. Great, Grace had told everyone that he stood her up and now everyone hated him. It didn't bother him too much if Carly never spoke to him, and Matt was so grumpy that Leon had no way of telling if he knew or not, but he could do without Grace having her ear bent by folks that disliked him. He promised himself to make an effort with Carly, although now didn't seem the time. As they passed seven thirty there were no early-bird customers, but there was also no Grace. Another ten minutes after that and Leon started to wonder if she might even be having a day off. There was no way he was going to ask Carly. She had already made her feelings known by rudely shoving a coffee in front of him, guessing that it was what he wanted, rather than interact with him. Great.

An elderly man that Leon had seen several times before, tied his dog up outside the diner, patted it on the head and sat at his usual seat at a table near the counter.

Finally, Grace arrived, jogging across the threshold and a little out of breath. She was looking at her watch as she came in, trying to establish exactly how many minutes late she was. As she looked up she caught sight of Leon and looked a little taken aback.

"Harry," she nodded to the elderly man at the table. The man responded by waving the crumpled newspaper that he had just extracted from his jacket pocket.

"Leon," she said, much more quietly as she walked past.

"Hi, Grace. I'm sorry. Look, can we…"

"Sorry, Leon. I'm late and I'm a bit busy here."

Leon looked at old Harry trying to flatten out his paper, and then to the door where precisely no people were trying to get in. Grace noticed his thought process.

"I'm at work," she said and disappeared through to the back room to clock in, or whatever it was they all did back there. He looked across to Carly who was glaring at him, arms folded. He wondered how Carly even knew. It had only been last night, and he always got the sense that Grace was not actually all that keen on her, certainly not enough to contact her outside of work hours as a shoulder to cry on.

Leon stayed for some time. He had a meeting at the canal boat yard later but not for a few hours. He was, however, not about to miss his second important date in the space of 24 hours. He guessed it was some sort of informal interview but it had been sold to him as a chat. It seemed unlikely that a business owner would waste half an hour of his valuable time having a chat unless he was gaining something from it. He wondered if Jenny was pulling in some sort of a favour to help him out. He was definitely warming to her but it seemed unlikely she would do that. Perhaps he had charmed her. That also seemed unlikely. He had never been charming and that was before spending sixteen years exclusively in the company of men.

Customers came and went. Leon nursed one coffee until it was cold, then another. Eventually, he saw an opportunity. He was the only customer at the counter and Carly was taking an order from the only occupied table. Grace had reacted to that situation by peering through the hatch for a meal that was clearly not being prepared.

"Grace."

"I've told you, Leon. This is where I work. I can't be bringing my…"

"Please. One minute. I'm really sorry. I couldn't get back. And you know I haven't got a phone. I should have. I felt terrible. I feel terrible, but I was…"

"Where were you that was so important that I ended up standing by the courts like a prick for half an hour? It was nearly dark when I left."

"I'm really sorry. Honestly."

"So?"

"Oh. I was in Liverpool."

There was a pause. She clearly wanted a better excuse than that. Why hadn't he thought of an excuse?

"I can't really say."

Grace turned away from him and moved back in the direction of the hatch.

"Grace."

"I don't need this Leon. I don't want any more drama. I've had enough of that."

"Can we try again?"

"Sorry."

"Please. I tell you what. Will you just give me your phone number? I'll leave you alone for a few days and then I'll ring you to see if you want to meet up for a coffee."

"You think I want to go for coffee after being in here all day?"

"Well, anywhere. As long as it's with me," he smiled. He hoped it looked charming but then had to remind himself again of the likeliness of that.

She shook her head. Whether it was a no or incredulity at his attempt to win her over, he was not sure.

"Just give me your number please," he pleaded.

"You don't have a phone, remember."

"If you give me your number I'll go and buy one now. Then I'll put your number in it. As long as someone in the shop shows me how to do it."

She suppressed a smile. Bloody hell, maybe he did have some charm after all. She scribbled it down on a paper napkin, balled it up and threw it towards him. Leon noticed Carly looking across disapprovingly.

"I'll think about it," said Grace, "but if you ever do anything like that again I'll shove your new mobile phone up your arse. Now sod off, you've been hogging that chair."

Leon flattened out the napkin, jumped down and left. He decided against saying anything in case it turned out to be the wrong thing.

Being throw out of an establishment had never felt so good.

## CHAPTER 40

Leon sat in the foyer, as instructed by the woman on reception. She was a fierce looking lady in her forties and her name badge told him that she was called Margaret. An excellent gatekeeper, thought Leon, with her no-nonsense, almost challenging approach. Leon had sat down immediately, as told. He took off his backpack and placed it beside him.

The website had stated that people were welcome to approach them for appointments to discuss employment opportunities and Leon had done just that. He had spent hours online investigating exactly what this company did and, to be honest, he still was not clear. The site was littered with high-level management speak and even the 'What we offer' page had just been a jumble of vague promises about portfolio enhancement, value creation, and solution focus.

At that point he realised a couple of things; he was going to have to learn to talk like that, and he was going to need an 'angle' to differentiate himself.

The angle was relatively straightforward. He could pitch himself as a change specialist in the world of higher education. Granted, it had been sixteen years since he had actually been involved in higher education, but he knew the basics, clued himself up on any changes to government policy, and hoped that the sector still developed at a snail's pace so would not be that different.

The language of consultancy was a bit more of a challenge. Hours of reading website blurb and watching promotional and instructive video clips had eventually made him realise that they were actually just talking shit. There seemed to be a requirement to use some current buzzwords such as narrative, journey, and emotional intelligence. Everything else could be covered using a list of recognised and unnecessary vocabulary or covered by resorting to cliché. In fact, it seemed to be the only line of work that actually encouraged banality, claiming it as insight. People were pushing envelopes, squaring circles and developing angles all over the shop.

He really didn't think he could do it, though. He simply wasn't convincing at it, despite practicing incessantly in front of the mirror. Still, he had to try. He looked at his watch, which showed him that it was ten past nine and, therefore, ten minutes after his appointment time. He glanced up and caught the receptionists' eye.

"Mr Williams will be with you shortly," she snapped, "he's rather busy with something at the moment."

Whatever that 'something' was, Margaret clearly believed it to be more important than Leon. He marvelled at the way she seemed to have reprimanded him without him actually having done anything wrong. Quite a skill.

The reception area of 'Golden Wings' agency was extremely quiet. Leon had been led to believe this was a vibrant, exciting hub of activity (via the website) and had half expected to see dozens of other wannabe consultants sat between 50 inch display monitors while employees zoomed around on scooters and descended floors by fireman poles.

Eventually, a man entered from the external door. He was around thirty and wore an expensive looking suit and tie, carried a retro sports bag and topped off his look with a pair of classic trainers. Leon thought it a stroke of genius on behalf of the sportswear companies that they had started remaking trainers they used to make twenty years ago and charging ten times the price. And people queued up to buy them. Leon looked at his own, more conventional shoes and his rather cheap back-pack on the seat next to him. Perhaps he should have made more of an effort.

Margaret nodded to the man as he entered, without raising a smile. He seemed to point at her and then rap a ringed finger on the side of the desk as he passed. Leon didn't know what he had just witnessed but it seemed to be some form of greeting.

Margaret glanced at Leon and then went back to whatever it was she was doing. Leon leaned forwards to watch the man. He walked into an office at the opening to a corridor and let the door swing closed. On it was a name plaque that read 'Oscar Williams'. Margaret noticed Leon looking and as he glanced towards her she was already wearing an expression that simply dared him to object. Leon sat back in his seat and prepared himself for a longer wait while Mr Williams got himself settled.

Leon looked at his watch and saw that it was now twenty five past nine. He considered this tardiness to be unacceptable but perhaps this was the way things were done. And who was he to criticise someone's timekeeping anyway? He sadly thought about Grace waiting for him at the park, alone with her anger. At least Mr Williams had actually turned up. He had just left her there without a word. He should have abandoned his plans in Liverpool. He would have had another chance and, after all, was there really such a sense of urgency that he had to stand her up like that?

Just as he was sinking further into introspection the main door opened again and another man entered. This man was considerably older than the first. In fact, Leon knew exactly how old he was. He was 59. He lived with his second wife. His first, with whom he had two teenage children, had divorced him. There had been much gossip about him having affairs, but the exact reason for the separation was not publicly known. With his second wife, now in her early thirties, he had a three-year-old son. The man that he was looking at was immaculately dressed and carried a shining briefcase. His patent leather shoes could have doubled as a shaving mirror. The man that he was looking at was called Gregor Baines. The man he was looking at might well be 'Alan'. Satan to his friends.

With the information Leon had at his disposal he had ascertained that Baines largely fit the profile of the man he was searching for. The demography and family history seemed to match Carl's description. The problem was that he did not know how accurate Carl's memory was or in fact whether he was making up some or all of it. And some things did not tally at all. Perhaps Carl had even based his story on Gregor's as he had a grudge against the man. Perhaps it was pure coincidence that Leon had found someone similar, and perhaps he had then just convinced himself this was Mystery Man. He wondered if Carl himself could be Mystery Man and it surprised him that he had not considered this before.

Leon was on his feet. This was a gift he could not pass over. He thrust out a hand. Baines reluctantly took it while looking across to Margaret.

"Margaret can you put Janine down to see me at two. I just saw her on the way up."

He looked back to Leon who had a moment of horror. He was now entering an area of complete improvisation and had not thought about whether or not Baines would recognise him. In a frantic internal dialogue, Leon told himself that it had been seventeen years and he barely recognised the old Leon himself.

Besides that, Baines may have never even seen what he looked like, so far removed did he keep himself from the 'unpleasantness'. And then, of course, this could all be a huge mistake and he might be talking to a man whose life had never impacted on his own.

"Mr Baines. Sorry to disturb you but I just wanted to say what an inspiration you have been for me. I'm a big fan, even if that sounds a bit embarrassing. I read your book and gave up my job. This is what I'm meant to do I think."

Baines' face softened. Leon knew that no matter how big and important the man, no matter how cynical or superior they believed themselves, no one was immune to a bit of flattery. Everyone likes to hear how good they are, from any source at any time.

"Well thank you…"

"Francis."

"Thank you, Francis. And good luck."

And with that brief exchange Baines headed off towards his office. Leon was panicking. He could not let this chance be wasted. Today was about playing a longer game, getting inside the company, finding out more about Baines. And here he was.

"Any tips Mr Baines?" asked Leon with a forced smile.

Baines stopped and turned to him.

"Just be yourself. If you are the sort of person we like, then you'll get your chance. We're all about giving chances to the right people."

"Values based recruitment," Leon needed to keep him talking. "I believe in that and I think that's what you are getting at in the reading I've done."

Suddenly Baines seemed interested.

"Yes. Although I don't think I have been particularly cryptic about that. It is the foundation of our recruitment method."

"Of course, sir. And I think my values match your company's."

Baines thought for a moment, "Who are you here to see?"

"Mr Williams."

Leon could have been mistaken but he thought he saw Baines' eyes roll upwards slightly.

"What time have I got board?"

"Ten," replied Margaret.

"Come with me," he said to Leon. Margaret raised her eyebrows to him. "Two minutes," he said, either to Leon or Margaret.

For all Leon's planning, he had never imagined this. To be sat in Baines' room was an enormous bonus. As they chatted his mind was working overtime on the spiel he had intended to give to Williams. He explained how Golden Wings was better than any of the agencies working in the higher education market. He explained that although his skills were transferable he felt that he could use his experience to help them into that new area. Embedded, aligned, synergised. They were all pouring out.

He talked about his experience in education and in industry, making sure that his story tallied with the work of fiction that was the curriculum vitae in his bag. The CV would fall apart under any genuine scrutiny, but he was banking on the fact that no one ever really checked them out.

And of course, he interspersed information about himself with more praise for Golden Wings and Baines in particular. He made sure that every line was delivered with as much enthusiasm as he could muster. Baines was pleasant enough and seemed to be enjoying Leon's company, littered with compliments as it was.

"Could I ask how you got started, Mr Baines?"

"Perhaps another time, Francis," he responded coolly, "not really time just now." Baines stroked his chin and looked at Leon. "Just wait here a minute. I'm just going to see if Oscar is ready to see you yet."

And with that Baines was gone. Leon had come prepared for any eventuality he could think of but this was getting better by the moment. He was at best expecting to gain entry to another office, at worst a toilet. The minute Baines left he began to fumble frantically with the zip of his backpack. He knew he had a matter of seconds and his eyes scanned the room as his fingers dipped inside the bag.

Baines re-entered the room dramatically and saw Leon sat there with his hand in his backpack. He looked at him with eyebrows raised. Leon pulled out his CV and showed it to Baines with a flourish.

"For Mr Williams," said Baines, "he will see you now."

"I can't tell you how much I appreciate this. It was really good of you." Although Leon was starting to feel a little nauseated by it, he knew that he should keep up the charm offensive for just a little longer.

He was shepherded out, wished good luck and pointed in the direction of Williams' office with a final shake of the hand.

Leon felt tension and pressure lift from his shoulders. He would simply give a repeat recital for Williams and be on his way. Despite his concerns he had clearly been convincing and Baines had liked him.

For all that, one crucial problem remained. He had found out little about Baines himself in order to ascertain whether or not he was 'Alan'. Leon's gut told him it was the right man, but on the other hand, he had seemed like a decent enough bloke.

Oscar Williams had proved himself to be utterly vacuous and was clearly a man who had talked himself into a senior position without having any discernible talent. It was clear from the start that Baines had given him instructions regarding Leon. But the interview's success or failure was the least of Leon's concerns.

Once Leon had bullshitted his way through his fake CV, Williams promised to call him soon with a decision and clearly wanted him to leave sooner rather than later. But Leon had not yet begun.

"So, Mr Baines…"

"Oh, Gregor? Yes…"

Leon could not tell how much of Williams' grin was part of his professional façade and how much was pleasure at being able to refer to his boss by his first name. Either way, Leon decided it was fucking pathetic. It was bizarre that Baines, the man who may or may not have ruined Leon's life, seemed quite likeable while Leon could have quite happily punched this bloke in the mouth.

"What's he like?"

"Personally, he's quite an inspiration, and I think you'd probably find that most people around here would say something similar. He *is* this company, to be honest. It's an impressive business but it is still essentially an extension of him." His dead eyes gave no indication as to whether or not this was a truth or an empty platitude.

"There's always something more special about people who have achieved that much when they came from nothing," agreed Leon.

Williams stood, clearly bored with the conversation now. "It was good to meet you."

Leon did not get up.

"He must have been through some rough times. Early on, I mean."

"Yeah. He certainly did," Williams seemed pleased to be able to demonstrate his knowledge of Baines as though it showed how close the two were.

"I heard he spent so much time here at one point that he bought a flat around the corner so he didn't have to go home."

Williams looked confused by the conversation's direction and Leon had to admit that he did not know what he was expecting to get out of this.

"Well, you'd need to ask him about that. That would have been in the old days before I knew him."

This was a dead end. Leon stood up, and then remembered something.

"What was it that his first wife did? Before they met. Wasn't she really successful too?"

Williams looked at him like he had two heads.

"I don't know why… I mean why do you…"

"Sorry, I also ask too many questions," Leon internally admonished himself. Why had he asked that? It sounded weird and suspicious.

Williams was now doing everything short of lay a hand on him in order to get him to the door. "If you are really that interested in finding out more you can read his story on line."

"Really?" Leon was shocked.

"Yeah. Although I'm fairly sure his living arrangements and wife's business interests aren't covered," Williams smiled, "Lots of people read it. I'm surprised you've not done that as preparation, to be honest. Most people can quote it by the time they get here. Anyhow, I really must…"

"I thought I'd read every bit of your website. How did I miss that?"

"Oh, it's not on our site. Gregor also runs a charitable organisation that helps young, up and coming entrepreneurs. He does a phenomenal amount of charity work of course, but that one's his baby. Silver Wings." Thomas proudly delivered this as though the variation on its parent company's name was the height of wit.

"Yes, I see," Leon disappointed Williams by not seeming to find the name extremely clever.

"Anyway," continued Williams, "details on there if you're that interested."

"That's great. Thanks for your time," Leon shook Williams' hand vigorously. To the man's evident relief, Leon finally headed for the door.

## CHAPTER 41

The arsehole in the shop had not seemed to find it at all strange when Leon bought two identical phones. He had just seemed pissed off that they were the cheapest model in the shop and had both been purchased with pay as you go SIM cards. The young lad with the short-sleeved white shirt, red tie, and chunky fake gold bracelet had looked close to tears as Leon continued to rebuff his offers of text bundles and 4G on spectacularly expensive handsets. Leon felt no sympathy for the man who made Oscar Williams look like a genuine, down-to-earth good bloke. The more expensive of the phones were so good, according to him, that he claimed to have bought almost every model for one or another of his family. Perhaps it was standard practice as when he listened to the other salesmen's patter they had also been equipping all their relatives with pricey handsets. Leon wondered why the shop even needed to open to non-staff, such was the level of employee purchasing. He also found it counter-intuitive that the top of the range models seemed almost the size of a football pitch.

Such was the scale of incredulity that he did not want a smart phone, whatever that meant, that he thought the kid's head might explode. Leon decided not to tell him that he would not have known how to use all the free texts he was being promised.

Leon got the salesman to type in the number Grace had given him by which stage he looked like he'd lost the will to live. Upon leaving the shop Leon proceeded to leave two messages on her voicemail before she curtly answered at the third attempt, telling him she was at work and he should just text in future.

Oscar Williams had rung him earlier in the day to say that they were glad to be able to offer him a position on their books. Thankfully for Leon they were "not currently in a position" to offer him any work. Leon was unsurprised by the news and grateful that he did not have to actually go and do any consultancy to maintain his cover.

Baines' website had revealed almost nothing. Leon sat down to read it with his heart galloping and his hands sweating, but it was devastatingly unexciting fare. It was a very factual and dry account of the company's beginnings with liberal doses of Baines's personal qualities that had enabled him to achieve. No real personal history to speak of, and no mention at all of his family.

The rest of the site offered advice and services to people wanting to set up their own businesses. Added to the numerous links to other charities supported by Baines and Golden Wings, the man virtually came across as a saint.

He had intended to paint a landscape but incrementally and almost imperceptibly it appeared that his mind had other ideas.

His head was aching with thoughts of Baines, Carl, Oscar Williams and wings of both golden and silver varieties. Meanwhile, his hand was sketching out in charcoal a scene that would offer little in the way of pleasing aesthetics. It would not have his customary natural beauty, green fields or moody lighting. In short this preliminary sketch was not like anything he had done before. Perhaps it was a good thing to broaden his portfolio, but arguably not with this.

He looked at the lines on the canvas. He always loved this stage of the process; the embryonic draft that promised so much. He knew that his end product was never quite as good as what he saw in his mind's eye at this point. But he also knew that he was reasonably good, would have a decent stab at it, and was likely to be fairly proud of the result.

There was another first for Leon concerning this particular piece. It was the first time he had drawn his outline completely from scratch. Previously he had always had a starting point, whether that was a photograph he had taken himself or found elsewhere or a basic drawing he had done in situ. He would normally clip this to the mirror, which he could see behind his easel. This time, he kept habitually looking at the mirror only to see only his own eyes staring back at him over the top of the canvas.

The piece was of a real location but he had mapped out its shape purely from memory. He stood back to take an early look and absorb the shape of things. The war memorial looked about right. He wasn't entirely sure if some of the side streets were in exactly the right place but he thought it was pretty close. Taking up a good chunk of the foreground was the top half of a figure, featureless but seemingly looking into the scene. He leaned in with his fat pencil to add some texture. Some brief strokes to add shape were all that was needed to show that this was some sort of coat from behind. He looked across at his paints. It was far too early to be adding colour to the palette but he was thinking ahead as he did not want to be caught out later. Despite having four different shades of yellow he did not feel any of them was accurate enough. With some careful mixing, he would probably get there, though.

## CHAPTER 42

Day one at the boat yard had been great. He headed home with more of a sense of satisfaction than he could remember having in quite some time. He had arrived there at eight o'clock, as requested, and worked hard until four thirty, with only a lunch break and another short tea break in between.

He had met a decent set of lads who had given him a warm welcome. He suspected that was largely because their last labourer had left a week ago and the joiners and welders had been running around to fill in the gaps rather than getting on with their main roles. It also didn't hurt that his predecessor was universally thought to be a 'complete twat'. But still, they seemed a good bunch and they had appreciated his work ethic, which had become immediately apparent.

On arrival, he noticed what a dangerous looking enterprise it was. Welders lay underneath enormous steel canal boats that would squash them like a tomato if any of the stands – hammered roughly into place by their colleagues – had toppled. In the next section, joiners heaved enormous pieces of timber onto circular saw tables that seemed to have guards missing. He guessed that someone might have helped them if they could see through the fog of sawdust particles which danced around the building in front of his eyes before being inhaled by the eight or so men in the wood workshop.

He had been led to believe that the world had gone 'health and safety mad' in recent years but, if that was the case, then the outside world had yet to influence the premises of his new employer.

He had been told upon arrival by Brian, the owner that had interviewed him (if that was the right term) that he could take off as many sick days as he wanted but needed to realise he wouldn't get paid for them. Leon wondered if this was the sort of fine detail he should have asked about on his first visit, but he didn't really mind. He was lucky to have a job and he couldn't bear the thought of doing something cooped up in an office.

So he spent the day in the warehouse and out in the yard, carrying, lifting and dragging around different items of varying weight, as well as being set off drilling and screwing wood to steel shells. He ached all over but he was satisfied by the fact that he was a working, contributing member of society, with a feeling of self-worth.

He knew he would be sore in the morning. Leon was fit and had trained inside sufficiently that, upon release, he was probably in the best shape he had ever been in. But today had involved tasks and muscle groups he was not used to exercising. In time, though, he would take it in his stride.

On his way home he passed along the main street and stopped outside Beans as he passed. He had no idea why; he wasn't remotely interested in Guy's whereabouts or welfare. Guy was nowhere to be seen anyway. He wondered if he should treat himself to a coffee. He had just finished his first day at work and it was early. There was no reason for him to go home yet. He didn't feel like painting and he needed to give his aching limbs a rest anyway. A flex of his sore fingers confirmed it.

Even if Guy wasn't visible, Leon didn't want to risk seeing him, and he did not want to go to the diner either. He had texted Grace (texted!) and she had tentatively agreed to meet up. She said she would pick the place this time as she needed to be somewhere where she didn't look like a tragic arse if he stood her up again. Harsh but fair, he had thought. But he didn't want to ruin things by heading there and doing something wrong.

He could not think of another coffee shop nearby. They were a strange phenomenon, these coffee shops. He could not see why they were so popular but, at the same time, he liked them. If he had seen one years ago he would have thought it an abomination and dismissed anyone going into one as a total idiot, going into an establishment full of other idiots, all paying a fortune for pretentiously sized, outrageously priced variations on what was essentially a very simple drink – a cup of coffee. But they were somewhere for him to sit and while away some time in the company of others. They were, to that end, a surrogate for the bars he could no longer inhabit. He would still have been far happier in a pub with a cup of coffee, where he presumably would not have to decide what temperature he would like the milk to be, but it was a tough environment for someone wrestling with a drink problem.

He wouldn't go in. Guy might just be taking a break and emerge as soon as he sat down, and he could not be doing with that. No, he would head home and hope that on the way he would pass some other establishment that he had not previously noticed.

Just as he decided to move on the door swung inwards and a woman emerged holding an enormous cardboard cup of coffee.

"Sorry," they both said simultaneously in a very British manner and without knowing what each of them had done wrong.

The woman half jogged away in front of him, clearly scalding herself with some slopping coffee and having to change hand. She reached a shop up ahead, found a key and unlocked the door before entering. As Leon approached he saw a flash of movement as the sign flipped from Closed to Open.

Leon stopped and stared at the closed door that was now inviting visitors. He did not know how long he stood there but it was a long while. The few other pedestrians in the street moved around him as though he were an inanimate object. Perhaps everything in this world really was connected, as people claimed – he did not profess to know the answer to that – but all he knew was, at that particular moment, he was not connected to anyone or anything. He was in the eye of a storm.

What little was left of his thought process tried to connect the dots and establish whether he was in the early grip of a seizure. He did not feel like there was any sense of déjà vu but he was feeling so alienated that he could not have sworn to that.

He breathed as deeply and slowly as possible and still felt as though he was merely sipping air. He needed to get this under control as he was feeling light headed. He wanted to go somewhere to sit down but could not bring himself to walk away from the exact spot he was in outside the charity shop. What if he moved and everything changed? Through his spinning vision, he could make out a horrific old-lady coat on a stand, next to some probably incomplete jigsaws and a pair of sandals that Jesus would have thought unfashionable.

He had to act now, whether his senses were prepared or not. He felt that if he dithered this moment would be snatched away from him. Before he could allow himself any further thought he saw his own hand pushing open the door and jumped slightly as a small bell tinkled above his head. The bell had returned him to his senses somewhat, although his eyes were playing catch up. The shop was dark compared to the street outside and initially his vision was blotchy and indistinct. He heard a distant voice saying 'Hi' and he grunted a response. He pretended to look at a threadbare shirt on a chunky plastic hanger until he sorted himself out. He should have waited outside.

He willed his legs to take him to the counter. He moved around a carousel of stiff jeans, past a single shelf of DVDs whose contents had never been near a cinema, and reached his destination. The woman behind the counter was crouched over, retrieving donated bric-à-brac from a black bin liner and sipping her newly acquired coffee.

Sensing rather than hearing his presence in front of her, she stood up to face him and he looked into her green eyes. They were now framed by a much-altered face, but one that he would have recognised sooner than his own. Time had been far from unkind to it but it still bore the irreversible signs of a life of hardship, vulnerability and living hand-to-mouth. It was a gentle face, creased now with lines and dotted with occasional blemishes. Her hair was pulled back in a way that gave her an appealing air of indifference. He could not have explained how he had known just from a brief, almost-encounter on the path. But without a fraction of doubt, he had known.

He fell into the eyes. The bottomless eyes that promised so much but told him nothing. Looking into them properly for the first time made him dizzy and he could not speak.

She wiped her spare hand on her jeans and stood up straight, carefully placing her coffee on the counter. She looked at Leon's hands, presumably expecting him to have brought in something to donate.

"Can I help you?"

"It's you. I have pulled my life apart trying to find you. I have destroyed every aspect of it in the process; my career, relationship, home, dignity, freedom. All for this one moment. Was it worth it?... No, I would have to say that it wasn't, and I always knew that would be the case. Did I have to do it? Yes. I didn't want to. I *had* to.

"I convinced myself that I had wrecked your life, if not ended it. I have ended up letting you inadvertently wreck mine. I threw it all away as knowingly as I did helplessly. You've been the most constant part of my life and yet you don't even know who I am.

"People always regret not taking another path. I had no choice. I am going to leave now. I just wanted to know that you are alive."

"Hello?"

Leon jolted and realised in surprise that he was yet to speak. But he did not want to speak, not now that he had heard the craziness of the words in his head. He felt a tightness in his chest, throat, head, and struggled to keep himself under control. He felt his hands shaking and pushed them into his pockets. His throat felt parched and he wondered if he should ask for a glass of water. He needed a few seconds, if nothing else to make sure that he did not start crying. He tried to breathe. He could not believe that he was actually in this position and his primary thought, which now took an almost physical form in his head was the word 'WHY?'

"Can I help with something? Are you alright?"

She glanced through the window, perhaps to gauge how vulnerable she was at this moment with a man acting so strangely in her presence. But at the same time, she did not look worried.

Leon tried several times to speak, each unsuccessful. Any concern that she did show was purely for his welfare.

"Is there somebody I can ring?"

"No... No, I'm..." he had no idea how to continue but, as she did not respond he felt that he must.

"I know you. You're Marie."

Marie's eyebrows raised a notch but there was still no sense of alarm. She looked at Leon, almost challenging him to continue.

"I should say I *knew* you."

Here it was. The moment had arrived. Leon had always said to himself that he would hang himself out there and tell her the truth, as bizarre as it sounded. If she thought him a stalker then so be it. If she ran a mile then that was fine. He just needed to tell her.

Now though… now, with her stood there looking at him. Now that he was staring into those eyes that he felt could see his soul. Now it was different. It seemed inconceivable to tell her everything. She would not understand. No one would understand. He didn't even understand it himself. Years with an unscratchable itch, a burning flame haunting his days. All because of an instant that anyone else would have forgotten in a heart beat. He had even forgotten it himself all for those years until he was hit by the thunderbolt while collecting his belongings.

"It was forty years ago."

Marie raised her eyebrows.

"I don't think either of us were in much of a state then," Leon continued, "In fact I wouldn't be surprised if you…"

"Sorry, no I don't remember you," Marie said cautiously, but there was a sincere element of apology in there too.

"Long time ago…" Leon conceded, "long time."

"Yes."

She certainly wasn't giving anything away and Leon wondered how to proceed. He was already into a lie he had not wanted to start.

"So are you doing OK?" he eventually asked.

"Fine thanks. Not too bad. Well, you know…" she glanced around the shop, "you?"

"Oh yeah, good thanks." This was excruciating. "Listen, this is going to sound really weird, but the last time I ever saw you was at the war memorial in town. I was chatting to you. You *definitely* wouldn't remember that, if you know what I mean," he said with a small smile.

The smile was not returned. Probably, like him, she had only made it this far by leaving the booze behind and didn't much care to be reminded of it.

"I remember you had just been to the doctor that morning, got some tablets. You weren't feeling well. We weren't that close really but, you know, we used to chat."

"Chat?"

"Chat. Nothing else, mind you, if that's what you're thinking."

"It's not," she said coldly.

"Oh. No. Course not. Like I say, we weren't even that close."

"But you remember me after all this time? You remember my name? How old are you?"

Oh shit, she was on to him. She had seen straight through his pathetic bluff. Why had he not just stuck with the truth? He had abandoned his Plan A just at the crucial moment and he'd blown it.

"Some things just stick," he shrugged, "I spent a lot of time trying to find you at the time. You were good to me. I was new to the streets and you were the first person that showed me any sort of kindness."

She shrugged as though that could be possible. Leon was relieved.

Leon wittered for the next few minutes. He was still not sure that Marie bought his story but she had not asked him to leave yet which was a major positive. But the conversation was going nowhere and they were rapidly heading back to the 'how have you been doing?' awkwardness of earlier. An elderly lady entered the shop, dragging her wheeled shopping bag across the threshold. Perhaps she had been enticed in by the hideous dress in the window. Leon waited for her to struggle past and start looking at a rack of indeterminate brown clothing towards the rear.

"So anyway, like I was saying before, I've not seen you since that day at the war memorial. We both headed off separately. I remember getting a distance away and turning round. I saw you'd left your handbag on the concrete steps and I remembered you would have your tablets in there. I couldn't see you so I headed back to pick it up. When I was almost there this kid came out of nowhere, swiped your bag and ran off. I chased him for a while but I wasn't exactly in the best shape at that point. I went looking for you but I didn't know where you lived or anything. I always worried about it. You'd told me about the tablets, you see. And over the weeks, I never saw you again which made me worry even more."

Marie did now seem to be getting uncomfortable. Leon glanced around at the old lady who seemed to be heading their way with a thick woollen cardigan in her hand.

"How much is this?" she growled, thrusting the cardigan onto the counter, "It's got no price on it."

Marie searched for a price and realised that there was no ticket.

"Three fifty."

Unbelievably, the woman grunted, shook her head and wandered back into the treasure trove of horrors, leaving the cardigan where it was. Marie was unperturbed. This was clearly not unusual. A tinkling of the bell announced the entrance of a middle-aged couple. Leon realised he was in real danger of losing what little momentum he had built up. He would be far better off taking this conversation elsewhere.

"So I was wondering if you maybe fancied catching up for a chat at some point," he ventured, noting that Marie did not look comfortable with the idea. "Can I buy you a coffee across the road there?"

"No thanks, you're OK."

"OK, could I call back here one day then?"

"I can't stop anyone coming into the shop. But you need to know I've moved on with my life. I'm not in the habit of catching up with people from… then. Sorry." The slight bite in Marie's tone was picked up by the old lady's in-built radar and she started to listen. Witnessing a good argument would give her at least a week's worth of gossip. There was silence for a moment and, worried that she was missing something, she pretended to look at a rail that gave her a decent view of them both.

Leon stood there and wondered what to do. He did not want to leave now she was here in front of him, nor did he want to piss her off so much that she refused to see him ever again. He raised the palm of his hand to her in defeat and started to move slowly towards the door. He knew it was the smart move even though his mind was screaming at him to stay put.

"I'm sorry," he muttered, turning and heading for the door. He walked towards it and tried to stop the emotion creeping back up his throat. In the reflection of the window, he caught sight of himself. But the strange thing was that it was not the image of a life-hardened grown man that returned his gaze. It was a fifteen-year-old kid with more swagger than sense. A young punk who had seen too much television and believed that a path of self-destruction somehow made him tragic-romantic and cool at the same time. The kid had anger in his eyes, which simply signified a desire to be angry, rather than a particular reason for it. The kid was clueless about where life would take him. If he changed his ways he could become anything. If he did not then he might find himself four decades later being unwelcome in a charity shop, having thrown away his life.

He looked to the next windowpane and saw in the angled reflection a young woman with a natural beauty only partially hidden by her straggly hair and cut lip. Even the reflection of her eyes almost burned holes through the glass. Her potential smouldered like an aura around her. She was tough but her destiny was held in the balance. Leon knew which way that destiny would go but at that moment it promised the world.

"Wait," she whispered.

Leon turned to look at her. She was staring directly into her own mirror image in the window. She did not look back to him. Had she seen the same thing he had just witnessed? That was barely credible but in that moment he somehow felt that she had.

He looked at her but she did not break eye contact with her other self. Leon could not speak in case he broke the spell, if that was what was happening here. The elderly lady decided she had had quite enough of this weird shit and trundled her bag towards the door. This would not make a good anecdote even if she understood what it was she was seeing. She would have to try the post office. She pulled the door and the little bell's ring pulled Marie back into this world. She looked momentarily crestfallen that it had. She looked at Leon, glanced briefly back at her reflection and then back to him.

"What exactly *is* it that you want?"

Leon shook his head gently. He had no idea how to answer her question.

"Where do you live?" he asked eventually.

"You can fuck off," she said gently, but there appeared to be a trace of humour in it.

"All right… Do you have a home?"

"Yes, thanks."

"Listen, I'm not sure how to do this, but I want to speak to you. Please, will you give me your number? An email address?"

She shook her head.

"What was your story, Marie?"

"Why do you want to know?"

"Because I thought about you a lot. At first, anyway. Obviously, I've not really thought much about it for years," he lied, "but then here you are all of a sudden and it's all come back."

"But I don't *know* you."

"Can't you just give me a break and accept it matters to me. You were nice to me. I was scared and you were the only one. That leaves a mark."

"How old were you?" she asked again.

"Fifteen. Thereabouts."

She shook her head sadly. "Why?"

The lie was about to get away from him. He had not intended to lie but now he was in too deep. If he admitted his deception at this point she would definitely throw him out. If she found out later she would be even more furious. All that mattered though was now. This moment. Later could wait. He may never have another chance.

"Never got on with my dad," he said quietly, which was not entirely untrue, "and then one day it just, you know, got too much for me. I was fifteen. I was a dickhead. I went out one morning. They knew I wasn't going to go to school but they'd given up caring. As long as I didn't come home in a police car they considered it a good day by that point. I was a terrible son."

Leon felt genuine sadness. Although his tale was mostly fabrication, some of it was certainly true and he felt more grief than ever in that moment for all that he had put his parents through. They were never openly affectionate but he knew they loved him unconditionally. It had broken their hearts that they only located their estranged son when he was arrested for crimes they could not comprehend.

He had been a burden to them up until the age of around eighteen when he had begun to make up for his mistakes, but even then he never felt close to them. Then he had drifted away later in life until they were little more than a backdrop to his childhood memories. He could never forgive himself. He certainly could not atone for it; both of them had died while he was inside. There was less than a year between their departures and at his mother's funeral his father had been so riddled with Alzheimer's that it was difficult to know if he even recognised his son. Leon had felt on a couple of occasions that day that the old man *had* recognised him. But a lack of acknowledgement either meant that he was wrong or his dad did not want to speak to this virtual stranger who was the centre of attention to the small crowd at the funeral. Every time he looked around people averted their gaze, embarrassed to have been caught whispering about the man with the guard.

"And that was it really. I went back before long. And that's it, that's my story. It's been played out thousands of times by other idiot kids and it's embarrassing."

He glanced up at Marie who was staring intently at the counter top. He wondered if she was looking at anything, but if there was something there he could not see it. Perhaps she had been judging his little story for authenticity.

"What about you?" he tried to keep the desperation out of his voice.

To his surprise, she started to talk down as though addressing the counter. "Different story. Still a cliché I guess. I ran away from home, but not until long after I should have done. I stayed because of my little brother. I suppose I thought I could protect him but of course I couldn't. I was seventeen when I left and he was thirteen. I would have gone earlier but I had to be sure. I had to be sure he was safe in that house. I had to be sure that the old man was not interested in Stephen in the same was that he was interested in me."

She almost spat out the last few words. Leon sighed, almost a groan.

"Is your dad…" Leon began to ask.

Marie shrugged indifferently. "Couldn't care less," she said, although there was a definite tensing in her body, "I always blamed her more than him anyway. She could have stopped it all. It doesn't make any sense but she's the one I really hope is dead."

"Your brother?"

"I don't know."

"You didn't ever..?"

"It's too late for that," she snapped.

Leon was at risk of stopping her flow but he could not help himself. "It's never too late. I could help you."

"You should probably keep out of it," she said, even more sharply, "I hope he's happy and I don't want to impact on that."

"Sorry."

She shrugged again. "So there I was, suddenly on the street. I half expected someone to come looking for me, thought I'd have to hide... but they didn't. I suddenly realised I didn't know what to do," she smiled sadly. "I found most accommodation wasn't safe for a young girl. I hit the street, found a leisure centre where the manager let me use the facilities. Before I knew it, that was my new life. Spiced up with some begging and minor shoplifting."

She paused for some time. Leon felt that the conversation was on a knife-edge and breathed quietly as though hoping Marie would forget he was there.

"I never talk about this stuff you know? Never."

"Me neither," said Leon.

"I know exactly when you are talking about," she said.

He was momentarily confused but then it dawned on him.

"The bag?"

"I'm sorry, I still don't remember you, and I don't remember the war memorial or any of that other stuff. But I remember the state I was in when I got those tablets. Never really had any good experiences back then but I'd had a really fucking bad one and I'd come close to the edge. Don't know if I'd have actually gone through with anything drastic, you know, but that's what the tablets were for. In the end, I don't think I ever got any more or took a single one."

"What had happened?"

Marie lifted her gaze and stared hard at him. Leon actually felt fear as her eyes seemed to glow and bore into him.

"Another day maybe."

Leon knew he should leave. Come back another day. He shouldn't ask. But if not now then when? When it was too late? "I just need to ask you one more thing. It's a bit weird."

"Jesus, I can't wait for this then."

Did you ever come across a bloke. A rich bloke. Took homeless kids from the street."

Marie was silent for a while. "I haven't thought about him in a long time," she muttered, almost to herself.

"When?"

"Wow, I don't know. 90s at some point."

"Did you see him?"

"No."

"But it was happening?"

Marie seemed lost in thought. "Yes. I don't know. Maybe." She looked up at Leon and saw his confusion. "It wasn't really my part of town but there were always rumours. Stories of young lads that went missing. The stories were so awful that even if they were true most people wouldn't have admitted being victims. Although there were also some crazies who claimed they had been taken. Most people thought the Cap Man was a myth?"

"The who?"

"Sorry, the Cap Man. He was supposed to wear a cap pulled right down over his eyes so you couldn't see his face. But it was all hearsay really. He was a ghost story. Something people liked to scare each other with at night. Especially new young lads appearing on the street. It was cruel, but some people enjoyed scaring the crap out of them. But whether he was real... I knew plenty of people said they'd seen him but I don't know. Nah, probably not."

This seemed to be a definite close to their conversation. Leon reluctantly moved further towards the door, half hoping she would call him back, and half hoping to get away while he still might be welcome to visit again.

As he was about to offer a goodbye a thought seemed to hit Marie.

"You've not put ads in the Big Issue to look for me have you?" she asked accusingly

Leon felt himself tense and tried to force a smile. "What?...*No*. It's not like I was *obsessed* or anything." He tried to affect a chuckle but no sound emerged.

## CHAPTER 43

His mind could not keep up. He would have moments of clarity where he thought he was in control, then he would realise that was just the pause in momentum before the rollercoaster dropped into another dizzying spin.

Between picking over the previous afternoon's conversation with Marie and wondering how the following evening's activity would pan out, he could barely concentrate on anything he was doing. But at the same time, he felt that he had to keep as busy as possible in order to at least stay on some sort of even track. He had already taken wood panelling to the wrong boat and found himself in several places without knowing why he had gone there.

He knew the boat yard and its myriad dangers was the last place to be when floating around on autopilot and he tried to scare himself by imagining terrible accidents he could cause to himself and the others if he did not concentrate. Perhaps losing an arm or disembowelling himself on the circular saw, crushing someone flat under a boat. It didn't work.

When should he pay Marie another visit? After he left did she wonder why she had humoured her strange visitor and vow not to do it again?

He had arranged to meet Grace? Yes, Saturday. Bloody hell. He had forgotten all about that. He could not let her down again. Although it was possible he could be back in a cell by then.

He daydreamed of a man in a cap floating silently through the darkened streets, looking for his prey. The face was always Baines'.

He needed to get the bus across town tomorrow immediately after finishing work.

He really struggled to be in the bait cabin with the others at lunchtime. They laughed and joked, ribbed each other and Leon, and seemed a little surprised when he did not join in. But he couldn't. He could almost see his thoughts bouncing around the inside of the disgustingly grimy prefabricated building they had to eat in.

All those years ago, Marie had done the only thing she could which was to disappear. How had her first days been? How scared would she have been? What happened to her family?

He needed to catch that bus if he was to have the best chance of carrying his plan out. The next one was not for another twenty minutes and, in Friday traffic, that could very well be too late. It all needed to be timed just right.

There was still half of the thirty-minute break left when he walked back into the workshop and started to work. And work he certainly did. He had set himself a target of ballasting and first-fixing a whole thirty five footer before he went home which would be a hell of a tough afternoon by anyone's standards. He was aware of the lads looking at him with concern and interest out of the windows of the cabin. They would be discussing him. Gossiping? He wasn't able to care about that.

Had Mystery Man ever found Marie all those years ago? Had he got someone to watch her? Was there ever even a chance he was in a position to tell Leon where she was? Having pondered these questions long and hard while inside, he was almost certain the answer was no.

The sweat stung his eyes and tickled his cheeks as he laid felt into the boat's base. The material was cold and damp and its rough surface scraped against his knuckles as the Stanley knife glided across the oiled metal beneath. He would need to wait for Keith to come out of the cabin before loading the concrete slabs but at least he could keep occupied until then. He tried to work out how many lengths of felt he had cut in order to fit out all the boats he had done since he started working here. But his mind knew it was being tricked and ignored him. Another bead trickled down the side of his nose and it reminded him of yesterday's tears.

Upon leaving the shop he had rushed to a nearby park where he had sat and sobbed. He was not even sure about what. Marie's life? His own? The fact that he had finally found his holy grail? Or perhaps a realisation of how futile the obsession that had controlled his life had been. He did not know, but the tears had helped and by the time they dried up he felt purged and lighter.

Leon could not for the life of him imagine how he was going to get through another day and a half at work before he could finally carry out his plan. It was an eternity. He looked up and saw Keith stand up inside the cabin and rinse out his mug. That was good – he could get started on the ballast.

## CHAPTER 44

Leon looked at his hands. He already knew that they were shaking but for some reason, he needed to check with his eyes. Seeing his uncontrolled tremors made him feel even more nervous.

He told himself that he had prepared thoroughly. There would always be scope for error but it would not be due to carelessness. He only had this one chance to do it cleanly. If things did not go to plan then events might slip from his control. He would at best give away his competitive advantage, at worst end up dead. His hands shook a little more.

He scanned the alley in which he had taken up his position. It was in a pretty disgusting state. The hotel on one side and shop on the other were well enough presented from the front but the alley between had obviously become something of a neglected no-man's land. There were black bin bags dumped on both sides of this narrow passage. They had clearly been there for some time and Leon was fairly sure that moving them would uncover all kinds of life. He thought back to when this would have represented a decent enough place to get his head down for the night. It still seemed alien to him. It was like remembering a childhood television show that had seemed real enough at the time but now appeared nonsensical.

The large industrial wheelie bin was over-flowing and produced a gag-inducing stench when he got close. God knows what was in there or what state of decomposition it was in. Still, standing behind it provided him with a decent vantage point from which he could not be easily seen. He trained his compact binoculars on a particular second-floor window across the street. Although there were still a few lights on there was very little sign of life in the offices of Golden Wings. The only people Leon could see were one secretary and the man whose head he was staring at the back of.

Leon had taken up his position early in order to be prepared but that had just meant that his nerves had lots of time to dig in their claws and start to vibrate in agitation. He clapped his hands together even though he was not cold. If anything he was starting to wish he had worn a thinner jacket as he could feel his shirt clinging to his damp back. He did not know whether the nausea was from the smell or his anxiety.

The secretary walked into Gregor Baines's office. She took some papers from him and they spoke briefly before she left the room. Leon silently cursed – she had been given some more work to do and so would be there a while longer. Leon had prepared for a potentially long wait. The length of time was no problem but the rising agitation was. He tried to control his breathing, which was becoming too shallow for comfort. The last time he had felt like this was his first night in prison.

He remembered his giant bear of a cellmate on that first night. Franks was a terrifying proposition who hardly spoke. To say that Leon slept with one eye open on that first, endless night was not strictly true; he had simply not slept. Franks had surprisingly turned out to be Leon's biggest ally in those early days. Leon had always promised himself that he would look up the big man, who had been released over a decade ago when he got out himself. He had not done so now that he was over the fence. It no longer seemed an appropriate thing to do.

He told himself to concentrate on the present and was relieved to see the secretary place her papers somewhere out of sight below the window frame, take her coat and bag, and head for the door. Even though he had scanned the rest of the offices dozens of times already he did so again to make sure. There still seemed to be a security guard on the ground floor but Baines was the only sign of life still left on his floor.

A light flicked off on the floor below. Those offices belonged to Golden Wings too, but it seemed very unlikely that anyone would bother the CEO this late on a Friday. They would surely be heading home.

Leon placed his binoculars on the top of the bin but they slid down the straining lid that could not contain its load. He stuck them in his jacket pocket. He needed to be absolutely certain that he did not leave anything behind in this alley. He pulled out his mobile phone and went through the menus until he found the only number that was programmed into it. He did not want to pause. He had rehearsed things so much that any last minute preparations were pure procrastination. He pressed the green dial button and then immediately saw the secretary emerge from the building. He dropped quickly behind the bin, frantically searching for the red button to hang up. He managed to do so.

He watched her exit. She seemed to spot someone following her out and held open the door, smiling. A second woman caught her up and they chatted as they came out onto the street. This colleague flicked a glance across the street towards Leon but her gaze did not stop on him. His mouth dropped open. Sandra. It had been a long time but he was certain. Wasn't he? But why would his ex partner be leaving the offices of Golden Wings? He saw her in profile, talking to the secretary. Had he seen her name when researching the company? He couldn't remember but she might well have a married name now anyway.

Except, of course, it could not be a coincidence. It rushed at him all at once. She had told someone of his obsession, that information had reached Baines, he had contacted Sandra and rewarded her with lucrative employment while surreptitiously pumping her for details. She would have had no problem crying on the shoulder of her generous new employer about her weird ex and his all-consuming obsession with a missing woman.

She glanced back round and he knew for certain that he was looking at the woman with whom he had once lived.

Baines arched his back in his ergonomically designed chair and sighed. That was enough. The weekend beckoned. He grabbed the mouse to begin the process of shutting down his computer and was surprised to hear the phone start ringing.

Leon heard the ring tone start and then noticed Baines' head look to the side of the desk. It was happening. But Baines continued to just look. After a few seconds he returned to face his PC. Shit - he wasn't going to answer his phone. Leon had not considered this. Men of Baines' stature did not answer their own telephone and the person that did this menial task for him had now left for the evening. Leon had made a mistake already and he cursed himself for it.

A click was followed by a slight dull hiss as an answering machine kicked in. Leon hung up. This was bad. He tried again. Baines looked to be tidying up a few things as the phone rang out again. Leon did not have a backup plan for this. All that planning had been for nothing. The thought of re-planning the whole operation was too much. He pushed the green button again and stared at the back of the head of the man he so desperately wanted to pick up the damned phone. Perhaps if he stared hard enough it would somehow be enough for him to do it.

The fifth ring. Shit. Leon now knew that he only had one more ring before he heard the dreaded click once more.

"Yes?" the slightly irritated voice said.

Leon jumped. He had not seen Baines pick up the receiver.

"What is it? You're clearly desperate to get hold of me."

Baines was not holding a receiver. Presumably, he was using a speakerphone of some sort. Leon did not falter but clicked into gear with what he had been preparing.

"You don't know me, but it is really important that you listen to what I've got to say," Leon tried to deliver this in a way that did not make him sound like a character from a crap action film. He did not succeed.

"What's this shit? Who the fuck are you?" Baines snapped.

"Just listen."

"You have ten seconds to tell me what you want or tell me this is a wind-up before I hang up."

"Don't do that."

"Why?"

"I know who you are, Gregor. I know what you've done."

There was a brief pause.

"I know *you*," Gregor growled back.

Leon had not for a second thought that Baines would recognise his voice. He must be bluffing. Either way, it knocked Leon back a step. "Yeah, yeah, I know you," Baines continued, "It'll come."

Leon was suddenly very worried. But there was only one way to go now, and that was forwards.

"You don't know me," Leon was aware that he had slightly dropped his voice. As if that would throw him off the scent. His worries were confirmed when Baines chuckled. Did he know?

"I'm going," stated Baines, and for an awful moment, Leon thought he had hung up.

"Wait! I know about your flat. What you did there. Look in the cupboard in your office."

"What?"

"Beneath the cabinet with the trophies is a small cupboard with two doors. Look in the left one. On the top shelf is a DVD."

There was a long, long pause. Baines was clearly working out if his caller was crazy and if he posed any sort of problem. He glanced back over his shoulder out of the window.

Leon had his phone pressed to his ear and the other hand held his binoculars focused on the office window. He felt a little vulnerable as it was difficult to scope out his immediate surroundings with the field glasses pressed against his eye sockets, but he could not take them down, such was his need to watch the man on the other end of the line. Baines had yet to move from his chair.

"The cupboard. The DVD." Leon did not want to push too hard but he desperately wanted to get things moving. He was sure that once he had Baines playing along then he would be hooked in for the duration of the call.

Baines was silent and still. Was he still trying to place Leon's voice? Why had he not disguised it? Because Baines must meet fifty people a week and not for a moment did he think that he would remember every single one of them. Leon left a slight gap at the top of his binoculars and a stream of sweat streamed into his eye. After an age, the man stood up and walked across the office. Leon lost sight of him. He emerged back into view, staring at a re-recordable DVD in a clear plastic sleeve as he rounded the desk.

"That's it," said Leon, talking to himself as much as anything, "just put it in the machine."

Baines spun round to stare out of the window. Through the binoculars, Leon saw the man's eyes lock onto his own. They stood like that for a while. Leon was furious with himself. Now Baines knew he was being watched, and there were limited options as to where he could be being watched from. Leon did not dare move. It seemed that Baines was staring directly at him but logically it seemed unlikely. Leon desperately wanted to crouch behind the bin but was terrified of making any movement.

"Why are you looking out of the window, Mr Baines?" he asked eventually, "Surely you don't think I'm across the street."

Baines turned back into his office.

"I am watching you, I'll admit, but I'm not physically there. Do you think I'm an idiot?"

He saw Baines looking around the walls and ceiling of his room. Hopefully, he was looking for a hidden camera and Leon had somehow managed to bluff his way out of it. Baines sat in his chair.

"So what's on the disk?"

"Just put it on."

"I have. I'm an impatient man."

"Do you remember Tommy McCann? Of course you don't. You probably won't even recognise him, but if you listen to what he has to say I'm sure he can jog your memory."

Leon listened intently to a series of mouse clicks. Then he heard a tinny-sounding voice. A voice that he knew belonged to Tommy McCann.

Finding Tommy had started out as a seemingly impossible task. Leon knew that the chances of him even being alive weren't great. No doubt that having been given a new chance of life by dodging a bottle of poisoned vodka he had proceeded to kill himself by some other route within a matter of months, accidentally or otherwise.

The thing that Leon had going for him was that the homeless life had not changed in the time he had been away. It was untouched by the technological advances that had shaped the way in which most people lived their lives. It was free from cultural shifts and fads, by political movements or current affairs. It just remained. It simply was.

Leon had done the legwork and soon got up to speed with the current food provision arrangements. But that had been followed by a huge piece of fortune. Randomly asking folks if they knew a man that had last been seen seventeen years ago, of whom he had no picture or real description, no known associates or hang-outs had seemed utterly pointless. But there was one thing that was in his favour; Tommy's red hair. An old, eccentric homeless man wearing what had once been a cravat knew a ginger man called Tommy that fitted the age profile. Leon tried not to get too excited. Half the people living rough had monikers such as Tommy, Jimmy, and Billy which had unknown origins and bore no resemblance to their actual names. The man with the cravat, William (very definitely not a Billy), had taken him to meet his acquaintance and Leon knew from the first instance that he had found his man.

So the pursuit had been simple, the persuasion not so. At first, Tommy denied that he had ever had the experiences that

Leon referred to. He had no memory of the abuse at the flat. He did not know a thing about the vodka in the park all those years later. Leon could well believe the second claim, but if this man was Tommy then he could not possibly forget his time in terrifying captivity. But Leon was fairly sure this was the man he had almost murdered. Yes, he looked different but he would have bet his life on it. Which was possibly exactly what he was about to do.

After the first meeting, Leon had left empty handed but he returned without William the following evening to the same doorway and found Tommy there again. Tommy eventually opened up a bit more without William's eavesdropping presence and admitted that he was the man Leon was looking for.

Leon told him everything, including the fact that he had been ordered to kill Tommy. He did not mention the fact that he had seriously considered it but dwelt rather on the fact that he hadn't. If Tommy felt any gratitude he certainly did not show it. In fact, Tommy appeared to have little feeling of any sort left in him. Presumably, it had leeched out of him into the various areas of muck and filth he had slept on for night after night, year after year. And by the breaking of his mind over three days, a lifetime ago.

Leon had sat in a darkened doorway with Tommy for almost three hours. Over this time, the man initially crumbled but then gradually became more and more animated. Leon could see he had absolutely nothing left to live for, so why not this? It was a cause. It was revenge. More than anything, most importantly for a street dweller, it was *something to do*.

The third meeting of the two men was arranged for the following afternoon as soon as Leon finished work. In preparation, he bought a video camera, purchased upon receipt of his first wage from the boat builders.

Leon cupped his hand around the mobile phone. There was no wind to speak of but he was desperately trying to hear the noise through the speakers of Baines' PC. He heard the tinny voice reciting some of the words he knew by heart as being those spoken by Tommy.

Leon had thought at first that Tommy was not going to turn up. Eventually, he stumbled into view along the riverbank. Leon had chosen this location as he presumed it would be quiet and so far it was. But he was worried about the ginger man's gait. He was walking unsteadily and almost dragging one leg behind him. He looked hammered which meant that this was definitely not going to work.

"Afternoon," said Tommy, raising one hand slightly in greeting.

He seemed fine. Leon realised that he had so far only met Tommy while sitting down and he appeared to have some sort of limp. He was not going to ask what had caused that as there would undoubtedly be some gut-wrenching tragedy attached.

No sooner had Tommy sat down than Leon had the camera out. He had been practising with it in order not to have any mishaps or delays. He had Tommy talking before the bloke had any time to back out.

"My name is Tommy McCann. I don't know what to call you. All I know is that I am speaking to this person," Tommy held a picture of Gregor Baines up to the camera. "I don't care what you call yourself, or about the fact that you have changed a bit over the years. I know it's you. I'm not likely to forget you. I still sometimes see you at night. I still sometimes feel what you did to me. James Potter never forgot you either. Right up until you had him killed."

Leon had helped Tommy out with what to say, but the emotion was all his.

The back of Baines' head was motionless but Leon was certain he heard a sigh over the speakerphone which he could picture sat on the desk, picking up sound waves from the wealthy businessman and the wretched tramp that may well bring him down.

"My friend here," Tommy continued, nodding to the person behind the camera, "knows everything."

Sat on the riverbank, Leon tried to keep the camera steady while leaning backwards to check that the red dot was visible and the time bar was escalating; the two things that assured him he was capturing this. Tommy was doing better than he could have ever imagined and he did not want to miss a second.

"He has found others as well. They have good memories too. Memories of the man in the cap."

Leon heard a mouse click and the sound stop.

"What is this shit?" Baines had composed himself and sounded loud and confident.

"I think it speaks for itself. Keep watching"

"I think this filthy bastard is suggesting I did something but I don't know what that is, and to be honest I am finding this a giant waste of fucking time. I don't know him. I don't know what either of you are talking about and as this looks like attempted blackmail I think I'll take it to the police. Do you have any idea how many people have tried to lay accusations at my door over the years? I'm rich. I'm very rich. And that's what you all see isn't it? A chance to have some of that. Money that I have worked my fingers to the bone for and you think you should be able to take. You make me sick. What you don't realise is that I can use that money to take you apart in a court of law, and if I ever hear from you again that's exactly what I'll do."

Leon had to consider that Baines could be telling the truth, and it was not just the man's escalating sense of confidence that worried him. He had always accepted the possibility that this was a mistake. Tommy would probably have confirmed the identity of any photo he had been shown. And everything else was circumstantial. Plus, of course, they were bluffing about having others too. They were in big trouble unless they were right. He was losing his nerve. He could be chasing this guy while the man he really wanted was a stranger in a different city. Or dead.

He wished he had brought something to drink. His mouth was parched and he thought about an icy trickle of water flowing down his throat. He tried to generate some moisture but nothing came. He had read once of a trick whereby one could suck on a pebble and build up saliva that way, but there was no chance of him putting anything in his mouth that might have been in this alley.

Baines was still looking around the fittings in his office but trying to act as though he wasn't. He was eyeing the ostentatious chandelier that hung from the high ceiling.

"OK, so you've had your fun now and I'm tired of you. I am going to hang up this phone now, put this DVD in an envelope and have my PA send it to a friend of mine at the police first thing in the morning." He sounded confident, believing he had gained control of the conversation.

"You don't need to send it. I am going to drop it off there now," replied Leon. And we'll see how loyal Carl Wallers is when he has to choose between supporting his family or saving you. We also know why James Potter had to die."

"I don't know any of these names."

Perhaps he did not, but he hadn't hung up the phone.

"I doubt you've forgotten James Potter," Leon continued. "You had me kill him in a fire."

Baines went quiet. If he was guilty then he would now know exactly who he was talking to.

"Sounds like you need to take the rap on that one, son," he tried to sound casual.

"I did it, I admitted it, I served my time in jail. I can't be touched any more. That's the major advantage I have over you, Gregor. I have nothing to lose and you have everything."

"My advantage is that I know who you are and I will find you," he growled.

Leon decided that if Baines was innocent then he was bluffing. If he was guilty then he had just realised that Leon was the poor bastard he had set up and forgotten about many years ago. Leon's head was spinning. He somehow felt that he was losing here. He had expected to feel in control throughout this exchange but his confidence was leaving him. His throat was screaming for water in a way that he had only ever craved alcohol when the rats were at their most rampant.

"Your family," he croaked, "what do you think they will think of you when they find out? You must realise that this will just be the beginning. Once folks hear what has happened they will be crawling out of your past to bring you down. There'll be victims who were homeless then, but they could be quite credible by now. I bet you've abused a lot of people in a lot of ways. They will have watched you with hate all this time, feeling powerless. But knowing they're not alone will spur them on; give them the confidence they need. How many were there Gregor?"

"What is it you are trying to do here?"

Was Gregor's voice wavering? Leon felt once more on the front foot, buoyed by every further second that Baines failed to follow through with his threat of hanging up.

"What do you think Matthew and Sophia will think of their dad? Can you imagine Matthew's life once people find out his old man raped young boys? Maybe *still* rapes young boys, who knows? We'll have to wait until the investigation starts before we find that out."

"You're not asking for money are you." he stated rhetorically.

Leon wondered how he knew.

"You would have mentioned money by now if you wanted it," Baines continued.

"And what about the current Mrs. Baines? I can't even imagine the sort of life she enjoys and the social circles she mixes with. I bet she spends two hundred quid on lunch and spends her nights dolled up at fund-raising dinners. How do you think she'll cope as a pariah once you're disgraced."

"I don't know who did the things you are talking about," Gregor hissed, "but I didn't do them, so it's either in your head or you have got the wrong person. But I have been recording the last part of this conversation and what with that and this video you have given me I will have you rotting in a cell in no time. And believe me, I am going to make sure you do *not* enjoy yourself in there. You don't have any idea who you're fucking with but I'm going to show you."

"Here's the deal," Leon felt that he was going to have to get to the point now that he had used all his artillery, "if you are still alive by the end of the evening then the video, the statements and Tommy himself are delivered to the coppers. You can't find him in the meantime so don't try. Copies of everything will also go to one local and one national newspaper, just in case you get your claws into your mates in the police or the local rag. There will probably be a campaign to find others that you have attacked. It will be very public and very thorough."

Leon paused but there was no response.

"But you can make sure that I never use any of this information. I will destroy the DVD and get rid of the documents. If you're not around Tommy and the others will have no need to tell their story. Why would they? There would be no sense in them opening up to their pasts for no reason. And your family. Think of them. Picture them."

Leon felt cruel and could hardly believe he was doing this to another human being. *What if it wasn't him?* What if a decent man was now panicking about the indelible stain this could leave on him?

"They'll be upset for a while. But you can make sure they live the rest of their lives in peace. They can enjoy their lives without hiding every day from the shame, the taunts, the abuse. What kind of a life do you want for Matthew, Gregor?"

There was complete silence. Leon ploughed on.

"In the cupboard to the left of the one where you found the DVD. Go on, open it."

Baines stood as he was told and moved across the office. He bent down out of sight and then his head emerged as he stood up, looking at something in his hands. Leon could not see it but he knew that Baines was staring at a three-quarter inch thick rope. Just in case there was any room for confusion one end was already tied in a noose.

"How the hell did you get in here?" he asked weakly.

Leon was surprised that it was the first question on his mind. It seemed a fairly irrelevant detail in the grand scheme of things. Baines sounded broken.

But Leon had heard the question before. From Baines. And Leon had been stood in this alley. Whatever had happened next had been horrendous. A ball of doom started to rise from his abdomen. He shook his head to get rid of the déjà vu and managed to swallow the ball. He needed to progress quickly in case it returned.

"You have time," Leon managed to say, "Leave a note if you want to. All this will disappear. You'll have to trust me on that. But I don't have anything to gain from pulling your family apart. You can save them. I'm going now. Bye."

And with that, Leon had gained the psychological advantage of being the one that ended the conversation on his terms. He was glad he had rehearsed the speech as his head was spinning and he felt light-headed. He could barely remember the conversation that had just happened. He felt himself tipping backwards and grabbed the filthy bin lid to steady himself. He went down on his haunches and felt as though he had left his mind behind.

This had happened before. And it ended in death.

## CHAPTER 45

All he was aware of was a faint hissing noise. As he gradually came to he realised it was car wheels spraying through the water lying on the nearby road. It had started raining. How long ago? He was calm but confused. He raised a hand to confirm that his face and hair were soaked. He was sat in the wet filth of the alley, which had taken on an even more foul smell as it got damper.

He gathered himself a little and looked nervously around him. About twenty yards along the alley was a homeless man lying up against the wall. He had clearly come here to wrap himself in cardboard as protection against the recent rain. Had he been there the whole time since Leon arrived? Surely not; Leon would have seen him. Had he been watching while Leon was out of it? Very probably. Leon automatically checked his pockets, confirming that he had not been robbed.

Leon's chest emptied and the rising ball brought up a new wave of déjà vu telling him that disaster was imminent. Just an after-shock. He needed to stay calm. He shook his head and slapped himself in the face to try and concentrate. Everything was so unclear…woolly.

He needed a drink, but no longer was his desire for water. He wanted to find a bar and drink quickly. Was this feeling real?

Or part of his episode? He realised that he wanted it to calm his nerves after speaking to Baines. The rats weren't really there.

It rushed back to him. How had the conversation ended? He couldn't quite recall – it was just out of reach. It would return as his mind remoulded itself but he needed to know immediately. He looked up at Baines' window but its emptiness told him nothing. He collected his phone from the floor next to where he had ended up.

He tried to evaluate how things had gone. What he could remember indicated that it had gone well but he could not yet trust his own thoughts or memories. He was remembering more and more but, again, with reservations. He had stayed strong on the phone but he was now less certain of Baines' guilt than he had been before the afternoon started. How was that?

He wondered if he could safely leave the alley yet. He had no idea how much time had elapsed so checked on his phone. At a rough estimate, about ten minutes. That was a decent-sized one. He would sit behind the bin in the stinking mess for ten or fifteen minutes more and hope that the tramp did not see him. He removed and snapped the SIM card from his phone and put the pieces in his pocket along with the now dead hand piece. He did not want to leave it anywhere that it might be found. He would dispose of it later.

He still couldn't see any sign of life in Baines' office and wondered if the man had left to go home. If he was still there then surely the lights would still be on. Had Baines called the police to report a blackmailer? Was he ringing his heavies to come and hunt Leon down? At this moment either seemed plausible. And that was why he needed a pint. Just the one.

He thought about ringing Grace, using his 'other' phone. He needed something to 'ground' him. Something real. So paranoid was he about getting his phones mixed up this evening that he had almost not brought it. He was hoping to meet her the following night but their arrangements had been vague and he wanted to firm them up. But he couldn't speak to her in his current state. He wouldn't be able to listen to a word she had to say. He rubbed his forehead. He tried to breathe deeply. He wondered if Baines had started the search for Tommy. What if he actually found him? Leon had been very firm with Tommy that he needed to disappear for a few days. But Tommy at times seemed to be dancing to a different tune to everyone else, his life having damaged his mind so much that his subconscious sometimes had to take the wheel.

Leon stood directly across the road from Golden Wings. It was not what he should have done – he should not have broken cover - but he simply stood out in the open looking up. The chair was still as it had been except that its occupant was missing.

What had Leon been expecting? He wasn't sure. He cursed that he had not seen where the man went on leaving. He would have to fight the nerves, try to be patient and see how things panned out. He squeezed his eyes as though it would help him see into the gloom but could not see anything. Regardless of what happened he would find Tommy as arranged and tell him he could do whatever he wanted with his allegations. Leon had told Baines that he himself would destroy the DVD but he had given no assurances about Tommy and the copy he had. And if they implicated Carl then he couldn't help that either.

But it was not at that stage yet. Baines might try to bring them all down first. It would be a nerve-racking time ahead.

Leon thought he saw a movement. But then nothing. He was about to leave when he remembered he had his binoculars in his pocket. He pulled them out and trained them on the window. Just the chair, the computer, and a dark empty office.

And then he saw them. Two brown polished shoes, attached to two navy-suited lower legs, swaying in the air ever so slightly, the rest of their owner obscured above the window frame.

Leon stood and stared, holding his breath. He had to reach for the bin to steady himself when he eventually got dizzy. He snapped out of it and walked away.

Leon took his remaining mobile from his pocket and scrolled through to find Grace's number. He was slightly numb from what he had just seen but he still had a chance at life and he wanted very much to live it. He did not want to dwell on right or wrong. There wasn't a moment to waste.

-THE END-

# ACKNOWLEDGEMENTS

Thanks to Gemma for her support and eagle-eyed proof-reading, both of which were vital, particularly the former.

I must thank two fantastic ex-colleagues at Northumbria University – Dr Jamie Harding and Adele Irving. They are both as generous as they are knowledgeable. And they know an awful lot – especially about homelessness. Any inaccuracies in that area are entirely mine and not theirs.

Thanks to Roger Crackett (*Enigma Graphics*) for designing the cover and generally being a very lovely cousin (this is me trying to get him to do the next one too).

And thanks to my parents and my friends for their moral support, especially Ben Salisbury for reading the draft, offering invaluable feedback and much needed words of encouragement.

And finally, thanks to anyone that takes the time to read this book.

Printed in Poland
by Amazon Fulfillment
Poland Sp. z o.o., Wrocław